RIGHTFUL PLACES

Athena Matthews

WRITTEN BY
ATHENA MATTHEWS

Registration No. 1141766

ISBN: 978-1-387-10529-8

Dedication

I am dedicating this novel to my husband Bradley Matthews, without his support and belief in me, this novel would just be a memory locked in the storage of my computer, or ashes as I would have burned all evidence. As well as dedicate it to my friends and family who have supported my love for writing all these years, thank you.

Rightful Place's

During great wars, many lives are sacrificed for one or many different peoples view of the world held by their leaders. Sometimes these leaders claim the gods told them, others leaders claim they are gods. For whatever reason, when humanoids wage war on each other innocent men, women and children are the ones to pay the ultimate price.

Sadly, this is one of those stories. This story truly begins at the end of a great war, on the night the Mountain Kingdom fell.

To bring down the stronghold that was once the Great Mountain Kingdom, it took a war that lasted fourteen years with a final siege that took months to plan and execute. By this point more than ten thousand lives had been whisked off the earth and sent to the void of the afterlife; and yet, still many more were yet to join those who had fallen.

The tyrant king of the Mountain Kingdom was Edmond Ironfist, a name that would stand the test of time. He ruled over this kingdom for twenty-two years. His sword dove heavy into the skulls and throats of all who stood in his way, kin or otherwise. To secure of a long and healthy reign, he slaughtered his brothers, sisters and father one by one until he was all alone. Edmond was a cruel and twisted man; power hungry and filled with greed. He could never have enough. whether it was gold, land or beautiful women he always needed more while he starved and tormented those beneath him.

He would order his men to burn down the crops of the villagers who could not pay their taxes. This action was considered a warning. If they then still could not produce the amount he wished for he would order their family to be raped, beaten, murdered, only then to seize their possessions.

As Edmond's desire for more land and power grew, he began targeting the smaller kingdoms of Tasryn, claiming their land as his own. After only reigning for a short five years, Edmond found himself in the midst of many great and formidable foes from this great land.

Edmond surprisingly had a wife, a wife who loved him dearly. She was a beautiful creature; a priestess, she was given to Edmond as a peace offering from a sanctuary to the east of the Black Cavern, hidden in the woods of the Twin Mountains. Lady Castriel Duvol was her title, she was an elegant and fitting queen. Even though she was forced into Edmonds arms, she did love him till the end of her days. He gave her something the sanctuary never could, a family. Three beautiful children; Katherine, Jasmine and their only son Allister, the rightful heir to the Mountain Kingdom.

Lady Castriel passed away five years after giving birth to their son, an illness swept over their lands. She died happy with Allister tucked tightly into her arms. She whispered her hopes and dreams for her son in his ear, trying to soothe the sobbing child in her last moments. Her two daughters stood at the edge of the bed, keeping a brave face knowing their mother was leaving them very soon. Lady Castriel looked into her son's innocent glimmering eyes for the last time as her own began to fade and dull.

"Become a gentleman, someone I would be proud of, my son. Break your father's curse on these lands and show these people the kindness they deserve." She forced her last breath with those words as Allister and Jasmine cried in mourning, Katherine biting her lip and holding her younger sister in her arms for support.

The queen died knowing that she was a loving and caring mother. Luckily, she never had to face the pain of watching her first daughter Katherine, being sold off to a rich king from across the great blood sea, or of her second daughter being mutilated and murdered in retaliation for her husband's war.

Prince Allister was almost twelve when the Mountain kingdom fell; he was Edmond's prize possession, Edmonds heir, his successor. He would one day have taken the throne from him and he wanted the boy to be ready for what Edmond himself had to face. After the passing of Lady Castriel Allister was forced to attend all executions and even accompany his father on the bloodied battlefield; only after the battle was won, of course, he had to keep his prize protected. Allister had to trek through fields of corpses, as his father tried to turn him from this gentle child his mother had raised, into a brutal monster of a king like himself, hoping that young Allister would absorb it all in. But the glimmer that his mother once saw stayed in the boy's eyes. He had witnessed true horror, he had to watch hundreds of people die and watch them beg for mercy as his father just laid waste to all those who opposed him, but the young Allister stayed passive, he stayed innocent. Something in him, maybe it was his age, or maybe it was something else that saved him from having his father's cruelty.

The night that the Mountain Kingdom gates fell was a night to remember. it was a night bards would sing and men would tell tales about for years to come. The four-waring kingdoms were The Volcanic Spire, The Crystalline Colonies and The Elves of Spirt lake as they had finally reached an agreement to siege the Mountain Kingdom, together as one. After arguing on the plan of attack for months, the three kingdoms decided and waited till the winter's last snow had melted away before they began their hunt for the king's head.

When the day came and they finally struck their armies as one unit marched towards the gates; the surprising factor of this siege was the Mountain kingdom was in the dark, not even one rumor had reached the tyrant kings ear in warning. Even as the approaching armies walked through King Edmonds lands, no one cared to call warning to their king, they just watched in silence as the soldiers made their way through. The three kingdoms all had different duties to achieve; The Elven folk from the Spirt Lake were the first in the gates, they were to break in and silently disarm and eliminate the first line of The Mountain Kingdom's defense, the Volcanic Spire soldiers were the second to charge into battle, they were to brutally make their way through the sea of now charging men and take control making their way to the throne room, the Crystalline soldiers were to calculatedly make their way through the wreckage, controlling the passive characters in this war, mostly the maids and butlers. A small selected group of Crystalline soldiers had the mission of capturing and containing the King. Ordered to take him to the throne room and one particularly selected soldier had the job of containing the prince and doing the same.

When the gates fell; the Volcanic Spire soldiers stormed through and the war alarm was sounded and young Allister was awakened from his slumber before being barricaded in his room along with eight well-armed and well-trained guardsmen. Allister sat in a corner far from the door and away from the huge glass doorway leading to the balcony. The guardsmen stood at the ready, seven of them facing the door, hands on their holstered blades, their captain kept one eye on Allister as the young boy panicked silently, his hands over his ears, trying to keep the sounds of screaming people being brutally murdered, that echoed throughout the kingdoms halls.

The captain of the guards was Jessie Silvermouth; he was very young for a captain, dirty blonde with a scruffy red colored beard, his armor had already been battle worn and the marks were there to prove it. Jessie knelt down next to the boy and placed his hand on the boy's head, roughing up Allister's hair slightly, trying to ease the boy's worry, "Don't fret, the Mountain's walls have never failed us before. This kingdom has stood for hundreds of years; it will not fall tonight." Jessie smiled as he patted Allister on the head, the boy just nodded and tried to give a smile, but he was just overwhelmed with his fear, tears were streaming down his face, as he trembled uncontrollably.

Jessie turned back towards the door, just as his fellow soldiers drew their swords. A clash of steel on steel, followed by a few loud thumps echoed through the thick wood of the door. The men readied themselves taking a step closer towards the sound, Jessie turned around and placed his finger to his lips. Hush, he told Allister as the boy crawled away from his location and stepped into his wardrobe, closing the door tightly behind him, with his hand over his mouth, drawing a small knife from his shirt.

The front door to the bedroom spammed opened and an elven man in blood stained black leather armor stepped in; he was silent as a ghost, a small curved sword in one hand and a straight cut dagger in the other. He was wearing no helm and his long black hair was tied loosely behind him, showing off his long elven ears, his face was dead white and his eyes were passively staring at through the soldiers. The elven man spoke calmly, "Stand down, I am here for the boy. No one needs to be harmed." He lowered his weapons to his side, waiting for their response. It was eight against one, the elven man seemed to be the one at the disadvantage and the guards charged foolishly. The elven man kicked the first, his foot hitting the man square in the chest, knocking him into three others, while placing his weapons in his sheath, he disarmed the next by breaking their wrist, twisting it behind the guards back and with one quick hit to the back of the man's head, the soldier fell unconscious with a loud thud. The attacker dropped down as the next guard took a swing at him, sweeping the guard off his feet, the elf landed and uppercut with the hilt of his now drawn dagger and again another soldier was out cold as the soldier's blade tumbled to the floor. The elven man made his way through seven of the men without drawing fatal blow or receiving a single wound to himself. Finally, he spoke directly towards Jessie; who stood dead still, almost in awe at the man before him, "I give you one last chance to leave, I have my orders to bring the boy, I do not wish to harm you or the child."

"We both have our own orders and duties sir. Draw your sword soldier, you are not taking the prince without a fight." Finally, out of his trance of awe, Jessie held his sword out towards the elven man in challenge.

The elven man shrugged and impatiently drew his sword, "I understand it's your duty to protect the boy. I admire that," the man said, waiting as the soldier charged. Their swords clashed against each other, Jesse was the first to draw blood, slicing the elven man across his face, as well as across the forearm. The elven man seemed unimpressed and unenthused about their engagement, but after a few minutes he finally took the assault, slipping past Jessie's defensives he stepped up behind him, the elven soldier took the hilt of his sword and cracked Jessie on the back of the head. Jessie slumped forward, but he wasn't done yet. Rolling over, he stood again, facing the elven man, he was struggling to stand disoriented by the blow, as the elven man placed his weapons back in his sheath. The head wound caused Jessie's vision to sway, as he recklessly dove at the man, the elven soldier took a step to the side and punched Jessie square in the nose, finally, Jessie dropped to the ground, defeated. His eyes rolled to the back of his head and he spoke Allister's name before he went into the blackness of unconsciousness.

Allister heard everything as he trembled silently in the wardrobe he was unsure how the interaction between soldiers unfolded, so he placed his ear against the wood, listening carefully as footsteps approached. Allister held his knife out towards the door and tried to hold it steady. The door to the wardrobe opened and the elven man looked down at Allister who just froze in fear. "You don't need to fear me; I am not going to hurt you." The elven man put his hands out towards the boy, as Allister just held the blade out towards him, but he didn't move to attack or strike the elven man. The man took the blade from Allister's hand and pulled him out of the wardrobe. "I am going to tie your hands now, but don't be afraid. I promise I will not hurt you." Allister was still frozen the elven man put Allister's wrist together and tied them loosely. Allister finally looked over the soldier's shoulder and he could see his guardsmen all laying on the floor lifelessly. Allister's lips trembled and he looked up at the man in horror.

"You killed them all." Allister started to cry, as his legs buckled under him.

The elven man ignored the child's cry as he caught his prisoner before he could stumble to the floor, "Can you walk?" He nodded as the elven man lead him out of the room, closing the door behind him, the elven man snapped the handle off the door and tossed it down the hall.

Allister tried to stop his crying, but the tears wouldn't stop falling down his face, he sobbed painfully, but the soldier just led him down the halls as quickly as the distraught boy could move his feet. Walking through the halls; the stone walls were stained with blood and the screams of more victims being murdered echoed loudly. Allister hyperventilated and vomited at the sight of first corpse that laid in their path, the woman had her throat slit and her clothes removed. The elven man looked over the corpse, Allister studied the almost sad, yet detached man who gave Allister a moment to recover before continuing.

Stopping at the entrance to the throne room, the elven man looked down at the boy, "You need to wipe your eyes." Allister did as the man asked and together they entered the throne room; it was overflowing with the conquering soldiers and the prisoners of war. The elven man whispered to Allister, his voice was almost calming, in a weird stern way. "Stay silent and stand tall. Be brave young one." Allister turned and looked up at his captor before biting down on his lip, as he was pushed forward.

Walking towards the throne, Allister could barely see his father through the crowd; he was beaten and tied, kneeling at the foot of his throne, his face was covered in his own blood and his one eye was swollen closed, he glared towards the Volcanic soldiers who were taunting and poking at the man with their blades, playing with his crown that they removed from his head.

The captain of the Volcanic Spire smiled as the boy was pushed towards him, he jumped off the throne and adjusted his chest plate, a black dragon was burned into the gold plated metal, striding towards the boy. "Oh Zavier," he spoke slyly, "what took you so long? Did a boy cause you that much trouble?" he mocked.

Zavier; the elven soldier, held the boy tightly by the shoulder as the Volcanic Spire soldier knelt down in front of the child, a wicked grin crossed his face, "King Edmond, how do you wish to die? Letting your son watch you die a pathetic coward, begging like a dog, or should I allow you to watch the boy beg like a scared little girl, crying and pissing himself?" The Volcanic Spire's captain placed his sword to Allister's throat as he laughed/

Zavier stepped forward grabbing the blade in his hand he gripped it tightly as he spoke sternly, "Jason, the plan wasn't to kill the boy."

Jason smirked standing up, the blade sliced through Zavier's hand blood dripping from the now open wound, Allister's eyes locked onto the wound, it had to have been painful, but the Elven man didn't seem to care, or wince to the pain. Jason spoke with a chuckle, "The plan wasn't to spare him either, this is war Zavier. What did you expect to happen?" The soldier stood up and pushed Zavier back away from the boy, spitting at the elven man. Zavier just stared back at the man and stepped in between Allister and Jason once again.

"We only need to kill the king, the boy had nothing to do with this. The death of a boy will not end this war."

"And sparing his life wont either."

The two men locked stares as the king laughed, "Bickering among men, how pathetic."

"Be quiet, your child's life is in jeopardy." Zavier pushed Jason back away from the boy, that was the first sign of emotion in the man's voice and even than it was detached, "End this war with the head of a corrupt king of a spike, not with the blood of an innocent child." In Zavier's eyes, there was determination, even if it was just the slightest hint reflecting in his eyes.

Jason snorted at Zavier, pushing passed Zavier and grabbing Allister by the hair, two Volcanic Spire soldiers placed their swords against Zavier's throat as he tried to push forward again. Zavier stopped in his tracks, standing tall and emotionless he watched as Jason walked towards the king, dragging the boy along with him, he kicked the king once in the crotch, laughing as the old king kneeled over, "Will you beg for your son's life?" as he forced Allister to his knees placing his sword to the child's throat.

Edmond stiffened and sat up straight, staring right back at his tormentor, "I will not beg like a dog, I am a king and my son shall die a prince!"

Edmond proclaimed loudly spitting at the Volcanic Spire Captain, hitting him dead in the eye.

Allister's heart skipped a beat, he held his breath to prevent himself from hyperventilating, he held back his tears as his fear took over. He was going to die. The boy expected the man to remove his head the moment his father had opened his mouth. Out of fear Allister closed his eyes while his lips trembled, but Jason just laughed and slapped the king on the back, grabbing Allister by his blouse he tossed the boy back into Zavier, the two soldiers removed their swords from the mans throat, slicing their blades against his skin, the bleed was minimal. "Zavier, for once you may be right. Edmonds death will do tonight, having the king realize in his last moments that his heir to his throne is going to grow old, as a miserable slave gives me enough pleasure for tonight."

Allister stumbled backward, tripping over his own feet, Zavier caught him and pulled the boy into his chest keeping him upright. Allister faced his father, their eyes met. Jason walked behind the king and pulled Edmond up by the hair, placing his sword to the king's throat. The crowd went crazy, cheering echoed all around, Jason smiled towards Allister who just stared at the blade being held against his father's throat. "Allister, watch and remem-" The king was quite literally cut off, as Jason's sword sliced cleanly through Allister's father's neck as the blade of Jason's sword clanked against the Mountain Throne. Blood gurgled and oozed from the king's mouth as Jason decapitated the king, raising the head well above his own, again the crowd roared. The tyrant king was dead; the war was over. Zavier quickly picked Allister up and headed out of the throne room, Allister was in total shock; he was soaked in his father's life blood. His hands trembled. He was alone now.

Zavier knew he had to remove the boy from the castle grounds or he too would die tonight in the victory celebration. Once outside the castle gates, Allister looked back towards his home. The place he was born, the only place he really knew. He watched as soldiers began to set it ablaze, all his father's banners, paintings and everything valuable were being taken or destroyed. Allister's lips trembled, this would be the last time he would see his home he thought sadly.

"I know it's hard to lose a parent, but now is not the time to cry, these soldiers. They will feed off your moments of weakness, force them to go hungry, boy."

"Why does it matter anymore?" Allister asked putting his head down and turning away from his home, Zavier placed the boy down, walking straight as Allister's whole body went seemingly numb.

After three hours of walking, the pair reached the caravan where all the horses, as well as the weapons and supply carts waited. Zavier lifted the boy up and placed him on the back of one of the supply carts; it was the first of many in a long line, cutting the boy's binds. Allister curled up with his face against his knees, Zavier saw it in the boy's eyes, as he spoke softly, "Now is the time." Almost as if on cue Allister began to cry. He was now alone in this big world and nothing mattered anymore.

The man's expression never changed, from the moment Allister saw him, to even now as he watched this boy cry his little eyes out. He just stood next to the boy and the cart, standing at the ready. Even though to the untrained eye, Zavier's expression never changed, he did feel terrible sorrow for the boy and currently, he had to protect him.

Zavier as the morning sun rose tied his charcoal cloak onto himself and placed the hood up covering himself from the sun. He looked at the boy who slept curled up, cheeks still wet from the tears. Zavier walked over to his horse and pulled a wool quilt from a bag and gently tossing it over the sleeping child. That whole night Zavier contemplated his actions as he stitched his arm and hand. Was sparing the boy from Jason's wrath really the right decision? Yes, the boy didn't deserve to die, but how was the young boy who was born to be a king adjust to living as a commoner? As an orphaned child. Zavier was accustomed to the terrible way people treated an outcast like him and he could only imagine that people would treat the child of the man who murdered hundreds worse than himself. And even though Zavier managed to get Jason to spare Allister's life, the boy still had more people to convince. This young child who was covered in the dry blood of his father still had struggles ahead, he still had many battles to fight. How was he going to cope with all this? Zavier asked himself.

Allister jolted awake hours later, the sun was just peeking through the hills in the distance and tossed the quilt off himself; his heart raced, as panic filled his face, he looked at Zavier's calm face, his captor and slowly began to calm himself down.

"Morning," Zavier said as he picked the quilt off the ground, folding it and tucking it under his arm, he just inspected the boy and asked. "Are you in need of anything?" Zavier's voice was calming to the boy.

Allister tucked his legs back to his chest are stared right back at Zavier, "Water, please and a cloth." Allister hesitated to speak as he looked away from the elven man, his eyes locking on his blood-stained arms and clothing.

"No problem." Zavier walked over to this beautiful red and white horse, placing the blanket in one of the satchels and grabbing a canteen and a rag. "Are you hungry?"

Allister shook his head as he took the water, placing his legs down hanging over the edge of the cart, watching the man closely, "Who are you?" Allister asked as he took a long drink before soaking the rag, squeezing it in his hands.

Zavier placed his hands on the hilts of his blades and stared through the boy, "My name is Zavier; I am the elected commander of the soldiers from the Crystalline forest."

"No last name?"

"None."

"Are you a soldier?"

"No," Zavier responded quickly as his horse nudged him with his nose.

"Then why are you here?"

"My fighting skills were required. I was asked to fight for the freedom and safety of the people of the Crystalline Colonies."

Allister looked at the man, his lips trembled as tears began to form in the corner of his eyes, "Why do people have to fight for anything. Who has the right to decide who gets to live and who gets to die?" Allister began to sob once again, as Zavier looking down away from the boy.

Zavier didn't hesitate to answer, "No one should have that right. Even your father in my own opinion didn't even deserve to die this night. He deserved to be punished for his crimes, but not killed and not in that way, but I had no say in that matter." Zavier was a pure pacifist. Maybe it was his elven nature, or just because he knows how cruel life can really be.

Allister wiped his eyes, only as more tears fell, "You killed tonight, you killed to get what you were ordered to get."

"I didn't kill any of your soldiers if that is what you were referring towards. My sword didn't take a single life this night. I broke the handle off the door so when your guards woke, they could leave, but it would be difficult for anyone to enter while they laid unconscious."

Allister sniffled and rubbed his red eyes dried, "But why?

"As I said no one should have the right to choose who gets to live and who gets to die."

With that Allister froze, this man, this elven man who spared his life confused him. Allister began to frantically clean the blood off his arms, he was rubbing his skin raw. Zavier reached out and placed his hand on the boy's and said nothing. Allister's face crunched as he began to cry again. He wanted everything to be normal again. Something that would never be so.

Zavier sat on the other side of the cart, he had given Allister a change of clothes, nothing he had could fit the young boy, but Allister wanted to be out of his blood-stained ones. He asked Zavier to keep the garments. Together Allister and Zavier sat alone for five days and nights, finally the soldiers returned from the conquered kingdom, cheering and dragging along miles and miles of women, slaves, some soldiers they spared and the heads of their victims; at the head of the pack was the Volcanic Spires men, Jason, the fourth son of the Volcanic Spire's King, Gregory Nightshade, held Edmond's head up high on a pike with the Volcanic Spire's flag waving in the wind. Everyone was covered in the blood of their enemies and ecstatic beyond belief, Zavier was repulsed by these people, but he dared not show it, he dared not to show anything. Even the people he called neighbors were cheering as they were soaked in blood. Zavier turned his face from them, "Would you rather ride with me, or in the cart, Allister?"

Allister watched in horror as his father's head was paraded towards him, "I don't want to ride with you." Zavier nodded and turned towards his horse, "As you wish," Jason marched right to the cart and flaunted Allister's dead father's head in the boy's face. "Leave him alone Jason," Zavier said as he stepped between the man and the boy.

Jason glared and backhanded the elven man, Zavier didn't move a muscle as the man's armored hand connected with his face. It reopened his wound from Jessie earlier. "If I wasn't so happy about being the man who single-handedly slew the tyrant king, I would cut out your tongue for speaking to a prince of the Volcanic Spire like that. Remember your place, Bastard." Jason spat in Zavier's face, but again the elven man didn't flinch. Jason growled as he taunted the boy one last time before turning away.

Zavier turned towards Allister who curled up against the cart looking blankly ahead of him.

Just before noon they were on the road: The Volcanic Spire lead the pack, followed by the Crystalline soldiers and the prisoners of war, as the elves from Spirt Lake held up the back. Allister was alone in the cart, the other people that were taken as prisoners of war were attached to the carts and chained along together. Among them was Allister's caregiver and his late mother's midwife, a dwarven woman Savanna Grey. She taught

Allister everything he knew. She was an older woman; her head was full of gray hairs with tints of the fire blonde she once had in her youth. She was the only person who could get away with calling Allister out for anything, or punishing him for behaviour. She was the closest thing he had to a mother since his real mother's passing.

"Allister, stop sulking! How many times have I told you to keep your back straight." Savanna barked, whistling for the boy's attention, she was three prisoners down from his cart. Allister just nodded and followed the woman's orders sitting up straighter, "You are a prince Allister, stand tall and proud. You're from the Mountain Kingdoms!"

"I am not a prince anymore," Allister mumbled looking down at his hands, even though the blood had been cleaned and the stains were gone, he still felt dirty. He still felt his fathers blood soaked into his skin.

"Rubbish, they can take your land and they can take your families lives, but they cannot take away where you come from." The dwarven woman was correct, but these words were not comforting and would eventually become Allister's burden. No one will ever forget who Allister's father was.

"Savanna, what is going to happen to me?" Allister's lip trembled, he fought the urge to cry again.

She snorted angrily and turned her head towards Zavier who was riding slowly beside the cart, keeping an eye on Allister. "Hey you! Soldier on the horse!"

Zavier turned his head towards the loud dwarven woman as he regarded Allister's question, "We are headed towards Travelers Valley, the Capital of the Crystalline Colonies, where the high council will decide your and his fate. I have no control over the counsel, but regarding Allister, I'll plead to them to spare the boy's life as I've already done. Likely of they allow, he will be placed in someone's care." Allister looked at the man who turned his head away from the pair, Savanna snorted at the idea but than silence fell over them because as much as she hated the idea, she had no say in the matter.

It was a long stressful ride for Allister, between his grief and the torment, poor Allister was exhausted and mentally drained. It was two full weeks before the Elves of Spirit Lake parted ways with the caravan and another three weeks before the Volcanic Spire soldiers marched away and only after three more long uneventful months, of bouncing along in a car while being verbally abused by other soldiers, while also watching in confusion as Zavier was verbally abused by his fellow men.

Finally, they reached Travelers Valley the place where he would be judged for crimes he didn't commit.

Chapter 2

The Crystalline soldiers reached home. The dirt road leading to the entrance was well kept, as perfectly aligned down the path where were thirty green lush maple trees, not a single leaf dirtied the road before the soldiers. The iron-barred gates creaked open and the sound of cheers came to the soldier's ears as the villagers saw their arrival. They knew the war was over.

Allister peeked over the cart curiously and saw at the villagers crowding the gates, clapping and tossing flowers at their soldier's feet. Allister was in awe of the town, it was huge, even larger than the towns of the Mountain Kingdom. Allister was petrified; he could see the angry glares directed towards him. Some men parted from the group to go off and be with their family, but the bulk of them kept on going making their way to the town hall, this was where the counsel waited for them.

The cart stopped just before the door entrance and Allister looked at Zavier who got off his horse and tied it to a post before returning. He helped Allister out of the cart while the other soldiers untied and unchained the other prisoners. Allister turned back at Savanna who gave him the motion to go with Zavier.

Zavier spoke as he lead Allister away from the cart, on hand softly on his shoulder. "Try not to say anything unless you are spoken directly to."

Allister nodded and Zavier removed his hand as Allister followed keeping very close as he saw the stares he was getting from the other soldiers. "This will be difficult, they don't need a reason to execute you. Give them a reason to spare you."

Allister just looked up at Zavier in silence and took a step closer to him, trying to get farther away from everyone else. The elven man had a cold towards everyone, but Allister was oddly reassured by the man walking next to him and found some reserved bravery while standing next to the tall man.

Zavier took Allister inside and made his way to the back of the audience, sitting him down nicely on the wooden bench.

Allister was once again in awe at the large church like building, its walls were decorated with coloured panels of glass and large fabric drapes of different shades of greens with the Crystalline Colonies sigil, the three crows stitched into each. The ceilings were vaulted almost as high as the throne room from Allister old home. It was stunning. Allister held his breath as he sat up tall looking over the layers of people who were watching the center of the room; there were five dressed chairs, they were all handcrafted and different in many ways; the colour of the dressing, the type of wood used and the detailed markings that were carved into the armrests.

The room went dead silent as the sound of shuffling feet echoed through the building and five people in red cotton robes slowly headed towards the chairs, their movements in sync with one another.

Zavier looked at the boy who stared in confusion and spoke quietly, so only Allister would hear, "The first person approaching is Lady Adrianna

Sliverstep; she is the last of the forest nymphs and controls the Mage District." She was the embodiment of grace, her hair was golden in colour that flowed down past her waist, she was slim and her skin was glowing with bountiful youth. "Next it Grundilyn Bolderfist, he controls the Dwarven District," he was an older dwarven man, with fire red hair, his beard hung passed his knees and was braided tightly, "Lilian and Cristopher Lynch control the Traders District," these two were an older elven couple, their hair was grey in colour and their face was wrinkled but soft, Lilian had a blindfold wrapped loosely around her eyes, "And the last, is Desmond Wolfblood, do not anger that man and you will be fine." Zavier warned, "He controls the Elven District." This was a very tall and slim elven man; he looked as if he couldn't break a twig, but there was a bitter, coldness that washed over the room as he walked across the floor and he drained all colour from Allister's face. Even though the man was looking straight ahead, Allister could almost feel his eyes piercing through his soul.

Zavier knelt beside Allister, ensuring that no one else could see him as he placed his hand on the boy's shoulder in comfort, "You will be fine, you don't have to be afraid of them." There was a small smile, for the first time since Allister had met this man he actually changed his facial expression! Looking up at the man and took a deep breath. That one momentary smile calmed all Allister's nerves. Allister smiled weakly and took another deep breath, trying to calm himself finally looking away from the man.

Adrianna, Grundilyn, Lilian, Cristopher and Desmond made up what the town called the four districts; the mage district, the dwarven district, the traders district and the elven district. The five of them held judgment over all of the districts. First, they were to regard the fate of the dead king's followers, the soldiers and servants alike, Desmond waved them forward; Savanna and many of the other house workers stood tall and patient, waiting for the man to speak. Some of Allister's father's soldiers were even there, still chained up to their captors with their captor's swords drawn to them. Desmond turned his nose to the men and women, his voice loud, as it echoed throughout the audience, "Slaves and housemaids of the house Ironfist, if you pledge no alliance towards your fallen house, you are free to live out your days where ever you feel fit. However," his tone of voice changed completely as he turned towards Edmonds soldiers, "the soldiers do not get the same kindness as I give the workers. You all shall be executed before midnight tonight." The room went dead silent for a moment until the guards marching the soldiers out the door with Desmond's judgment, the workers started yelling that they had no alliance towards the house of Ironfist, Allister's stomach dropped, no one was going to fight for these soldier's lives? These were people just following their king's orders! They were doing the same duty their captors' did when they killed all those other soldiers, other innocent lives! Sweat dripped down Allister's face as his heart began to beat louder.

Lilian frowned and when she spoke, her voice didn't echo like that of Desmond's, it was almost like a squeak, "We have one other issue to deal with this day it seems." She grabbed Cristopher's arm, "We have a boy in the audience who should come forth now. Zavier? Bring him forward please."

Zavier stood up and pushed Allister forward as they walked towards the Council, the crowd erupted from their silence, into roars of hateful slurs, as a few members of the audience began to tossed things in the direction of the two, Zavier made sure to protect Allister from all the projectiles by positioning himself between the crowd and him.

Adrianna spoke next turning towards the boy in her seat. She cocked her head and raised her brow, "Speak your name child." Her voice was like a song, it just flowed off the tip of her tongue with a strange, inviting elegance.

Zavier saw the boy freeze and spoke softly to him nudging him slightly, "Tell them who you are." Allister stood tall and stiff, his face went white as he spoke quickly, "I am Allister Ironfist, the only born son of Edmond and Castriel Ironfist." His voice cracked nervously. Allister could feel the sweat on his face as Desmond and Grundilyn stared right through him with a bitter, cold rage. Allister went to take a step back as all eyes were on him, but Zavier stopped him with his body.

The room still had not silenced. Until Lilian's voice broke through the crowd of anger, "Such a young boy to be facing us the council and for such terrible crimes that are being held against you." Sympathy was in her voice.

Grundilyn snorted rather loudly and leaned forward in his seat, his voice was cold and cracked, "Age means nothing in war! He's probably just like his father, standing beside his father in battle, aiding in the slaughtering many hundreds of our good men!" He was furious as he spoke and Allister trembled, trying not to cry in fear, "He's an Ironfist and he should be put down like a scum of the earth he is." Allister lost his breath as he was stared down by the dwarven man, everyone in the room watched as the child before them trembled, Zavier's heart sank for the boy, he could do nothing to console the child.

Adrianna laughed and cut in on Grundilyn's rant, "Do only the victors in war get their story told? Both sides in war taint their swords and their souls with the blood of innocents, but to the victors is it really for the greater good? No. Both sides can be wrong, as well as both sides can be right. Hasn't your son aided you in many battles? Laying waste too many men by the end of his own sword?" She was coy but honest, everything she said rang true. "The question we here have to answer today, is do the crimes of thy father burden thy son? He is but a child, I doubt he could even hold a sword in battle, let alone fight in one. Should a boy really be sentenced to death because of the man that bore him?"

Desmond and Grundilyn rolled their eyes at her empathy towards the child. Desmond's eyes never left Allister's as he spoke aloud, "The boy is twelve, which is old enough to know what is right and what is immoral. He could have defied his father, or at least aided in his fall." The man crossed hands over his lap and sat up straighter, his nose held high out towards Allister, "If you had the power, would you have stopped this war your father started?" The crowd was silenced by the question.

With all eyes again on him Allister froze, turning his head towards Zavier who whispered to him, "Just be honest with them."

Allister took a breath and turned back to the council, "No sir. I most likely wouldn't have."

The crowd again went into an uproar, they screamed, He's guilty, hang him! He has no remorse, he's a monster like his father! Kill him! Allister slumped his shoulders and fell back into Zavier who just placed a calming hand on the boy's shoulder again, his legs shook and he wiped his eyes trying to stop himself from crying as he trembled.

The council tried to wave them into silence, but as it was unsuccessful till Desmond yelled for calm and the room went dead, except for the footsteps behind the boy, Savanna stepped forward, Grundilyn eyed the dwarven woman up and down and smiled sheepishly, "And who might you be?"

"I am Savanna Darvish, past midwife to Queen Castriel of the Mountain Kingdom and caregiver to the boy you have on trial here. I just wish to speak before you judge this young child's answer, sir." She bowed low, knowing when to give respect, she was a lady of the court after all. The council nodded allowing her to speak her mind, "Grundilyn, this question is towards you. If your son, questioned your actions no matter how terrible they might be, wouldn't he be punished for his defiance? And I ask the same to you Desmond Wolfblood if your son refused you, wouldn't he be punished harshly?"

Desmond stormed from his seat pointing his boney fingers at the woman, "The difference in my sons are dead and that is because of this boy's father." He attempted to stare down the woman down but seeing the stubborn woman unmoving he sat back down hesitantly, he lost to the woman's stare.

"Yes, because of his father, not because of Allister," In that momentary fit of rage, Desmond lost his argument, "it might be hard for you to see, but Allister in a good boy."

Lilian spoke softly, "This woman makes a valid point, you have to agree. Desmond and Grundilyn, as much as you would hate to admit. Edmond slayed his father and all his siblings to secure the throne for himself, if he saw defiance in his own son, the punishment may have been great." Lilian placed her hand on Cristopher and her voiced changed completely, it was manlike and deep, "This boy has the blood of the Ironfist, even if we do not execute him, what kind of life would this boy lead? If we do not kill him, some stranger in the night would surely take his anger out of the boy. What kind of life will a prince from another kingdom have here, as an orphan child? No one would likely take him under their roof, unless for possible malicious reasoning's. It would be merciful of us to kill him."

Zavier cleared his throat, "If I may speak council?" They nodded towards him and he stepped in front of the boy, "I offer to take the boy under my roof at the school, I am the one who-"

The council waved Zavier into silence before he could even finish, a true sign of their disrespect for the man and spoke among themselves. Allister turned his head and looked at Zavier, who just stood their emotionless waiting for a response. He was confused; why did this man care what happened to him? Why was he going out of his way for a kid that he barely knew? Allister only turned back to the sound of a voice. Adrianna spoke again, "We will grant your request Zavier, maybe one day under your guidance, the Ironfist name will be able to atone for his family's sins."

The crowd re-awoke in furry, but Zavier remained silent and bowed respectfully low towards the council. Leading Allister out of the room quickly, just before they reached the door Desmond called outstanding from his chair again, "Zavier, remember this. Whatever crimes this boy will face; you too will suffer the same consequences."

Zavier didn't stop to answer the man, he just pushed the boy out the door into the empty streets. Untying his horse, he placed Allister up on the saddle and walked the horse through the town along the back streets. They didn't run into many people on their way through the town, but when they did people would toss rocks and yell profanities; this confused Allister though, they didn't really aim for him, they were aiming everything at Zavier and the calm, emotionless man just took the abuse. Even as one large stone hit Zavier in the face, cutting just above his eye the man didn't even flinch or retaliate as blood soaked the right side of his face. Allister just looked at the man and watched this blank unmoving expression that was Zavier's face. What causes a man to put up with this abuse he wondered?

Finally, after a ten-minute walk, Zavier and Allister reached a large rusted gate and a few yards beyond it was a large stone building, it was almost build to resemble a church, it had small glass windows all along the front and a pair of large oak doors. The front yard was well kept, the grass was cut perfectly even and the yard was kept tidy, the only thing around to clutter were the racks upon racks of practice weapons, most were made of wood and a few of cheap dulled metal.

Zavier looked up at Allister, "Do you need help off the horse?" he asked as he walked the horse through the metal gates, blood dripping down his neck.

Allister shook his head, dismounted easily from the horse. He was a prince. Horseback riding was mandatory.

The main doors to the building opened and this small, red-headed girl poked her head out of the door, a huge smile on her face as she ran over to Zavier wrapping her arms around his legs, before taking a step back, placing her hands to the side and taking a quick bow, "Welcome back Brother teacher." Her ear to ear smile disappeared as she looked at her brother's face, she noticed a few more scars and the blood what was dripping down his face was cause of concern for her. Zavier wiped some of the blood away and showed the little girl, that it was just a small wound and her smiled appeared back on the girl's face and she peered around the man, now looking at Allister. He met her gaze and blushed awkwardly. This girl was Valkyrie Dragonsbreath, she was almost eleven years old, with long curly red hair and bright green eyes, her skin was lightly tanned and her smile was full of innocence and respect for Zavier, she was Zavier's half-sister, on their late mother's side.

Valkyrie waved at Allister excitedly, "This is the boy right, brother?"

"Allister, this is Valkyrie Dragonsbreath. She also lives at the school with me, as you will now."

Valkyrie walked around her brother a stuck her hand out, "Hello Allister, nice to meet you."

He stared at the girl for a second and looked at Zavier who just nodded before taking her hand.

"Valkyrie, can you take Allister to the tower bedroom? The top floor will be a better fit for you, Allister, away from all the other students."

"But brother?" She began to question, but Zavier waved her off, Valkyrie just shrugged her shoulders, "Yes, Teacher Brother!" Valkyrie smiled and gripped Allister's hand dragging him along behind her. Zavier attempted to wipe the rest of the blood off his face onto his shirt before leading his horse to the stables.

Allister and Valkyrie stepped into the building and in the large main hall there were many benches and tables, grand weapons on display and a few banners with different family crests hung on the wall; it was rather plain for Allister's standards.

"So, if you haven't guessed, or been told already, this is a fighting school. No other school stands close to brothers in ability! People will travel for months just to enroll their child to fight along with my brother, the best weapons master alive." Valkyrie turned and smiled at Allister as they headed up the spiral stone stairs, "You are really quiet for a prince, why don't you say much?"

Allister shrugged, "For a lady, you talk a lot." He responded quickly.

Valkyrie smiled and laughed as she pointed her finger to the sky in protest, "I am not a lady; I am a warrior!" Allister managed a small smile. "My brother is a really good man; he will put his neck out for anyone. Don't abuse his trust." Her smile was filled with a sinister intent, which caused a shiver to go down Allister's spine.

Allister looked at the girl with fear, but she smiled again taking his hand she dragged him up the last few steps. It was just a thick oak door with a lot of wear and tear over the years, with a brass door knob. Valkyrie opened the door and beckoned Allister inside. "This is actually Zavier's bedroom; he doesn't really use it much. There is a wood stove, Zavier keeps wood stocked in the wardrobe. Zavier or I will bring you some stuff from storage to make it your own."

Walking into the room he looked around in shock, his father's servant quarters were more elaborate than this room, but Allister studied the writing desk filled with blank paper stacked neatly, the woodstove was close to the bed, hadn't been used in a while, made sense, Zavier had been at war for however long. There wasn't even proper bedding on, just a quilt folded neatly. Allister walked over to the wooden writing desk and placed his hand over it, "Thank you Valkyrie, but I would like to be alone now if you don't mind."

"If you need anything, I am one floor down last room at the end of the hall. Zavier will probably be in his office which is on the main hall, hard to miss or outside in the court yard." Valkyrie paused looking at the saddened boy, she hesitated, thinking she should say something, or do something, but left it at that, closing the door behind her.

Finally, Allister was alone and the tears began to fall, it was uncontrollable and painful as his eyes burned red, he threw himself on the bed, burying his face into the quilt as he curled up into the fetal position. Allister found himself crying for hours until finally, sleep took him; he hoped the pain of everything would be better, but his dreams were filled with the same nightmares he was facing in his wake.

Zavier had collected Allister some clothes and blankets and headed up to the bedroom, he knocked on the door and waited. Hearing nothing, he opened the door and peeked inside, "Allister?" He whispered quietly, then upon seeing the boy asleep on the bed, Zavier allowed himself to smile for a second. Stepping into the room Zavier placed the clothes in the wardrobe, removing the two outfits he had hanging and carefully placed the blankets over Allister, making sure not to wake the sleeping child. He could see the drying tears on the boy's face, this will be the first of many sad nights. Zavier thought to himself as he started a small fire to kill the draft and left without disturbing the young boys slumber. Valkyrie stood outside the door as he exited. "Yes, Valkyrie? Do you need something?" he asked looking down at the curious girl.

"Is he okay, brother? He looked really sad earlier." She asked as she fiddled with one of her curls.

Zavier walked forward turning the girl around as she started to walk alongside him, "He will need time; remember how you were when you felt you lost everything?"

Valkyrie turned her head and frowned, she understood what he was going through and her heart ached more for the boy.

"And remember try to not call me brother in public," Zavier spoke placing his hand on Valkyrie's shoulder turning her around as they walked down the stairs together. Zavier didn't wish for his half-sister to share in his torment.

The next few days were normal; for Zavier and Valkyrie that is. They started their preparations for the new arrival of students and did their regular chores. While Allister didn't leave his room. Zavier and Valkyrie brought him food and drinks, but that was the only socializing that he could stand for those first few days. Zavier was sitting in his office looking at the parchments of all the students that were going to be arriving in the next few days when he got a knock at his door. Putting the papers down he looked towards the door, standing up from his desk as Valkyrie opened it, "Sorry to bother you brother. I mean, Teacher Zavier, but there is a Lady wishing to speak with you about Allister."

Before Zavier could answer Savanna pushed past the girl rudely, "Prince Allister to you girl, he is of royal blood and you should respect him as such." Valkyrie just stared at the woman and stuck her tongue out, as the Dwarven woman stepped towards Zavier, she barely stood past his waist line. "Where is he?"

"Care to sit?" Zavier asked, pointing to a chair on the opposite side of the desk, calmingly taking his own seat.

"I asked you a question, where is Prince Allister." She demanded, her lip twitching with annoyance. Zavier nodded, "Allister is most likely in his room."

"Thank you for keeping him safe for now, but I am taking him with me, I can teach him how to one-day rule a kingdom, teach him to make a place for himself, what can you teach him? How to murder and kill more innocent people, to become like his father?"

Zavier crossed his fingers on the table and looked the woman in the eye, "Valkyrie, go and finish your duties please."

"Yes, teacher." She didn't hesitate.

Once the door was closed Zavier waited until he could hear no more footsteps, "Lady Savanna, I have no disrespect for you, I get what you are trying to do. But no one will sit on the Mountain throne again. Allister is a prince by blood, but he has no claim to the throne anymore. If he tries to claim it, he will be killed and no one will be able to protect him from that fate. I can teach the boy to survive and live out his life however he chooses, as a commoner. I can make it so maybe he will be accepted if that's what he chooses."

"I can teach him to lead an army, he would be able to take the kingdom back and he could make it better, he is a good boy, he is not like his father." She was stern and angry.

"You don't understand the situation here when the three kingdoms allied together to take on the Mountain kingdom, a treaty was signed stating no one shall ever reclaim the kingdom. If someone shall, war will break once again and more people would die, do you want Allister to restart a war that ended with his father's death and nearly his own?"

Savanna glared at the man; they both locked stares, both waiting for the other to break. Savanna snorted angrily as she turned her head from the stubborn elven man, as he began to speak again towards her, still calm and unaffected by emotions.

"I am not holding Allister against his will. If you honestly believe it is in the boy's best interest that you take him into your custody you may go ask him to go with you, or you may take him by force if that is your wish. Though I do have another option for you, you may stay here, keep an eye on him. Legally the council placed him under my protection, so under their rule, I am responsible for anything regarding him and his actions."

Savanna thought for a moment, "I shall take a room here, I will clean and I will teach Allister his normal lessons, but I shall respect that you are legally responsible for the boy, for now." She growled unpleased as she spoke.

Zavier nodded and stood up with a small bow, "Do you wish to see him? Then I can show you your new chambers?"

Savanna grumbled in annoyance, but she nodded in agreement and headed for the door allowing Zavier ahead once into the main hall.

Once upstairs they knocked on Allister's door he answered; he had changed into black trousers and a red loose cotton shirt, he looked up at Savanna with his large tired eyes, he was shocked and excited to see her, "Savanna, why are you here?"

She glared at the boy, "Is that any way to talk to me, Prince Allister?"

"Uh, sorry Lady Savanna, it is very good to see you again." He managed a smile, but it was weak and fake, as he gave her a quick respectful bow.

"Are you being treated well?" Savanna asked shooting a look at Zavier, who took a few steps back away from the door, his head in more paperwork he brought along.

"Yes, Zavier and Valkyrie have been quite nice to me and very helpful."

"Now don't lie to me boy, if they aren't treating you right, you tell me." She pointed her thick fingers in Allister's face.

"Honest, they are nice to me." Allister gave Savanna a hug and smiled at her, "Thank you for worrying about me Lady Savanna."

Savanna smiled and started grooming Allister's hair, her dwarven toughness melted away, as her motherly affections for the boy kicked in, "You know I will always worry about you. You look like a normal child in those garments." Savanna turned around and saw Zavier reading his papers, "Zavier," hearing his name he lifted his eyes from his work as Savanna continued to speak, "I just wish to thank you for sparing Allister's life. Speaking for him when no one else would."

"I did nothing extraordinary and you spoke for him as well. You probably convinced the council more than I." Savanna glared at him and Zavier just gave a nod of his head, "I would gladly do it again if needed. Allister if I may take Savanna to her room now?"

Allister nodded, Savanna and Zavier turned away from the boy; were things turning around for Allister? It seemed even though he lost so much in these last months, but he seemed to be gaining something different every day and he slowly watched the pain lessen with every passing moment.

Chapter 3

Finally, after three weeks of being at the school Allister managed to pull together some emotional strength to exit his room; though only at night when he knew the other students had already gone to sleep. He would just wander the hallways. Exploring his new surroundings, his new home, trying to find his place in this maze of a school.

Most nights he found himself sneaking around watching Zavier, the man was always awake! He would bring all the weapons and armor out of storage to sharpen and polish them until dawn, then he would place them all back where they belonged or place them out for that morning lessons.

Zavier never spoke while he worked, he just stood there in silence carefully inspecting every blade and piece of armor as if it was a piece art.

On the fifth consecutive night of Allister spying on Zavier from the shadows when elven man spoke with almost a tired voice, "Allister, is there a reason you feel the need to spy on me? Am I that terrifying that you cannot approach me?"

Allister was shocked and his knees clanked together nervously, "How long have you known I've been here?"

"Five nights ago, when you first began to spy on me." He didn't look away from the blade in his hand as the sharpening rock grinded against the metal. "I am elven; our hearing is more in tune than other races. Over many years, I have trained myself to detect even the most carefully placed footsteps."

"Why would you have to train yourself for that?" He asked innocently.

Zavier sat down on the bench and waved Allister forward, he listened and sat down beside the man. Zavier handed him a cloth as Allister helped polish the armor alongside him, "The reason why," There was a small pause as he dared not to look at the curious boy, "is because people are cruel and when they see something that doesn't fall into their idea of a perfect world, they try to eliminate it, torment it, or forget it. Many people have tried to eliminate me from existence in my lifetime. Quite a few had come close in my younger years." Zavier looked at the boy and hesitated to say the rest, but he did felt the boy might understand if not now, later he would, "There has been a few times I nearly took my own life. In my childish theory to make it easier for the world that hated me." Allister's eyes were locked on Zavier's face; the story he was being told was tragic and hit close to home for the young boy. Zavier could see the anxiety building in Allister's face, "I'm sorry, I should have realized this wouldn't be a story you'd wish to hear right now."

"No, please continue." Even as this story seemed sad and terrible Allister knew he needed to hear.

"How much do you want to hear?"

"All of it," Allister said as he placed the chest plate on his leg, looking at Zavier intensely.

Zavier cocked his head and sighed, "Well, I may not tell you everything, but we will see. The two of us have some things in common Allister. We are both hated for things that we cannot control." Allister didn't dare speak as he watched the elven man, sit there calmly blade still in his hand "I am a bastard son. My mother was raped by my unnamed father. She was very young and the elder man left her for dead. In my mother's village, bastard children were a sin, she knew she couldn't let those around her know that she was carrying a child of the man who raped her. She traveled for six months, alone, till she made it here. My mother cared for her new child for three months, before she gave me up to the Mistress of the weapons master who use to reside here. Being a bastard, I wasn't allowed to train with a person of higher status and having no status everyone was higher than I. People of status can physically abuse known bastards, publicly, or privately, in any which way they wish." Zavier paused watching, trying to see what was too much for the young boy, keeping details to a minimal, "Growing up, pretty much anyone could get away with doing anything they wanted to me." Allister again looked horrified, Zavier tried to reassure the boy with the slightest hint of a smile, "All the trials I went through, made me stronger in the end. If I had learned my fighting and stealth skills from the weapons master I wouldn't be the fighter I am today."

"How did you learn to fight then?"

Zavier looked at his reflection in the metal of the sword, "I had to learn to fight, to defend myself, To survive, I studied from afar, but mostly I adapted to the abuse. Now for someone of lower status to lay a hand on anyone with a status that was a punishable offense. It didn't matter if it was in defensive or not."

"How were you punished? Why were you punished, you would have been defending yourself?" Allister was confused and angered over this story as his voice rose.

Zavier handed the blade over to Allister and took another sword in his hand "That is a story for another time." He placed a warm hand on the young boys' shoulder, "Do you want to learn to fight?"

Allister shrugged, "I've been trained to fight, but I was never good at it."

"If you wish to spectate on this morning's lessons you may and maybe you will change your mind." Yes, Zavier rarely changed his facial expressions, but you could see the hint of a smile it in his eyes, a hint of compassion and understanding; it was soft and warming and maybe the only thing that could reassure Allister at that point.

Allister nodded and smiled weakly; he found himself studying the elven man and even in the dim candlelight he could start to see the outlines of many scars, trailing up and down Zavier's arms and on his bare neck. How many scars did this man have? Allister asked himself, trying to not stare. What all did Zavier have to go through to end up the way he was today?

Allister was growing ever more tired as he continued to pester Zavier with questions between yawns, he rested his head on the table watching the elven man work and listening to him speak until sleep took him slowly. Once he was in a deep sleep, softly snoring Zavier turned and looked down at the boy, he chuckled slightly and if you looked closely at his face, you could see smile wrinkles in the corner of his eyes. He put his work down and picked the sleeping boy up, placing Allister's arms over his shoulders and carefully took him up the stairs to Allister's room. Laying him on the bed, he placed the blanket over the sleeping boy and left the room. He still had more work to do before the night was over.

That morning was bright, the sun was shining and the smell of flowers filled the air; it was a great day to make the students sweat. Zavier wanted to smile as he hung the last practice sword in its rightful place and grabbed his own sword and running the freshly cleaned metal against his hand the smooth steel felt comforting against his hand closing his eyes he took a minute to center himself. As he started to swing the sword, but it wasn't like fighting, it wasn't filled with anger, it was calm, it was precise. The sword and he moved as one, it was almost a dance between steel and man. Every movement was for a reason, not one step out of place. Zavier stopped and placed the weapon back in its sheath before opening his eyes, he turned towards Valkyrie who was standing there with her hands behind her back and a smile on her face, "Good morning, Valkyrie. Take a position and wait patiently for the other students."

She smiled wider and bowed grabbing a practice sword, "Yes teacher!" Valkyrie sat down in the soft grass and stared up at her brother, he the only person she truly respected, trusted.

Ten minutes had passed and all the students were outside and in position, Zavier started the lesson, all the boys and girls that were in the class were new besides Valkyrie, so the lesson went agonizingly slow, Zavier focused on the fundamentals of welding a weapon and respecting the weapon, but even so most of them were still sweating by the halfway point.

All of the students were high-class children, they had some experience with swords and other forms of weaponry, but none showed any real promise, yet. Zavier instructed and watched to place each of them in categories, depending on where they excelled and where they failed to make notes, for later training after the first month.

Around the end of the lesson when the students were just practicing what they learned Allister peered around the corner keeping his distance from the group, Valkyrie smiled and waved, only to be scorn for going out of position by Zavier.

Allister laughed as Valkyrie give Zavier a funny face when his back was turned, Zavier knew what she was doing, it was written all over his half attempt to hide a smirk.

"Place your weapons away and you are dismissed for today students." Zavier made his way to the front of the class and tipped his head to the students, they all bowed respectfully and then they dismissed from the courtyard.

Valkyrie stayed back, helping Zavier place all the weapons in their proper place as Allister approached slowly now that the students were out of view. "I have never seen a lesson like that before," Allister noted. "Brother, I mean teacher," Valkyrie corrected herself as Zavier looked down at her, "He doesn't teach us to fight, he teaches us to be one with the blade, he shows us how to master it, not to kill," Valkyrie smiled as she looked up at her brother, who just looked down at her.

"You make it sound so much more than it really is Valkyrie."

"Teacher is just silly, he is the best weapons master ever! He can teach anyone to be flawless with a blade." Her smile was ear to ear and Zavier just shook his head at the girl and placed the last weapon away.

Valkyrie walked over and took Allister's hand and squeezed it nicely, "Want to come play with me?" Allister looked at Zavier who just nodded hiding his smile from the too, "Sure."

Valkyrie beamed dragged the un-expecting boy along behind her, "We are going to climb!"

She looked up at this large willow tree at the far end of the school and smiled widely, "Have you climbed a tree before?" Allister just shook his head and she just laughed, "I expected so! You are going to have fun!" She let go of his hand and jumped up grabbing the first branch, swinging herself up she reached her hand down, "Grab it; trust me." She smiled sweetly, Allister at first hesitated, but as he looked deep into her smile he found his hand reaching for her even before his brain knew what was happening. His face went red as their hands locked and he was pulled up towards her, grabbing the branch she helped him up, inches apart she laughed as he looked down at the ground. "Don't be scared silly, now come on that was the hard part." She continued up the tree and Allister grabbed onto the trunk of the tree as she became out of reach, not hearing him behind her she looked down, "Come on, just one step at a time!" She took a few steps down and reached out to him, "I won't let you fall." She laughed at him, but Allister took her hand and made her way up the tree along behind her. "What was is like living in the Mountain Kingdom? I've never been there, I've only heard stories. It's like a sea of tree and stone I've heard, is that true?" There was excitement in her voice as she questioned.

"More like a prison of tree and stone, it surrounded the place, suffocated everything it touched. There was almost no reason to have walls because the trees themselves protected the kingdom from a lot."

"You think that badly of your home?"

Allister thought for a second, during these last few weeks where his whole world changed and he began to adjust to his new, home, he actually had the chance to reflect on his past. See things in a different light and he looked at the girl who was only a few feet away from him and honestly told her what he thought, "It wasn't terrible, it was just lonely. I didn't see other kids my age, besides young slaves and they wouldn't even look at me. Which I understand but it was lonely."

Valkyrie looked at him and her smile disappeared as she grabbed his hand again, "Now you won't have to be lonely anymore." Allister broke eye contact and pulled his hand away from Valkyrie his face blushed red. "I'm sorry, did I say something wrong?" She asked confused by his reaction.

"No, I just want down. I'm sorry." Allister started to slowly step down, he was doing fine and Valkyrie was just a step steps behind him, but when he got to the last two branches his foot slipped and he lost his grip of the tree, Allister tumbled, Valkyrie tried to reach for his hand but only inches short she missed and nearly fell out herself.

Allister managed to land on his feet, but the force caused his legs to buckle and his ankle to twist, he fell to the ground his head connecting with the dirt. He laid there looking up at Valkyrie whose face was worry stricken, Allister lost consciousness for just a moment as she called down to him, "Are you okay Allister?" She jumped down beside him.

He just nodded and tried to stand Valkyrie tried to take his hand but he just pulled away from her and smiled, "I am fine." He pushed himself to his feet, not placing any weight on his left ankle that twisted badly as the pain intensified.

"You might not be in a few minutes." Allister and Valkyrie turned to see a group of five boys' and one girl standing around them. They were all locals, from the Traders district, Zackary Reignwater, son of Jax, his father was the owner of all the mines around the town; he was a rich and powerful man, with a lot of influence in the city.

Valkyrie picked her head up and stepped between Zack and Allister, "What do you want Zack?"

"Valkyrie why are you hanging out with a demon?" Zackary poked Valkyrie who crossed her arms and took a step back from the group. The girl in the back spoke, Melony Cooms, "I heard that the Ironfist were cursed, they need to kill or they wither and die."

Valkyrie turned her head and looked at Allister who was looking down at his feet, "Allister isn't cursed, he's nice, why would you even say something like that?" Valkyrie was confused, Allister hadn't hurt or even spoken to these people before, why were they trying to start something with someone they didn't know?

Zack smiled funny and stepped towards Valkyrie placing his hand on her shirt, "We are here to make sure he isn't a demon, because you know demons don't bleed, right?"

Valkyrie smacked Zack's hand away, "Just leave him alone, he didn't do anything to you."

Zack smack Valkyrie across the face, the sound echoed slightly, as he then pushed her over, "Don't touch me, girl!"

She went to get up but three of the boys jumped on her and held her in place, one sat on her chest and placed a firm hand on her face forcing her to watch the scene unfolding, unable to do anything about it. "Get off me!" She screamed as Zack just smiled taking another step towards Allister.

Allister just backed up, tripping over his twisted ankle he fell into the trunk of the tree, still standing and keeping one eye on Valkyrie, "Leave her alone." He finally managed to speak, "Fight me and leave her out of it."

Valkyrie kicked and screamed as Jack cracked his knuckle and punched the defenseless Allister in the face, he stumbled to the ground as Jack and the two-remaining boys' started to kick the poor boy in the face and stomach. Allister just covered his face with his hands and took it, Valkyrie still screaming for them to stop.   It only took minutes and Zavier came running around the corner, he pushed his way through the kids grabbing Jack by the arm and raising it above the boys' head, "If you want to fight, take it out in class, not after." Zavier held the boy tightly as he tried to pull away. All the others disappeared as Zavier just held stronger. "Allister, Valkyrie are you alright?"

Allister wiped the blood from his face and nodded still not getting up from the ground, "Zackary Reignwater, go pack your stuff, you are dismissed from my school."

Finally, Zavier dropped the boy, who stumbled to the ground and scurried away, "You'll pay for that!" He yelled back.

Zavier turned and helped Valkyrie up and then turned to Allister, "Are you sure you are alright?"

Allister just nodded and turned his head, not wanting to show either of them his face, as he was riddled with emotions, dirt and blood, "May I be dismissed to my chambers."

There was a hesitation, but Zavier nodded "Okay, I will come check on you in a little then." Allister just nodded, struggling to stand he limped his way out of sight as quickly as he could, not saying another word. Valkyrie watched in devastation and nearly found herself about to cry. "Valkyrie there was nothing more you could have done to stop it," Zavier said looking down at her.

"I should have." Her lip trembled looking up at her brother.

Zavier knelt down and pulled his half-sister in for a hug wrapping his arms around her, "You were brave for trying to stand up for him."

Valkyrie just frowned and pushed away from her brother, "Yes teacher."

Zavier placed his hand on her shoulder and looked down at the girl, "Try not to worry too much Valkyrie, I need to go deal with the others involved in the confrontation. Okay?" Valkyrie just nodded and ran off out of sight wiping her eyes, Zavier watched her for a moment before he headed inside.

Zavier didn't care if he lost money, all the kids involved in the fight were taken out of the program and he took them all to their houses that evening; no answers were given to the parents, Zavier just said they were not welcome at the school any longer. He knew the problem wouldn't be solved with just that, if they again wanted to threaten Allister it wouldn't take much effort to do so and there was another problem to be brought into light….

That night while Zavier was working he heard the soft and untrained footsteps of Allister as he made his way down the stairs, still limping as

he peered around the corner. Zavier turned, "Come sit over here Allister."
Zavier looked him over; his face was covered in a large bruise and he had
a small cut on his cheek, all minor and healing already it, "Are you
okay?" Zavier asked as he placed his sword down and crossed his arms.
Allister just stared at his shoes.

"It doesn't hurt if that is what you are asking. My ankle is sore, but
fine."

"I was asking if you were okay, not if it hurt."

Allister looked at the man and then back towards his swollen bandaged
foot, "I did nothing to stop it. I've been trained to fight, but I froze and
maybe for a moment thought... Thought I deserved it."

Zavier picked up the sword again and stared deeply into the shining
steel. "Sometimes it takes a stronger man to not partake in juvenile
quarrels, then it does to throw a punch. Be thankful you didn't throw a
punch at the boy, there would be some painful repercussions coming
your way if you did."

"Even though I didn't, you laid a hand on him?"
"I do realize that."

"What is going to happen to you then?"

Zavier started to polish and clean the next blade, "You don't need to
worry about that Allister."

Allister grabbed a cloth and started to polish and clean the blades
alongside Zavier, "Will you teach me to wield the sword as you do?"

"If you wish, I would gladly train you."

Allister smiled weakly, "How many people have you killed, Zavier?"

Zavier paused, it was almost like he froze in time for the moment as he thought of his answer, "I do not generally enjoy reflecting on that subject. I have been forced into quite a few wars in my short-lived existence where death and murder are sadly a part of war. With that in mind would you believe me if I told you that I have only killed three people through my military career and in my lifetime?"

Allister laughed, "There is no way you only killed three people." He looked at Zavier's face and could see this sadness in his eyes as the elven man didn't meet the curious boy's gaze.

"Honestly. The first person I killed," He cleared his throat, "He was an older man. I was soaked my own and others blood, I was in a frenzy and I just kept attacking the man. He was skilled and managed to parry most of my swings, but my blade slid up his and my blade went right into the man's jugular, he was dead before he hit the dirt." Zavier's stared ahead, Allister could see the discomfort in the elven mans face, he clearly didn't enjoy telling these stories, "The second person I killed was a younger man, I had been separated from the other soldiers and I was ambushed by sixteen of your father's soldiers. Even before that fight, I had obtained a few minor but painful injuries. I quickly disarmed and removed the soldiers from the fight one by one, it came to just me and the last soldier. I was exhausted… The soldier lunged faster than I could parry at that point and sliced right through my armour," Zavier lifted his shirt and Allister looked at the horrible scar that took up most of his abdomen, "I was losing a lot of blood and my vision was going, I just stabbed my sword when I saw the man grow near, he must have thought I was down for the count as he didn't even attempt to dodge my blade. It went right through him. His helm fell off as his limp body fell on top of me. I had lost so much blood I didn't even have the strength to push him off me. He was probably the age I am now when he died." Zavier concentrated on the blade in his hand "I was in a medical tent for two weeks. My captain wanted me alive. I was his perfect weapon, so he personally paid the healers worked on me until I could stand on my own again, only to once again throw me out into the fight."

Allister was confused, "You nearly died to that man and you still feel guilty for his death?"

Zavier nodded, "No man should take another's life."

"I think that's extreme!" Allister began to protest, "if you didn't kill him, you would have been dead."

"Even though I did kill him, I still would have died without the aid of the healers," Zavier explained, but Allister still didn't understand why he had these morals about himself. It seemed so weird to a boy who witnessed his father and his men kill thousands.

Zavier placed the sword down and stood up placing his hands behind his back, as he gripped his wrist tightly, that story always made him uneasy and Zavier was struggling to hold in his emotions, "I'm surprised you have managed to stay up this late every night Allister, are you use to restless nights?" He tried to change the subject.

Allister picked up another blade and fiddled with it, "I could always hear the screams of all my dad's prisoners. They would scream and cry, begging to be freed… I would stay up and think about who all these people would be leaving behind."

Zavier looked at the sadness in the young boy's eyes and shook his head, "Maybe you should get some sleep. If you are going to be prepared for training tomorrow; you will need some rest."

Allister placed the blade down, "Yes sir." He smiled and headed up for the room, Zavier wondered what kind of man this boy would become, would the world around him taint his innocence, or would he manage to prove them all wrong? Zavier closed his eyes and took a deep breath, collecting himself.

Chapter 4

With the group of students gone from his class Zavier was able to focus more on each of the students, working with what strengths and weakness' each of them had. Allister hid in the back away from the other classmates, but he showed great promise. He wasn't sure if it was anger or fear that was channeling this talent. He had such power in his swing, poorly trained, he would drop his shoulders with every thrust and his footing was weak that with any resistance he would just stumble to the ground. Easily fixed problems though, Zavier noted.

Valkyrie was skillful; she already had her preferred weapons and style, short swords and daggers. She would rather work on her footing and finesse than her force with the blades, which suited her petite frame. If Valkyrie got behind any opponent, even Zavier she could take them down and she had only been training for three years. She was going to be one talented lady, Zavier knew and he knew that if she harnessed her skills, she would be unstoppable.

Zavier froze and took a deep breath. He could hear horses coming to a stop at the gates, then the faintest sound of footsteps. Zavier clapped his hands and addressed the students, "Class is over for the day, drop your weapons where you stand and dismiss immediately."

Valkyrie was the only one who saw the red flags in her brother's request; her brother had always taught his students to treat their blades as their own arm, to treat it with respect. Laying a blade in the dirt, even a fake one was a weapon master's sin, Valkyrie just placed her weapon at her hip and stood tall looking at her brother. Allister was going to place his sword on the weapons rack until he saw Valkyrie still standing at attention, he then walked over to Valkyrie and copied her stance, looking at Zavier.

Zavier walked over to the two disobeying students and looked down at them, "I said you were dismissed. Go do what you wish."

Valkyrie frowned, "I wish to stay here."

Zavier refused to scorn the girl, or show any emotion, he just straightened his shirt and stood tall. "Valkyrie, you are a smart girl, you can probably assume what is going to happen. You will not want to watch this again."

With that Valkyrie heard the footsteps and turned around, her face dropped and her lip trembled slightly as she grabbed Allister's hand stepped behind her brother dragging Allister along with her. He was going to say something only to have Valkyrie snapped at him.

A group of soldiers and a short, fat man in red silk robes holding a rolled-up piece of parchment in his fat stubby hands came into view. The man was the ambassador for the trader's district, Yohan Grey. When it came to small offenses regarding his district he would deal with the punishments, rather than take minor dispute to the counsel.

This man knew Zavier well. Yohan smirked, "Zavier, you stand before be accused of placing a hand on the Son of Jax Reignwater. How do you plead?"

"I do not deny the charges laid against me."

The man smiled, "Good, the only good thing about you is you make my job easy. My only question Zavier, being that you are oh so smart. Why to go through the trouble of protecting that little monster?" Yohan stepped forward reaching out for Allister who just stumbled back with Valkyrie holding on to him. Zavier stepped forward and locked his hand on Yohan forearm.

Yohan stopped and froze looking after Zavier, within seconds the guards grabbed hold of Zavier's arms, one of the guards punching Zavier in the face. Dropping the fat man's arm the guards chained Zavier's hands in front of him and pulled him off Yohan. Zavier didn't fight he just stood tall and looked down at the man, "As much as you might not agree with me, you have no right to lay a hand on the boy."

Yohan granted and snapped his fingers. The soldiers lead Zavier away; Zavier didn't fight or resist, he just stood tall with his head held high, he had done this walk all before.

Valkyrie waited till her brother was out of sight, she squeezed her weapon as her knuckles turned pale. She at least understood what was going on, while Allister was in the dark. He looked at her in confusion as he shook her shoulder, "Valkyrie, what's going on?

Valkyrie frowned and entwined her fingers into Allister's not giving him any answer, as she pulled him along. They made their way from the school grounds to the center of the trader's district. Valkyrie lead them through the alleyways and hoped up on a fence, Valkyrie knew she didn't want any of the villagers noticing Allister and as much as Zavier was going to be angry that she was there, she had to watch, even if it hurt her. Helping Allister up onto the fence, he hung onto her and the fence post as he looked over the large sea of spectators. In the center of the people was a large wooden pole with a hook and chains attached to it. The soldier's shackled Zavier to the poll, his back towards the people, as they forced him to his knees. Allister suddenly knew what was going on, his stomach sank and he grew nauseous.

Zavier didn't speak, he just breathed silently with his eyes concentrating on the post waiting for this to start.

A man dressed in full black approached a large whip in hand. He was tall and muscular, his face covered in a dark leather mask. Valkyrie held her breath and held onto Allister's hand tightly. Allister watched in horror. He was the reason this was happening.

The man took his whip raising it above his head, it cracked loud as it broke through the air and struck Zavier's back, tearing through his shirt and skin. The crowd roared with excitement, Allister was horrified. Were they enjoying watching an innocent man being whipped? How were they any better than his deceased father? He thought silently, trembling. Valkyrie could see Allister's urge to go forward and do or say something, so she broke her silence. "Allister, all we can do is watch. If you go forward and try to do something you will just be there alongside brother and it would hurt him more not being able to protect you from that then this is going to physically hurt him."

Allister just looked at her and then back to Zavier to watch the horror, taking her hand again, he sqeezed it reassuringly. It had only been minutes and already his shirt was nearly torn off and soaked in blood. The crowd still cheered, but Zavier just knelt there gripping the chains, his head held high; he wouldn't stumble, he would stand tall before these men and never show them weakness.

This went on for three hours straight. Three hours of lashing for stopping someone from hurting another, for protecting a child that he is responsible for! The only time the punishment stopped was when the punisher was switching hands. The amount of blood, fabric and flesh that laid on the ground was repulsive, the bone was even visible, Allister had to turn his head from the scene as he held his breath not to be sick, he had seen executions before, but this was something different, this was just morbid.

Valkyrie tried as hard as she could not to cry, but she couldn't stop the tears, as she silently sobbed holding onto Allister's hand.

After an hour, the crowd slowly started to disappear only a few stragglers were left by the time the punishment was over.

The man placed his whip away and unchained Zavier from the post, he gripped the post as tight as he could, taking a moment. The man said nothing as he walked away from the podium.

Zavier stood up slowly and tore off what was left of his shirt. Zavier went to take a step and the world spun and he nearly stumbled, but he caught himself and closed his eyes taking another moment. Valkyrie jumped from the fence and rushed over to her brothers' side. Allister followed sluggishly, the guilt hit him hard as he couldn't find the strength to look at Zavier as they approached.

Valkyrie tucked herself under her brother's arm, positing herself to support her brother. Zavier just looked down and shook his head, trying to push her away, "I told you not to watch this, it only makes you upset." Valkyrie buried her face into his side, making sure not to touch his wounds, even though her arm was already covered in his blood. Zavier looked at the pale and devastated boy, Zavier tried to reassure Allister but the boy was too distraught to even listen to his words, "This isn't your fault."

Allister just nodded weakly and wiped his eyes; he didn't believe it, but he wasn't going to argue with the man, as tears began to brew behind his eyes. Zavier placed his hand on the top of the boy's head and roughed up Allister's hair, "Don't worry, all wounds heal in time." Allister finally looked up at him then pushed himself into Zavier's side, also supporting him. Together, the three of them walked back to the school. Valkyrie was sobbing into Zavier's hip, Allister was guilt ridden and just walked barely aware of the world and Zavier had to put all his energy into every step.

By the time, they reached the front gates Valkyrie could see the pain written on Zavier face, he tried to write it off, but it was obvious every step was agony. Savanna was just inside the front door, pacing back and forth impatiently.

She was about to ream Zavier about Allister missing his lessons with her, but before she could say her first word her jaw dropped, the floor was already covered in his blood that was dripping down his body. Zavier pushed Valkyrie and Allister away and placed a hand on his half-sister's shoulder to keep her at arm's reach, "I am sorry Savanna; I know Allister missed his lesson. It won't happen again."

Savanna shook her head in disbelief, "What happened?" she went to help him stand but Zavier just waved his hand at her.

"Nothing to worry about, I will be in my study if anyone needs me." Zavier just slowly walked passed everyone without another word. He stumbled using one of the tables for support as he made his way to his study.

Allister dismissed himself without a word, he couldn't look at anyone as he ran up the stairs; he was the cause of all that abuse.

Finally, alone Zavier closed the door tightly and placed his face against the wood, the stinging pain in his back made his chest tight as he struggled to take a breath. Zavier exhaled loudly and stumbled over to his desk chair, falling forward into it and having to pull himself up onto it. Sitting down he looked into the glass mirror beside him. It wasn't the worst he had suffered, didn't mean that it was painless.

He laid his head on the desk, closing his eyes he tried to forget the pain. He wanted to get up and dress his wounds, but his body was tired and weak. After about twenty minutes of peace and quiet, the door slammed open. Savanna walked in carrying a bucket of water, clean clothes and bandages as she kicked the door closed behind her. Zavier instantly sat up and acted as if nothing was wrong. She just rolled her eyes and dropped the bucket at his feet. Her heavy dwarven accent made Zavier smirk, "You don't have to play the strong man in front of me." She just stood there with a stern expression waiting for him to relax. Realizing that he wasn't going to win with this woman he leaned his head back down on the table, "Valkyrie explained what happened. You are a brave, but stupid man. You could have just let the boy's settle it themselves, Allister should have been able to defend himself. He has been trained for these things."

"He wasn't defending himself and he is lucky he didn't, or he too could be in the same position as I."

Savanna pulled a cloth out of the bucket of water and strained it before carefully beginning to clean the blood off Zavier's back and his wounds, "Why do you do this to yourself?" As the water washed away the blood Savanna was mortified at the scars that were appearing through the blood and wounds.

Zavier just took a deep breath, "I know how it feels to be judged for things you had no power in controlling, people like Allister don't deserve to be punished for someone else's wrongdoings."

Savanna shook her head and frowned. She had no words to say, just from looking at the scars she understood Zavier so much more than words and questions could ever answer. There was a strange innocence about him, but it was brought on through many years and years of pain. The way he cares for the people who have no place in a perfect society is only brought on by the fact he doesn't fit in a perfect society. He is a man with no name, no place rather than in the back where people can easily forget their mistakes, Savanna found that rather sad about Human and elven culture; dwarven folk would take pride in the bastard kin, even if born out of wedlock or other, they were still children with their blood running through their veins and blood was thicker than water, something the elven and human people seemed to have forgotten. We are all brothers and sisters.

Zavier fought with Savanna about bandaging his back, trying to tell her it would make it seem a lot worse than it really was, but she just smacked him on the back of the head and told him to be quiet until he let her work. He finally submitting again and closed his eyes, resting on the desk.

Savanna tied the last bandage and placed everything in the bloody bucket before taking a step back from Zavier, her arms crossed she stared down at the man, who stretched and worked out the stiffness of the bandages.

He stood up, nearly toppling himself over in the process as he became light headed, Savanna studied him before stepping back again, "What happened when no one else was here to help you?"

Zavier paused and thought back as she sat him back down in the chair, "When I was younger, if I was too weak to make it back here I would just pass out in an alley, sometimes I would wake that morning, others I'd lose track of how many days had passed." Zavier reflected his eyes distant, as Savanna just smacked him on the back of the head again, Zavier looked at her and smiled, he had never been scolded by anyone before, it was a humorous change of pace.

"Well, take it easy and rest, I am assuming you won't listen to my advice, but with good conscience, I have to mention."

"Thank you, Savanna. I do admire your heart."

Savanna just sighed at him, "I don't want to make this a normal happening."

"I cannot promise anything." With that Savanna sighed and left the room. Zavier just sat there looking at the closed door, this was strange, someone going out of their way for him. He had to actually put effort not to smile.

When night fell Zavier decided to put in a half night, only polish and tidy up the things that hadn't been done that day and actually get some sleep. He was mostly done his shirt was off and his bandages were bloodied from all the movement when he heard footsteps approaching. Zavier looked up and of course saw Allister peeking around the corner, guilt was unhidden on his face. He saw the blood and froze at the bottom step.

Zavier waved Allister over with a small soft smile, "What is on your mind, Allister?"

Allister slumped over and sat down beside Zavier, trying not to look at the blood-stained bandages he asked, "Does it hurt?"

"I am not going to lie, it does but I've experienced worse." Zavier could see that wasn't comforting, "Don't worry about it, Allister."

Allister just looked away, "I'm sorry. You got punished because I wasn't able to defend myself and then again you got punished for defending me. It's my fault you got hurt."

"You know I would do that for anyone under my care. I've defended Valkyrie in the same way and honestly, I get myself into this kind of trouble from time to time still, on my own." Zavier shook his fingers through Allister's hair trying to get a smile, "Cheer up Allister. All wounds heal in time and they make us stronger in the end." Allister just looked up at the elven man, even though he must have been in an enormous amount of pain, he was still just worried about Allister.

Allister wiped his eyes clear of tears, "Can I help change your bandages?"

"You really don't-"

"Please?" Allister asked, Zavier hesitated, but just nodded his head. Allister and he sat in silence as Allister bandaged all of Zavier's wounds, before both of them headed to bed.

That night while Valkyrie slept her dreams were plagued with visions of a future and the past melted into one confusing mess. Valkyrie wasn't just a normal girl, she had visions and when she had these visions, it was like she was a spirit being able to walk through someone's memories un-interrupting their pasts, or walking through someone's future as a ghost, but with her untrained mind, she could only see a few seconds in clips.

First she was standing in front of Allister as he knelt on the floor, his hands tied and Zavier's hand on the boy's shoulder, they seemed to be looking right her, but she turned around and a man swung his sword at her, she screamed and ducked, as blood sprayed and the last thing she was Allister's terrified face covered in blood as she was then thrown from this memory just as fast as she was placed in it.

Next, she was in the dark, she stumbled around trying to see where she was, when a single candle was lite in the darkness, she walked over to the candle and looked as a man appeared his head hung low and he was strapped into a chair, he was badly beaten and covered in fresh and dry blood, his clothes were ripped and it looked as if he had been tortured for weeks. Valkyrie only knew who she was looking at when they spoke, "You won't find them, Allister and Valkyrie are long gone. You will never find them." She tripped as she stepped back and it was almost as if the Zavier from the vision knew she was there, he lifted his head and looked right at her, as a shadow came up behind Zavier and slit his throat, blood pooled down her brother's chest and she screamed before again being physically thrown from the vision.

This time Valkyrie was woken, she screamed. Panicked, she breathed heavily, tears running down her tan cheeks, she was in a full-on panic attack and she couldn't control herself. Her body just shook and she could feel herself losing feeling in her fingers, she just pulled her legs into her chest and wrapped her blankets around herself. Even though she knew she was telling herself a lie, she kept telling herself it was only a dream; there was a slim chance her vision could be wrong, there was a small chance that fate could change. After twenty minutes of panicking she finally cried herself back to sleep. First thing in the morning she would run to Zavier and tell her what she saw that night.

Chapter 5

The next morning Valkyrie dressed and ran outside, knowing her brother would be already preparing for the day's lessons. Tears were streaming down her face she ran into Zavier's arms. Confused, he didn't reject her affection, instead just stood there and placed his hands on her back and listened to the girl's hysterical explanations. Finally, she took a step back from her half-brother and looked up at him with red eyes, "Allister is going to be the reason I lose you, I don't want to be alone again brother. Please don't leave me, don't let him take you away from me!" She sobbed painfully.

Zavier shook his head, knowing that she was talking about, "These premonitions are just dreams, which have a chance of coming true, just because you saw it doesn't mean it will happen. Even if it does, it would not be Allister's fault. Do you understand? Allister is just a child like yourself, who has been subjected to some terrible circumstances, again such like yourself Valkyrie." He knelt down to be face to face with the girl, as he wiped her eyes clear of tears, "You will hear some terrible things about Allister, people are going to say many terrible things, but don't believe everything you are told, okay? You don't believe that people say about me, why would you believe what others say about Allister? Only believe what you physically see before you."

Zavier was making a valid point to the young girl, but Valkyrie was too young to really understand all she knew in her mind was Allister was the reason that her brother was going to be killed and tortured, that was enough for her to begin to hate him. For the next few days Zavier forced Valkyrie and Allister together   in class and while doing chores around the house, trying to show Valkyrie that Allister isn't this monster that everyone assumed he would become, but every time she would look at Allister near Zavier, she could only see the imagine of her brother tied to the chair, beaten, bloodied and that was hard for the girl to disassociate Allister from the stigma and everything slowly began to take over and she just became bitter and eventually stopped listening to Zavier on the subject of Allister.

Zavier felt terrible for Allister; the boy was still feeling guilty for the punishment that Zavier endured and now the one person his age he thought was his friend was now rejecting him, for reasons he did not know of, couldn't control or understand.

Allister wasn't stupid, or blind and he could see that Valkyrie was pushing away from him, Allister didn't fight it. His depression started to seep in and affect his mind. Allister found himself just wondering the city streets alone in his spare time, attempting to keep to the back of the alleyways, away from prying eyes. There was something in him that hoped he would be noticed once he left the safety of the school grounds, there was something growing in him that welcomed the punishment, because for the most part, if someone older noticed Allister's presence they would release their hatred for the Ironfist name by beating Allister to the point he could no longer stand. Most days Allister would end up crying behind some buildings, bleeding all over himself, having to wait for Zavier to finally find him and carry him home. Allister never defended himself from his attackers, he thought that by letting them vent their hatred for his father through him, that maybe he was doing some good. And now that Valkyrie was beginning to hate him he began to believe that maybe his family were monsters, maybe that was what he deserved. Zavier tried to help him understand that what those people were saying was out of anger not truth, but it grew harder and harder to reach the boy. But saying all that, not all days were that bad. Sometimes he would be the one to come out of hiding; Allister was kind at heart and when he saw someone in need, he would go a help, most of the time, his body would regret his decision in revealing himself, but his soul didn't.

More than a few times if he saw someone struggling to carry their things, he would go a help. Sometimes they would refuse and spit at him, cursing at him to bugger off, but the majority of the time, they would thank him, seeing the child and not just the name and most people he helped saw something different than the stigma of what people said about him.

Allister even from time to time risked his life to helping those in need. One afternoon Allister rushed out of the safety that was the alleyways to the sound of people screaming in terror. A horse got spooked and along with the cart it was carrying was running ramped through the town central. No one knew how to stop the petrified horse. Allister heard a woman screech as he made his way into view, a woman had fallen in the path of the horse, twisting her ankle she froze in terror. No one went to help the woman as the horse sped closer towards her. Allister pushed his way through the people and rushed towards the woman. "Get up miss!" He yelled pulling on her hand she snapped out of her trance and looked and the boy standing up with his help, Allister pushed her ahead of him just as the horse and cart zipped passed them. Allister was clipped by the cart and he was thrown to the ground, his arm broke and he could feel his flesh being scrapped off his elbow. Allister grabbed his now broken arm and tucked it into himself self, he turned away from the scene about to head back into the alleyway away from the scene

When someone screamed that he had assaulted the woman, who was now sitting down, nursing her twisted ankle. One man grabbed Allister by his broken arm and pulled it up above the boy's head, Allister cried out as he could feel the bones wrongly adjusting in his arm, he tried to pull away but the man's grip was too tight. Allister's arm was already turning purple as a bruise formed, but the man didn't let go until the woman stood up and limped over. She poked the large man's chest and scowled him, "You back away from this poor boy." Just by her accent, Allister knew she wasn't from around here, maybe some how she didn't know who he was. He was shocked that she was defending him, but he was thankful as the man then removed his hand Allister dropped to the ground and the woman helped the boy up, "Thank you, young man."

Allister looked up, terrified and all she did was smile at him, he just nodded and then just ran away without another word. He wasn't really looking where he was going he was just running, after turning back for just a moment, he looked forward again, only to crash into someone. Falling back onto his butt, still holding his broken arm, he looked up in horror, just his luck was the only thing that ran through his head as she stared up at Desmond, the counselor of the elven district.

"I haven't done anything wrong, sir, I swear." Allister trembled and dared not to stand back up.

Desmond looked down at the boy, his face aged and wrinkled, even though, he still scared Allister; but the man just reached his hand out and helped the boy up, "I saw what you did there. That was rather brave of you. I am glad to see that you have proved that I and the other council members made the right decision in sparing your life that fateful day."

Allister held his arm and smiled slightly at the elven man, "Thank you, Sir." Suddenly Allister didn't see this scary man, he just saw a man standing before him. With that Desmond dismissed the boy and Allister rushed back to the school grounds. After that day, Allister slowly started to fear less of what people wanted him to become and started looking at who he was really becoming and so did some of the other villagers.

Savanna after Allister's fifteenth birthday felt she had to move on, she had done all she could for the boy, she went back to do what she loved, being a midwife, in a faraway town. Allister was devastated when she left, she was the one thing from his true home he was able to hold on too and now there was nothing.

After that seven more good years passed by quickly for Zavier, Valkyrie and Allister, the two children grew into young adults and for Allister, these years with Zavier and Valkyrie ended up being better for him than the life he would have had with his father and he knew that. Allister didn't have to grow up with the mantle of the throne above his head; no executions, no death, he could do what he wanted and he could make a difference. Unfortunately, he grew to look a lot like his father; he was tall and muscular, his hair was dark as the midnight sky, but his eyes stayed light blue, almost cloudy by the amount of white layered in them, just like his mothers, thought Allister never knew that.

Valkyrie outgrew her awkward height, only being a little bit shorter then Allister, her long red hair was curled and unmanageable besides when she tied it back with a leather strap, her large green eyes could see everything.

Their fighting abilities also grew stronger with age; Valkyrie could now even sneak up on Zavier when she really tried and her duel wielding combat was flawless when it came to one on one.

Allister was talented with a sword, matching almost every opponent he faced, but his talent actually came from a distance, he could hit a bullseye from a hundred feet away with no effort at all and with a bow in his hand he was a threat to be reckoned with.

Even though they were both trained under the influence of Zavier, Valkyrie didn't share her brother's moral's on taking a life and Allister sometimes saw what Valkyrie did when it came to taking a life but Valkyrie had no hesitation when it came to someone standing against her. Allister on the other had was always scared, knowing that people were still judging him for his father's actions, he only took a life when it came down to either him or them and even than he sometimes would just listen to Zavier's voice in his head and retreat. Allister had gotten himself into many fights in the few years, some he won and some he lost, but he always took everything as a lesson, as a reminder that his past hasn't been unwritten. He was still an Ironfist and many people lost loved ones due to his family line. Allister's depression became manageable for the most part. He found things to keep his mind occupied, Valkyrie's childhood hatred deflated slightly, but there was still that bitterness she held deep inside her, the image of her dead brother still stuck in her mind.

Chapter 6

Valkyrie had been gone for two weeks on a bounty; it was a rather simple one, kill the target. The man's name was Frey, no last name given, not that she cared. He was a man who stole from the wrong man and they wanted him dead and they wanted what he stole back. Once she got to his last known location it didn't take her long to locate her man, she was in a small fishing village just south of the Volcanic Spire, Valkyrie hated being around here, she could smell the sulfur wafting over from the Volcanic Spires stronghold and it always made her nauseated. But the job paid well enough for her trouble.

Valkyrie waited in the back of a tavern, her tan face fully hidden by the shadows, she waited and watched for her target to leave the building, another thing the young woman was good at, being patient and waiting for the perfect moment. She had been sitting there for three hours. The only thing to keep her busy was laughing at the drunken men stumble out of the building with skimpily dressed woman, it almost scared her knowing that if Zavier wasn't around to raise her after her parent's death, she might have been forced into that lifestyle, but she placed her lite pipe to her lips and took a puff, thanking that she didn't have to deal with that. Finally, she perked up and smiled, the man she was looking for; a skinny and short man, with a scar distinctive across his face. He had a woman at his side as he staggered along the street with her, hoping to take her back to his room at the inn down the street.

Valkyrie got up from her seat and walked down the street, quite a while behind them, her hood over her face and her footsteps silent. Hidden in the shadows she crept closer, she could hear the man telling the lady of all the great things he could buy her, Valkyrie smiled thinking to herself; you won't be able to buy her a thing when I remove your head.

Frey and the woman kept a slowly staggered pace, as the man was rather drunk which bored Valkyrie she was hoping for some kind of a fight. She stepped behind them right as they were stepping into an alleyway, Valkyrie placed her blade to the man's throat and covered his mouth with her hand she spoke softly into the pairs ear, "Girly, run along, silently while Mr. Frey comes with me."

The girl ran off and disappeared into the night leaving Valkyrie alone with Mr. Frey.

Pulling him into the alley she pushed him into the back wall, his face inches from her as she kept the blade against his skin. "Now you have an item that I am currently searching for, an item that you stole. Do you know what I am looking for?" Mr. Frey shook his head and Valkyrie smiled pressing the blade harder against his skin, "Does the name Firewielder ring any bells?"

Instantly the man froze and started to stutter, "I know, I know what you want, I can get it for you, it's in my room, I swear!"

Valkyrie smiled and pulled out a necklace from her pouch, studded with rubies and diamonds, it sparkled even in the dim lighting. "I kind of helped myself, but the Firewielder's prefer to make sure you can't bother them again with your thieving." There was an awful smile across her face as she slit the man's throat, nothing but gargling and sound of blood pooling on the floor of Valkyrie's feet. Her smile faded and removed the man's head from his shoulders, cleanly and placed his decapitated head in a thick sack. Valkyrie placed it on her belt and headed to the tavern for a quick drink before heading back home in the morning.

Walking into the building Valkyrie sat at her table in the back and the taverns woman brought Valkyrie a drink, just sitting in the corner relaxing she closed her eyes for a moment.

She could feel someone approach and sit down on the chair across from her, the air in the room shifted, he had the smell of the sea and miles on him. Valkyrie opened her eyes and stared at the man, she could only see a small scar on his lip as his dark crimson hood covered most of his face and his eyes, he was in all black, thick leather armor, he had at least three weapons strapped across his chest and a long, military sword at his hip. He was a soldier at one point, but he wore no badge claiming where he came from, he was clearly uncomfortable in his leather, he fidgeted uneasily in the seat. Valkyrie was about to ask who he was and why he sat down with her, but he started to speak before she was able to say or do anything, "Just sit down and listen, I have some worrisome news for people you keep in your company. There is word where I come from, that the Volcanic Spire is seeking Allister Ironfist's head."

"Why do you care?" Valkyrie leaned into the table slightly, trying to look under the man's hood, lighting her pipe taking a puff, trying to seem disinterested in his news, as she tried to calm her nerves.

He looked down more, seeing that she was trying to ID him, "I am an old friend of Allister's. Take my warning to heart. He might only have a few weeks before they are in a full assault for his capture."

Valkyrie cocked her eyebrow, the man didn't sound very old, but she was intrigued by what he had to say, "What reason would they want with him at this point?"

"It is said that one of the Volcanic Spire Princes in wishing to claim the Mountain throne for himself, Jason Nightshade, he wants to take out the Ironfist bloodline to make a solid foundation for his claim."

"Claiming the Mountain throne with or without Allister's death will result in a war, there is a peace treaty that was signed by all the kingdoms including the Volcanic Spire."

"It's the Volcanic Spire, do you think that matters to them? They live for war."

The man made a point, "Not unlike Edmond Ironfist himself." Valkyrie took a long drink and leaned back in her chair with a long sigh seeing the disappointment in the man's posture, "Can I at least have your name, sir?"

The man just stood up from his seat quickly, "I cannot stay any longer. Valkyrie, you need to be careful yourself, they will get rid of anyone who stands in their way." And with that, the stranger was gone in the crowd of drunken men and woman. Valkyrie got up from her seat in an attempt to follow him, but he was gone by the time she reached the door through the crowd.

With a lift from a trader heading to the Crystalline Colonies, Valkyrie made it back in less than a week, thanking the man she made her way through the town; autumn was in full, the trees were going bare as their crimson and golden leaves coated the streets, the people were dressed in more layers as the hard winds from the seas made their way towards the town. Valkyrie had been living there for more than half her life, but she still never felt this town was home, she felt at home in the school's walls. All the women here were ladies hoping to find a high-class husband to bare him many sons, in a lovely house; those women always turned their nose to Valkyrie. She just wasn't that kind of girl; she was beautiful and she was graceful, two things that would have made her a lovely wife, but the sound of being stuck under one man's rules made her cringe. She was a fighter, she was born to fight for herself, to fight for survival, not for anyone else. Her mother gave birth to her early while on the road, they were relocating after their village got raided, then when she was six, again their village was taken from Valkyrie, along with her father's life and the last time she faced losing a home she lost her mother as well, but even after all that, Valkyrie still stood tall and strong. With the help of Zavier, Valkyrie fought all the emotional pain and struggles. Even the way she overall looked pointed her out in a crowd, her red hair was untameable and she didn't try, she loved her fiery locks, the one thing she got from her late mother. She was always dressed dark leather armor, with a long black cloak and hood, maybe a dark blouse over top, no other woman beside some of the prostitutes dared to carry weapons, were Valkyrie never left the house without them, but she was okay with all that. She didn't need the company of those from this town, she knew all their dirty secrets. They were all cowards and hypocrites.

Surprisingly enough Allister heard Valkyrie approaching and that's when he began wondering what was wrong. He looked up as she jumped over the school's wall and landing with a crunch in the dead leaves, her cloak fanned out around her as she landed, like black wings of a fallen angel and then fell back into place as she continued forward passed Allister, she removed her hood.

There was anger, determination and something else trapped in the girl's face, Allister followed the girl with his eyes and asked, "Did the bounty not go well?"

Valkyrie just tossed the sack with her targets head at him and spoke, "We need to talk to Zavier, now." There was urgency in her tone.

Allister paused looking at the sack, it already began to smell, turning his nose to it, he picked up the sack and followed Valkyrie into the house without another word.

Zavier was in his office just working on his normal paperwork when Valkyrie just stormed in, again instantly, he knew something was up. He just sat there and turned towards her in silence waiting for her to speak rather than asking a question she was clearly just going to state.

"I heard a little rumor from… An apparent old friend of Allister's." She seemed puzzled by her own opening, but the boys just looked at her and listened.

After Valkyrie explained what she told by the cloaked man, Zavier was just frozen in contemplation, his chin resting in his hand eyes not leaving Valkyrie, Allister just stood behind her petrified, about what he had just heard. Already in those few minutes, he listened to Valkyrie explain he had pictured the many ways he was going to be killed and mutilated about sixty times.

Zavier didn't leave Valkyrie's stare trying to dictate how accurate her story must have been, "Allister, breathe." Allister's face was going blue as he exhaled calmly, "No need to panic, yes this can possibly be rather serious, but we need to figure how serious this stranger's claim is and we should address the counsel about these rumors. If the Volcanic Spire is planning to claim the throne, then there is a war that we need to be looking out for." Zavier stood up and grabbed his cloak, "I will be gone for a few days, keep your head down and don't make yourself overly noticed Allister, if you see or hear anything out of normal, retreat, do not stand to fight. That means you as well Valkyrie." His eyes met hers again.

Valkyrie pushed herself in front of Zavier not allowing him to exit the room, "Where are you going?"

"I'm going to find more information."

"I would be better at it than you," Valkyrie spoke quickly and instantly regretted speaking out as she did, as he just stared down at her tying his cloak with his brow raised.

Zavier placed his hands-on Valkyrie's shoulders and forcefully moved her aside, "Allister, take over the lessons until I am back. If I am gone more than five nights, the students should be heading home before winter hits, so stop with the lessons."

"Yes, Zavier." Allister said without hesitation, Zavier walked passed Valkyrie and Allister disappearing down the stairs to his armory, Valkyrie smacked Allister, hard, glaring at him, "What was that for?"

"Why are you letting him go off on his own, without a fight? We should be there, us, or more you should be getting to the bottom of this, it is about your life! Your mess! Zavier shouldn't even be involving himself!" Valkyrie was anxious, Allister assumed it was about being left in the background, she wanted to be at the front of every mission, every class; sitting and waiting for answers wasn't her style, but the truth was the thought of her childhood premonitions had been on her mind since the stranger spoke to her.

Allister just placed his hands in his pockets and looked behind him where Zavier left from minutes ago, "Do you not trust Zavier's abilities to collect this information?"

"Well no, but-"

"There is no but, Zavier is quite capable of handling things himself and he said don't make ourselves noticed, as long as we keep doing his lessons for him, who says we can't make our own discoveries?" Allister gave a slight grin and Valkyrie's expression didn't change, she was still annoyed but at least Allister had a good idea.

She punched him in the shoulder, "At least you are thinking, for once." She smiled smugly, as Allister nudged her back and headed towards the schools' entrance.

The two made it outside to see Zavier on his black steed, weapons dangling from his hip, Zavier stopped at the gate and turned around, "Don't cause trouble you two."

Allister and Valkyrie nodded, as he rode off into the crowd of the afternoon villagers, them all just quickly moving to the side as the horse trotted their way.

That night Valkyrie and Allister headed out; they knew of a few taverns just outside the wall where people traveling from all around Tasryn would go; mostly looking for a fight, or for information about other towns; they knew Zavier would be going closer to the source of the rumors rather than bothering with the odd whisperings of strangers, so they knew there wasn't much fear of seeing him there. Taking Valkyrie's horse, a chestnut colored, Peruvian Paso, Crimson, she was young, well trained and quite fond of Valkyrie. Valkyrie was in her black leather pants, with a forest green shirt over it, mostly to hide her weapons and a low-cut corset revealing an abundance of cleavage for her own advantages and replacing her normally black cloak with a blood red one, Allister was dressed in all tan leather, with a white blouse over top and a dark blue cloak, his long sword strapped on his back and a whole range of throwing weapons at his hips.

Valkyrie pulled herself up on the saddle and adjusted herself, she looked back at him and laughed slightly, "That's what you are wearing?"

Allister stepped up on the horse behind her, his chest just inches from her back as he placed his hand on the back of the saddle, "Yes, why?" Valkyrie didn't answer she just laughed again and they were off into the darkness, the sound of the horse's hooves clicking on the stone ground was just one noise in many as the wind howled and called to the night.

Within the hour the two reached the Tavern, The Blackeye; one of the few Valkyrie and Allister knew in the area.

Once inside Allister and Valkyrie separated, Valkyrie taking a seat in the back next to some large men who were highly intoxicated already, she rested her arms over two of the men as she jumped in on their conversation. Allister watched her as he took a seat at the bar, his hood still over his face.

The barkeep walked over with a mug and cloth in his hand "Ale for you boy?"

Allister nodded and tossed the man some coin, his eyes still on Valkyrie who was already downing her first drink as the men cheered her on, she was a lot better with people than Allister, which made this all the easier for her.

The barkeep was a middle-aged man, with a large beard and a ginger mustache, his eyes were dark and hazed over. Placing the drink down, Allister perked up, "Barkeep, have you seen any soldiers from the Volcanic Spire around these parts? Or news of them recently?"

The barkeep paused for a moment before picking up another glass cleaning it, he stared at Allister's shadowed face closely, he knew there was something about the boy's face that was familiar but he couldn't pinpoint it, "Volcanic Spire soldiers?" The man question as he thought, "They don't normally come around these parts," He was hesitating, so Allister placed a few more coins down on the table and stared the man in the eyes, his tongue loosened easily, "About two weeks ago. There was a small scouting group, they didn't say who they were looking for, but I did hear them congratulating each other on locating their target. Even though when they left they didn't have any captives in their possession."

"Volcanic Spire soldiers don't usually take prisoners. But they said nothing about who they were after?"

The barkeep shook his head and placed the coins in his pocket still looking at Allister, "No names, but where do I know you from, boy?"

Allister put the drink to his mouth and smiled, "I just have one of those faces." Every day Allister looked at himself in the mirror he knew what everyone else saw, they saw his father and Allister even sometimes saw his father when he just caught a glimpse of his reflection and he hated himself for it. His broad features would have fit well with a military lifestyle, but no, he was happy in the shadows. He turned his head to see Valkyrie, she already drew her dagger having it placed against one of the men's throats, they all looked nervous as they grew quiet. Valkyrie had a smile from ear to ear as her arms draped back over two of their shoulders again, the dagger just swaying in the face of one of them. Allister laugh, she is sadly better with people than I, he repeated in his head. Allister finished his drink and leaned back in the chair watching as things went down on Valkyrie's side, she was either getting somewhere good, or nowhere at all and you could never know until it ended with her. Allister couldn't help but smile as the girl worked her magic of intimidation. How could six large men fear that tiny little red head? Pure skill and the power of word of mouth. Pretty much everyone knew her as the ruthless huntress, who would kill and loot anyone for a price. Not once had she ever failed a mission and not once had she been defeated, that they knew of. Allister took pride in taking her down a few times in his lifetime, even if she would never admit it.

Allister could see eyes on him from some of the other customers of the bar and he just adjusted his hood and took another large drink for his mug, as a man stood up and sat next to Allister his large bald head, covered in poorly done tattoos got in the way of Allister's view of Valkyrie. Allister sat up straight and pretended not to notice the man.

But the bold man leaned in closer, his nose right against Allister's face, "Where do I know you from?" His breath reeked of booze and smoke, Allister turned to face the man; his five o'clock shadow couldn't hide the scars that painted the man's face with disfigurements. The man grabbed Allister's hood and ripped it off him, holding it tightly in his grip, the large man pulled Allister closer, "I asked you a question."

The barkeep turned away from the scuffle as Allister looked the man in the eye, calming he shrugged placing his hand behind his back grabbing one of his throwing knives in his left hand expecting things to get worse. "I don't know, never seen you before in my life, maybe I just have one of those faces." He said with a coy shrug.

The man lifted Allister up from his seat and glared, Allister pulled the knife out and spun it around in his fingers a few times, before stabbing it into the man's leg. Removing the bloodied blade, the large man dropped Allister and took a few stumbling steps backward, he was clearly unhappy with how his confrontation was going, so he threw a poorly placed punch, Allister stepped to the side and the large man fell into the chair with a loud crash, crushing the chair with his weight, with that the tavern was in an uproar. Allister sighed as men were tossing each other over tables, screaming and pulling out their weapons. Valkyrie was on one of the tables, smiling at Allister who just made his way through the crowd of men towards her. Valkyrie jumped on the first man who dared look her in the eye, wrapping her legs around his throat, forcing him to tumble, then she kicked in his nose, before moving onto her next victim.

Valkyrie made her way through four men when one guy grabbed her by the shoulder and cracked her once in the face; the room froze and Allister just stopped and watched the scene unfold. Valkyrie's eyes went wide and her smile turned into a twisted grin, she turned towards the man and swiftly she slipped under the man's feet, with the hilt of her blade she shattered his kneecap, the man toppled to the ground screaming in pain and Valkyrie placed him in a headlock between her tights as she continually punched the man. He was out cold and she was still punching the poor guy, her fists covered in the man's blood, finally after five full minutes Allister grabbed her by the arm and just nodded at her, she frowned but stood up wiping the blood onto her skirt. They made their way out of the tavern unnoticed, Allister and her pretty much unharmed from the brawl. Stepping out of the tavern Valkyrie shrugged heading towards the horse, "I always knew your face was so ugly it could start fights." Valkyrie teased, Allister just lifted a brow to her, "And why do you always have stop the fight just before it gets good?"

"What would Zavier think he if saw you try to beat a man to death?" Still keeping his emotionless expression locked on his face.

"He is already rather disappointed in my methods anyway, why do you think it would change now? I've done worse." She was rather smug about this and Allister couldn't help but smile at her pride. She was talented in a very scary way. Valkyrie mounted her horse and waited for Allister, "Are you coming?" She was already getting annoyed with Allister, she couldn't stand being around him for too long anymore. Allister just looked at her and stepped up behind her and off the two went in silence.

The night was still young, but the pair still decided to end their search for the night and head back to the school to calculate what information they had now and decide whether they should work together or turn and go separate ways tomorrow night.

Making it to the school they walked into the silent empty halls,

Valkyrie dropped her hood and untied her cloak dropping it into her hands turning her head towards Allister. He kept heading towards the stairwell, "Meet in my room after you put all your stuff away?"

"Yeah, sure." He turned around and looked back at her, as she tossed her wild hair out of her eyes.

Continuing up the stairs as Valkyrie just watched him leave, she couldn't help but dread their current events, she remembered her visions when she was younger too well. And recently she had been having more visions in relation to that one all those years ago. They were coming and she wasn't sure if she could protect her brother from what was coming for them, for Allister. She crossed her arms and thought silently as she made her way to her room, maybe she should have fought to go with Zavier, or go in his place, what if this is how he gets captured by the Volcanic Spire? Valkyrie turned and punched the wall angrily, her knuckles cracking painfully, but she didn't care; all her hatred for Allister was building up in her mind again, he was the man who was going to possibly get her brother killed, if not killed, tortured to the point of breaking, he was going to get Zavier destroyed. If this did happen what was Valkyrie going to do? Even the thought was putting this bitter notion in her head towards Allister and even though he wouldn't be the one to physically harm Zavier, he was going to be the reason for this. Through the years that she had known of this fate, she tried to tell herself that it wasn't for certain, just as Zavier always told her, it was a small possibility in a sea of changing faces, no fate was solid as stone. She tried to tell herself that if it did happen, it wouldn't be anyone's fault, but now hearing that they want Allister's head to start a war, to claim his once families throne, she knows that Zavier would give his life for Allister's and herself. She knew that given the chance to let them escape he would recklessly put his life in jeopardy. It saddened and enraged Valkyrie in more ways than she could understand.

Finally reaching her room, she changed into a loose white blouse and black trousers, placing her armor and weapons carefully away, her dreaded visions still in her mind, her hands trembled bitterly, she clenched her fist and sat next to the fire poking it with a stick waiting for Allister to join her, trying to calm herself down before he entered.

She laid on the dark furred bear rug, as the fire toasted her cold face, she sighed loudly as she tasseled her hair around in her fingers, letting the wild red curls tangle together, she rolled over on the ground staring at her ceiling she waited for Allister to join her.

Allister after fifteen minutes finally knocked on Valkyrie's door, she just grunted loudly and he entered, he stared down at her as she laid on the floor her hand draped over her eyes dramatically, "Sorry I took so long, Valkyrie."

"Don't you know it's rude to keep a woman waiting?" Valkyrie sighed lifting her head, she tried to smile but it didn't show through her clouded eyes. "Did you learn anything from the barkeep?"

"He said there was a small group of Volcanic Spire soldiers around a couple weeks ago, they didn't leave with anyone, but apparently, they found their target he said. That was all."

Valkyrie sighed, "No wonder Zavier didn't want us to come with him. You suck at gathering information." She sat up and crossed her legs, "The guys I was talking too said the group was looking for the Last

Ironfist, so confirmed again they are after you. They were looking to pay people off in the town to use as a distraction to get through someone they find a threat, which would probably be Zavier because the Volcanic Spire know him well, a lot of the soldiers now trained here when Zavier was younger and the prince who is trying to claim the Mountain throne is Jason the second born of the Volcanic Spire king and again he knows Zavier well."

"I even know him well enough to understand." Allister crossed his arms over his chest and looked down at himself.

Valkyrie paused and looked at Allister, she could see guilt and worry in his eyes and for those moments she forgot about her bitterness, "They didn't tell me who or if they managed to pay off someone off, but they are planning on coming back with a bigger group of men to take you back with them, apparently Jason wants to make a huge spectacle about this. He wants to start this war, he knows the allied nations won't allow someone to claim the kingdom without a fight, he wants to fight and him and his brothers have plans to take out all the kingdoms and claim them for themselves, this is a big thing, Allister and we are tied in the middle."

"How do these men know so much?"

"Boy's talking a lot when they drink? I don't know if I can really trust all that they said, it's mostly just speculation I'd assume, but most of it makes sense, but how could one kingdom defeat the other allied nations? Your father failed, they too would likely fail."

Allister ran his fingers through his thick dark hair, "My father almost succeeded remember. If the nations don't rally together and make a full front attack like they did when the Mountain Kingdom fell, they do have a chance and those soldiers are ruthless, do you think the other allied nations would have been able to defeat my father without them? They train for war all their lives; people elsewhere train for other fields, no one else trains their children hoping for a war like the Volcanic Spire do. We have to tell someone about this."

"Who is going to believe us? Two little orphans and one is the son of a man who started all this, the son of the man people still hate to this day."

Allister swallowed hard and shook his head, "We have to do something. This could be another full all-out war."

Valkyrie crossed her arms, "Is there much we can do? Besides hide you away, without the mountain kingdom their plan is flawed. It's a stronghold, which they would need if they wanted to take the rest of the kingdoms."

"I don't see why they need me to start this war, I am not the prince of anything anymore."

"You are the last born of the royal bloodline, if they wanted to truly strong claim, all the royal bloodline would have to be dead."

Allister frowned, "Does it seem that they really care for technicalities?" Valkyrie shrugged, "It doesn't make sense, but if this is what they are going to do and then the only thing we can probably do is keep you from them."

"I think we should at least try to warn someone about this."

"You are too much like Zavier, we will wait for Zavier and then get to see what he thinks. Do you think we should go out again tomorrow and find more information? Maybe someone knows when this is happening?"

"Maybe we should just wait for Zavier, we got a lot, well you got a lot. I don't know what else we will be able to find out without capturing ourselves someone from the Volcanic Spire."

Valkyrie nodded sadly, "Don't worry Allister, we will figure it out." He just looked away from her, a similar thing that was worrying Valkyrie was worrying Allister, was Valkyrie and Zavier going to put themselves in harm's way to protect him from a fate he slipped passed once before? Chances where he wouldn't slip passed it again. Valkyrie could see him thinking, she stood up and tossed another piece of wood on the fire. "What's on your mind Allister? Are you scared?"

Allister just shook his head, "I don't like being reminded that your brother's kindness towards me gets him in more trouble than I am worth. And the fact that I am going to possibly cause a war doesn't make me feel the greatest if I am being honest."

Valkyrie tried to smile, hoping she could attempt to be a little supportive knowing he was upset, but she couldn't, she just looked away from him while she spoke, "Well, Zavier would do it for anyone. You are our family now, we are supposed to protect each other, so we will protect you, okay?"

Those words didn't make Allister feel any better, if anything it made him feel worse; was he really so weak still that he needed to be protected? He just nodded in compliance. It wasn't until Valkyrie started to yawn did Allister make his leave.

Chapter 7

Zavier, found himself alone hidden in the shadows of the trees as he watched the Volcanic Spire soldiers taking a rest for the night. Their camp was busy; ten tents, which held at least six soldiers in each, five fires blazed high and as the soldiers were still wide awake and moving about the camp, drinking and talking rather obnoxiously. Silently he made his way around the perimeter, listening to the guard's talk.

"How much longer are we going to wait before we advance and take the boy? I get that Prince Jason wants this to go flawlessly, but really! How much trouble could one man and two kids be? We are a skilled army, they are nothing!" He sluggishly yelled.

One of the soldiers laughed as he drank from a mug snobbishly, "You don't know this Zavier fellow; he doesn't care if he lives or dies and a man who isn't afraid to die; that is a man to fear. He was living at the school back when Prince Jason was learning to fight as a child, Jason and this elf got into many quarrels as children. Some people even say that this Zavier fellow is a far better fighter than Prince Jason himself."

There was a sour laugh behind the group of soldiers, as Prince Jason stepped into view. Zavier's eyes locked on the man as he held his breath.

"Zavier is nothing, I could defeat him with one hand tied behind my back," Jason proclaimed loudly adjusting his shirt. "Some of you on the other hand would struggle against him."

The soldier was clearly embarrassed as their prince took a seat beside them, he smiled as he took his sword out of its sheath, "I want to wait. I want to ensure that my plan goes exactly as I want it too, I want Zavier to suffer and I want the boy's head publicly on a pike, as I did too his father. If you have a problem with how I manage my time-"

"No, my prince, I meant no offense sir."

Jason waved the man into silence and took another drink from his mug, silence washed over the camp and Zavier just watched from the shadows until the camp fell dead before retreating.

As he made his way back to his horse he was uneased by the lack of scouts around the camp; there were guards at the entrance and that was all? He would have easily been able to get in the tents if Zavier really wanted too. There prince was here, why are they slacking now? Something was up, Zavier noted. Maybe they knew something he didn't. Turning his back from the camp he silently made his way through the trees, silently as he avoided the dried dead leaves, the wind was whistling past his ears as he placed his hood back over his head, holding it in place. Pausing, he heard voices and saw the light of torches ahead of him. Zavier looked around and crouched low, proceeding with cautiously.

Finally, directly ahead of him he spotted a scouting group that was just returning to camp, they must have been just returning from a mission, as they no longer stood tall and on guard, they slugged around with almost pride at a job well done, even though they seemed empty handed.

They all were clearly exhausted from their journey as none of them spoke to each other nor where they paying attention to their surroundings as they crunched loudly through the woods, but unnoticed to them the scouts were heading directing towards Zavier. Thinking quickly Zavier jumped up into the tree and hid along the branches. He watched them breathlessly as he pressed himself against the tree. He looked directly down as one of the soldiers stopped right below the tree. Something alerted the man, as he looked around franticly. He didn't utter a word, he just stopped and peered around. Zavier continued to hold his breath and watched as the man shook his head before continuing forward. Zavier's heart pounded heavy in his chest as he took a calm, soundless breath. He just kept himself against the tree, waiting for a few extra minutes to pass before descending from his hideout and rushing towards his camp.

Zavier stopped and his body froze as when he finally managed back to his camp; it had been ransacked. The only thing not tossed around was his horse who just snorted angrily and stomped her feet. Zavier walked over and placed his hand on her muzzle, trying to calm the large horse down before grabbing what was left of his supplies. Jumping on his horse Zavier headed back to town as quickly as he could, he had been discovered.

The ground was wet against the horse's hooves as rain began to fall. The rushing wind tossed his dark hair around and wisped loudly in his ears as the cold nipped at him. Zavier tried to think about the situation, tried to calculate his next move clearly, they discovered someone was scouting them, he knew that Jason would push their plans forward the moment the information relayed and if somehow, they found out who was scouting them, Jason would be moving tonight.

With the little information, he received he knew that they were after Allister for certain and they weren't planning on continuing their mission until they had the boy. Fear washed over Zavier. If Jason and the Volcanic Spire wanted something, they would die out trying to get it.

By the time the sun peaked over the rooftops on the fourth day of Zavier's absence Allister and Valkyrie had morning lessons prepared and were just waiting on the damp grass for the students to arrive. Valkyrie bent over stretching, her hair tossing around, "Do you want to check out the Horseman's Hall tonight, or the Roosters' Bed?" They had only investigated three taverns, the second and third places didn't come up with any answers, but Valkyrie was still hopefully for this night.

Allister picked up one of the practice weapons and held it tightly in his hand inspecting it carefully, it had been a few years since he had handled a fake weapon like this, he almost forgot to respond to Valkyrie's question. He only realized she was still expecting an answer when she turned her head towards him, her long locks touching the dirt as she continued her stretch. "Oh, well the Horsemen's Hall gets more travelers than the Roosters' Bed. The Horseman's Hall would be our best option."

Valkyrie just nodded as the first wave of students began to enter the courtyard, the two together taught the class and then watched as the majority were picked up by their parents. There were only four kids left by the end of the day and they all were back in their rooms well before nightfall.

Allister sat in the main hall he was wearing a loose blouse and tight dark green trousers, he had only one small dagger strapped to his back and his cloak already tied around his neck as he waited for Valkyrie to come down the stairs.

When she finally did, Allister was in awe; her long red curls tasseled to one side, her lips were ruby red, wearing a dark red dress, with riding pants underneath. She walked off the last step and placed her hand on her hip and a grin on her face, "What? People at the Horsemen's Hall might not know me, I can possibly use my ladylike charm to get my answers."

Allister laughed as he stood up from the bench, "I didn't know you were a lady, what happened you I'm not a lady, I am a fighter?" He teased as she punched him in the shoulder hard.

They turned to head for the door when Zavier walked in, he was soaked from head to toe from the rain that they could now hear pouring down on the city and there was a nervous gleam in his eyes, as he was too tired to hide it.

Valkyrie was the first to speak turning to him with a half-smile. "Did you get any answers? I thought you'd be gone a few more days at least?"

Zavier tore off his hood and ran his fingers through his hair, "I ran into some trouble, in a sense. Allister, Valkyrie you both need to leave tonight."

Valkyrie paused looking at her brother in confusion, "Wait, what happened? Are you okay?"

"I found the information to prove that you were right, they have plans to move within the week." He lied as he assumed they were already on their way.

Allister just froze unable to speak, he clichéd his lips closed, worried that if he tried to speak his lips might quiver.

Valkyrie's eyes were wide, she was the one to first hear this rumor, but until now it was just that, a rumor, now it was a proven fact. "What are we going to do then?" She asked her eyes bouncing between her brother and Allister.

Zavier tossed his hair again with his fingers and straightened his posture; composing himself. "Valkyrie, you are going to take Allister to your secure location. I need to stay and wait for the last students to leave and then I will meet up with you two." Zavier placed his hand on Valkyrie's shoulder.

"No!" She protested pushing him away from her, "You should be coming with us."

"Valkyrie listen to me, you two go pack. I'll prepare the horses." She whimpered, as they just stood there until Zavier pushed Valkyrie towards the stairs, "Go, hurry."

"Okay, okay!" Valkyrie said as she grabbed Allister by the arm and dragged him up the stairs furiously.

Together the two of them went to Valkyrie's room first, she quickly tossed off her clothes the second she walked through the door standing there in just her undergarments her tan and toned body nearly bare, as she dug around for her black leather armor. Once tossed on she covered herself in a dark green blouse and began placing things roughly into a large satchel; bandages, clothes, potions, weapons and more.

Allister was silenced. He blankly stared into nothing using the wall to support himself as he felt weak in the knees, he had to shake this feeling. Things were going be fine. He had nothing to worry about, he kept lying to himself. But the guilt began to seep into his mind and his depression reminded him that if anything happened to Zavier or Valkyrie it was his fault.

Valkyrie stuffed the last thing in her bags and tossed it over her shoulder before standing up, her hair that she worked so hard to contain was now tangled wildly, she smiled uneasily and shook Allister's shoulder, "Come on. Let's go grab your stuff."

Allister didn't bother changing, he just placed his armor at the top of his bag and shoved as many supplies he thought would be useful. Valkyrie just stood there her eyes looking towards the stairwell, she wasn't even paying attention to Allister.

Allister finally picked up his bag and turned heading out his door without a word, Valkyrie following the moment he passed, the two placed their cloaks on and headed to the back of the building. Zavier was there with two horses saddled and ready to leave. He looked at the pair who quickly stepped towards him, "There is some food and gold in the pouches, try to keep out of sight. When they find out that Allister isn't here they will come looking for you."

Valkyrie couldn't see the change in Zavier's expression. He was the same calm and collected Zavier that she grew up to love, but there was something that she didn't understand that was a difference somewhere. "You are going to be right behind us, right?"

Zavier looked at grown up sister and wrapped his arms around her, embracing her tightly, his body was warm, "Don't worry, I will."

Valkyrie left it at that. She dared not to cry as she knew there were things not being said.

Zavier let go of his sister and turned to Allister placing a firm hand on his shoulder while speaking quietly so Valkyrie wouldn't overhear him, "You will protect her for me, right?"

Allister nodded as their hands clasped together, finally Zavier stepped aside as they two mounted their horses.

Valkyrie held tightly onto her horse's reins as they moved forward, "Zavier, you know where we will be?"

Zavier broke as he smiled towards the pair; they both saw it, the undeniable sadness that washed over their guardian's face. "Yes, I know where your safe place is a little sister." He smacked her horse on the butt and off he went trotting away, Valkyrie turned her head as the rain poured down and her brother disappeared from their sight as the pair rode off into the storm.

Valkyrie knew what ever Zavier was leaving unsaid was dangerous as he actually genuinely held her tightly, he called her his sister, but through her doubts she tried to remain hopeful, even as the thought of her visions from her younger years dwelled heavy on her mind. Was this the beginning ripples that would in the end lead towards Zavier's torture and death?

The two rode hard throughout the night and well into morning. Valkyrie was only a few seconds ahead of Allister who kept his head down and his mouth shut, the hood of his cloak fell, as he let the rain wash away his angered tears. He was also thinking of the worse possible outcome.

Why did even bother running? He asked himself as he watched the passing scenery, the leaves no longer crunched under the horses as the storm moistened everything it touched. Allister continued to speak to himself, if I run, I am risking everyone who is or will help me. I should just turn back, give myself into the Volcanic Spire soldiers and end this before it gets any worse. End this before those around me get hurt. The wind whistled high in his ears as the trees rustling around them silenced the sounds of the horses' hooves.

Valkyrie turned her head to ensuring that Allister was still following behind as she observed the expression look on his face, she could read his every conflicting emotion as it was written all over his face. She stopped and turned her horse around, patting the beautiful horse on the side softly, "Allister, talk to me."

"Just keep riding, Valkyrie." Allister looked away from her as his horse stopped, nudging Valkyrie's horse.

Valkyrie just stared at him, her horse getting antsy, "I know that's a lie, Allister. I'm not stupid, are you scared? Are worrying about Zavier? He said he would be leaving as soon as the kids are gone and they should be gone tomorrow afternoon, he knows where to find us, he will come join us."

"That's what he said, but what if something happens before that? Or what if the Volcanic Spire soldiers catch up to us, I don't want you or Zavier to suffer any more then you already have for me over these years. You've always been right to hate me, all I do is cause suffering."

Valkyrie held her tongue and really studied Allister's face for emotions, there was true honest guilt and nothing had happened, yet. "Allister, I can't promise no one will get hurt during this, but you are Zavier's family, you are my family. We need to protect each other." She reached out and grabbed Allister's hand squeezing his hand slightly, she gave him a weak smile.

Allister just nodded and pulled his hand away from her, giving her a fake smile to try to ease her worry, before following at her side. Only to once again ride in silence.

Chapter 8

As the sun set over the second day Zavier sat alone in the school. He was beginning to feel guilty. He wasn't use to lying to Valkyrie like that. He knew he had to do something more to help them, even if the only thing he could do was waste the Volcanic Soldier's time. Zavier sat at the back wall; one blade in his sheath, while his other firmly in his hand the sound of the metal scraping against the sharpening stone, it was comforting sound, him alone in silent solitary. He took a deep breath and placed his blade away. His time was running out, he had heard rumors that Volcanic Spire soldiers were patrolling the outskirts of the city earlier that morning; he knew it was only a matter of hours before they would be charging in and he was ready for the worse they could give him.

Two more hours passed. He could hear the horses outside and metal of the soldier's armour as they approached the door. He blew out the torch and pulled this blades from his sheaths. They pounded on the door, he could see the glow from their torches peeking through the cracks of the door, as the wood slowly but surely began to give under the stress of their battering ram.

Zavier took another deep breath and tucked his chair back under the table standing up against the wall, his blades held at his side as the door finally gave in. Soldiers poured into the room with weapons drawn. They swarmed the first half of the room, leaving the center opened; a man in blood red armour walked through the door. Jason, the prince of the Volcanic Spire walked through his hand resting on the hilt of his sword. As he stared right at Zavier, as their eyes met.

Jason smiled, "Zavier, it's almost like you knew we were coming." He toyed, "Just give us the boy and I promise to make this less painful then I have planned."

"If you assumed that I knew you were coming, would you really think Allister would still be anywhere near here?"

Jason stepped forward waving his soldiers to step forward with caution, some listened while others advanced to far, "Honestly, I was expecting you to be gone with them, but then again you always did enjoy a little beating now and then. You welcome death more than you lead on, don't you Zavier? All those times that I left you near death and you just clung on, maybe you just needed one last push."

With that the first man swung his blade at Zavier, who just simply dodged to the side and cut the man's hand off from the wrist, the man dropped to the ground and Zavier elbowed the next man in the throat, he also dropped to the ground, Zavier stepped forward and Jason's men stepped back realizing their mistake in underestimating the man who stood before them.

Zavier scanned everyone in the room, even the subtlest movement the soldiers made, he saw. Jason frowned, he knew this was going to be difficult if he played fair, but when did he ever play fair? He snapped his fingers and his men moved in on Zavier, all of them charged; besides his five personal guards who made a wall between Jason and Zavier jumped in, swords swinging wildly at Zavier. It was just blur, the fury of blades, blood and flesh, Zavier cut them down to size as quickly as he could, making sure none of them would be standing against him again, but he wasn't fast enough to deal with them all. He made his way through fifteen of them before they landed their first hit on him. The swordsmen got him deep in the shoulder blade and instantly his whole arm went dead, dropping his blade he quickly dropped low and swung with his good arm taking the man out by the legs and knocking him out with a swift hit to the jaw. Taking a step backward Zavier went into a defensive stance, blood poured down his arm and the soldiers took the opportunity of his weakened state and pushed hard on him. He knew by this point he wasn't going to make it much longer, it was easier for the soldiers to make superficial wounds now and it seemed that Zavier hadn't even thinned the group by any measurable amount.

He managed to take down ten more before he stumbled, the pain and the loss of blood made his chest tight and breathing difficult. Falling to his knee he wiped the blood from his mouth and clutched the blade tightly in his hand. The men still hesitated moving forward, but Jason ordered them to push harder. Zavier fought back the best he could, but his body was weak and there was too many. They cut, kicked and beat Zavier down, finally, Jason called them back as they stood tall, making an entrance for their Prince. Zavier panted heavy on his hands and knees, holding back his urge to gag on the blood in his mouth. He looked up and watched as Jason walked forward. He kicked Zavier's blade off to the side and his heart pounded heavy in his ears as the Prince stepped closer. Zavier pushed himself from his hands and stared up at the man, his face was empty, the pain didn't show through, the guilt, all his emotions were absent from his expression, as the large man in red stepped forward. Jason smiled, his hand still on his hilt; he stared down at Zavier with pride, "Tie him up and then search the school, there is a small chance they could be somewhere."

"Yes, my Prince!" His men called out, six of them grabbed, forcing him face first onto the floor as they bound his hands tightly behind his back before wrapping the rope around his throat. Every time Zavier attempted to struggle the rope around his neck would tighten, but at this point, Zavier didn't have any strength to struggle. The six men plus Jason waited in the main hall, along with the injured men, as the others ripped through the school, they tore off the banners, broke everything in their path, looking for possible hidden rooms, making sure to check every door. If Zavier had the strength he might have laughed, as they found none of the hidden entrances in their two-hour long search of the building.

Once Jason was satisfied that Allister and Valkyrie weren't in the building, he walked back over to Zavier and knelt beside him and leaned in close, Zavier could feel the man's breath on his neck as he spoke, "You could have just made it simple on yourself, run off with your pretty little half-sister, leaving Allister as a gift, wrapped just for us. If you would have done that, I would have had no reason to harm her or you, but now, because of your actions against me I am going to make sure she suffers just as greatly as you and Allister will, I'll force you to watch me take the life from her pretty little eyes." Zavier just stared straight ahead, taking a calming breath, "I just wanted you to think about that hard." He stood up and walked towards the door, "Kill all the soldiers who won't be able to move out and get our guest on a horse and let's move out."

Zavier was pulled to his feet and forced forward, he was pushed through the threshold of the school and he walked the steps for what he was assuming for the last time. Pushed up on a horse his binds were tied to the saddle, Zavier took a deeply pained breath as he rode in the center pack of the army, he was now a prisoner. He was a prisoner to a man which tried to make his life a living hell from the moment he met him. Still bleeding out, Zavier wasn't hopefully for the days to come.

A week after leaving the school Valkyrie and Allister finally reached their destination. A small fishing village as far as you can go east; it was called Kel'mare, named after the goddess of the sea and ironically the place where Valkyrie got her information about the hunt for Allister's head and met the strange unmarked soldier. Valkyrie knew this town well, most of the fishermen who lived there were wanted criminals from other parts of Tasryn; there was an unspoken law around Kel'mare. No one dared to spread rumors around these parts, or they would find themselves dead in the ocean. It was the only place Valkyrie knew they would be safe from the Volcanic Spire getting word of their location.

Allister cautiously kept his hood up and a scarf around the lower half of his face to hide his identity. Valkyrie, on the other hand threw her hood off and pulled her hair from under her clothes, giving it a good toss around between her hands. "If we head for the docks, there is a tavern with an underground Inn, mostly criminal's hideout there waiting for a boat to take them to one of the other islands."

"Staying with criminals? Sounds like a great plan and why again won't they rat us out the minute they have the opportunity?" Allister questioned as he rode up next to her.

Valkyrie turned her head and looked around at the small crowd of people, some carrying baskets of fish, while others just stood to the side staring at the pair, "Most of these people are hiding from things too, why give someone else up, when themselves are possibly worth a fortune and most rats can't swim to well if you know what I mean." Allister just shook his head, unsure if this plan was the right way to go or not, but he followed her.

Reaching the tavern, the Fishers Beginning; it was a large, old building, the dark oak wood was tarnished by the salted air. when the pair walked in the door the floor creaked with every step and the intense musty smell of old men and wine filled the air. The moment Valkyrie walked in everyone in the tavern tensed up, even this far out she was known? That was the moment that made Allister think twice about questioning her decision on coming here. She walked straight up the tavern keep and leaned against the counter. The man was a rather lean and older fellow with thick gray hair and a concerned look on his face, "You know I've seen nothing and I've heard nothing, so why you here Valkyrie?"

"Harrison, I'm not here looking for anyone this time. I just need a room. Two beds, downstairs." Valkyrie whispered low making sure only he heard her, the man nodded and poured Valkyrie and Allister a drink, he stared at Allister for a long moment as he took off the scarf covering his face, Allister stared back at the man, but Harrison either didn't recognize Allister, or he didn't care who he was. He knew Valkyrie would pay well and it's not in his business to ask questions. After he placed the drinks down, he nodded at Valkyrie and turned away back towards his other customers. Valkyrie took a long drink from the mug and turned towards Allister, "We either wait around here till the tavern gets quiet, or come back later tonight, which would you rather?"

Allister just shrugged taking a drink, "I can go find somewhere to house the horses'."

"They have a stable here."

"It would be better to keep them a real stable."

"We can both go," Valkyrie quickly added as she stood up from her seat.

"No, I think it's better if we don't wonder around together too much..." Allister just stood up and walked out, placing the scarf back over his face and readjusting his hood before leaving the tavern, Valkyrie just stood there, unable to say anything to him, she didn't know what to say and she didn't fight him. She didn't want to fight him.

Jumping into his saddle, he grabbed the reins of Valkyrie's horse Crimson and slowly made his way through the town. No one gave him a second glance, they looked and turned, regarding that someone was coming, but no questions were ever asked, no one glared at him, this was the first time he went through a crowd without being judged, at least on the surface.

Reaching the stable he dismounted and walked the horses inside; there was a young woman with long blonde hair tending to the horses she turned and with a tired smile, spoke robotically, "Two horses, twenty copper a night."

Allister hood off his hood and reached for his coin pouch, handing her two silver. "I will be back to check on them every other day when possible."

The woman took the coins in her hand and slipped them into her pocket, "Going to be here a while?" Allister didn't respond, "Is there a name I should file them under?"

Allister thought for a moment, "Allister."

"No last name?"

"None worth mentioning."

The woman smiled coyly, "Understood, follow me." She took Allister's horse's reins and led him to the far stalls. Unsaddling the first horse and taking off his bridle, as Allister lead the other horse behind, doing the same. Once both horses were undressed Allister patted the horses and stepped out of the stall.

The woman leaned against the wood and looked at the man, "Do your horses have names? They are beautiful, don't see many beautiful creatures like these around these parts."

"The red one is Crimson and the black one is Nightmare, they were bought in from another land a few years ago as a gift for a-" Allister paused, "For a friend of mine." For Zavier.

The woman laughed slightly as the horses came closer as she handed them both some snacks from her pocket, "What original names they lave."

"They weren't my horses to name, but they are good. Take good care of them please." Allister sighed, rubbing his forehead, "Need anything else from me?"

The woman shook her head, "Anything you feel I need to know before you leave?" He shook his head and turned away, "My name is Nina. I'll maybe see you around, Allister."

Allister just kept walking, he didn't bother placing his hood back on, he just walked through the town, observing the town in silence. People here didn't ever seem busy? They just kept on moving at a slow, but purposeful pace.

Allister would just periodically stop and look around, no one gave him weird looks and no one cursed towards him. He was just another stranger in the crowd, something he had never experienced before. He was comforted in being alone in this large, strange crowd. Allister just took a deep breath and took it all in, he wondered around aimlessly for a few hours, but he knew Valkyrie would have been worrying about his whereabouts as it grew closer to closing time.

He watched as the sailors walk the docks and the straddling ships docking into the port, the moon sparkled pale blue on the ocean waves, the full moon was clear in the midnight sky. The stars coated the never-ending blackness that was across the skies and Allister turned and make his way back towards the tavern.

He didn't even have to walk inside before he found Valkyrie, she was sitting in the front open window, with a pipe in her mouth and a mug of ale in her hand she turned her hazed gaze towards Allister and spoke, "Did you enjoy it? Not being recognized?"

Allister just shrugged and untied his cloak before opening the door. Valkyrie ran her finger through her hair as she took another puff from her pipe, the bar was empty this night, she looked towards the barkeep and he just nodded at her. Valkyrie placed her mug down and suffocated her pipe before slipping it back into her pocket. Standing up she walked over to Allister and took his arm, leading him towards the end of the bar.

The barkeep looked around quickly and opened up the door leading to the back of the bar and then pulled a few boards leading to a trap door. Valkyrie pulled the door opened and walked down the ladder, Allister and then the barkeep followed. Closing the trap door behind him, they made their way down towards the well-lit halls. Allister was amazed of the number of rooms hidden underneath this one little tavern.

The barkeep pulled out a ring of brass keys from his pocket and handed one to Valkyrie, "You room is the last one down the hall, no one is around your room, but there are people in some of the rooms down here, but they will also be keeping to themselves. You promise you are not here to make trouble for them this time, Valkyrie?"

Valkyrie nodded and took the key from the man's hand "I am here for my own reasons, I swear on my parent's graves that I am not here to apprehend anyone."

The man nodded, "If you need anything, send notes during the day, preferably morning, not the evening and if you need to leave, use to emergency escape in your room. It leads down to underground sewers and then heads towards the shoreline."

"Thank you, Harrison," Valkyrie smiled and turned away walking towards the door, Allister sluggishly followed.

Once inside the tiny room, Allister just stood lost in the entrance way. There were two beds at the far side of the room, at separate wall corners, in between the two beds was a small table with a brass candelabra with unlit candles placed in it. There was a square wooden table with four chairs around it; the craftsmanship was terrible, there were scratch marks from blades and pieces missing from the table. Valkyrie took a seat at the table and rummaged through the cabinets that were placed directly behind her at the table, there was a basket with food and plenty of alcohol. Valkyrie dove right into the booze, pulling the cork out and downing a good quarter of the bottle. Allister went to the bed farthest from her and sat, elbows on his knees, his hands limp, looking down at his feet. The silence continued over the pair, as neither of them knew or wanted to say what was on their minds.

As the night continued Valkyrie continued to drink her pain away, Allister just laid on the bed in silence, almost waiting for something to happen, just anything to happen. Finally, as the bottles began to empty one after another Valkyrie's emotions started to become uncontrollable as she found herself sobbing to herself. Leaning her head on the table, the nearly empty bottle clasped in her hand she painfully sobbed. The only person she ever really cared about was gone and she had to protect the one person she blamed for this.

Quickly her sadness turned into anger, she lifted her head and tossed one of the empty bottles against the wall, the glass shattered and she lifted her head, wiping her eyes clean of tears she looked at Allister, who now was sitting up in the bed arms crossed over his chest, he couldn't look at her. "Valkyrie. I'm sorry. I am sorry for everything."

"If you hadn't come into Zavier and my life." She could barely hold the tears back as she yelled at him, "he and I would be happy right now. Safe back at the school! But no, I am currently here with you and he... " She sighed hard, unable to calm her voice, "I had all the warnings, I saw this coming and I still couldn't keep him from staying, I still couldn't protect him from the burden you placed upon him." She didn't even fight for him to come with them.

Allister turned and looked at her, her words confused him, "What do you mean by saw this coming?" Valkyrie struggled as she tried to open her next bottle of alcohol, tears bubbling down her face, as she tried to wipe them away. Allister stood up from the bed and removed the bottle from her hand "What do you mean Valkyrie?" His tone stern.

She bit her lip and glared coldly at him, "I see things. I physically saw Zavier being imprisoned and tortured by the Volcanic Spire, because they wanted you, they wanted our location to get to you. When I was younger I had to watch my brother be murdered to protect you for nights on end. Zavier always told me, that these visions were always just possibilities, one path in a sea of options… But my visions have never been wrong. I knew this day would come, but I wanted to believe Zavier's optimism, I wanted to trust my brother. And now because I wanted to trust my brother's optimism I have possibly lost him for good!"

Allister's eyes widened and his lips trembled slightly as he placed the bottle down on the table. Allister grabbed his cloak and headed towards the door, "I'm sorry for everything." It was the only thing that could come out of his mouth, he was in disbelief.

"You better not fucking leave me, Allister!" Valkyrie screamed as she pulled herself from her seat turning and facing Allister tossing an empty bottle against the wall, "If I am going to do anything, I'm going to keep you safe for Zavier, because it was the last thing he asked for. If he is dead, or being put through something terrible I don't want it to be for nothing. So you are not running from this Allister." She trembled with anger as she reached for another empty bottle, threatening to hit him with it this time.

"I'm not running away… I just need some air. Your hatred is suffocating me." Their eyes met..

She knew she should stop him, but looking at his face, even as she saw the pure distraught, the sadness in his eyes, it still made her furious. She pointed to a small hatch behind the table. "There is the exit. I'll leave it open and a candle lit so you can find your way back." She managed to calmly say as she wiped the last of her tears away.

Without another word Allister took a lit candle and jumped through the hatch blindly, with a splash he found himself under the city, a water removal tunnel. Along the edges were paths above the water lines. Allister picked a hanging torch from the wall and lit it with the candle before following the flowing water to the tunnel exit. Allister could smell the sea and finally, hear the waves crashing against the shore. Turning one last corner he saw the ocean. Taking a deep breath, he jumped down into the sand. The crashing waves muffling the sounds of his footsteps he walked closer to the shoreline and took a seat at the edge of the dry sand looking out into the water, the moon large and glistening on the ocean surface hiding behind Allister. He looked up towards the stars, almost looking for an answer. He broke down. Allister could feel the warm tears on his cold, wind-kissed cheeks. He was alone now and he had a chance to break down and be venerable to the world. He tucked his face into his knees and wrapped his arms around his legs just holding himself in a ball, listening to the sounds of the waves, masking his pained tears as he sobbed to himself. The wind knocked his hood off and he looked back up at the stars and called out, "Zavier, I'm sorry. I feel like all I have ever done is hurt you and fail you and Valkyrie. All I ever wanted was for people to forget where I came from and just see me for who I am now... But it seems that I can't hide from it. I am a monster..."

"Who's Zavier?"

Allister jumped up and turned to find himself face to face with the stable girl, Nina. He wiped his eyes and placed his hood back over his head, ashamed that this stranger just witnessed him cry and speaking to the sky. "How long have you been standing there?"

"I heard someone talking, so I came to investigate." Nina studied the young man under the hood and smiled, "You okay?" She asked obviously knowing the answer.

Allister looked at her and questioned how to answer, "Honestly, I am not." He finally said.

"Do you want to talk about it? I know talking to a stranger isn't normal, but it's better than sitting in the sand alone, self-loathing oneself."

Allister's instincts were to tell her no and walk away but he looked at her and for a moment realized he didn't want to be alone. He just didn't want to see the hatred in Valkyrie's drunken eyes anymore. "I'd appreciate the company," Allister answered defeated.

"Just a little bit that way there is an abandoned dock, we could go sit by and wait for the sun to come up." Allister just nodded and followed the girl. Walking side by side Nina broke the silence, "We could play a game? I tell you something and then you tell me something about yourself to keep it fair?" Allister nodded behind his hood, Nina smiled,

"Okay, Allister ask me anything."

Allister thought for a moment, his head still blurry from the tears and the guilt, "Do you have a family?"

Nina looked ahead of her and thought about the question carefully, "I use to be a mother. I had a beautiful son and a husband."

"What happened to them?" Allister asked instantly.

Nina smiled and shook her finger in his face with a coy smile, "Only one question at a time. So, who is Zavier?"

Not wanting to really answer this question, he answered as straight as possible. "Zavier was my teacher and my guardian. He's saved me many times over and in more ways than he has realized…" Allister looked down at his feet fighting back his imagination. If Zavier was still alive, was he free? Or was he a prisoner of the Volcanic Spire? If that, what torment was he being objected too?

"Now you ask me another question." Nina was trying to get Allister out of his own head.

"What was your son's name?"

"His name was Richard." She smiled sadly, "Is Zavier deceased?"

"I don't know. If he is it's my fault and if he isn't there is a good chance he is suffering again, because of me." Allister rubbed his eyes with the palms of his hands and shook his head clear, "What happened to your son and husband?"

Nina knew the question was going to reappear so she smiled sadly knowing it was only fair and answered as they walked on the old, worn wooden dock. Taking a seat at the end of pier her feet dangling off the edge she answered, "My husband. He killed our son, still holding the bloody knife he turned to me and swung. I grabbed a knife and stabbed him." She smiled again looking at the near un-shocked Allister who was now looked at her. "Wow, normally when I tell someone I murdered my husband they show some sort of emotion."

Allister shrugged, "You did what you had too."

"If only I had done it sooner, I'd still have my son." Letting out a long sigh, "Who does the other horse belong too?"

Allister was almost thrown off by this question, but he answered after a hesitant moment, "Technically neither of them belong to me, but Crimson is Zavier's sister's horse, Valkyrie. We grew up together, we were friends a very long time ago." Allister paused thinking about the first time he met Valkyrie, her innocent smile, her genuine happiness towards him. She didn't care who he was, or who his father was, she didn't care what people were saying about him, she just wanted to be his friend. She wanted to make him feel better. Allister could see Nina looking him in the eye and smiling sweetly, "What are you looking at?"

"A hurting, oblivious man in love. So, Mr. Allister with no last name to note on, what are you running from?"

"Isn't it my turn to ask the question?"

Nina smiled and looked out onto the water as the sun was beginning to rise in the distance, "Nope, you asked me what I was looking at. So, Allister? What are you running from to bring you to this dead-end town?"

Allister froze, was he really going to tell her? Just bluntly tell a stranger? "Without all the deals. I am running from persons who do not like my heritage. My father was a terrible man and these persons believe, that I need to suffer for my father's crimes, even after all these years. They are currently hunting me and those who ally themselves with me."

"That's terrible, I'm sorry Allister."

Allister stood up from the dock, "it's late. I really need to return, thank you for talking to me Nina."

Nina stood up and smiled wiping the wet moss from her dress. "Maybe we can talk again another night? Just come find me."

"Maybe." Was all Allister said as he turned and walked away from Nina and the pier.

Walking through the tunnels in silence Allister reached the open hatch, the flickering of a candle still lingered above. Allister took a long silent sigh and climbed up into the room. Valkyrie was passed out on the table, the near empty fifth bottle still gripped loosely in her hand. Allister looked at the girl, her cheeks were still wet from her tears. Allister took the bottle from her hand and lifted the sleeping Valkyrie carefully and carried her to the bed. Placing her down, he picked the quilt up going to place it over her, but he paused. Her hair tossed angelically around her head, she looked at peace, no longer did she look angry, or stern. He smiled weakly at the girl and he wondered if what Nina said held any truth, was he in love with her? The girl who hated everything about him... The one he was hurting just by being alive. What a sad romance he was living if it was true. Shaking his head, he placed the blanket over her and laid on the other bed, rolling away from Valkyrie.

Valkyrie found herself thrown into a nightmare, another premonition? She walked out onto a dark lake, the water was thick with ash and steam, she couldn't see three feet before her face as she walked on top of the murky water. She just wondered walking across the cold, dark waves. She could hear the wind howling and groaning in the distance, she tried to follow the sounds blindly, unsure what to expect. When she finally reached the groaning, her heart skipped two beats and her ghost like a hand reached her mouth, she tried to hide her expression almost feeling as if he could see her, even though she knew it was just an image. In the boat was a beaten, bound and bloody Zavier, his head held high with the last remaining strength. She could see the expression holding on his face, she knew that he wouldn't break to them. Her ghost like body rushed towards him, her hand reaching towards her brother's shoulder, she tried to hold on to him, but her hand just ran right through him. The moment her hand connected, Zavier turned his head and stared right at her, Valkyrie jumped back, could this image of her brother see her? He looked her right at her, he tried not to show emotion, but she could see regret, guilt in his eyes. He whispered her name to the wind, a hand grabbed Zavier by the hair and placed a blade to his throat, Zavier didn't struggle, he didn't dare breathe. Valkyrie's body froze and she just watched as the boat continued forward without her, tears filled her eyes.

Suddenly the wind picked up again and a swirling mist formed around her, knocking her off her feet. The water absorbed her, her body sunk and she could feel the presser forcing her to let go of her breath. Once she did the water disappeared and she was standing in a small house, Valkyrie had never seen this building before, it was rather simple but well kept, the house had quite a few grand furnishings, a large fire pit, wood stove, a large oak dining table, shelves of books, weapons hung neatly on the walls, furs from exotic animal's she had never seen before and a dark iron desk filled with papers. She was alone at first, she just looked around the house, running her fingers along the furnishings, trying to find out what she was supposed to see here.

Valkyrie turned around and nearly fell over as there was a dark haired boy sat on the floor, his legs were crossed and head was down, it was almost like he was speaking to Valkyrie again, but when Valkyrie blinked there was a faceless woman kneeling down in front of the child, through her ghostly body, she could only see a sad smile across the woman's pale face, "Did dad die for a reason?"

The woman ran her fingers through the child's hair, "Your father was a great man and when he died, he managed to change people. He died for something he was proud to die for. Always remember that your father sacrificed himself for the better of his people."

Valkyrie looked down at the child studying him carefully, there was something about the young boy's face, his light blue eyes that sparkled, never truly content or not thinking about something, she had seen this in someone before, but no face, no name came to mind.

Again the mist formed around her, tossing her into the never ending darkness. When she finally woke, she tossed the blankets off herself and pulled her legs into her chest. She attempted to hold back her tears, but they just fell uncontrollably, she knew now that Zavier wasn't coming, she knew that his fate was sealed; the Volcanic Spire either had or will capture Zavier before he ever reached them.

Chapter 9

Zavier knew how to take a beating. His body had been put through many forms of torture in his lifetime and this was no different; his hands were bound behind his back, his face in the dirt and an armored foot against his cheek. There were five of Jason's personal guard's around him, while the other soldiers rested and restocked. Zavier had this shirt ripped off his back, blood soaked through his pants, he was caked in old, dry blood, mud and dirt. His shoulder gash from the school was infected with dirt, slowing the healing process as it reopened once again.

One guard continuously kicked Zavier in the stomach and ribcage, Zavier could feel with every blow his bones weakening finally, he felt one of his ribs crack. Biting down on the inside of his lip, he refused to give these men the satisfaction of seeing the pain in his face, he refused to break under their presser.

The one with his foot on Zavier's face stomped down on him, before kneeling his foot still firm on Zavier's cheek, listening carefully to the sound of Zavier's breathing, the guard's breath reeked of bad ale and old food.

"You aren't that tough. If you were really as tough as they say you are, you would have killed all our men. You are just the same scared little boy from back when I still went to the school, you are just a bastard who never learned his place." The man moved his foot from Zavier's face, his mistake as Zavier jerked his forehead up into the man's nose.

The soldier stumbled to the dirt, his hand over his bloody nose, as he kicked Zavier in the face, "Fucking ass."

One of the soldier's pulled Zavier to his knees holding him up by his arms, while the others continued to beat him.

Zavier took every punch with grace, when they finally grew tired, his face was a swollen purple and bloodied, he could feel at least three cracked or broken ribs, a dislocated shoulder. Breathing, blinking, any form of movement was painful, but Zavier just managed to keep his head up and just stare forward, watching the guards grinning with a job well done.

"Take him closer to the fire, I think he's ready for us to begin asking questions."

Zavier took a deep, painful breath as they pushed him forward, tossing him into a chair one placed him into a headlock keeping him in place, while the man with the broken nose dared to lean in again on Zavier. "I know we have asked you a million times, but we are going to ask a million times more. Where did the little bitch and the bastard Prince run off too?" Zavier just looked the man in the eye, the soldier clenched up his fist and knocked Zavier in the jaw, "I'm going to ask again, Zavier. Where did they go?" They had been at this for days, Zavier wondered if they'd ever realize that he wasn't going to give them the information they were looking for, "I get it, you don't want your sister to be hurt in this mess, but the longer you keep the information of the bastard Prince's whereabouts, the worse it's going to be for you and her. No matter what you do, we are going to find him and your pretty, little sister and I will make sure she pays for our wasted time here. Do you want to see us violate her because you want to be the big tough guy?"

Zavier looked the man in the eye, "She would kill you before you ever got the chance to hurt her. You won't find them, not without my help and I am not going to tell you anything."

The soldier turned and paced around Zavier for a few seconds, cracking his knuckles before again hitting Zavier in the face, "Tell us what we want, you fucking bastard. Why do you feel the need to defy us? Just give us what we want!"

Zavier held back his smile, these men got annoyed very easily, the Volcanic Spire were never known for their patients and they were at the point where they were getting reckless; Zavier was waiting for it, hoping they would take it too far and kill him, end this. He knew there is always a point, a breaking point. The point where he's too beaten and battered not to tell them, or they'd somehow hover something over him, something that he couldn't refuse, all these nightmarish thoughts ran through his head as he took it.

The beating continued until Zavier was a dazed, bloody mess, he couldn't feel his face, he could barely breathe, he could no longer keep his head up, still pretending that everything was fine, that he wasn't in pain. He knew even though he was weak and pained beyond belief, that he didn't lose this battle with them and they knew that too and with that Zavier smiled inside. As they walked away, leaving him sitting in the chair, watching from a few feet away. Closing his eye's he just welcomed the warmth of the fire on his cold bruised body and waited for the night to end.

Zavier managed some sleep, at least thirty minutes before the sun was in his eyes and soldiers were reaching for him, pulling him to his feet; Zavier could barely open his eyes, they were so swollen, but he could clearly see Jason mounting his horse and looking his way, he seemed furious. Jason could see that even with this amount of force and torture he was still getting nowhere with his interrogations, Zavier let out a small smile.

Jason walked his horse towards Zavier and his soldiers speaking loudly, "We will be branching off into scouting groups, group one head west towards the Spirit Lake, group two head towards Jez'barian borders, group three you are coming with me and our prisoner back to our Kingdom and group four head east towards Kel'mare before making your way up towards home," Everyone missed it, but the moment the city Kel'mare was mentioned Zavier's face froze, it was only for a second as his heart stopped and all time froze, shaking it off he looked Jason in the eye, making sure that he was dead calm. Jason didn't suspect anything. But with a scouting group heading towards Kel'mare, it wouldn't be hard for a scouting group to make their way through the fishing village and it wouldn't be hard for them to intimidate their way through for information on the pair.

Zavier was pushed and yanked back onto the horse where they secured him with ropes and waited for their prince's lead.

The other parties had already departed before Jason led his group out.

Every movement on the horse there was a sharp, shooting pain through his ribcage, there were a few points during the trek where he fully lost the ability to breathe for a moment or two and at least three times during the first day he blacked out from the pain and lack of air, Zavier couldn't track where they were, or what direction they were going, as his head spun, but he still knew where they were heading and with that knowledge, he knew this was just the beginning of a very painful journey for him. But the only things that could run through his nauseated head was the question if Valkyrie and Allister were safe, that is all he could think about and that was all he cared about, they could shatter every bone in his body, they could mutilate and torture him for days, months without end. He would endure it, even with the hope that it would save them, he knew it was in a way selfish; putting Valkyrie through this, she probably saw this future for him and she'll probably wake up from nightmares, having to watch what he would be going through, if she hadn't already. He also knew Allister well after all these years, he would be blaming himself, the moment Allister realizes that he wasn't making it back to them, he would be hurting, feeling that he would be responsible for this, but Zavier didn't blame him and he never would blame him for this. Allister wouldn't understand he was young, stubborn, hard headed and when he had something in his head, it was nearly impossible to change it.

When the night was starting to fall over the skies, the march stopped and Zavier was pushed from the horse, landing painfully on his side, knocking the air from his lungs, he tried to pull himself off the ground but was pulled up before he could manage himself. Two guards dragged him towards a tree and rebound his arms around the trunk, leaving his back exposed to the guards. Kneeling in the dirt and roots of the tree Zavier pressed his forehead against the tree and concentrated on his breathing, he was expecting another beating and interrogation today, but it seemed the guards had grown tired of him, at least for the night. The fall wind was harsh against his bare back, it howled in his ears all night, the cold was nice on his wounds but with his body tensed up against the cold, it numbed some of the pain and he managed a few hours of sleep, waking up to the sounds of birds chirping loudly in the tree above him. Zavier just watched the small blue birds bouncing along the branches above him, but the blissful silence didn't last long as the other guards slowly started to awake from their sleep and trek around the camp, the birds flew off within minutes of guards waking.

Three guards approached Zavier, unbinding him from the tree and rebinding his hands in front of him, before punching him once in the jaw and tossing him some scrap bread before backing away again. Zavier just looked at the bread and wiped his mouth with the back of his hand feeling the fresh blood, breaking the bread in half he stuck half in his bloody pockets before biting into the other half, his mouth was sore and chewing was more painful than his hunger. The guards continued to around their camp for two more hours before they continued their trek forward, it was another painful ride for Zavier, as the days and nights just repeated.

Five days and nights had passed. Valkyrie was sitting at the table with another bottle of wine in her hands, already it was half gone. She looked over to the occupied bed as Allister viciously tossed and turned under the covers. Every night since arriving here it had been the same for him, Valkyrie noted on. She knew soon he'd wake up, toss the blanket off him, sweat pouring down his face, pale and panting. She'd have an urge to ask him if he was okay, what he was dreaming about, but her stubbornness to be angry at him would keep her from saying anything to him. She'd just watch from her chair still drinking from her bottle as the boy tried to compose himself, as he tried to play off that he was alright. This day was different.

When Allister woke, he tossed the blanket off him and sat up on the bed, his hands over his eyes, Valkyrie could see the tears that were falling from his face and in the moment her resentment for him disappeared again and she managed to speak, "Allister,"

In between catching his breath, Allister spoke, his voice harsher than Valkyrie had ever heard from him before, "Don't even try to be nice to be right now. Don't lie to me about not hating me. Don't pretend to care about me. I destroyed everything Zavier and you had."

"I don't hate you." She wanted to lie, but the words refused come out of her mouth. Did she hate him? Looking at him now, she didn't, but was that only because she saw a sad broken boy here? Was it the truth? She just turned away from him and took another drink from the bottle.

Hours of awkward silence washed over the pair until finally, Valkyrie blacked out into another drunken sleep, Allister moved her to the other bed and placed the quilt over her. Allister leaned his back against the wall. Looking up at the ceiling above them, every night he was plagued with the same images, the same haunting story… Zavier's dead body. Valkyrie's teary eyes, her anger as she screamed at him, she screamed what Allister thought was the truth. Everything will always be his fault. He will never not be to blame for this. They would never be safe from his past.

Looking over and seeing Valkyrie sleeping peacefully across the room,

Allister made up his mind in that moment. As a final gift to Zavier he was going to keep her safe and the only way he knew to keep Valkyrie safe in his diluted guilty mind, was to be as far away from her as possible. If he wasn't here, they'd have no reason to come after her. As long as Allister was close to her, she wasn't safe.

Taking Valkyrie's last unopened bottle of wine, he uncorked it and downed half the bottle, holding back the urge to vomit as the bitter liquid went down his throat. He looked back over at Valkyrie who tossed uneasily in her sleep. Allister took some parchment out of his pack and jotted down a quick note.

Valkyrie, I know you hate apologies, but this is a true one. I am sorry for all the pain I have caused you over these years, all the pain Zavier has suffered for me. I am not running from this fate any longer. I am going to face it head on. Don't bother coming after me out of obligation to your brother. The last thing he asked was for me to protect you, so that is what I am doing. As you said, we are family and it's my job to protect you. I am clearly not worth protecting in your books anyways.

Signed

Allister Ironfist – the bastard prince

Placing the folded paper on his bed, he grabbed his supplies and some food and jumped through the escape hatch. The water was higher than the days before, rain water washed its way through the system. Allister's legs were soaked, as he stomped his way through the dark tunnel, making his way out to the stormy sea, as the rain poured down on him. He paused as he looked over the ocean as the sun was beginning to rise, the rain clouds covered up its beauty with their dark thunderous mass. It was perfect; Allister looked up to the sky as is washed over him and he cried the rain washing away all evidence. Holding his breath, he fixed the hood over his head and made his way to the stables.

Nina was already in the stalls dealing with the horses when Allister arrived, he soaking wet from the rain.

"Oh, Allister." Nina jumped slightly as she turned around to face the soaked man standing behind her, a smile appeared on her face, but for only a moment as she looked hard at Allister.

"Sorry for startling you, Nina. I just need Nightmare and then I'll be gone."

Nina paused and leaned her back against the stall. "Not both of them?" Allister didn't respond, he just grabbed the halter from the rack and turned around to her unamused expression. "Are you running away?"

"I'm am a monster. All I have ever done is get those around me hurt or hurt myself. I'm tired of being the author of all this pain and suffering. I need to face these demons alone."

"Allister, the people around us, they are what make us strong in terrible situations like what you are going," Nina stepped forward and placed her hand on Allister's arm, "You don't need to face anything alone."

Allister shrugged away from her and stepped towards the stall. Nightmare walked forward and nudged Allister with his nose, snorting loudly into Allister's ear, there was almost a sense of disapproval in the horse. Allister ignored it and placed the halter on the horse and unlocked the stable, leading him out. "Thank you for everything, Nina. Goodbye." Allister went to walk out of the stable, alone, with his horse, but Nina grabbed his arm again.

"Can I at least walk you out? Have a real goodbye?" Nina had desperation in her eyes, she knew that he was walking out to his death in some way, but what she didn't know was how close it really was.

Allister nodded, gripping the reigns tightly in his hands, as they walked out towards the city central.

Nina sighed loudly, "Am I the reason you decided to leave your friend? Because I told you that you were in love with her?"

Allister's memory went back to that conversation, *an obvious man in love*. Maybe it was true, maybe he had loved her all along and maybe that's why he knew he had to leave her. Seeing how he destroyed everything she ever cared for. Allister lied to Nina, "No, it was just a matter of time before I realized this was the only way."

The two of them paused, dead in the street. A large crowd had formed, which was odd for this early in the morning. Allister's heart started to race as he heard voices overhead, Volcanic Spire soldiers?

A group of six soldiers had dragged two persons out of their home questioning them and those around them, the first soldier spoke, "We are looking for two persons, a man and a woman. Would have come in on horseback a few days back." He had the middle-aged man by the throat as he shoved a crudely drawn photo of Allister, in the man's face.

He trembled with his hands in the air, "I swear sir I haven't seen anyone." The soldier punched the man in the face, before reaching for the man's wife.

She screamed in terror as he gripped her blouse, the man tried to reason with the soldier, swearing on his life that he hadn't seen anyone, the soldier went to raise his hand towards the wife and Allister pushed through the crowd, dropping Nightmare's reigns and leaving Nina in shock lost in the crowd.

"Enough! I am Allister Ironfist. I am the man you are searching for." Allister could hear his heart beating in his ears as the soldier dropped the wife and the six of them stepped towards Allister. The first held up the sketch of Allister as the others walked forward.

"Yes, it's him." The man said as the soldiers grabbed Allister by the arms forcing him to his knees and tying Allister's hands behind his back. The soldier stepped forward and grabbed Allister's chin tightly in his hand forcing the young man to look him in the eye. "Everyone was so worried you'd be hard to capture and you just handed yourself to us?" He bent down to be eye level as Allister broke contact with the man, "Now tell me, where is the sister?"

Allister looked away but said nothing, the man smiled and stood up again, cracking his knuckles before knocking Allister forcefully in the jaw. Allister was knocked to the ground, dazed from the blow, the two soldiers standing behind him quickly pulled him from the dirt and returned him to his previous position. Allister's cheek had been ripped open by the man's metal plated glove and warm blood pooled down his face, the rain water stung his open wound. The two soldiers held Allister in place while the first soldier continuously punched Allister in the gut and face.

After a few minutes, Allister's face was numb from the pain and all he could taste was his blood in his mouth. The soldier grabbed Allister's face again lifting it to his eye level, "I'll ask you again, where is the girl?"

Allister took a deep breath and pulled his face away from the man, "She's not a part of this. You have what you came here for." The soldier cracked Allister in the ribcage, Allister kneeled over coughing up his own blood, panting, "She's not here! I left her, just take me and leave!" The pain was starting to become overwhelming for Allister, the soldier scratched his own chin and looked down at his prisoner.

One of the soldiers holding on to Allister asked, "Do you think he's telling the truth Jaz?"

The now named soldier Jaz answered after a moment, "I'm not convinced, but we have time to waste. Rough him up, see if his story changes at all, while Lenard, Marcus and I continue to search the area. Someone here knows something."

Another soldier stepped forward and took a swing at Allister, cutting him right above the eye. Instantly he could feel the swelling and the blood pooled down his face, as the man continued to beat the senses out of him while the ever-growing crowd watched.

Valkyrie sat up in her bed, biting down on her thumbnail, without even looking over she began talking, "Allister… Don't say anything until I finish what I have to say. I just want to apologize for how I have been treating you. This isn't your fault. If Zavier has taught me anything; it should be that someone's past doesn't matter, who their parents were doesn't matter. Where they come from doesn't matter, the only thing that matters is your own action, their own actions. I am just trying to deal with everything and I am not doing it in the right way…" That's when a bell rang through the room, Valkyrie tossed the blanket off her, jumping out of the bed she turned towards where she was expecting to see Allister, where she only saw the folded letter on the neatly made bed. Her heart skipped a beat and her fingers trembled as she snatched the letter, clenching it in her hand. She didn't have time to read it, so she stuffed the parchment in her blouse, grabbing her gear, before jumping down the escape hatch. Instantly she was soaked to the knees, but she didn't care, she tied her cloak around her neck and tied her armor mid stride as she made her way through the tunnel. Soaked, she easily found her way to the shore, panting as she sprinted through the sand Allister you idiot. Where the fuck are you? Where the fuck did you go? She asked herself as she made her way towards the stables, that was the first place to check, she prayed to whoever would listen that he at least wouldn't be far, that she still had time to stop him. Making her way through the town, hidden in the shadows, as she rushed down the alleyways in silence, the heavy rainfall muffling her hasted footsteps. Swinging the door open to the stable, it was empty. No one watching the horses and Nightmare was gone. Quickly she grabbed Crimson and led her out of the stall.

Two women walked by, their faces pale as if they were going to be sick, using each other for support, the smaller one spoke, "I know they said he's an Ironfist, but he's just a boy. What terrible thing could someone his age, have done to deserve that?"

Valkyrie stepped up to them her eyes flared red with anger, "Where is this happening?" The two women pointed towards the city center and

Valkyrie quickly made her way, Crimson following closely behind nudging Valkyrie every few steps; the horse was keeping Valkyrie calm, keeping her mind in the moment.

In the back of the crowd that formed was a girl, holding tightly onto Nightmare's reigns, Valkyrie grabbed the woman's arm and turned her around, their faces inches from each other.

Nina held her breath as the angered woman pointed her finger at her, Valkyrie was the first to speak as she lowered her voice, "What happened and why do you have my horse?" She growled at the still in shock Nina.

"Allister, he saw someone being harassed so he just ran in. I wanted to reason with him, but he just ran out there so fast." Nina stuttered, her eyes not leaving Valkyrie's face.

Valkyrie rolled her eyes, she couldn't see anything over the crowd so she leaned in and whispered to Nina, "This is how you are going to help me. Take the horses around that side of the crowd, I'll go handle the soldiers and get Allister to you. Deal?" Nina just nodded and Valkyrie threw her hood back over her head and snuck her way through the crowd, Nina hushed the two horses the other way around the crowd.

Valkyrie could see the crowd cringe and she could now hear someone gagging, gasping for air and she could hear the repeated sound of a fist connecting with flesh and even the crush of bones.

Valkyrie listened to the whispers from the crowd, is anyone going to do anything? Is anyone going to help the poor boy? Finally, Valkyrie saw him; the soldiers had to prop him up as the other continuously punched Allister in the stomach, blood drooled out of Allister's mouth, gagging on his own blood he looked defeated and that was when she snapped. Valkyrie's weapons were already in her hands before she even thought about them and she forcefully pushed her way through the crowd. Her eyes locked on the soldiers as she turned her blades in her hands. Her red hair fanned out around her head as she pushed her way through the last layer of the crowd, the wind knocking her hood off; the soldiers were so preoccupied with Allister that they didn't even see Valkyrie until it was too late for the first soldier. She slipped her blade under his helm, up into the back of his skull. The soldier who was beating Allister mouth dropped, as he rushed towards Valkyrie, while the remaining living soldier grabbed Allister and pulled him away from the fight.

Allister could barely keep himself standing as the man's arm wrapped around Allister's throat, a blade pulled and pressed against Allister's already bloody and numb cheek.

Valkyrie and the soldier's weapons clashed, she forced the man back as she swung hard again at him. He stumbled and she drove again, with more ferocity. The soldier tripped as she pushed him again and she took the opportunity jumping on the man and plunging her blade into his chest. Valkyrie twisted the blade still staring deep into the soldier's dying eyes.

The soldier held Allister in a head lock, his dagger against Allister's flesh just above his stomach, dead center of his ribcage.

Valkyrie ripped her blade out of her victim's chest plate and turned to the last remaining soldier and Allister. The rain poured down on, cleaning Valkyrie's blood drenched blade, her dark, determined eyes locked onto her next victim as he stared back at her, he hid his fear behind his helm as he yelled back to Valkyrie, pressing his blade against Allister's flesh, piercing just slightly, Valkyrie could see Allister cringe as the blade dug slightly deeper, "Drop your weapons!"

Valkyrie cracked her neck and stepped forward, not falling for his bluff. He wasn't going to kill Allister, not right here, not right now.

The soldier was naive and expected his bluff would work, but what he didn't expect was for Allister to regain enough straight to swing the back of his head, into the un-expecting soldier's face. The man flinched and unintentionally jabbed his dagger deep into Allister. Allister gasped, as the soldier dropped him and fell backward, grabbing his face. The soldier only began putting the pieces of his mistake together when Allister hit the ground hard, unmoving and as he looked at his empty blood soaked hands. He looked up in horror as Valkyrie charged him, her blade high in the air as she dove down, her blade easily slipping into the eye socket of the soldier's helm, piercing his brain and killing him swiftly. Ripping her blade from his skull, brain matter pooled out with it. She turned to Allister and dropped to her knees next to him, placing one hand around the blade and the other blood-soaked hand against his face. More blood gurgled from Allister's now quivering lips as he groaned, her hands are so soft Allister thought he looked up at Valkyrie horror filled tears reached the corner of her deep green eyes and as blood pooled from his mouth, he choked and gargled, wondering was this the last time he was going to look upon her beautiful face? Would this be his last image of her? Allister's eyes rolled to the back of his head and he blacked out. "Allister," Valkyrie called to him, placing her blood soaked hands on his shoulder trying to shake him awake. "Allister, wake up! Don't die! Don't die, I'm sorry, I'm sorry for treating you terribly. Wake up!" She screamed, it was in anger, not sadness as she looked down at his bloody, water soaked body. She cut his binds as Nina approached with the horses.

Nina covered her mouth and dropped the reign's, Crimson and Nightmare stepping forward; Nightmare nudging Allister's face. Nina trembled, "Is he?"

"No," Valkyrie said as she looked at the blade still stuck in Allister's stomach, without hesitation she pulled it straight out, quickly and cleanly. Ripping her cloak, she bunched up the fabric and tore off her belt. Placing the cloth over the wound she looked around for more soldiers as she wrapped and tightened the belt around Allister, holding the cloth tightly around the deep wound., "He's alive, I just need to get him somewhere safe." Tossing Allister's arm over her shoulder she stood up taking on his dead weight.

"There are at least three more soldiers here in the city, searching for you."

"Help me get him on the horse, we just need to get out of here." Together Valkyrie and Nina pulled Allister onto Nightmare wrapping his hands with the reigns and leaning him forward Valkyrie jumped on Crimson and grabbed her reigns and Nightmare's lead. Turning back towards Nina, she quickly spoke as she could see the other soldier's returning, "Go hide. Get out of this town, if they find out that you helped him, they will kill you."

Nina nodded and grabbed Valkyrie's hand "Keep him safe. He really does care about you Valkyrie. You are one lucky girl to have him do this for you." Their eyes locked as an arrow wisped passed Valkyrie's ear, quickly Crimson jolted, causing Nightmare to follow quickly behind, as they rushed towards the woods, away from the town.

The rain would make it easy for the soldiers to track than on the muddy path, Valkyrie had to lead the horses through the thick brush, but even than it would be easy for them to track, what she needed was to get Allister somewhere safe. Then she could fall back and deal with the remaining soldiers, but she needed Allister safe first. Her head wasn't clear as she found herself turning around and making sure Allister was still on the horse every few minutes, which turned to seconds. It poured heavy on the pair and she had no clue what to do. Where to go, she was lost and distraught, was he dead? Was she too late, was this all for nothing? Tears started to run down her face as she tightened her grip around the reigns, her heart pounded, finally she stopped and she told herself, I need to be calm right now, I need to be level headed. Take a deep breath Valkyrie, this isn't ending like this.

Valkyrie didn't even know how much time had passed, the tears and the cloudy skies made it impossible, she could still feel her hangover, now that her heart had calmed down and the adrenaline had dissipated from her body. At least the rain stopped and she still hadn't heard any pursuing soldiers, she hoped she lost them. She stopped the horses and jumped from Crimson and quickly walked over to Nightmare placing her hand on Allister's bruised bloody face, he was cold, but he was still breathing, even if it was harsh and strenuous, blood still drooling from the corner of his mouth. Valkyrie brushed his hair out of his face and frowned, "Allister, I need you to fight. Fight to live, you don't need to die here, not like this."

Crimson snorted loudly and Valkyrie turned around her blade already drawn. There standing not even three feet from there was a woman, in a long green dress and a black cloak that was draped over her face, carrying a large wicker basket filled with herbs and flowers. Her dark skin and her piercing amber eyes were locked onto Allister's face. She raised her hands up, revealing herself unarmed and spoke; her voice was soft, yet stern and very foreign. "I can see the obvious, your friend there needs some assistance. I have a cottage not far from here. I can attempt to treat whatever ailment or wound affects him currently there."

"Why should I trust you?" Valkyrie asked, her voice was uneasy as her heart started to race once again.

"You have no reason to trust me, or not to trust me, you are smart not to but unwise to not take the assistance." The woman said bluntly, Crimson walked forward and placed her nose into the woman's chest. The woman in green smiled and placed her hand on the side of the horse's face.

That was the moment Valkyrie decided to trust the woman, Crimson disliked everyone. "Okay, I'll trust you for now," Valkyrie spoke turning back to Allister who was still unresponsive.

"My name is Dayla, follow me." Crimson followed behind the woman without even a nudge of being told to do so and Nightmare followed only after giving Valkyrie a reassuring neigh. Valkyrie took Allister hand and squeezed it, holding onto him as she followed Crimson and Dayla.

Finally breaking from the wooded forest, they fell upon a small stone cottage with an enclosed stable, with a fence that encircled around her property. Opening the fence door, Dayla removed her hood, revealing her large black elven ears.

Valkyrie took a step back from the Night elf.

Dayla laughed, "Even after all these years' people are still afraid of my kind? Really? And should the woman caring for the Ironfist boy really be judging someone for their heritage?" She turned around and gave a disappointed smile, "If I was like my kin, I would have killed you, left your friend out to die and steal your horses, but clearly I do not care about who you are, or who he is."

Valkyrie looked down almost ashamed of herself, but she stopped and looked at the woman confused, "I'm not afraid of your kind, I have just never seen a Night elf in person, but how do you know who he is?"

Dayla waved her off, "Most people know who he is, but that doesn't matter right now, let's get him in the house and whatever wound or ailment affecting him dealt with and then we can talk." Valkyrie was hesitant, but she didn't have an option here, so she still trusted the woman. Together they dragged Allister's limp body from the horse and carried him into the house.

Chapter 10

Together Valkyrie and Dayla carried Allister into the house.
Dayla directed her to a small bed next to a wood burning stove. "Let's
place him down on his back, we'll need to prop him up with pillows."

Valkyrie after laying Allister down studied her surroundings; it was
small cottage, perfect size for someone living alone, there was a kitchen,
a small oak desk with papers and unmarked books scattered all over the
place, stacked up high. There were two chairs facing the fire, with
handmade quilts draped over them and a large animal skin rug laid in the
center of the room. This place was quite strange to Valkyrie, none of the
details were Elven, they were more reminiscent of Barbaric origin if
anything. Valkyrie tossed her confusion from her mind and brushed
Allister's hair back from his face, he was the only thing that mattered
right now. Sticky sweat coated his forehead. He was burning up.

Worry filled her eyes and Dayla noted on it, "How about you go place
the horses in my stable, my horse is friendly. I'll grab and prepare the
medical supplies while you do that." Valkyrie just looked at Dayla, so
she spoke again, "I won't harm him, I cannot do anything worse then the
state he already is in. You can trust that."

Valkyrie nodded and walked out of the cottage, once gone Dayla
grabbed her medical supplies, along with a bucket of water and pulled
one of her chairs up to the bedside, as she began untying Allister's armor.
Carefully she peeled the soaked leather from his skin. His wound was

still bleeding, so she placed a clean towel into the bucket of hot water, strained it and placed it forcefully on his wound. Allister's hands gripped the sheets and then his body went limp again. With one hand still pressing the towel into the wound, she found her cleaning salt. Removing the towel, the blood had slowed. Dayla rubbed her hand with the cleaning salt and placed two fingers in the wound. Allister's whole body jerked, his breathing became labored and he dug his nails into the bed once again. She braced him down on the bed, as she felt around his wound, it was deep, but it seemed to have missed all major organs. Dayla packed the wound with cleaning salt and herbs before placing the towel back over his wound. The bleeding stopped completely and Dayla grabbed a needle and some thick thread stitching up his wound tightly. Sitting him up, leaning him against her body she wrapped his stomach up with clean bandages, before laying him back down carefully, still propping him up with the thick pillows. Dayla took a few moments to inspect him; she ran her hands down his bare chest, feeling each of his ribs, trying to feel for breakage. She could feel some weak points and with the colour of bruising appearing on his pale skin, she assumed that there were some fractured, but at least no full breaks that would need realigning, that was a positive. His face was torn up and bruised, but again, no bones seem broken. She pulled out some more threat and cleaned the large gash that was on his cheek and above his eye. While stitching his face, Valkyrie walked into the house, the worry was just locked on her face. Dayla cleaned her stitching and stood up from her chair, she was covered in Allister's blood, she walked over to the pot on the stove and placed a clean towel in the water washing her hands and arms.

The jittery Valkyrie rushed back over to Allister's side kneeling down next to him. She held his face in her hand as she inspected him, he was blue and purple; his breathing was nearly nonexistent. All Valkyrie wanted was just some reaction from Allister, but he just laid there limply. Dayla let out a long sigh as she placed the towel down, grabbing Valkyrie towel to dry herself off and sat down in the other chair still across from the fire, "The bleeding stopped, but he has lost a lot of blood. That is likely why he is having trouble breathing and why he's unconscious. The clear beating that he took didn't help his situation. I can't be sure if there are any underlying problems until he wakes up." Dayla motioned Valkyrie into the chair, as she sat on the other, at the other side of the bed. "He might have few fractured ribs, or they could just be bruised, but it doesn't seem like any bones are broken. It would be best to keep him propped up to help him breathe."

Dayla looked so calm, so sad? Valkyrie noted on as she looked at the woman, "Thank you for everything. Dayla, I really mean it. I don't think Allister would have much of a chance without what you have done. But we don't have time to wait for him to wake up, the Volcanic Spire soldiers could be right on our tails by now." Valkyrie buried her face in the towel, rubbing her tired eyes as she drained her hair into the soft fabric. She was so tired; she was so angry, so drunk only a few hours ago, it seemed. She hated him only a few hours ago and now the thought of losing Allister was dragging heavy on her heart. She had to fight back the tears, all she wanted to do was break down and cry. Allister couldn't die, he couldn't die thinking she hated him, she didn't want to be alone. She selfishly needed someone…

"There is a spelled casted over this cottage. So even if the soldiers were on your tail, it would take a lot of luck and time to find these dwellings. You are safe for now."

Valkyrie looked up hopefully and then spoke aloud. "I don't mean to sound ungrateful, but why have you gone out of your way to help a stranger? Someone who could get you hurt, or killed."

Dayla bit her lip and scoffed slightly as the image of a man appeared in her own mind, she turned her gaze towards Allister and spoke, "A very long time ago, when I was new to these lands a very kind man saved me. Together we traveled all over Tasryn and he taught me unbiased kindness. He was the type of man who'd go out of his way for anyone." Dayla crossed her hands over her check and inspected Valkyrie's face for a long moment before changing the subject, "I see the conflicting feelings you have for Allister in your eyes. Is he not turning out to be the boy you've hated from a distance all these years?"

Valkyrie stared at her confused, "How did you?"

"I have a gift," She said looking into the fire, "Quite similar to yours, but I can read people very well, my people would call it fate weaving. Want me to show you the real boy who you've hated all these years?" She extended her long dark hand towards Valkyrie, hesitantly Valkyrie took the woman's hand. Dayla leaned in towards Allister and placed three of her fingers on Allister's face, "Close your eyes and I'll show you."

Valkyrie took a deep breath as she closed her eyes and allowed Dayla's magic to transport her into Allister's past.

Standing in a large courtyard, once of which Valkyrie had never seen before stood a blond-haired boy, sitting next to a gravestone. Three dozen roses laid next to the stone head, as the boy pulled his knees to his chest. Valkyrie and Dayla appeared as ghosts, behind the six-year-old Allister who cried painfully next to his mother's grave. A man came and walked up behind the boy, grabbing him forcefully by the arm. Allister tried to fight with the large man, only to be struck across the face with the back of the man's hand. The man, Edward Ironfist spoke, his voice echoed loudly in Valkyrie's ears, "No son of mine will be caught crying over a simple death." A red mark from Edwards grip formed around Allister's forearm, but Allister stopped crying and looked down towards the grass. "Yes, father." He said submissively as the man walked away, beckoning the boy to follow, again submissively the young Allister followed his father, placing his hand over the mark made by his father.

Dayla took Valkyrie's hand as they drifted into another transition, smoke dusted around them, it was smooth and it was calming, unlike Valkyrie's premonition's transitions, where it was chaotic and confusing. Standing in a throne room, the Ironfist sigil hung behind young Allister, Edward and a girl, she had dark almost raven hair, strangely even darker than Edwards. Valkyrie watched Allister's expression, he was trying to be strong, but his body trembled and he kept looking towards his father for support, for strength but the man was too far gone. This dark anger filled Edward's face, as Valkyrie and Dayla turned around to see the scene before them. A young girl's body was carried into the throne room, her golden blonde hair, coated in her own blood, her throat was slit and her head hung limply in the guard's arms. Her clothes had been torn off her body, the soldier's cloak the only thing covering the child, clear signs of struggle and assault was written all over the young girl's body.

The girl with the raven hair turned to Edward with hatred, "How could you let them do this to her, father! Jasmine didn't deserve this! You do! Not her!" No tears, just anger forced on the girl's strong face.

Edward went to raise his hand towards his daughter, but stopped and walked towards the corpse of his middle child. "Katherine, go pack your bags, you leave tomorrow to your soon to be husband's kingdom."

Katherine stomped her feet and turned towards her brother, there was empathy in her eyes as she walked over to Allister and wrapped him tightly in her arms. "I never wanted to leave you with this monster of a man." Katherine looked at their father as she spoke the words aloud.

Allister latched onto his sister and whispered, "Please don't leave me with him." Allister trembled with fear.

Edward turned and matched back over towards Allister and Katherine, ripping them apart he grabbed Allister by the shoulder dragging them apart, heading out the room.

Valkyrie and Dayla found themselves floating into another transition; Valkyrie recognized this place. It was the marketplace back home. It had been a few years after Allister first arrived at the school.

Allister had his back against a wall as three kids formed a semi-circle around him, Allister looked away from the other boy's, blood dripped from a small cut on his lip where one of the kids had punched him. "You guys are just jealous because Valkyrie is stronger and a better fighter than yourselves."

The middle boy came in and punched Allister in the gut, Allister didn't even dodge the punch, he just keeled over in pain. The boy spoke with a laugh, "She's just going to be an ugly street whore, just like her mother probably was."

Allister looked up and lunged at the boy, knocking the boy to the ground Allister punched him in the face, "Don't you dare say anything like that about Valkyrie!" The two other boys grabbed Allister's arms and pulled him off the one kid, pinning him back against the wall. The kid got up as the three of them continued to beat on Allister, who again didn't dodge any of their attacks.

Finally, they walked away from Allister leaving him bleeding and curled up in the alleyway. After a while passed Allister picked himself up off the ground and stumbled away from the back alleyway.

The image disappeared, Valkyrie and Dayla were standing in the hideaway room. Valkyrie saw herself sleeping, while Allister sat up in his bed, they could hear his thoughts as he looked towards Valkyrie, "Is Nina right? Am I really in love with Valkyrie?"

Dayla and Valkyrie were tossed from his memories, as Allister stirred in the bed. Dayla smiled and placed the back of her hand on Allister's forehead, he was burning up, "Normally I would have asked said person for permission, but I felt you needed to see some of that." Standing up she went and found a clean cloth and dipped it in a bucket of cold water before sitting back down, she folded it and placed it on Allister's forehead. "You have a letter to read, don't you?"

Valkyrie looked down at herself and felt the paper stabbing her in the breast. Pulling the folded parchment from her blouse she held it in her hand. Dayla smiled and walked away leaving the house, giving Valkyrie some space. Valkyrie fought whether she should read it as she looked over Allister.

Zavier knew they were closing in on the Volcanic Spire boarders as the smell of sulfur filled his lungs and he could hear the water crashing against the shores, it was well after midnight, the moon was full and the volcanic mountain in the distance lite lightly with the soft embers of its core.

The horses stopped and a soldier pushed Zavier from the horse, at this point he was too tired and weak that he didn't even attempt to catch himself, his head hit the ground first, his ears rang painfully as he rolled over in the dust, everything went black in the darkness, only to reappear as a torch flared in his face, two soldiers lifted him off the ground and pushed him forward. Zavier's leg buckled, he tried to push himself from the ground, only to be grabbed and held up by the same two soldiers who just laughed at their prisoner.

Every step he took it was like his body was filled with needles, Zavier just tried to keep his expression straight and his eyes forward, as they marched towards the shores, marched towards the Volcanic Spires Kingdom.

Torches were lit as they approached the docks, from across the murky water Zavier could see the well-lit city in the darkness and just beyond that, hidden mostly in the smoke and ash was the volcanic castle, build out of the base of the only active volcano left on Tasryn. Zavier held his breath and closed his eyes, this is the place where I am going to die. As they approached the edge of the dock Zavier glanced down at the murky waters, there was an urge to fall in, the appeal of just disappearing under the waves. One of the soldiers saw the look in Zavier's eyes and they must have known what was going through his head as he was kicked down onto the wooden dock, his chest against the cold, wet, grimy panels.

The man whispered quietly in Zavier's ear before lifting him back up and holding him tightly by the hair, "You even make a move towards the edge of the boat and you will wish that we were nice enough to let you just drown." leading him towards the boat two soldiers already in the row boat grabbed Zavier's arms and pulled him in. Forcing him into the center seat. Two more soldiers entered the boat, one placing a sword on Zavier's back, as they kicked off from the dock.

Zavier kept his head high and just stared at the city in the distance as it grew nearer and nearer. About halfway through the boat ride, Zavier felt a hand reach for him, he turned his head towards the blackness of lake. Valkyrie's name crossed his lips before he could even think of anything. The soldier behind him snapped, grabbing his hair and pushing his head down, there was a painful crack in his neck. Zavier just closed his eyes and hoped, hoped that this wasn't a sign that Valkyrie would be see this. The rest of the boat ride he stared at the bottom of the boat, the soldier's hand squeezing down on the back of his neck. With this angle his ribs dug deeply into his chest, he could feel this chest tightening with every second as he tried to breathe calmly and slowly. He knew that the minute he stepped foot on the shores of the Volcanic Spire city his suffering was just going to intensify; he just closed his eyes tightly and waited.

Two hours had passed, as they reached the docks horns blew loudly;

Zavier was barely conscious when the boat jolted to a stop, the soldiers behind Zavier pulled him up to a sitting position, before lifting him to his feet and tossing him from the boat. Again, Zavier's head hit the dock first this time, the hit knocked the wind out of him, he just gasped quietly and pushed himself up to his knees, staring forward as the city exploded with people.

Whole families exited their homes to watch as their prince and their soldiers returned, with to their naive judgment they thought it had been a successful mission. The soldiers grabbed their prisoner and pushed him towards the cheering crowd. Zavier found remaining strength to hold his head high and make his way through the crowd without a slip-up.

Mothers and children screamed at him, tossed rocks and other heavy objects at his face, while the other men knowing that Zavier wasn't the prisoner they were hoping for just saluted the soldiers and their prince in silence.

They reached the cold steel gates and were greeted by guards who opened-up as they approached, bowing to their prince. One of the guards stood straight and spoke directly to Jason, "Our king, your father wishes to speak to you and your prisoner my prince."

Jason turned back and stared at Zavier, there wasn't the pride in the kill anymore, there was bitter angry in his eyes knowing that his father would see this as it was, a true failure. Zavier was a nothing, Jason was after the Hire to the Mountain kingdom and he came home empty handed.

Jason turned back to the guard and nodded, "Very well, if that is what my father wishes." He snarled bitterly, "Are my brothers going to be there as well?"

"Your oldest brother Harald will be present, but your brothers Tristan and Ragnar will be absent."

Jason rolled his eyes and pushed his through his guards towards Zavier, wrapping his hand around Zavier's throat, he squeezed digging his nails into the soft bruised skin, "Gag him, I don't want our prisoner attempting to be coy, or smart in front of my father and my brother." Zavier and Jason locked glances; infuriating the prince, Jason grabbed Zavier by the back of the head and rammed his face into his knee before stepping to the side away from his prisoner, as one soldier quickly shoved a gag into Zavier's mouth, before pulling him back up right.

With a freshly bloodied nose, Zavier just stood tall and breathed, trying to forget his pain.

Once inside the palace, Zavier was silently in awe at the size. It was even grander than the Mountain Kingdom was all those years ago. Everything in the palace was overstated by its sheer size, the doors leading to the throne room were from floor to ceiling, made of pure red stained glass and a dark iron casing entwined throughout it, mimicking a tree.

Jason stopped, hand on the handle and paused he took an angry breath and straightened his posture before entering the grand hall.

Again the room was enormous; every wall had a painting of the king alongside his wife and on the two longest walls there were paintings of his four sons, drapery was also hung on the far walls, a black dragon engraved into the fabrics.

Six thrones waited at the end of the room, alongside a small wooden chair, the kings chair was made of gold coated bones, where the others were just black iron and plush fabrics, the king and his oldest son Harald, the Hire to the Volcanic Spire were the only ones in their chairs.

The volcanic Spire king was a large, older man, he was well out of his prime, as his large gut hung over. His long gray hair and beard were thinned in age, his dark eyes emotionless as his youngest son approached.

Harald, was a different man; he was much leaner than his brothers, resembling their mother more than the king himself, but he was the successor to the throne none the less and size didn't matter to this man; he was known for things other than strength. He was a manipulator, a torturer. He could twist anything out of anyone, he could break anyone, he was cold and ruthless, he was mostly known for his experiments' on people. Testing pain tolerance and much more. If Zavier was going to be afraid of anything, or anyone, it was going to be that man. He was a blond fellow and he carried no scars, unlike that of his father or brothers.

The king adjusted in his seat and stared down at his son's prisoner, "Is that all you have to present me, Jason? This isn't the Ironfist boy." The old king stated the obvious.

Jason turned and grabbed Zavier tossing him at his father's feet, "This man will lead us to the Ironfist boy. Just a matter of time for him to break."

Harald laughed in his seat, only to have their father hush him with the wave of his hand the old man leaned in as Zavier stared the man down. "I recognize him, who is he?"

"He's the bastard elven boy who took over the fighting school, the same elven soldier who caused Allister's life to be spared all those years ago, am I right brother?" Harald spoke with a snicker.

"Yes, he raised the boy at the school."

"Why is he gagged? If you want him to tell you where to look for the bastard prince, you need him to have the ability to speak."

"I understand that father, but-"

"Soldier, ungag the prisoner." The king ordered, him and Zavier still locked in eye contact. The soldier pulled the gag from Zavier's mouth and backed away again. "Bastard, tell us where the boy would be hiding and I will allow you to live after we have acquired the boy."

Zavier straightened and stared at the king, he contemplated on saying nothing, but he wanted to push Jason's buttons more than anything, knowing that if he was lucky enough to anger Jason enough, he would just be killed right there. Zavier grinned slightly, it was a strange feeling on his face, being smug didn't feel right, but already he could sense Jason's unease, "If you are hoping to get anything out of me, you are going to need stronger soldiers, your son included in that observation."

Jason kicked Zavier to the floor slamming his foot heavy on his head, he leaned in. "Answer his question, or don't speak at all, bastard." Jason spat at Zavier before moving off him ordering his guards to pick Zavier back off the floor. "Father, I will get him to talk, you have nothing to worry about."

The king smiled and turned his head towards Harald, "I give you a four days, if you have nothing by then I will leave the interrogations to your brother, he understands that a little more than you do. Take him away, you are dismissed."

Jason snarled and turned away, the soldiers grabbed Zavier and pushed him out of the throne room and down the many halls and corridors until they reached the most bottom level of the palace; they had to unlock six doors with different keys just to reach the prison, once there, it was a large room with four large barred cells. It was damp, covered in moss and the stone floor coated in water. The prison was intentionally placed near the shore line, so as the waves crashed over the kingdom, the prisoners would be soaked with the oceans spray.

The soldiers unlocked the center cell and chained Zavier's wrists to the bars on the window, giving him just enough leave way that he could kneel on the floor, but his hands would still be stuck above his head. Zavier just stood there in silence, staring Jason down.

Jason approached and reached for Zavier's throat; Zavier jerked towards him, as the prince jumped backward, the soldier's swords drawn and pointed to Zavier's throat in seconds. Zavier stepped into their blades, daring them to break his skin. Jason turned heading for the door. "Break his spirit, I want him ready to speak by morning."

Three soldiers stayed behind, they placed their weapons and armor outside of the cell door and locked themselves inside with Zavier. The three smiled at each other, as they lined up, each taking five minutes each to beat Zavier senseless, before moving onto the next.

By the time they made their third round Zavier collapsed to his knees, he could barely breathe as it felt like all his ribs had been shattered, he again was fully covered in his own blood, choking on his own blood painfully between every punch, he couldn't even see straight by the repeated blows to the head, as one grabbed him by the face and smashed the back of his head into the wall, but by this point the blows were nothing, his body was numb in agonizing pain.

This continued through most of the night, the soldiers left him shortly after the sun peeked through the small window, finally the salty waves gave up. His fresh wounds burning from the salt water.

After the soldiers left Zavier let go, leaning his body against the cold stone wall, he no longer had the strength to play tough. He tried to catch his breath. There wasn't a part of his body that wasn't covered in his own blood, or reeked in pain; his chest and legs were purple and red from the bruising that already set in.

Shortly after the noon bells rang Jason returned to his prisoner, Zavier was tied to a chair and pushed to the center of his cell, two guards stood with Jason as they attempted to beat the location out of Zavier, even after Jason and the guards grew tired of beating him, the numb Zavier still had told them nothing.

This happened for three days straight, soldiers would beat him throughout the night and the Jason would attempt to squeeze information out of him through the afternoon.

By the fourth day Jason was furious, Zavier couldn't even keep his eyes open, he was barely even aware that Jason was there, but he could feel the anger fuming from the man. He just sat in a chair across from him, "You are going to wish you told me where the Ironfist bastard is. My brother, he finds people's weaknesses and he twisted them. He'll make you witness your worst nightmares. I'm done beating you, I'm bored of you. One last time I asked you, where is Allister Ironfist?"

Zavier adjusted trying to open his eyes, only to spit blood at Jason, he missed by a mile. But Jason just exhaled, he was furious, but at this point he had nothing left in him to do, he was tired, his knuckles were bruised and bloodied from hitting the man so many times, if four days straight without food and water and repeated beatings weren't going to break him, Jason knew he wasn't going to break without more time, which he didn't have. Tomorrow morning, his prisoner, the person he hated the most was going to be passed onto his brother, his prisoner. Knowing his brother was being given Zavier to finish the job he couldn't complete himself, angered him more than not getting the information on Allister's whereabouts. He didn't even get the satisfaction of Zavier begging for this to end, or begging for him to stop. He got nothing but bruised, bloody hands.

This day Jason just left Zavier tied to the chair, he was too defeated to even re-chain him to the bars, so he walked away. Silence once again fell over the prison once again.

A week passed and the only people that ever entered the cell were the guards the next day to chain him back to the bars on the window and every other day when a girl in revealing purple robes, that would bring a small scrap of soft bread and a small bucket of water.

Zavier sat with his legs crossed, eyes closed taking deep breaths. His chest was still tight and hurt, as his ribs were attempting to heal. He only opened his eyes when he could hear footsteps heading down the stairs approaching the door, the girl entered as two guards followed, opening his cell before closing and locking it behind her.

The woman was carrying a bucket and bandages; she was a young thing, only a little older then Valkyrie, she was a pale, dirty blonde haired girl, her lips were full and red as she left nothing of her body to the imagination. The guards exited the prison leaving the girl locked in the cell with Zavier. For the first time, she spoke to him. "I am going to unchain you from the bars. You can threaten to kill or harm me," Her eyes dead and sad as she didn't even meet Zavier's eyes, "but I have no keys to release either of us from this cell and honestly I think the guards would find some sick pleasure in watching you kill me." She approached and placed the bucket and bandages on a small cloth she pulled out to keep them clean, "I'm just going to dress your wounds, I realize most have healed, but your broken or fractured bones should be addressed, they should have been addressed earlier, but they don't really care."

Zavier nodded as the girl approached when she unlocked his wrists from the chains; once his hands were free he rubbed the chafed area where the metal was tearing into his skin, still sitting cross-legged he watched her.

kneeling across from him, she pressed her lips together and inspected the practically naked man, the bruising on his ribs were still really bad, his left knee cap looked like it had been shattered and she wasn't sure if it was healing in the correct position. She just sighed and leaned into Zavier with the bandage wrapping it around his chest tightly, trying to carefully a line his ribs correctly, every time the bone moved, it felt like a dagger in Zavier's side, but he just looked forward and tried to forget it.

"One of the scout troops found your sister and the boy." The woman didn't look up at Zavier, but his heart fluttered and panic filled his head. "I'm not supposed to tell you this, but they did get away. Jason say's that his men are on their trail again though, he thinks it's a matter of days."

Hearing that they got away calmed him, but he was still worried if they found them once, it seemed likely that they would find them once again. "Why do you put your life on the line for someone who you aren't related too? I understand your sister, but the Ironfist boy. Didn't his father's war get your family killed?"

Zavier still just stared ahead, taking a deep breath he spoke, his voice cracked and was horse, the first time he spoke since he was chained up in here, "The Ironfist wars had nothing to do with me. I am responsible for him, just because he's not my blood, doesn't mean I would care less about him."

The girl smiled, "But you are putting his life, higher than your own. Wouldn't you rather live? That Ironfist boy will never have a full life, even if you don't give his location up, you could have a full life."

Zavier looked at the girl, there were confusion and curiosity written all over her face, "He still has the blood of Edmond Ironfist, he is still technically the heir to the Mountain throne, this is only again being brought into light because that's why they want him. They can't take a strong claim to the throne with knowing the bloodline still continues. Myself, I am just a bastard, something the world wants to forget. So yes, Allister," Zavier paused digging his name into the girl's mind, "the Ironfist boy's life is more important than mine if you are just looking at social standings." The woman wrapped Zavier's knee and started to wrap his still bleeding wrists after a quick wash in the hot water. "Don't try to play me, Silvia." The woman froze, she looked up at him stunned, Silvia was the only daughter of the king of the Volcanic Spire; she was born from one of the kings Mistresses. Rumors had it that the king treated the girl like she was a sex slave, himself even taking advantage of her, as well as allowing only his better soldiers to take advantage of the girl.

"How do you know my name? My face can't be recognizable."

"It's the way the soldiers tread around you, they hold some form of twisted respect, but they still look down on you. Almost the way people look at me now. So an educated guess." Zavier looked away from her, placing his hand on his rib cage and then his collarbone.

Silvia smiled and coyly laughed, "You are a smart man Zavier, yes I was told to be friendly with you. But maybe I have a soft spot for someone whose father doesn't recognize them as their own." Zavier refused to match her gaze as he looked away from himself as she continued to clean and bandage him. "Jason really hates you. What did you do to him to make him want to cause this much pain to you? Normally he would just hand his prisoners over to Harald when it comes to interrogation. He knows he doesn't have the patients for the messy things."

"He's hated me from the moment he met me. Maybe seeing a bastard anger's him and the fact that I haven't and I won't break to him just makes it all the worse for him."

Silvia laughed, "Anyone Jason hates is liked by me." After she finished to bandaging Zavier, she rechained Zavier, this time to one of the sidebars giving him more room to lay down and adjust. She banged loudly on the bars and the soldiers re-entered and released her from the cell and left without another word.

Every day after that Silvia returned, she stayed out of the cell besides checking the bandages, but she stayed just to talk. She asked him about his past, she told him secrets about her life, about her family, things no one else apparently ever knew. He knew what she was doing, she was trying to gain trust, hoping that he would reveal more than what he wanted, but Zavier kept his answers short, as much as he knew he shouldn't even speak to her. He wanted to talk to someone, even if it was a risk.

Chapter 11

A week after Allister and Valkyrie arrived at Dayla's cottage, Dayla found herself unable to trail far from the safety of her cottage's magical boundaries. Small scout groups of what she knew too well to be Volcanic Spire Soldiers marched and trampled through the woods. She noted they were not close enough to worry Valkyrie about their presents, at least not yet. Dayla realized the girl was already worried enough for her friend. She had to finally force Valkyrie to stop sitting at Allister's bedside, inspecting his breathing, his pulse and temperature every few minutes. It wasn't going to help Allister, so Valkyrie was tasked with small chores around the cottage. There was a lot of preparing before the bulk of winter storms took out the foot paths leading towards the villages.

That morning Valkyrie was outside dealing with the horses, when she found Dayla just standing by the gate with a bucket of water in her hand. She seemed just lost, staring out into the woods. She hadn't spoken to Valkyrie as of yet that morning, she cleaned Allister's wounds in silence, wrapped him in a warm wool blanket, while Valkyrie started the fire without a word. But now as she was staring out into nothing.

Valkyrie walked up behind her, with a bundle of wood in her hand "Dayla is something worrying you?"

Snapping out of her trance Dayla brushed her ebony fingers through her hair, "Oh, no child. Something… Correction someone is on my mind thing morning."

"What's his name?"

Dayla paused and frowned sadly, placing her bucket on the ground and rubbing her forehead with her long dark hands, she sighed long and sad, "Faren Blight, was his name. He and I were married, a very long time ago it seems. He drove me nuts, but he was kind hearted, playful and he understood people more than they understood themselves." She held her breath and wiped her eyes dry, "My apologies. He is not a subject I tend to speak of. It may have been many years since I have lost him, but the wounds of being without him still feel fresh."

Valkyrie turned towards the cottage door, where just beyond the pinewood door laid Allister. "I understand. The pains of losing someone you really care about never goes away, does it?"

Dayla smiled as she looked at Valkyrie, "Even more so when you love them." no longer was their hatred filled in Valkyrie's eyes, there was just compassion and fear for Allister, for his future, for their future.

The pair headed towards the house as their conversation ended. As they pushed the door open they could hear Allister mumbling in his unconsciousness. They both looked and each other before rushing to Allister's bedside, as he tossed in the bed furiously, his hands clenched tightly in the blanket. Allister spoke, his voice was raspy and there was a good forty-second pause between every word he managed to mumble, "Valkyrie, no… Zavier, please… Don't…. Please forgive… Me." He panted, sweat poured down his brow.

Valkyrie brushed his hair back, her lips trembled as she spoke softly to Allister, "Please wake up Allister. I forgive you. I forgive you for everything. I just need you to wake up, so then you can know there is nothing for you to be sorry about."

He gasped loudly and Valkyrie took his hand removing the bedding from his grip; she squeezed his hand tightly, hoping for a reaction, he lost his grip and his arm fell limply in her hand and silence fell back over Allister. Valkyrie stood up from the chair and leaned over Allister, she shook his shoulders lightly, "Allister! Allister wake up! Please!" Her whole body began to shake as she turned to Dayla, settling herself, "What is wrong with him?"

Dayla leaned over and placed the back of her hand on Allister's forehead and check his pulse on his neck; he had a high fever and his pulse was erratic. She grabbed a cloth and placed it in her bucket straining it before placing it on his forehead. "It's possible that he's having a nightmare, but he was responsive for a moment, that is a good sign."

Dayla's words were reassuring and before Valkyrie could even respond Allister jolted up in the bed. He was in a panic, he grabbed his chest with one hand and then his stomach with the other. Throwing the blanket off himself he pushed away from Dayla, he was hyperventilating, confused, disoriented and trembling from the amount of pain as he ripped his stitches open by tossing around. Standing up on the bed he winched still trying to catch his own breath, Valkyrie reached forward and took his hand. Allister's eyes wide as his head turned and he saw her standing there, worried filled in her eyes. "Allister it's okay. I promise. You need to calm down, please. Everything is okay."

Allister kneeled over gripping his stomach, eyes now locked on the strange woman on his bedside, Allister tried not to puke as he gagged on his own breath.

Dayla took a step back from the bed and reached her hand out with the still damp cloth. "You have a fever, I believe it would be in your best interest if you lay back down and we can attempt to get your temperature down."

Valkyrie placed her hand on Allister's back, beckoning him to take the cloth from Dayla. Hesitantly he took the cloth, as Valkyrie forced him back down into the pillows, taking the cloth from his hands and placing it on his forehead for him.

Allister rubbed his eyes. His eyesight went blurry, as he tried to take a deep breath; his chest was tight and the pain in his stomach was growing. "What happened?" He honestly didn't remember, the last thing he remembered was being in the underground hideaway… He didn't even remember why for that moment.

Valkyrie's face grew livid as she slapped Allister across the face, "What happened? What happened is that you are an inconsiderate asshole! That's what happened!" Finally, she exploded, all her worry about if he was going to wake up was gone and she just let everything out. "You gave yourself up to the Volcanic Spire soldiers. You're fucking lucky that I had got there when I did, they nearly killed you, Allister! You've been out, unconscious for a week if Dayla didn't find us you would have… You would have died, Allister. Do you understand that? What in the world were you thinking?"

Allister leaned forward on the bed and rubbed where the blade pierced him. Now he remembered. He could feel the metal inside him, he could feel their hands on him, Allister began to tremble, he looked down his bare bandaged chest and spoke, "I wanted to protect you." He couldn't even look at her, "I was hoping that my sacrificing myself you'd forgive me for everything." Allister turned his gaze towards Dayla who was trying to not watch the happenings going on. "Miss," Dayla turned around realizing he was regarding her, "Thank you for keeping her safe."

Dayla nodded with an emotionless smile, keeping her distance from the concerned Allister, "I didn't do much really, I kept her from going metal worrying about your health, but you are welcome."

Allister finally looked back at Valkyrie who was standing there with her arms crossed over her chest. She was worried he was going to black out again and maybe this time he wouldn't wake up.

"Can we all stop looking at me now?" Allister was embarrassed, ashamed. Even with everything that he tried to do, he's back where he started. Dayla and Valkyrie both turned their heads at the same time, Dayla walking towards her kitchen area, as she placed a pot of stew on the fire burning stone. Valkyrie turned away in her chair, her arms still crossed over her chest, still filled with rage. Her voice shook as she spoke to him, "Allister, I don't understand why you decided to face this alone." She grabbed the folded parchment and tossed it on the bed, "I didn't read it. But you need to understand something, you need to trust that we can do this together. I know I was mad and I was hurtful, but neither of us needs to face this alone. I can't lose both you and... Zavier."

It hurt Allister to hear Valkyrie say his name, he could hear the pain, the devastation in her voice. She couldn't hide it as much as she wished she could. It was written all over her face. Allister reached for her hand only to pull away at the last second before she even noticed him move. Allister spoke looking down at himself, he clenched the blanket, "I'm sorry. I thought this way I'd be able to protect you. I wanted you to stop hating, I needed you to forgive me... Maybe I wanted to earn your respect... But they want you as much as they want me right now." The guilt was overpowering; he was feeling worse now that he had left Valkyrie alone in the tavern. He was a coward. He ran because he was afraid. He abandoned her because he was scared that she hated him and that he was going to get her hurt.

Valkyrie bit her lower lip and caught a glance of Dayla who had turned just for a moment to watch the two. Valkyrie thought about her words before she spoke, "Allister. I'm sorry that I made you feel that you were at fault for this. This isn't your fault, none of it is, it's the soldiers that are after you, it's Jason that caused all this."

Allister shook his head, "Valkyrie you don't need to lie to me to make me feel better about this-"

"No, listen to be for a fucking second Allister." She leaned over the bed and placed her hand forcefully on his chin, turning his gaze towards her. "It's not your fault. It was unfair and immature of me to blame you for this. I will admit that I felt that you were to blame with Zavier being gone. But you aren't. It's their fault, they are the ones hurting us, hurting you. You aren't at fault for any of this, you don't deserve this."

They locked eyes and Allister froze. Right now, he couldn't see the truth in her words, he couldn't believe any of her words. It was his fault. His bloodline was at fault, Valkyrie could see the guilt still unchanging on his face, but she didn't know what else to say. If he wasn't going to believe her, what could she do to prove it to him? How could she prove to him that he was and could never actually be at fault for this? She removed her hand from his face and the two looked away from each other. Looking down the pair fell into silence.

Dayla smiled while facing away from the two, there was something hidden in their eyes, something which neither of them saw. Dayla poured them two bowls of stew and handed one to each of them. "Eat up and take as much as you like Allister. You haven't eaten in a week. If you two need anything I'm just out scouting the area, there has been a lot of activity heading towards the falls and now that you are awake, I need to restock on some of my herbs." Dayla grabbed her cloak throwing her hood over and grabbed her herb basket, "Valkyrie, make sure he stays in that bed." She smiled and walked out the door.

Allister waited until he assumed she was out of earshot of the cottage before tossing the blankets off himself and threw his legs over the bed, his feet touched the cold floor, "We need to leave, it can't be safe here. We've been here a week already." Pushing himself up from the bed, he could feel the already torn stitches and his chest went tightened with every motion he made, his legs buckled and he collapsed to the wooden floor. Grabbing his stomach and coughing for a breath he knelt there on his hands and knees.

Valkyrie jumped over the bed and placed her hands on his shoulders. "Allister, we are safe here for now. Just lay back down and rest for now. We will leave as soon as you've recovered." With Valkyrie's help, Allister got back on the bed, his legs felt like pins and needles as they were asleep and his muscles were sore, looking at his bare still bruised legs. He placed presser on his now blood covered bandages and looked away from Valkyrie as she spoke, "We need to have a plan at least before we leave."

Allister took a moment, the minute she said they needed a plan, he already had one in mind, but could he do it? He questioned himself. "If you bring me a map, I think I know of a safe place for us."

With slight hesitation Valkyrie stood up from her chair and walked over to her bag, searching around for her map. Sitting down on the edge of the bed handing Allister the map. He unrolled it quickly and paused, Valkyrie placed her finger on their rough where a bout's. Allister nodded and his finger trailed up through the map at the borderline of the Jez'barian Boarder's, his finger paused and he just looked at the map, lost in thought. Valkyrie looked at the unmarked location where Allister's finger laid; there were no villages, no towns, no marked temples, it was just a clearing close to the black cavern. Valkyrie cocked her head waiting for him to explain what they were looking at.

"There is an unmarked sanctuary located here. It's well hidden, away from main trails and paths and it guarded, at least last I've heard of it. Those who find themselves getting close are normally are escorted away and sometimes killed if they pose a threat. If we can get there the Volcanic Spire soldiers would struggle to get close. We might be able to stay until this blows over. If it ever does." Allister swallowed harshly and ran his fingers through his hair remembering a woman's face, vaguely. "That of course if they recognize me."

Valkyrie looked almost horrified, "That doesn't sound like a safe place. How do these people know you?"

It took Allister a few minutes to answer, he still couldn't look at Valkyrie at this point. "Lady Castriel Far'mel. She was a priestess of the sanctuary many years ago. She was respected, love and she shouldn't have been forgotten. Even after years of her being absent from the compound, the moment she walked through their gates, it had been like she never left. Even people she had never met just swarmed her and fell in love with her grace." He wiped his eyes, he could feel his body temperature rising and his eyes grew heavy, it had been a long time since he thought of her.

Valkyrie tried to solve the puzzle before her, the name Far'mel didn't ring any bells, but Castriel did. Still, she asked, "Who is Lady Castriel Far'mel? Will she help us?"

"She's very long gone. She was later referred to as Queen Castriel Ironfist." Allister paused, Valkyrie already understood who she was, but he wasn't saying it for her. "She was my mother." Valkyrie held her tongue as sadness was written all over Allister's still bruised face, the sadness was lost in his eyes, even the soft sparkle that was always in the corner were gone. "Since she was highly respected, they should accept us into the compound under their rules on Sanctuary. I've been there once, just before my mother's passing. I barely remember anything honestly. But I do remember the happiness that was in my mother's eyes, it was her home. Something that I don't remember ever seeing in her before."

Valkyrie sat uncomfortably in her chair, she had to pause and really look at Allister, he was emitting this tortured sadness and it really hit her as she finally understood how hard this was for Allister. Once again, he was being prosecuted for his heritage; he had no blood family to lean on and the few people he cares about were being hunted down alongside him, just for being close to him. It broke her heart in the moment as she realized how terrible she had been to him. She reached over and grabbed his hand entangling her fingers in his, she squeezed tightly. She paused, she just held his hand tightly in silence, only when he tried to pull away from her, she managed to speak, "You've never spoken of your mother before."

Placing his free hand on his reopened wound, Allister took a deep, long breath, "I don't remember her well. I don't even think I could describe her face to you. She died when I was five, only a few months after visiting the Sanctuary with me and my sisters… While I was unconscious… Healing. I think I dreamt of her." Allister laughed sadly, "Maybe the gods were sending me a sign, telling me that's where we will be safe." He joked.

Valkyrie bit down on her lip and really looked at Allister. There was something so innocent and still so young about him, something she felt she lost many years ago, "Okay, I think that plan is the best we got. But you need to rest more and allow yourself to heal. Winter is getting closer. With how your injuries are right now, I doubt you'd be able to ride for an hour and a full day would be out of the question."

"I'm fine Valkyrie."

"Listen to me Allister. If we are going to get out of this area, both alive, we are going to need to ride all day and all night, the Twin Mountain paths get very dangerous once the snow starts to fall. If we are going to get there before that and before the Volcanic Spire, you need to be healed." Valkyrie pointed to his bloodied bandages. "Can I rewrap you?"

Allister nodded as he freed his hand his face blushed red, from the embarrassment of the whole situation and the fever that was taking over his body. As Valkyrie cut the bandages and cleaned the wound, Allister spoke business, "We are going to need more supplies to even make it that far. Winter, even before the snow begins to fall will be harsh. Harsher the closer we get to the top. We won't make it halfway to the mountain top with what we currently have."

"There is a village a day ride from here, Dayla goes there for supplies every now and then, I can maybe go and pick up supplies for us."

Allister shook his head and winced as Valkyrie placed the hot water on the wound trying to stop the bleeding again. "No, Dayla said that there has been a lot of activity around here. It wouldn't be safe for you to go. The only option would be having to ask Dayla to get us our supplies, we give her all our coin." Valkyrie tied the bandage and Allister laid down into the bed, sitting up as his ribs dug into his lungs. Gasping he adjusted.

Valkyrie holding the bloodied bandages in her hand looked away from Allister as she spoke, "That would be the smartest option I suppose… But Allister," He rolled away from her as she continued to speak, her voice was hesitant, "If there is anything you need to talk about. I know you probably feel that I haven't always been there for you because truthfully, I haven't. But I am here now and I want you to know that whatever you need, anything at all. I want to help you, you just need to talk to me, okay?" Allister didn't even look at her, she sighed.

"Valkyrie… I need to rest as you said."

Taking the empty bowls, she just nodded, "Okay. I am sorry Allister, sleep well." Valkyrie was smarter than that, she knew he wasn't going to rest, but she took the hint and exited the house, going to deal with the horses.

Once he couldn't hear her, he dragged himself from the bed, using the wall for the support he stood up. His whole body cracked and ached painfully that tears were forming in Allister's eyes, he groaned and tried to catch his breath. Every step he managed to make made the pins and needles slowly go away. Allister stumbled and fell to the floor a few times, but he'd keep pushing himself up. He wasn't going to rest, he needed to get his body back into shape, he didn't want to be the reason Valkyrie got hurt and he wasn't going to be what keeps them there for much longer.

Late in the evening Dayla returned and Valkyrie joined her into the house, Allister acted like he slept the day away, but Valkyrie knew better. She knew Allister more than either of them realized.

There was concern written on Dayla's face, as she bit her fingernails, staring out the window into the darkening woods. She was mostly ignoring the fact that Allister and Valkyrie were even there and the night was mostly silent between the three of them.

Finally, as the night crept over the house Dayla finally settled her nerves. She took a seat at the desk and went through some papers, she wasn't reading them, she was just keeping her hands busy, remembering the image of Faren sitting at this desk all those many years ago.

Valkyrie finally spoke up, walking towards Dayla, "Would it be possible for you to do a gear run for Allister and me? I would do it myself, but Allister doesn't feel like it would be safe for me to go out. We need some winter clothes and blankets, as once Allister is healed up we are heading towards the Twin Mountains."

Dayla paused and then shook her head, realizing that Valkyrie was speaking to her, "Yes, yes, I can do that for you. I agree it wouldn't be safe for you to travel alone. Just make me a list. I was going to head into town tomorrow anyways." She turned around in her chair and looked at the two whose eyes were on her, "I don't wish to worry about you. But while I was out I nearly ran into three soldiers, they aren't close enough to start worrying, yet, but a little close for my personal comfort."

The information didn't scare Allister, he was expecting it, Valkyrie had fear written all over her face as she turned to Allister. He wasn't in any condition to leave and if they were getting close to the cottage what if it got to the point where they didn't have a choice.

"Do you think they will find this place?" Valkyrie asked.

"There is always a chance. The spell over this place is more like a veil, it blurs your vision. If you search around the same area long enough you see the details that you missed the first few times. Maybe when I go to the village I can find out if there are any rumors on the Volcanic Spire soldiers or rumors on your whereabouts."

"Do you think it would be safer for us to leave now?" Allister asked eagerly, sitting up on the bed and tossing his feet off the bed.

Dayla and Valkyrie both flashed him a glare, but Dayla was the one to speak with reason, "I think if you tried to leave today, you'd die, or be captured by those same soldiers. Like I said the Volcanic Spire soldiers were close. Your injuries were worse then you are making them out to be. You were comatose for a week, Allister. Think about that. Trying to push yourself out of fear isn't going to make this go away, or any better." Dayla stood up, arms crossed over her chest, with a long sigh she stared back at Allister who felt uncomfortable as the two strong women glared coldly at him. "Your mother would be rather disappointed that you value your own life so lowly. She has very high expectations of what she wanted her son to become. Pushing yourself beyond your physical limits and going out searching for your own death isn't what she had in mind Allister Ironfist."

The whole room froze as the words left the woman's mouth and Allister's jaw clenched. He was unsure how to react to the woman's works and he just stared hard at her, "Who are you really?"

Dayla took a few seconds to respond moving in between the door and Allister as his eyes jolted towards the exit. "Many years ago, I met your mother and in a sense, I met you. You were just a small baby still forming in a beautiful woman's stomach. She was heading back home, towards the Mountain Kingdoms, back towards your father. My husband and I, we were a fortune teller and a writer. We weren't worth giving a second glance to, but she stopped. She was kind hearted. So, I told her a story of the young man named Allister Ironfist." Dayla shook her head, there was more to her story that she wished not to tell, "She was a very kind queen and she cared about everyone who crossed paths with her. I allowed her to fall in love with the son she wouldn't get to see grow up."

Allister zoned the two ladies out, his legs hanged emotionlessly over the edge of the bed, Dayla's words were stuck in his mind, his mother was lost in his mind.

Valkyrie was frozen in the moment, Allister's face was just filled with so many emotions that she couldn't even sort them out and Dayla just looked mortified that she even said anything, reminding someone who was already clearly distraught about the loss of his mother. She had been gone many years, but being truly alone like Allister would have had to face, without a family, those scars would never truly heal. Something all three of them knew too well.

Allister couldn't look at the girls, he just sat up putting more presser on his stomach, hoping the pain would help him snap out of his emotional state. He needed to grow up, he was an Ironfist, Ironfist boys don't cry over death. Those words rang heavy in his head, he wondered why that memory popped into his mind. He hadn't met anyone who knew his mother after his father's execution. Most people didn't even remember her, she was long gone before the end of the war and that's all people ever remembered of his family. No one remembered the kind, gentle woman she was, they just remembered the harsh cruel man that his father was. He tried to hold everything in, he held his breath, but all these emotions were washing over him. All he wanted to do was cry, scream and even run away again, he held his urge to shake in. After being out for a week, the dreams of his mother, his sisters and even his father, everything was just overwhelming. Allister wasn't like Zavier, even though now he wished he was. He could feel the worried expression on Valkyrie's face without even looking at her.

Dayla finally spoke, "I think it would be best for the two of you to move up into the loft. The soldiers have a slim to none chance of finding this place in the dark but just encase. There is a hidden escape hatch behind the back wall that leads into the stable from up there."

Allister didn't fight, or argue, or say anything. Valkyrie just helped him up into the loft.

A few hours had passed; Valkyrie was asleep on the bed next to Allister. The loft had one hidden window, a large wooden wardrobe and just one large bed. It clearly hadn't been used in a long time as it smelled of dust and was stiff. Allister sat up in the bed, trying not to wake Valkyrie who snored softly behind him. He closed his eyes listening to Dayla walking around below them. He was trying to forget his pain, forget his emotions.

Allister made his way down to the main floor. He caught Dayla pacing, there was a sad smile on her face as she read the page in her book. The last step of the latter creaked and she turned around closing the book in the same motion as she faced Allister. "You should be resting."

"You knew my mother. Could you tell me what you remember about her?"

Dayla looked at the leather-bound book that was still in her hands as she spoke, "I only met her once, a very long time ago. I don't know if I have any answers for you."

"Anything would do. Honestly…"

Dayla saw the loneliness in Allister's eyes. Pulling out the chair at her desk she motioned Allister to come forward and sit. She sat on the desk, placing her book down, she grabbed Allister's hands and closed her eyes, "Are you sure you want to see what I have to show you?" Allister nodded, "Close your eyes and relax. My people have always had this ability to tap into the lifeline of a person. If we focus we can almost see anything, someone's past, even their ancestor's pasts. Focus on what you want me to show you, what you want me to remind you of, or who you want to remember and maybe together we can see what you need to see."

Allister closed his eyes and nodded again. Dayla held his hands tightly and together they searched through his mind, through his bloodline, his past, Dayla even saw a glimpse of his future but did not show him the image.

Finally, a solid image appeared.

A young woman in gold and white robes stood at the edge of the black cavern looking over the great abyss. She was beautiful, her face was soft, joy and youth glowed on her unaged face. Her long curly blonde locks blew against her body as the wind tried to lift her away. Gripping a small red amulet in her hands, she dropped it into the nothing of the cavern. There was symbolism in her offering, she was leaving her home. She was promised to a man, a great powerful man. Many people feared for the young woman's life, but Castriel wasn't afraid. She saw something in the man's eyes, something she knew no one else cared to see. The man she was to be married too was destined for great things. Dayla's voice echoed in Allister's man, telling him this story that was unfolding. As the woman in gold brushed her hair out of her eyes, lifting her skirt and walking away from the cavern edge.

The vision in Allister's mind switched and everything disappeared in a wisp of smoke, now the woman was a few years older. She was still the simple innocent, glowing woman from before, but her glow seemed to be grander, with purpose she walked into the throne room with a bounce in her step, her head held high and a sweet smile across her face, it was the Mountain Kingdom throne room. Her belly was round, as she rubbed her hands softly over her stomach, "Edward, whatever our child is going to be, he or she is going to be an active little angel. They haven't stopped kicking me all day." She smiled so sweetly and lovingly as Edward

Ironfist, Allister's father turned around.

There was something in Edward that Allister never saw before, he was nothing like Allister remembered. His harsh coldness seemed to be absent and there was a softness, a kindness in the man's eyes that Allister had never known.

Allister's father stepped forward and wrapped his wife up in his large arms, kissing her on the forehead, "Well when our child comes out, they are grounded for a lifetime for kicking my beautiful wife."

Again, the images changed and Allister was beginning to become disoriented, the haunting image of his murdered sister appeared and Allister tried to pull away from Dayla, but she held on and the images cleared again.

Castriel was aged, still graceful and beautiful, but aged. There was a tired soul, which consumed her face, again she held her swollen stomach, she was expecting once again. "Edward, my love. Have you seen Katherine? She got scared last night when she heard the battle alarm. Did any get in?"

"I am a king, Queen Castriel. Call me by my title, but no I haven't seen her. It is not my job to follow our daughter around. None of the enemy soldiers managed to get through the gates. They didn't even get all the way through the town." There was something lost in Edmonds' eyes, there wasn't that happiness or softness like in the vision before. Allister could see that the war had gotten to him and was slowly changing him into the man Allister knew too well.

Suddenly Castriel fainted, falling to the ground. Edward rushed over to her, taking his wife in his arms, the harshness disappeared in that moment, as worry took over. Guards swarmed her and doctors appeared. Flashing forward only a few hours, Lady Castriel was lying in a bed, sobbing her beautiful eyes out. Even in her misery, there was grace in her face. Edward sat at the edge of her bed, his hands covered in blood, his head down looking at himself. Castriel spoke between her sobs of pain, "Edward I'm sorry. I'm so sorry Edward." Edward just reached out and took his wife's hand. They trembled as the nurses took their leave with the blood splattered blanket and the baby which they lost.

Allister pulled away and Dayla opened her eyes and studied Allister for clear signs of distress. He looked sad, but okay, "If you think you can mentally handle it, there is something I saw, which I think you'd like to see. Just one more memory?" Allister wiped his eyes, tears were already falling, but he took Dayla's hands and nodded. She smiled and squeezed his hands tightly, reassuring he wasn't facing these memories alone.

The memory unfolded into the scene the moment they closed their eyes.

Lady Castriel laid in a large oak bed, she was dressed in all white, her long blonde hair limping hung at her side, she was pale and clearly fatigue, but she was glowing, happiness just washed over her as in her hands she held a baby, wrapped tightly in a dark red blanket. Standing around the scene were Allister's sisters, faces he could never forget. Katherine, who looked like their father, with their mother's beauty and Jasmine, she was just like their mother. Jasmine was six at the time and Katherine was already thirteen years old. The pair leaned over the bed trying to look at the baby in their mother's arms. Jasmine giggled, "Mommy, he looks funny."

"All babies look funny, you had a squished nose when you were first born." Lady Castriel laughed as she poked her youngest daughter little nose, with a smile.

Katherine leaned over reached out for the baby, as Castriel handed the child to her daughter. Katherine held her new sibling in her arms. Instantly there was a bond that was created towards him. "Have you thought of a name yet mother?"

"I have a name in mind. But it's your father's choice to name the heir of his kingdom.

Katherine rocked the baby softly in her arms, as she spoke to him, "Little baby boy, you have a lot riding on your tiny little shoulders. You have a lot to fix after your father's doings. One day you will be destined to rule the Mountain Kingdom. But take my heed little brother. Sometimes compassion and kindness goes farther than fear itself." She kissed her brother's forehead and smiled, hugging him tightly in her arms. "I'll protect you baby brother.

Katherine handed the baby back to her mother and Castriel whispered so only the baby could hear, "Your father will name you Allister and you will do great things for our world my son."

Dayla broke the connection, but Allister held tightly onto her hands. He didn't open his eyes, he just sat there holding onto the woman, his face red from crying, he couldn't hold it back. Seeing his family, the people he loved, seeing these memories that he never got to experience, seeing the love they had towards each other. Seeing them happy. Remembering his fallen mother, his sisters and even his father in a new light, it was so hard to take in, that he just cried.

Dayla just sat there, she waited for him to break the connection, letting him calm himself down and just take in everything that he just witnessed.

Chapter 12

After a full week of undisturbed healing Zavier could manage to breathe and think clearly again; clear enough to know that the worse was yet to come. They wanted him fit for whatever they had planned next. He hadn't seen Jason at all that week, Silvia would arrive daily, even when she most likely wasn't supposed too, but when she came to visit, she tried to be kind towards Zavier. He knew there was another reason to her visits, but he just couldn't be sure of what.

That morning the wind howled harshly as the waves kept washing over the window, Zavier shivered as the cold cut right through his body. Where he laid in his cell he was protected from the majority of the splash but he couldn't avoid the pools that where forming on the ground around him. Standing up slowly Zavier stretched his leg. His knee was still healing, but at least it was healing in the correct position, his ribs were now just tender and that was all he could complain about. Zavier tried to regain his body strength, trying to do a few arm and leg workouts that his range would allow him. If he had a chance to escape he was going to take it.

It was late, Silvia hadn't arrived this day and the sun was already setting, Zavier wondered what they were planning on doing with him. He knew Harold was known for his interrogations, there were never details on what he did to those people as Volcanic Spire doesn't release prisoners.

They execute their prisoners. Zavier felt blind for once, he didn't know what to expect, or what to prepare himself for besides pain.

After the sun had fully set over the Volcanic Spire, four guards entered the room. Two unlocked the cell door and approached, "Stand." Zavier just looked at them and did as they asked. Grabbing him they unchained their prisoner from the bars and twisted his arms behind his back and slamming him against the brick wall, before tying his wrists together and pushing him towards the door. Zavier didn't fight the guards, he just followed and listened to their orders. They placed a burlap sack over his head and lead him away from the dungeon; Zavier was almost certain that they had been taking him down the same hallways and backtracking just to disorient him, who of course was trying to plot out the route in his mind. He was unable to track their footsteps, but they didn't succeed in disorienting Zavier. It may have worked for people with smaller brain capacity, but not for him. Finally, they stopped. A large, metal door creaked loudly as it scraped opened and it smell of dust and musty air washed over. This room hadn't been opened in months, maybe longer just by the scents that filled Zavier's nostrils.

The soldiers pushed through the doorway and forced him down into a chair, his feet were then strapped to the wooden legs of the chair with leather buckles and after his arms were positioned behind the chairs back, a leather strap was tightened around his chest holding him in position; Zavier twisted slightly just testing how much movement he had, they had strapped him in rather securely. He only had a matter of inches to squirm in the chair. Zavier faced forward and stood up tall in the chair, he could hear them walking around the room, no one said a word. It was rather daunting, there wasn't even a slight hue of light breaking through the burlap sack; no light, no sound, just the overwhelming presence of persons and the strong possibility of a painful night.

Thirty minutes had passed and finally the guards left the room sealing the door behind them. Zavier could hear at least three lock systems in place. Even though Zavier counted the footsteps leaving, there was a feeling that something else was in the room, it was strange. He heard nothing. Not even the sound of someone breaking, but he could feel their presence. Taking a deep breath, he stayed perfectly still, waiting, expecting something to happen. Finally, after an hour longer of nothing, the door opened and a single set of footsteps approached, Zavier again straightened himself and faced forward. He could feel the person breath on the back of his neck. He was being inspected by whoever had entered the room. A voice came out of the darkness, "You are a rather boring subject to watch from a distance." It was Harold, the oldest brother. Zavier stayed silent, he knew the man through many rumors. He was now mentally preparing himself for whatever the man had in store for him. "Jason tells me that you are stubborn." Harold dragged a chair behind him, the wood scratching loudly against the stone floor as he placed the chair inches from Zavier before sitting down.

Breathing silently Zavier continued to wait, he could hear that Harold had something in his hand. He was turning the object in his hand it was metal and every full turn it would make it scrapped against his fingers with a clink. "Why does my brother dislike you? Is it because you have a stronger will power than him? That can't be so, he would hate the whole world, even his slut of a half-sister. So, what about you makes him so bad? A normal bastard, elven man that angers my baby brother so much." With that comment, he removed the sack from Zavier's face. He was amused by the lack of reaction to being freed from the blindness and thrown into the dim light of the room.

Zavier took this moment to study his surroundings; in the room there were four small candles, a dusty old bed, at each post there were more leather straps, hooks on the walls with spiked chains, buckets of water and a thick rag hanging out of one of the buckets, rather empty but there was something about the room that gave Harold a twisted look in his eyes. "Are you just going to sit there or add something to our friendly conversation?" Harold placed his elbows on his knees and his head in his hands he looked deeply at Zavier, "Silvia told you that we had the Ironfist boy in our custody? Did she tell you that he surrendered himself to Jason's soldiers? Apparently, he begged for them to leave your sister out of this fight and they beat the kid, one soldier even admitted to stabbing the kid, unintentionally. Oh, but they beat him senseless. With how many injuries the boy abstained if he is still out in the woods with your sister, he probably won't make it. I can make a deal with you, Zavier. Are you interested? It will be the best deal you will ever get out of this." Zavier just stared the man down, he knew with or without an answer he was going to tell him the deal. "Silvia said you were rather talkative with her, not with me? I'm hurt." Harold sarcastically pouted, tracing as if a tear fell down his cheek, "Now, if you give me where the Ironfist boy and your sister will be heading, I will make sure the soldiers leave your sister alone. As of now, they are ordered to bring them both in, mostly your sister just to toy with you. They will torture and defile her in front of you.

But I can stop that, I can prevent that from happening to her. Just give us the boy. He means nothing, he is just an orphan who's caused you more pain and suffering than he's clearly worth, he even thinks that or he wouldn't have given himself up so easy to begin with."

Zavier thought for a moment and then broke his eye contact with the man, adjusting once again, "Allister and Valkyrie are smart, you won't find them again."

Harald smiled, "at least you aren't denying knowing where they will be heading, at least then I have something to break out of you." He rubbed his hands together and stood up, placing one hand on the bottom of the chair that Zavier was tied too, as he carefully laid the chair back onto the floor, Zavier rested his head against the stone and that's when the water buckets made sense to him. He dared not show it, but he was scared. Harold took his time moving the buckets of water closer to Zavier, dragging the metal buckets against the stone floor, whistling softly to himself. Zavier's body tensed up, the anticipation was agonizing and part of Harold's torment. Finally, Harold leaned down next to Zavier, who didn't even look at the man, "Before we start, I will give you another chance. Any idea where they will be heading after their stronghold in Kel'mare had been found?" Zavier took a deep breath and remained silent, Harold smiled, "Oh well, this will be fun none the less." Harold draped the cloth over Zavier's face and stepped on the edges holding Zavier's face in place with his legs for the inevitable struggle ahead.

Without struggling, Harold slowly poured the containments of the bucket over his face, he tried to hold his breath, but as the water slowly poured over his nose and mouth Zavier coughed and swallowed, the water kept coming over him; as irrational as it was, Zavier while drowning wondered if the bucket would never end. Finally, when it did, Harold removed the cloth and sat the chair up once again, taking his seat once again.

Zavier spat and coughed, inhaling painfully as the air was rushed back into his lungs, once he regained himself he sat straight again and stared the man down.

Harold smiled, "I like you. Most people even with the first bucket, they are squirming and begging the second they can take another breath, you on the other hand. You have composer, I love it. Now, has that loosened your tongue a little bit? Take in mind, I have about nineteen more buckets and I can get more." Zavier just kept his lips closed tightly, "Okay, well let's get started, I promise you this is going to be a long night." Harold laughed sinisterly as a smile appeared on his face smiled placing the back on the chair on the ground and draped the cloth back over Zavier's face, this time after three buckets, he sat Zavier up and repeated his questions, while Zavier just coughed and wheezed as he struggled to take a breath, but he didn't say anything. By the sixth bucket, Harold knew he wasn't going to get anywhere with this tactic, but how could he waste such an opportunity to see how long an elven man could last while being drowned like this? After that he just kept increasing the number of buckets before giving Zavier a break, he was amazed at Zavier, he managed to get through four buckets before even his composer was broken. Zavier clenched his fists and tried to shake his head, even though he knew that it wouldn't save him from the water washing over his face.

Finally, Harold pulled the chair back to the seated position and smiled taking a seat, "You are the first man to actually make it through all my buckets." He clapped three times getting comfortable in his chair, Zavier just coughed and wheezed trying to take in as many breaths as he could. Zavier's eyes still locked on the man as he panted. "Looks like I am going to have to use a few other technics to get anything out of you." The man looked deep into Zavier, watching as the man intensity before Zavier composed himself once again, sitting tall, staring right back at Harold, no anger, no fear in his eyes and that gave Harold this excitement he had never felt before. "I'll give you tomorrow and then we will play again." Harold stood up and placed the sack over Zavier's head, as he slowly walked out of the room.

Zavier closed his eyes and just listened as his heart pounding in his chest; one day before he would return, one day to dream up all the possible things that man could do to him, trying to get information out of him. Zavier at least could look at the positives, he had no idea where Valkyrie and Allister would be heading, there was nothing for Harold to break out of him.

Valkyrie dreamt that night; it was different from her normal visions; she wasn't sure it even was one. She was strapped to a chair with leather, she turned her head and looked around the room, but she could only see a man before her. He was engulfed in a hellfire, his face was just embers and every movement was just a blur before her eyes, the man spoke, he had a soft, mocking tone with every word that left his mouth, "Just tell me, you have proven your bravery and dedication towards the boy. Just give me a location and this could all be over."

Suddenly a light from behind him appeared and another man, who was smothered in darkness, there was something familiar in the man's voice as he mockingly spoke, placing one of his hands around her throat, "Your worst nightmare is about to come true, Zavier you have failed. Allister is being brought here as we speak. You went through all this torment, torture and pain for nothing. Apparently, my men had your sister begging on her knees."

Valkyrie froze as her spirit left the chair and she stood as an entity behind her brother, was this a warning? Is this what is to become... Valkyrie stumbled back and placed her hand over her mouth, she trembled, was this all for not? Maybe there was a chance, was it a blessing that Zavier was at least alive? Or was it a curse... Valkyrie reached forward and placed her wrapped her arms around her brother's shoulders and whispered in his ear, "Brother, I am sorry. I'm scared, I'm scared I lost you, that I may never see you again, what is going to happen to me if I lose Allister as well? What is going to happen if the Volcanic Spire start their war? Tell me what to do, somehow tell me..."

Zavier straightened himself up in the chair and stared the men down, "Never underestimate those two children. They are stronger than you even understand. How does it make you feel that two children have been able to outsmart you for this long? And knowing them, they are going to outsmart you again and again. They will not make this easy on you, you may think you have won, but you haven't even come close."

The man pushed back from Zavier, with a good amount of force, his foot connected with Zavier's chest, knocking the chair to the ground, the

back of Zavier's head hit the floor and instantly Valkyrie could see blood
and Zavier stopped moving. Valkyrie's heart stopped and she was
forcefully pulled from the image. It was almost like she was caught in a
whirlwind, everything was a white blur and Valkyrie just turned and
turned around trying to escape. Images of Allister and Zavier appeared
before her as two paths; Allister was being escorted towards the gallows
by four armed guards, a noose set and waiting for him. Fear was stricken
on his face as he struggled with the men, the other Zavier's neck was
locked in a guillotine, there was regret, maybe even guilt washed over his
face, as he looked over the crowd. Valkyrie started to reach out towards
Zavier and then pulled her hand back towards her chest, hesitation as she
wanted to step towards Allister. "What does this mean?!" She screamed
out to whoever forced these images upon her.

A reply she didn't expect, she jumped and fell backward onto her butt as
a voice boomed loudly in her ears, "You child hold these fates in your
hands, your actions will cause the death of these who you care most
about, but your actions may save many more lives."

"Is there a chance I can save both of them?"

The voice laughed, "No, at least one has die. You have the chance to
save one, but even if one of these men are spared, the repercussions could
be worse than just losing them both."

"Will you tell me what I need to do to save one of them?" Valkyrie
begged, there were tears in her eyes as she fell to her knees, whipping her
eyes raw.

"When the time comes when you have to decide whose life is more
important, you will know the answer then, child. In the meantime, spend

your time with who you have wisely, they could be their last moments at any given time."

Finally, the wind stopped and Valkyrie was awake in the bed. Allister was sitting up in the bed just inches from her, woken by her stirring, he was watching over her while she slept.

"Valkyrie, are you okay?"

Her heart was beating rapidly in her chest, but she took a deep breath and nodded, whipping her eyes clear, as the man's voice echoed softly in her foggy head, beckoning her towards Allister. She tossed the blankets off her and stood up on the bed. Her bare legs and the long shirt that barely covered her lower half as it slid off one of her shoulders. Something took over her and her legs trembled at the thought of what she wanted to do. "Valkyrie?" Allister asked, as their eyes locked on each other. Valkyrie hovered over him and knelt down straddling him as she tore the blankets off of him. Allister was frozen and confused. He swallowed hard as the beautiful woman sat on top of him, pinning him to the bed with her body. Valkyrie leaned in and closed her eyes, as she forced her and Allister's lips together. Her lips were soft against his chapped and cracked ones. Something sparked and Allister got scared as he tried to push her away. But Valkyrie wrapped her arms around Allister's neck and pulled him into her and he couldn't resist the temptation, the spark. Finally, Allister wrapped his arms around her and traced his hands up and down her back, his hands gripped tightly around her firm buttocks. Their lips never left each other as she traced her hands down his strong toned chest. She followed the indents of his muscles, stopping at his bandaged wound, only to open her eyes and pause, they both looked at each other and took a long breath, before Valkyrie returned to his lips and untying his trousers. Allister pushed away holding her arms as Valkyrie hand his pants nearly off his crotch. They took another breath and he asked, "What brought this on?"

Valkyrie grabbed his face with both her hands and pulled him closer to her face, they breathed in each other as she spoke, "We need to live in the moment. Let's live like tomorrow is the day we are going to die and let's just love each other tonight." Valkyrie forced her lips back on his and tore off his trousers. Again, the two erupted into this hormonal passion.

She tossed his trousers far off the bed and Allister wrapped his arms around her lifting her and tossing her forcefully down on the bed, he was just inches apart from her body, she bit her lip as she looked at the man hovering over her, his dick throbbing before her.

Valkyrie pulled off her shirt as Allister started to kiss his way down her tanned body, his lips and his tongue tracing down every sensitive spot down to her thighs. Valkyrie grabbed hold of his hair and forced him down into her. She quivered and gasped. Finally pulling him back up to her face, he pushed himself softly inside her, biting her own lips she tried not to moan. Allister kissed her neck softly, as she scratched down his back, leaving red marks. He thrust inside her between her legs, as they held tightly on to each other. Moving together in every motion.

Time was irrelevant as the two entangled passionately between the bed sheets; when they finally finished the two of them flopped off each other and laid their sweaty and panting next to each other on the bed. Valkyrie just laid there, her fingers tracing her lips were Allister's had just been, her stare blankly into the ceiling, as a pleased smile was stuck on her red flustered face.

Allister had rolled his feet off the bed, both still undressed. He placed his hand on his wound, he could feel the wound trying to tear open again, but he didn't care. The pair was still in awe of what had just overcome them. Neither of them spoke a word.

Valkyrie stumbled around pulled her oversized shirt back over her naked body, she grabbed her pipe and lit it, walking over to the small hidden window. Dayla had been gone for a whole day already and the sun was just peeking over the tree line. Valkyrie could feel Allister's eyes on her, she bit her lip gently thinking about everything and turned around her back against the wall. "Do you have to keep staring at me?" She teased him with her body.

Allister just smiled at her, "I'm sorry, I'm just a little shocked that's all. One minute I'm watching you having a nightmare or something and then next thing I know you are all over me."

Valkyrie smiled coyly as she took another toke from her pipe, "Me? I'm a lady Allister I'd never do such a thing." Allister gave her a look and she smiled sweetly back towards him. "Like I said, we need to live like tomorrow is our last day. Nothing more to it, right? It was just sex." Valkyrie didn't believe that and neither did Allister. Something happened as they were entangled in each other, nothing but skin, sweat and passion between them. For a moment she lost herself in that thought, in that memory, a memory she hoped to never forget. Only to be shaken from it as Allister got up from the bed and walked over to her. He grabbed her waist with one hand and then slipped his fingers into her right hand. She placed her pipe down on the window, she looked into Allister's eyes,

"What are you doing?"

"I don't know," Allister responded with a smile, he pulled her close him and their lips were just inches from each other again. Valkyrie could feel the beating heart that was Allister's through her chest as she tried to keep her composer, but her heart fluttered and matched his. She fought the redness she could feel trying to blush her cheeks, as she brushed her bangs back, finally pushing away from Allister, arms crossed she smiled looking down, "Maybe you should help around outside a bit? See how well your body holds up to moving around."

His boyish smile never left his face, but he nodded turning away from Valkyrie as they two dressed and head out to the front yard.

Valkyrie that day kept a close eye on Allister. Even if he wasn't struggling to do something she would force her help onto him. Allister realized that no matter what he said she was going to help him, so he smiled and stayed quiet. Watching her just as much as she was watching him.

Chapter 13

Every time Dayla had to venture towards the town it was always an awkward encounter for her; the townsfolk only tolerated her being there because it gave them business and Dayla hated human interaction, but it was a necessary evil and both sides of this interaction realized that.

It was high noon by the time she reached the town, a little later than she had hoped, but the town was active and lively. She had already dismounted her horse fifteen minutes back, she just loosened her hood and pulled her hair out from under her collar.

Dayla started with her usual buys; dried fruits, vegetables, some meat, horse feed, restock on bandages and ointments, it wasn't too suspicious for her to be buying winter cloaks and supplies; it was odd for her to be buying in groups of three rather than one, but no one overly questioned anything. Until she got to a man name Elias, out of everyone in the town, he annoyed her the most, but at the same time he was the only person who ever spoke to her outside of bartering between them, he only sold cloaks; today he had some good, thick wool ones, Dayla inspected them carefully and grabbed three of roughly the same size.

"Three, wanting something different to wear?"

Dayla just grabbed the coins from her purse and studied the man, "You have good thick winter cloaks, not going to pass them up and last year one of mine ripped halfway through the winter, better safe than sorry right?" She smiled innocently handing the coins over to him.

Elias inspected the supplies in her cart that she had already purchased, "Grabbing a lot than normal, aren't you?"

"I'm expecting a harsh winter, grabbing what I can before the paths are too rough for my horse to make it safely. She is rather old and if she loses her footing and hurts herself, I'm in a bad situation for the rest of the year." Elias nodded, he seemed a little hyped on something and she knew that there was something he was wanting to say, "Is there something on your mind Mr. Elias?"

"Yes, you missed a lot of excitement lately. Volcanic spire soldiers say that two people should be either passing through here, or already have. Apparently, they have set up a pretty steep perimeter and they are closing in on their targets. Rather exciting don't you think?

Dayla looked disinterested on his news, "When have I cared about what the Volcanic Spire was doing? Let alone anyone else."

Elias smiled, "True very true Dayla, the Volcanic Spire soldiers are giving people pretty good rewards if they can give them information on the where a bouts. You are pretty close to the side trails, in between us and Kelmare aren't you? Haven't seen or heard anything, anyone?"

"Actually, I have. It was those soldiers running around in the bushes like crazed animals, but like I said. I don't care to worry about other person's problems."

Elias nodded again, fiddling with the coins, rolling them back and forth in his hands. There was suspicion in the man's eyes as he looked her up and down, but Dayla just walked away from the conversation, grabbing a few more things before she headed towards the exit, but Dayla was stopped. Ten Volcanic Spire guards surrounded her, all at the ready to draw their weapons.

Dayla placed her hand on the nose of her horse and waited patiently for the guards to address her.

"Witch, we have reason to believe that two criminals have crossed your path."

"Witch?" Dayla laughed sourly, "That's a name I haven't heard in ages. And which criminals do you speak of, sir." Dayla tightened her grip on the reigns and stared back at the soldier.

Two men came up behind Dayla and placed a shackle on her wrist, "I don't know anything." She growled, not struggling with the soldiers.

"If you have nothing to hide, you won't mind showing us your home. Your friend Elias says you live somewhere around where we set up camp, yet we haven't found a house?" He stepped forward and placed his hand around her throat and smiled, "Just a precaution, right?" He tossed a small coin purse towards Elias, "If anything comes from this lead, there is more where that comes." Smiling again, he placed his hand through Dayla's hair, the man leaned in and whispered in her ear as a sick feeling filled her stomach. "You are going to ride with me, any funny business and you will regret it, witch." The man just grabbed Dayla's arm and forced her up on his lap, "let's head out men." He ordered, one soldier grabbed Dayla's horse as they left the town, grabbing their mounts they headed to the rough location of Dayla's house.

The soldier had one hand on the reigns and his other hand was wrapped around Dayla, he would slip his hands under her blouse, or into her pants, he enjoyed feeling her try to squirm away from him, his body was pressed fully up against her; Dayla just kept her mouth closed and concentrated on anything else. She knew what to do in her situation, as she had been in it maybe times before, she cringed at the memories but kept calm.

Night crept up on the soldiers and Dayla was almost relieved as they side tracked looking for the house and headed to camp for the night; Dayla hoped that if Valkyrie and Allister realized that she wasn't back today, that something went wrong and they would leave.

Dayla's arm was grabbed and she was pulled from the horse by the man who she had been forcefully riding with, he smiled and brushed her hair back before pulling her along to the fire.

Their commander stepped forward and stared at the woman, grabbing Dayla by the arm and pulling her from the man's grip. Dayla stopped inches from the commander and stared back at him, the man spoke, "You were supposed to be bringing me the Prince and his friend."

"We won't find her house in the dark, she's a witch. She probably has magic's protecting her home."

Dayla flicked her hair back and stared back at the man behind her, "Just because I am a night elf, you humans always suspect that we are all into magic's, there are many night elves who were terrible with magic."

The commander squeezed her arm and jerked her into him, forcing her gaze back at him, "And were you one of those terrible with magic and witchcraft?"

Dayla smiled, "I was the best there was." Her coy tone was a challenge to the man.

Pushing Dayla back into the arms of the one soldier he turned away from her, "Make sure she is able to tell us where her home is tomorrow morning, do whatever you wish otherwise."

The soldier smiled and grabbed Dayla's chin, pushing her off towards his tents, Dayla didn't fight it and she just closed her eyes and hoped this night would be over quickly.

The following day Allister and Valkyrie tried to keep their minds off their sexual escapades. That night they just laid naked in each other's arms and now they couldn't forget their moment of passion together. Allister would just turn his head and see this beautiful woman that he wanted to ravish all over again, take her now and then. While Valkyrie saw this strong man that could easily engulf her into this strange ecstasy that she had never experienced before. Thought the two tried to keep their distance, Valkyrie would come over to him to help him if he seemed to be struggling, their hands would just brush up against each other and the spark would cause them to jump back. Valkyrie tried to play cool, that the sexual moment between the two of them was nothing, but Allister could see past her eyes, he could see the truth of her feelings, she felt something more than just physical enjoyment. Neither of them wanted to admit this to the other, at least not yet.

Finally, the pair could only think of the happy things. Valkyrie had almost forgot about her vision; they could only think about the feeling of their bodies entwined together.

It was getting late in the afternoon and Valkyrie could see that Allister was in pain and slowing down. He had one hand pressed against his stomach and every few steps he took he's winch in pain.

Valkyrie finished what she was doing and then walked to towards

Allister, "Allister let's head inside. I'm tired, we got a lot done today." She lied, trying to make it seem that she was the one who wanted to go inside.

Allister tried to hide the excitement, but his face lit up when the words left her mouth, "Yeah sure." He nodding placing the equipment back in the horse stall and Valkyrie did the same before heading back into the house together.

Sitting next to the fireplace, Allister tossed another log on the fire and watched it slowly catch ablaze. He closed his eyes and groaned as he rubbed his stomach, his ribcage had adjusted painfully and he kept breathing deeply trying to catch his breath, his chest was tight and his body was sore and stiff.

Valkyrie sat behind him and rubbed his shoulders softly, digging into his sore muscles. Allister went to argue, but her hands on him were just what he wanted, what he needed.

"Were you having a nightmare? Or a vision that night Valkyrie?"

Valkyrie stopped and rested her hands on Allister's neck, "Maybe just a little of both. It was confusing, to say the least."

"Do you want to talk about it?"

Valkyrie kissed the top of Allister's head, "It's nothing you need to worry about Allister."

Allister turned around and wrapped his arms around Valkyrie, pressing his lips against hers. She was nearly toppled over by his force, but she just melted into his arms. Kissing him back, she wrapped her arms around his neck and brought herself even closer to him. All thoughts just washed over the pair as they took each other's breaths in. Valkyrie was the first to push away, they looked deeply at each other and Valkyrie placed her hands on the side of his face and smiled. Her tough girl persona was no more as she melted in his gaze.

Allister just smiled and brushed her hair back, "I feel like I get to see you in a whole new light."

"Is that because we had sex?" Valkyrie laughed trying to distance the conversation of the heavy feelings overwhelming her at that moment. He just shook his head and looked deeper into her eyes, "No, it's something else. If anyone else was in this situation with me, they would have been gone the first chance they got. They would have left me to die at the hands of those soldiers. But you stayed and you are here with me and I appreciate it. You should have left me with the Volcanic Spire, saved yourself. I'd like to believe that it was for a reason, other than just guilt. I want you to know, that I left because I wanted to protect you." Allister sat on the bed and Valkyrie sat down next to him, as the pair just looked into the fire. "I was thinking that my life isn't important. Zavier and most of all you could have lived a normal life, if only I hadn't been in it."

Valkyrie hugged him tightly, "I should have hit you harder for that stunt then I did. Don't think that your life isn't important. If Zavier was here he would lecture you on how every life is important. He wouldn't have saved you all those many years ago and sacrificed himself for someone he didn't care about, for someone who wasn't important. You have a chance to do some good in this world, Allister." Valkyrie just held him tightly as he hugged her back, "When I woke up and you weren't there I was scared. I have terrified Allister. I can't even think about what would have happened if I didn't find you. This may be selfish of me, but I can't lose both you and Zavier. I need you, I need someone."

Allister broke awake from her and looked her in the eye, "I'm sorry, but I can't promise you I'll always be there. I will promise that I won't leave you like I did again. I swear on my life, I won't run away from you like that again."

After a few long moments of silence, they broke away from each other. Valkyrie felt emotionally drained. She rubbed her face and looked back towards Allister, who placed his elbows on his knees and rested his face in his hands.

The day finally ended for the pair and they stayed up waiting around for Dayla by the fire. It was well after midnight before they thought it would be best to rest. Maybe something kept her and she had to stay in the village for the night, they couldn't be sure. They decided it would be best to think positive and hope things were alright, there it was a daunting through that made their night rather restless. Before sleeping they gathered all their supplies and laid them next to their bed, the horse's saddles were even set up and ready to just hook up and leave in case they needed to head out in a hurry.

Allister laid down on the bed and moaned in pain as he kept readjusting himself, he wished he hadn't pushed himself so much today. Valkyrie was out cold the moment she closed her eyes, while Allister couldn't sleep most of the night, as he spent the hours staring at the back of her tangled beautiful head.

The uncertainty of Dayla being later than she had expected and his body tightened painfully again. It was nearly impossible for Allister to fall asleep and when he did manage to rest, he'd be woken by the wind howling in his ears, blowing wildly against the house.

The morning was near and Allister found himself walking through the house, he borrowed one of Dayla's books and read a few pages, he didn't know the name on the cover, Faren Blight. Whoever the writer was, he had an interesting insight on the world he lived in. He must have seen and been a part of many things in his lifetime. Allister rubbed his eyes and placed the book down as he could see the sun peering through the wooden blinds. Opening them he looked back at the beautiful late fall morning. The fruit trees on the outskirts of the fence were bare, it's red and golden yellow leaves that had fallen to the ground and the crystallized dew on the grass sparkled, the wind nipped at Allister's skin. As beautiful as the day seemed to be, with the sun shining brightly, today was going to be cold.

After opening the few windows to air out the place, Allister started the fire up again and placed some water on the stove to boil, waiting hopefully for Dayla to walk into the house, or Valkyrie to wake up, whichever came first. He grabbed the book again and sat down at Dayla's desk to read again.

It was nearly noon when Valkyrie finally strolled out from the loft, Allister had finished reading two of the many books that laid scattered on Dayla's desk by that time and he didn't even put the third down as Valkyrie walked up to him.

"Has Dayla returned yet?"

Allister finally looked up from the page and shook his head, "There is no sign of her still. Do you think something went wrong?"

Valkyrie shrugged and looked out the window. "I'm not comfortable staying here. Dayla was worried about the soldiers being so close to the house, maybe they stopped her." The unknown was worrying her, but the unknowing didn't last long for the pair.

Only a few minutes after their conversation did they pair hear the horse's approaching. Allister froze in fear and Valkyrie grabbed his arm, snapping him back into reality. The two rushed up into the loft and pulled the ladder up with them. Grabbing their bags and tying their leather armor onto themselves. Valkyrie looked out the window, there were twenty soldiers on horseback now in the front yard and another five walking, scouting the area behind them. Dayla was shackled, her neck, arms and face were covered in burns and she looked drained and exhausted. Valkyrie drew her sword, she itched to just run out there and fight them, but she realized it was a losing battle. They would execute Dayla before she even got to the first soldier.

Allister unlocked the escape hatch and reached out with his hand for Valkyrie, "We need to go, now."

Valkyrie looked out the window once more and grabbed Allister's hand jumping down the hatch landing in the horse stall. Crimson jumped and whinnied loudly. Valkyrie grabbed her reins and calmed the horse before saddling her. Allister already had the saddled the unstirred Nightmare. Allister unlocked the back door, while Valkyrie locked the door leading towards the front yard, as they crept out the back, silently they mounted the horses. They looked back at Dayla's cottage guilt written all over their faces, today Dayla was possibly going to lose her life for her kindness towards them. They prayed to any god that would listen that they would spare him life, but the gods did not answer that day.

Dayla was pulled off the horse while the armed soldiers broke open her door and started to go through her things; they tossed and ripped the books and pages on her desk. she cringed as she watched her late Husband's irreplaceable pages be turned into scraps.

The commander kept one hand tightly clasped on Dayla's arm as they went through every inch of her house, even the upper loft.

Finally, after searching everywhere and coming out empty handed the soldiers came back to their commander. The man wasn't convinced, though, "If no one has been here, how is there a stoked fire and water on onto boil?"

"I thought maybe you are your soldiers would like a cup of tea." Dayla coyly spoke as her tone didn't flutter as he swung her around forcefully, meeting her gaze.

The commander shook his head and pulled her to the desk, sitting her down in the chair. He looked through his papers and found something hiding upon the books, a map, with a small location circled softly in charcoal. The man smiled, "Planning a trip towards the Cavern?"

Dayla just looked over the map quickly and answered quickly, "My late husband lived around those parts. I was planning on going to see his memorial."

"Why would you need to map it out then?"

"Just was looking at other options of travel." Dayla knew she wasn't fooling him with her excuses, but she just looked down at the paper and whispered a few words in her elven tongue and it caught ablaze. Burning away the evidence and location on where Valkyrie and Allister were heading. The man dropped the map and tried to stomp it out, but as it wasn't a normal fire, something that couldn't be stomped out. The commander punched Dayla knocked her out of the chair, his hand wrapped around her frail neck and he began to squeeze. Dayla clawed at his hands, but with her wrist weakened by the cast iron she barely marked the large man. The commander removed one hand from her throat and pulled his engraved blade from his sheath, slipping the blade deep into her ribcage. Standing up he hovered over Dayla, as she gasped, as her life blood pooled on the floor. Tears began to fall from Dayla's face, as pain and nothingness slowly crept upon her.

The commander watched her struggle for a few moments as he ordered his men out of the house. The soldiers set Dayla's home ablaze, as they watched her home slowly turn to embers. Dayla was too far gone to feel the heat from the flames. She pulled a portrait from her blouse, she tried to smile, through the pain and the tears, "Faren, we shall be together again my love." Her lips trembled as she hugged onto the piece of paper, even has her body went limp and all life left Dayla, she still had the image of her late husband grasped in her hand next to her none beating heart. Within hours there was nothing but ashes and dust.

Valkyrie and Allister pushed the horses hard for a good few hours gaining a lot of distance from Dayla's cottage. They reached a high vantage point and only quickly looked back to see if they could see a scouting party or anything. And even though they were hours away from the cottage they could see smoke pouring from the where bouts of Dayla's home and the pair realized that Dayla was most likely gone.

Valkyrie paused. Giving a moment of silence for the helpful woman.

Allister placed one hand on the base of her back and spoke with distance, "We need to keep riding, we can't let her sacrifice be for nothing."

Valkyrie took a moment and nodded. Allister took Valkyrie's hand and held it tightly, not for just her ease, but his own as they continued back onto their path.

Even before the sun fully set over the trees, Valkyrie and Allister were shivering, the winter wind was already starting to kick in with a force. The pair lit their torches and continued through the night slowly, wanting to try and get as much distance as possible, knowing that they also were racing against time.

Valkyrie and Allister only stopped to feed and water the horses, besides that, the two were too scared to stop, too afraid to rest. thinking that somehow the Volcanic Spire soldiers would be right around the corner ready to surround them.

Slowing down as the sun again peeked over the treetops; Valkyrie couldn't feel her fingers as she rubbed them together, removing her hood. Her stomach grumbled loudly, her butt was painfully sore, she was cold and tired, but she didn't want to stop. Allister, on the other hand didn't care about how sore his butt was, or the frozen tips of his fingers, he was hankered by how painful it was to be riding for over twenty-four hours with fractured ribs and a stitched stomach. Allister maybe got every other breath in, he wasn't paying attention to where his horse was going and he knew that he could rely on Nightmare to keep, him in the right direction.

Valkyrie slowed even more and looked around she hadn't looked back at Allister in a long time, "Maybe there is a covered area close by that we can stop and set up a quick camp.

Allister just nodded, he was concentrating on catching his breath and holding on the horse, that he couldn't give her an audible response. Not hearing him, she finally turned her head and saw his face. Valkyrie fumed for a moment, as she reached over and grabbed Allister's arm, "Allister, if the ride was getting too difficult, you should have said something. Let's get to the clearing over there and stop, okay?"

Allister again just nodded, Valkyrie leading the way only by a few steps, keeping a closer eye on him.

Once they reached the clearing, Valkyrie helped Allister off the horse and they laid down together on the grass, while Allister inhaled and exhaled deeply. He found himself pulling at his shirt, trying everything to make his chest loosen, but nothing was working, he could feel his heart pounding heavy in his chest. Valkyrie just laid down on his stomach next to him, her cold hands against his sore and bleeding stitches hoping that it would help a little. Finally, after nearly twenty minutes and nearly blacking out from hyperventilating, Allister found it easier for him to catch his breath. Rubbing his hands through his hair, he started to stand up, only to be pushed down again by Valkyrie, "You aren't going anywhere. Just rest for a bit longer, please. I can handle the horses and start a fire." Allister starting to say something, but Valkyrie pressed her lips against his to shut him up and then walked away, not giving him the chance to argue.

Laying there, Nightmare and Crimson poked their noses at him, Allister smiled sleepily as he scratched their faces with his hands.

Valkyrie brought dry wood and started the fire, placed two filled water buckets on the ground for the horses and a pile of gain for the two, before placing their blankets over them. Allister sat up as she sat behind him placing her hands on his shoulders. The two moved closer to the fire, Valkyrie pulled out some dried meat and some bread and passed it to Allister, before putting the rest away. "I'm not sure how long what we have will last, we will have to do some hunting."

"We should try and keep as far from the main road as we can." Allister grabbed his bags and started looking for his map, after not finding it quickly he started to frantically search for it, "Valkyrie, do you have the map?"

Valkyrie looked through her own bags and found nothing, the pair just looked at each other and sighed, without a map it was another obstacle for them to pass. Valkyrie sat down and placed her face in her hands, "Fuck, we have no equipment, limited food and no map."

Allister just shook his head and placed a hand on Valkyrie's shoulder, "We at least have enough feed for the horses. If we follow the river it will lead us in the direction of the mountains' path, once close enough it will be impossible to miss."

"There is a village close to the mountain trail, Yargren. It's still at least a two-week ride and there isn't even a good chance they will be friendly towards us."

"We don't have a choice, with what we have, neither of us would last the climb up the mountain and neither will Crimson and Nightmare. Hopefully the little coin we have left will get us something."

"Yeah I know... Guess we will chance it when we get there right."

Valkyrie leaned into Allister, tucking her hands into her shirt and wrapping her cloak tightly around herself. Allister unrolled their blankets and tossed it over Valkyrie, she cuddled into him and closed her eyes; she was asleep in his arms in minutes.

Allister just smiled and brushed her hair back; at this point, Valkyrie was all that mattered, he needed to be there for her.

After a few hours, Valkyrie woke up and Allister took that chance to rest his eyes for an hour, before quickly packing up camp and continuing on their journey.

The ride this day was calm, they hadn't heard, or seen any movement behind them since leaving Dayla's home all those days ago, so they let the horses take it easy. Finding the river, they just slowly walked the banks and stopping for camp by nightfall.

Chapter 14

Zavier jolted awake and straightened himself as the door creaked open; whoever had entered the room took their time to approach him. There were at least three people by the sound of their footsteps and they were dragging something along with them. Zavier shook his head, shaking himself into alertness.

Someone reached down and untied his legs, while one person held tightly onto Zavier's shoulders another went to unchain his hands. He waited until the binds completely fell to the ground and then reached up with his legs and wrapped around the closest guy's neck, slipping out of the one man's grasp, he used that to throw himself over the ones shoulder, landing and stumbling Zavier tossed the sack off his face and went to turn on the door, only to feel something hard hit his head and blackness.

When Zavier awakened again, he realized that he made a mistake. How could he have missed the footsteps approaching the door? Now his head rang and he knew he wasn't going to get another chance like that.

Zavier was sprawled on his stomach out over a large metal table, his arms we chained and pulled tightly as far to the side as they could go, his feet were chained to something, that he could assume, as when he moved his feet they just caught and clanked. He lifted his head and saw the blood soaked on the table, Harold sitting down to the left of him, a metal rod with a sigil on it, in his hands and a medium sized fire pit burned low, with other metal rods sticking out of it; it didn't take much of an imagination for Zavier to realize what the man had in mind.

Harold stood up and stepped behind Zavier, teasing him as he placed the cold metal on his back, Zavier just held his composer not even flinching as he placed his forehead on the table and closed his eyes. "That was a good attempt. A little bit sloppy, but I will give you the benefit of a doubt due to your lack of practice in the last while. Maybe you will get another chance to show me your abilities." He smiled as he placed the cast-iron brand into the fire pit.

Valkyrie rubbed her eyes as she saddled the horse and brushed the horse's mane with her fingers, Nightmare nestled his nose into her chest and snorted loudly.

Allister kept rubbing his head; waking up cold, stiff and with a migraine just made the pain in his rib and stomach all the worse, he wasn't looking forward to this ride today. Crimson could sense that Allister was having a rough morning and kept placing her head down on his head and shoulder.

The pair gave each other a quick glance before mounting their horses, it hurt jumping up on the large horse, but Allister did it without complaints and heading off towards the river beds, the sounds of the rushing water leading their way.

With every hour that passed, the temperature slowly changed. Valkyrie and Allister soon would feel the harsh reality of the winter on their faces.

Valkyrie tucked her hair into her cloak and placed her hood up, as she could feel her ears turning red as the wind blew against her. Before their day was even halfway over, her nose was red and her lips were chapped, but today, Valkyrie felt optimistic. Something was in the air that made Valkyrie feel that their upcoming day's maybe even weeks would bring them at least some good fortune. Allister of course wasn't feeling her optimism, but had to smile at her cheerfulness. Valkyrie tightened her grip on the reigns and trotted up closer to Allister. "Together we can survive this Allister, we haven't seen or heard soldiers in pursuit, we've lost them. We are winning this battle." She smiled ever so pleased with herself.

Allister looked at Valkyrie for only a moment, dread was just written all over his face as he turned away; he wanted to believe Valkyrie's optimism, but he couldn't. The only end he really could see was more death and the Volcanic Spire getting what they wanted.

Valkyrie wasn't blind to his doubt, she rode up closer to him and slipped her fingers into his and squeezed his hand softly and just silently rode next to him. He appreciated the physical contact and just held on to her, for that moment, he just never wanted to let her go.

"Do you ever regret living with Zavier and myself all these years?"

Allister was instantly thrown from the question and stopped his horse and looked at Valkyrie.

Before he could even answer she spoke again, "It's not a bad thing if you do, just something that came to mind. That's all."

Allister shook his head, "The only thing I do regret is not being able to protect Zavier from a fate that he did not deserve. He should be here by your side, not I. But that doesn't mean I don't want to be by your side and that I am not thankful for being here... It's rather selfish to say, I'm terrified of what will happen to me when they capture me. It scares me not knowing what exactly they want from me." Allister looked ahead and they started moving on the horses once again. "I won't lie and tell you that I am not afraid right now. I have been playing out to be brave and strong, but I just want this to be over." Valkyrie just looked at the man as he bore all to her, it was weird seeing him act so vulnerable, "If I am captured by the Volcanic Spire and if they do what I am expecting them to do, I almost feel that my death won't matter. No one will care. They don't know me. I haven't done anything to them, all they will see is I am the son of my father. They won't know the man I have become and they won't care. I think I am more afraid of that, then anything else. No one is going to care that I am going to die and the only reason they won't care, is because of something I didn't do. Will they only see my father when they look at me? Or will they actually see, me? Have I even given anyone a reason to care? I haven't done anything remarkable with my life."

Valkyrie was speechless, what could she say? Allister just told her everything, she wasn't even sure that she was supposed to respond.

The mood was heavy and the skies reflected that. The gray late fall clouds had formed in, the tree leaves fell all around them and the branches swayed in the ever-growing wild storm. Allister placed his hand on his forehead, he was almost regretting saying all that he had just, only as he could feel the pity filled look that had filled in the beautiful Valkyrie's eyes.

"My biggest fear is being alone." Valkyrie began to just say, wanting to break the silence, "Which is funny right? When I think about it I pushed you and even sometimes Zavier away. When it really mattered at least, when I, or you need someone I pushed away. I try to be this independent person, but I am afraid. When people hear my name, they only think of two things really, yes I am a skilled bounty hunter, that isn't afraid to just kill. But even as the world feared me, there was still disrespect. I was the sister of the bastard elf and I was the friend of the damned Ironfist boy. When I first met you, I didn't care who you were, you were just another person. You were just a friend. But after I had the vision about Zavier being taken, the things people were saying about you started to really affect me, the way I looked at you. I hated being associated with you, but the reason I hated it so much was because in the end I never stopped caring about you. I cared about all the terrible things they were saying about you and none of them knew you. But I didn't do anything about it. Because I wanted to be accepted, if they didn't accept me in some part of their society, I was going to be alone... So, I pushed you as far away as I possibly could. It seems even though I wanted to push you away, we were just fated to be together for at least this moment and I feel we should make these few good moments, last. Cherish the little things, keep the fear at the back of our minds, without letting us forget that there is a threat to us."

Allister turned to Valkyrie and smiled, "You are afraid of being alone? Says the girl who would sometimes leave for two months at a time, without saying a word to Zavier or me?"

Valkyrie scrunched her nose and frowned feeling that she just opened herself up to him and he was mocking her, "Facing your fears is a good practice for everyone, Allister. I should be laughing at your fear, I have only heard stories of your father and you are nothing like those stories. You are a great person, just for some reason, you let the cloud that was your father hang over your head. I think it is you that needs to prove to yourself, that you are not like your father. Why does it really matter what others think of you? Your own opinion of yourself and the few people that do care for you are the only opinions that should matter."

"But they aren't. I know what other people think of me shouldn't matter, but it does. If what people thought of me didn't matter, we wouldn't be running would we? I'm not like you and Zavier, people judge you, but they can still see you as who you are. When people look at me, they don't see Allister, they see an Ironfist. They see my father. I wish I was like Zavier, be fearless and unbothered by anything, but I'm weak."

Valkyrie's face dropped a little, thinking of her brother once again, "A lot of things actually bothered him. Zavier just never wanted his emotions to show that what people said affected him. Zavier puts himself in a lot of danger for those he cares about, because the physical pain he can take better than emotional pain. But he cared a lot about what happened to you and he let a lot of the people's prejudice bother him. I remember sometimes I'd over listen him talk to himself and it was more like him just wishing that he could give you something more, he wished he could change the way people regarded you because he knew you were growing into a great man and you always have been a great person."

Allister pulled her hand up to his mouth and kissed her hand "You strangely know what to say." He looked into Valkyrie's eyes and smiled. "I think-" He stopped himself and turned away from her, releasing her hand and grabbing the reigns with both. "Never mind."

Valkyrie just shrugged it off and smiled, looking up towards the graying sky, "It seems like it might rain tonight. Do we want to look for some shelter before it comes down on us? Nightmare and Crimson won't like sleeping in the rain." Allister just smiled for a moment and nodded, he couldn't help but be glad that at least Valkyrie could genuinely smile even in darker times.

"If we are as far along as I think we are, there should be a cave just north of here close to the waterfall. It still might be a few hours from here, or it could be an hour."

"Okay, so just keep the way we are going pretty much," Valkyrie smiled, the dimples in her cheeks and the smile wrinkles around her eyes just made Allister start to really realize something about himself. He was in love with Valkyrie. She cocked her head at Allister, seeing that he was getting lost staring at her, "Want to race for a little bit?"

Allister smirked, "You are on." With that the two galloped off together, Valkyrie taking the early lead.

By the time that the rain started to pour down on the pair, they were already inside the cave, curled up next to a small roaring fire, after recovering the cave entrance with leaves and brush from around the waterfall. Valkyrie untied her hair and squeezed it dry as she sat closer to the fire, taking off her cloak she laid it out also to dry. Allister followed Valkyrie's lead with the cloaks and undressed the horses, feeding them and placing their blankets on before sitting down himself.

Sitting on the opposite side of Valkyrie he hugged his legs and stared into the small fire, while he was looking at the fire, Valkyrie was just looking at him. Valkyrie was remembering before all this, the time where they were both innocent in a world filled with cruelty, but her smile distinguished from her face as she remembered her vision from the many years before and how she let that one thing, ruin what could have been a beautiful thing between them. "I want to apologize to you."

He looked up from the fire and cocked his brow, "For what?"

"When we were growing up, I let what I thought would happen and then I allowed that the other people were saying about you form what I thought of you."

Allister frowned and looked back down at his feet, "It's fine Valkyrie, that all is behind us now."

Valkyrie got up and walked over to Allister, she placed her hand on his back and traced it to his shoulder sitting down on his lap their faces now inches from each other, Allister tried to look away, but Valkyrie grabbed his chin and forced him to look her in the eye. "No, Allister I really need you to listen to me. It was wrong of me, you are and you will always be a great person. You are a better person then I am, by far. I wish that I gave you more of a chance when we were younger. It took us in a dire situation together for me to really see you and it took one moment of passion to make me realize that."

Allister was thrown off, but he just took the moment for what it was, "Valkyrie, I think I'm in love with you." and with that he leaned in and pressed his lips against hers. Valkyrie pressed hers against him and leaned forward, forcing Allister onto his back, her arms wrapped around his neck, as his hands cascaded down her back and stopped firmly on her buttocks. The two tossed and turned on the ground wrestling each other's clothes off, it was like a test to see how much clothes they could get off without their lips ever leaving each others.

Allister forced himself on top of her, his hands roaming up and down her naked body, as the two panted, finally getting a full breath of air; Allister kissed down starting from her neck, softly he traced his lips and tongue on her nipples, Valkyrie closed her eyes and allowed the feelings to wash over her. She was hesitant as she slowly kissed lower down her body, he reached passed her belly button she tightened up, but Allister's hands rubbed her tights and in between her legs, Valkyrie relaxed again and just fell into natural sexual bliss.

It wasn't a silent night for them, claw marks were still red and fresh on their backs; neither of them slept, but they were satisfied by the night they had. The two of them just laid naked on the cave ground, Valkyrie curled up into Allister's warm chest and both just smiled.

Allister looked at the woman in his arms and kissed her forehead, "I wish that we could just be like this, till the end of time."

Valkyrie smiled and sat up reaching for her blouse, "Maybe we can do something like this till the end of time. Maybe the volcanic spire will give up and we can just spend our lives together, doing whatever we want. Things could get better for us, we could even leave here completely. Who says we need to stay on this forsaken land we have been fighting a losing battle from the moment we were born, it seems. Why stay?"

Allister thought about it, could he ever leave this place completely? He was connected to these lands, by many ways; even if not all of them he wanted to admit. "This is our home."

"We can make a home somewhere else."

Allister wanted to say yes, but he couldn't. There were many things forcing him to stay here, even if it seemed that no one wanted him here. "This is where I need to be, maybe one day it's possible, but not now." He didn't say it, but he knew that if given the chance he would trade his life in for Zavier's release. If he is still alive that is and as much as he knew it would now hurt Valkyrie, he hoped that would happen.

Valkyrie didn't stop smiling, but there was a hint of disappointment in her eyes, she understood what he meant, but she wasn't as sentimental towards this place as he was, since her parent's death, no place was ever home. Being with Zavier was home and now being with Allister was becoming home... She wanted to run away from Tasryn, sail far away, but she didn't want to run alone. She wished that Zavier, Allister and she were just together and had left this awful place years, but no... She didn't believe there was hope for Zavier, as much as it pained her to say, she just wanted hope for Allister now, it's what Zavier would have at least wanted. And he would have been proud to see what they had become. Whatever they were now.

The pair spent two more nights in the cave as rain poured down heavy from the clouds. They continuously checked their surroundings for any sign of soldiers as the days went by. After they got plenty of rest and exercise in a sense, their nerves got the better of them finally as they grew restless in the cave. The moment the rain gave up the two mounted up and headed back on their path. They hoped that the skies would stay clear for a few more weeks, giving them enough time to find a village and grab supplies before having to trek up the mountain, the first snow fall was approaching.

After a few long weeks of riding, they could really start to feel winter coming. Valkyrie's lips were chapped and breaking, every time they kissed, they almost began to bleed on her, some nights started to get so cold that their tangled, hair had icicles forming, it got to the point that they just rode together switching between horses, keeping each other warm with their body heat.

It was a freezing afternoon when Allister stopped the horse. Valkyrie paused holding tightly onto him for the moment, as the pair listened closely.

There was a rustling in the bushes just west of them. Allister got off the horse and ushered Valkyrie to stay. Valkyrie held tightly onto the reigns and beckoned, "We should move faster, what if it's someone catching up to us?"

"No, I don't think so. They are a little too quiet to be a group of soldiers but too loud to be just one. Just wait here a second." Valkyrie surprisingly listened to Allister.

Allister made his way through the bushes rather silently and the closer he got towards the rustling, he now could hear these soft little sobs, leaning over a bush, there was a little boy. He had dusty blond hair that was chopped short, wearing a thick dark blue cloak and he hugged his legs tightly.

"Are you lost?" Allister asked the moment the boy heard him speak he jumped up and backed away from the strange man. "Don't worry, I won't hurt you. Are you lost?"

The boy whipped his eyes with his sleeve and nodded.

Allister reached out for the boy's hand "We can help you find your way home."

The boy hesitated, but finally grabbed Allister's hand and let him lead him back towards Valkyrie.

Allister smiled and laughed a little while he spoke, "I found our big strong soldier trailing us Valkyrie." Valkyrie smiled as the boy came out of Allister's shadow.

"Oh dear, such a strong soldier, whatever are we going to do to face him."

The boy smiled and wiped his eyes again.

"Where you do live little boy?" Valkyrie asked adjusting in her seat.

"I live in the village of Toft."

"Why are you even out here all alone?" Allister asked placing him on the horse with Valkyrie.

"I was riding my horse, when she got spooked and ran off, I fell off and she just kept running. I hope she made it home." The boy sat in front of Valkyrie, she grabbed the reigns and looked at Allister.

"Toft, that's the village we were heading towards the right?" Allister just nodded, "What's your name?"

"Christopher."

"Well, Christopher, we will get you home," Valkyrie smiled at the boy and Allister mounted Nightmare and they headed off continuing in their original direction. It was nearing nightfall when they finally reached the village, Christopher was asleep in Valkyrie's arm before they even saw the torch lights.

"Allister put your hood up. I don't know how these people will react towards you."

He just nodded, like he really needed her to tell him that, as he placed his hood over his head and they slowly walked their horses into the village gates.

Allister rode up to the first person he saw and spoke softly, "Excuse me miss, my friend and I stumbled upon a boy in the woods today. Do you know where he might belong? His name is Christopher."

The older woman was carrying a torch and tried to look under Allister's cloak before answering him, "It's a miracle that you found the boy. He belongs to the widow woman in the last house down the way, the house with the broken wagon out front."

Allister adjusting his hood again, hiding his face from the curious woman, "Thank you." they then made their way to the house. Allister dismounted first, taking the boy from Valkyrie and walking towards the door not wanting to wake the sleeping child.

Allister didn't even knock on the old wooden door twice by the time a panicked woman answered the door, "Christopher?" Her eyes were wide and her hair was matted and tangled, she was a young woman, almost too young to have a child Christopher's age, but the relief that filled her eyes as she saw the boy in Allister's eyes made him smile.

"My friend and I found him lost in the woods."

"Oh bless you! Can you please, come in, come in the two of you?"

Allister was about to refuse, not seeing it as a good idea, but she grabbed him by the arm and pulled him into her home.

Valkyrie followed, "We really shouldn't stay ma'am."

"I can't let you leave at this time, unless you have a place to stay?" She took the boy in her arms, as he slowly started to wake up. "You saved my son, please let me at least offer you to stay the night."

Allister just looked at Valkyrie and she just smiled sweetly at the woman, "Thank you."

The woman walked off into another room with the boy in her arms and came back a few minutes later. Please, take a seat anywhere, I can hang your cloaks if you wish." There was such happiness in the woman's eyes, Valkyrie removed her hood and handed it to her, while Allister hesitated, but eventually gave in.

The woman was startled slightly when she looked at Allister, she clearly knew who he was, but she thought about her son, now asleep in his bed and just smiled again. "You can rest and I have some food if you are hungry."

"We have our own food, but thank you for the roof over our heads tonight," Allister spoke, trying not to stare at the slightly nervous woman.

The woman laughed awkwardly, "You seem more nervous to be here than myself. I won't tell anyone who you are, if you are worried about that. You saved my son, you could have left him in the woods to die, but you didn't." She grabbed a piece of paper from one of her counter tops and handed it directly to Allister. "A month or so ago, we were visited by Volcanic Spire soldiers." Allister looked at the paper, it was a crude drawing of him, with a description and a list of all the things his father had done. He forced himself to sit down, as he just blankly stared off, Valkyrie took the paper and quickly glanced over it as shredding the paper before crumpling the parchment and placing her hand on Allister's shoulder. The woman looked at him, "I don't think it's safe for you to stay here long and there is a reward out for your head. We are a poor village and some of the people would kill for that reward."

Valkyrie shook her head and placed the scraps of parchment down, "It's a good thing there is no information about me on this paper. I can gather supplies in the morning and you just stay out of sight."

"If this makes you feel any better." The woman spoke sitting down beside Allister, "Now that I have seen you, I don't believe any of the horror stories that those soldiers were trying to tell us. You are just a boy and if even half of that was true, you wouldn't have brought my son safely back to me."

"Thank you," Allister smiled towards the woman and she stood back up and walked out of the room.

Valkyrie sat down next to Allister, laying her head on him. Still nervous about staying in this house, the pair slept in sessions, Valkyrie first and then Allister slept till the morning.

Allister woke up, to the feeling of eyes staring at him, Christopher knelt on the ground and his face was inches from Allister's face. Sitting up and rubbing his eyes he looked back at the boy, "Good morning, Christopher."

"Good morning, Mr." Christopher smiled standing up. "Your pretty friend is already out in the village with mother. Mother told me to stay and not let anyone in the house today."

Allister looked towards the door and went to grab his cloak, tying it around his neck he placed the hood over his head and peeked out the window. For a small seeming village, it was packed with people, Allister couldn't even see Valkyrie's red untameable hair from where he was and that make him more nervous.

"Do you not like people, Mr?"

Allister turned around as the boy tugged on his cloak, he laughed slightly with a smug smile. "More like people don't like me, Christopher."

"Why?"

"Maybe one day I will ask them that myself." Allister smiled at the boy and looked back out the window, "Christopher, do you want to help me prepare the horses?"

The boy nodded and they headed out the door silently, Allister's cloak as tight around his face as he possibly could. As he saddled the two horses, making sure they had plenty to eat and drink, hoping that Valkyrie wouldn't be too long. Since even with his back turned towards the villages, he could feel their eyes on them, it's like some how they knew who he was.

Christopher just brushed the horses for Allister, he never stopped talking and asking Allister questions. It made him happier than he would care to admit, this child, showed no fear, no hate, he had no opinion of who Allister was, besides what he physically saw and felt towards him, it was a comfort Allister hadn't experienced from most people.

It was nearly noon, even as the sun shinned brightly, the winters bitter cold nipped down harder and the cold winds coming down the mountain tossed Allister's cloak around him. Allister's heart stopped, a villager approached the gate, "Christopher, who is your friend?" the strange man asked, as he inspected the back of Allister and the two horse's carefully, "Not from around these parts, by the look of your horses."

Allister held his breath and spoke calmly, "Just a friend passing through."

"Where you from?"

"Kel'mare area, I own a small farm just outside the fishing village."

Allister could feel the man not believing a word he was saying, so he just kept working on the horse's saddle.

"What's your name, I saw your lady friend walking around the village today with Sasha, she's a fiery little thing isn't she."

"My name is Zavier." Allister lied, it was the only name he could think of, but after saying the name he could hear the man pushing through the gate.

The man placed his hand on Allister's shoulder and turned him around, so they were face to face. Allister now stood a foot away from a tall, broad man; his face was darkened by the amount of dirt caked on his face, he had a thick black beard that took up all his lower half and dark piercing eyes. The moment this man got a look at Allister's face he smiled and grabbed him by the throat. Allister didn't fight, the man before him was just a farmer, not a soldier.

"It's the Ironfist boy!" The man yelled out and the village froze. Allister grabbed the man's wrist trying to loosen his grip as the man tightened around his throat, as he started to choke Allister.

Christopher pulled at the man's arms, "Leave him alone Anton!" The young boy demanded.

"Back off, Christopher." The farmer said as he backhanded the boy, knocking the small boy over. With that Allister pushed harder away from the man, grabbing and twisting his attacker's arm behind his back and dropping the older man to the ground holding him there.

Anton yelled and Allister was surrounded by other farmers, they all holding small knives, pointed at him. Placing his hands up and backing away from the man, Allister didn't even see as one of the men cracked him over the head with a sharp rock. Allister dropped to his hands and knees. Anton stood up and kicked Allister in the face. The world went black for Allister.

Chapter 15

Valkyrie and Sasha heard the commotion from the other side of the village; the two of them ran back to the house.

Two of the larger men dragged the unconscious Allister to a horse post in the middle of town and tied his hands tightly above his head. There was blood, dripping down Allister's back from where the rock hit him, Valkyrie went running over to him, but the crowd began to get too thick with cheers and Sasha held on to her arm, "You won't get him back by charging in. Come with me, he will be okay."

"But he's hurt."

"Trust me, please."

Valkyrie looked towards Allister as Sasha dragged her back to the house, where Christopher was crying. Sasha and Valkyrie came up with a simple plan.

Zavier was amazed that he was even still alive at this point, day and night meant nothing, he guessed at least two months had passed since he had been in captivity, but that was just a guess. He was so pale from no light, which he was almost like a ghost in the black room. His body was so weak, that they gave up even chaining him down completely. All they did was chained one of his ankles to the wall. He was just flesh and bones. Mentally he wasn't broken yet, Silvia would come in every other day and inform him of the lack of luck her brother's and father's men had in locating Allister and Valkyrie and that at least gave him hope and Zavier wondered if that was the only reason he was still alive... Jason wanted to see the moment that he would come with the news that Allister and Valkyrie had been taken into custody, he wanted to see the moment that Zavier's hope was forever shattered. Zavier had to remain hopefully, he didn't believe it would happen. He couldn't let himself believe that it would happen.

Harold had given up trying to look for information from Zavier, it was a small victory for him; he defeated the most notorious extractor, of any generation. Harold wasn't happy and every few days he could come in and try a new "experiment" on Zavier.

This day he wasn't sure what to expect, Silvia hadn't been into the room for a few days and Harold, even longer. He was waiting for something to happen.

When the door finally crept open, the light that flooded into the room was the first painful thing, Zavier just sat there his back against the wall, pretending that the light didn't burn.

Silvia was the first to stumble in, her knees hit the floor as she crawled on her hands and knees, tears were streaming down her face; she was in a pale blue dress that was covered in dirt and droplets of blood. Two soldiers walked in next, neither of them was wearing their uniforms, in just cotton trousers and opened shirts and they both shared a wicked grin, as they grabbed Silvia and pulled her off the ground tossing her towards the metal table. Silvia hit hard, sprawling her half over the table, the two guards grabbed her and held her there, her legs spread.

Silvia cried but didn't call out or tell them to stop.

Harold was the next to walk in. He was in his normal royal colours, standing tall and clean.

Zavier couldn't just watch this, his voice was cracked and horsed, "Stop this, it's your sister!" Zavier coughed loudly, he was surprised he was even able to speak.

Harold smiled, seeing that this gave him a reaction. "Stop them yourselves. This is the only reason why father keeps her around."

Zavier slowly stood up, his legs gave way a few times, but he stumbled and forced himself, "Stop, she doesn't deserve this." The two soldiers stopped and turned around and smiled.

"What are you going to do to stop us?"

Even just forcing himself to stand was causing him exhaustion, but Zavier stood his ground and raised his hands. Zavier knew he wasn't going to win against them, but he could at least distract them from Silvia. The soldiers laughed and cracked their fingers, stepping away from Silvia, who just rolled off the table and onto the floor watching in horror, "Zavier you don't need to do this!" She called out, but already the two guards were throwing swings at Zavier. Not having the room or the strength to dodge, he just kept throwing as many punches in as he could, one of the soldiers stumbled back, tripping over the other man's foot and landing on his back, while the other caught Zavier with a right hook and dropped him to the ground. Zavier just barely caught himself, as the soldier flipped him over and stomped down on Zavier's rib cage. Spitting blood, Zavier lost his breath coughing and gagging while the soldier sat down on Zavier's chest and repeatedly punched him in the face. He managed to still get a few good shots on the soldier and finally flipped the man off him, only to have the other grab him by the hair and hold him in place.

The first soldier was about to go in for another punch, when Harold yelled, "Stop." They released Zavier and he dropped back to the floor, trying to push himself off the stone, Harold knelt down in front of him and smiled, "Is that really the answer? Pain and torment are nothing to you, but seeing an innocent harmed, is too much? Was the answer really just staring me in the face this long?" He chuckled and snapped at the two soldiers to grab Silvia, they dragged her over to Harold and he grabbed his sister by the hair and forced her face inches from Zavier's, "What is it about innocent people that make you feel that you need to protect them?" Harold asked as he pulled a knife out of its sheath, placing it to his sister's throat. "Do you know where your sister and Allister would go after leaving Kel'mare?" Zavier just stared the man in the eye, silent still. "I am not afraid to kill her, she's nothing to me. I'd kill my brothers. A half-sister means nothing to me."

Zavier remained silent, but the second the blade began to slice against the crying girl's throat he spoke up, "I know nothing." His voice was just a defeated whisper, "It would have taken a lot for Valkyrie to leave Kel'mare, she doesn't have an official plan after that and I don't know where they would go. Just let her go." Zavier felt utter defeat in those moments and Harold just laughed releasing his sister as she crawled away from them.

Harold just sat on the floor and smiled at Zavier, he had won and he beat the unbeatable Zavier.

Someone knocked on the door and entered, it was two soldiers, they were both dressed in scouting gear and Jason stepped out from behind him, a grin from ear to ear painted on his face, "We know where Valkyrie and Allister are headed. Prepare Zavier for travel."

Zavier just pulled himself up to his hands and knees and hung his head low, he had failed. He broke and now if Jason was right, they could be close to capturing Allister and Valkyrie... What would be the point of all this if it was true? If something happened to Valkyrie and Allister, he had no reason to live.

Jason stepped towards Silvia and pulled her up by her arm, "Get Zavier some appropriate winter attire, he's weak and frail. I still want to see his face when we take his sister and Allister hostage. Bandage his wounds while you're at it, don't want blood all over the place." Jason, Harold and their men all left the room, Silva following behind them.

He was only alone for a few minutes as Silvia went to grab clothes and bandages, but in those few minutes Zavier just laid his body down on the cold damp floor, wondering if Valkyrie and Allister still had a chance. How could they have found them, where did they slip up? Where did Zavier's training fail them?

Zavier pulled himself up and shook his head clear, he had to keep telling himself to hold faith in their abilities, if he had taught Valkyrie and Allister one thing is to never give up; he managed a smile as he imagined what Valkyrie would say to him if she saw him like this, all he could see was the little red haired girl holding back the tears, trying to be scornful, trying to be strong.

Silvia walked in with a dark green cotton shirt and black pants, with a matching green cloak, her eyes were still filled with tears, as the guards locked the two inside, she stepped closer and handed Zavier the clothes wiping her eyes dry. "I'm sorry you had to defend me." She sat down in front of Zavier and extended her hand as she started to bandage his arm, before moving on to his chest and ribs.

"I am just happy you are alright," Zavier spoke weakly as Silvia found herself crying again, as her hand started to shake, Zavier reached and placed his hand on her hand and gave a small, but calming smile.

Silvia managed a smile and her hand stopped shaking, once she finished bandaging, she turned around while Zavier dressed himself, she helped tie the shirt and then she hands to bind his hands in front of him, whether on purpose or not, she loosely tied them together and then knocked on the door, signaling that she was finished. "I hope, that somehow you are spared from the torment my brother wishes upon you."

"I hope the same to you," Zavier responded as the guards piled in, grabbing both of Zavier's arms and dragging him out and down the halls.

Once outside they placed him in a caged cart and headed out onto one of their large boats, the wind caused for a bumping ride. Zavier just held onto one of the bars and sat silently as days turned into nights and nights turned back into days.

When Allister finally woke up, he was surrounded by villagers with weapons pointed at him, the world spun as the pain from his head intensified and caused him to vomit on the ground before him, going to wipe his mouth with his hand was when he felt the binds holding his arms above his head. He looked up and took a deeply pained breath.

The men and woman were whispering among each other, The Ironfist boy would have killed Anton if we weren't there, did you see the way he just savagely attacked him? Unprovoked and all! He looks just like his father. I bet somehow to demon soul of his father is infested inside him.

Allister chuckled, things never do change do them? He asked as he dared to speak up as he looked down at himself, "I didn't attack the man, he assaulted Christopher and so I stopped it." Allister coughed trying not to vomit again.

"Don't lie to us, we saw the whole thing."

"You are just lying to yourself, no matter what happened here today won't change the fact you have me tied to a post. Probably sending a message to the Volcanic Spire as I sit here, but I am not a liar. All these crimes I am again to face, are none my own." Allister just hung his head and stared down at himself, "can you at least tell me that my friend who was with me is alright?"

The villagers looked at each other thinking about what Allister had just said to them, a woman finally spoke. "Your friend is at Sasha's; we have no ill will towards the girl. Just you." The villagers agreed and Allister just went silent, staring down at himself, while the villagers continued to gossip among themselves. Too Allister's surprise, some of them even started to talk about what he said, but it was mostly in the younger mothers, the men wouldn't even consider what Allister spoke of.

Allister had to slightly laugh at the situation, Valkyrie and he had been running from Volcanic Spire soldiers for weeks, only to be captured by simple farmers. Allister leaned back against the wood, the blood was finally drying on the back of his neck. But the pain and the ringing didn't seem like it would go away anytime soon, but at least Valkyrie was alright and that's all that mattered to Allister in this moment.

Valkyrie paced back and forth inside the small house, Christopher sat next to the fire guilt written all across his face, while Sasha stood at the window checking to see if the crowd would slowly start too thin out around Allister.

Sasha turned around and looked at Valkyrie, "Don't worry. They won't harm him, he's captured and defenseless. They aren't the greatest people, but they aren't monsters."

"I just feel that I should push through the crowd and just forcefully take him and we can just be on our way."

"It's a whole village against you, that would be dangerous and Allister or you would probably get injured in the process. Just wait until nightfall. My plan will work."

Valkyrie placed her hands over her face and sighed angrily, trying to calm herself down, the feeling of being useless was overpowering once again. Trying to keep herself distracted for the time being as she looked at Christopher, sitting soundly staring at the fire, "Where is the boy's father?"

Sasha's face dropped and there was a hint of sadness, but she just smiled and looked Valkyrie in the eye, "His father could be right around the corner, or he could be villages away." Sasha smiled at Valkyrie's confusion and explained, "I am a prostitute, I have been forced into this profession rather early on in my life. One day I found out I was pregnant with him. Christopher is my blessing."

"Do the town treat you well?"

"They treat us as well as any other village would. I am a single mother, who is a whore." Sasha laughed at herself as she looked back out the window.

Valkyrie's heart sank as she looked at the boy, this boy child was probably going to grow up with the same fate that Zavier had. Valkyrie didn't get the abuse he did, only because her father claimed her. "When we leave, why don't you come with us? Just leave this place behind?" Sasha smiled, "That's a nice offer Valkyrie, but this is our home. It has its ups and downs, but it's still home."

Valkyrie hung her head and thought about that, it was the same of what Allister was saying, this place is a part of them.

They spend the day preparing the horses and keeping themselves busy, Sasha every now and then would go and check on Allister, still, the crowd was packed around their prisoner. He was alright, his head still rung loudly and the people still spun, but he was alright.

Finally, night fell over the town and the crowd at last left Allister in peace, only two of the larger farmers stayed to watch and they just sat a good few feet away from Allister, barely even keeping an eye on him.

Sasha was dressed in a short red dress, the skirt barely just brushed her knees and she tightened her corset, which made her breasts stand out more. Using ground up a poppy flower, she brushed the red onto her lips and quickly put Christopher to bed.

Valkyrie tied her cloak around her neck and placed the hood over herself, "Are you sure about this plan? I can fight them, you don't need to involve yourself, not that way."

"No it's alright, you need to worry about getting Allister and yourself out of here. I can handle myself." Sasha smiled and headed towards the door, "Just wait and watch, it shouldn't take long for me to distract them, they are regulars."

Valkyrie nodded as she watched Sasha leave the house, she followed slightly and stood next to the horses, hiding behind them, watching as the scene went down.

She could see Allister just limply sitting in the dirt, while the two farmers laughed at each other's conversation.

Sasha walked over to them and placed her arms over their shoulders, they turned their eyes towards her and placed their hands on her hips. It wasn't long after their conversation started that the three of them walked away, holding onto Sasha and that's when Valkyrie ran in silently.

Coming up behind Allister she pulled out her knife and cut the rope holding him to the post.

Allister scared for a moment as the sound of the blade shocked him, "Valkyrie, what are you doing?" He whispered softly looking up at her, as she pulled him to his feet.

"We don't have much time," She cut the rope that bound his wrists together and held him up, as his legs gave in, the dizziness washed over him once again. "Let's go, Sasha said she will be fine. Trust her."

Together they made their way back to the horses and got on and silently rode out of the village, once out of the gates they rushed into a gallop and were out of sight in minutes. The ride in the cold air numbed the pain, but the bouncing made the nausea ten times worth, having to stop every now and then just to vomit. Valkyrie was worried about

Allister, but she knew they didn't have time to stop yet, "Allister, how much longer do you think you can last riding tonight?"

Allister just wiped his mouth only to just vomit once again, "I'm fine," coughing a few times, he straightened up and placed his hand on the back of his head. "We need to get more distance."

Valkyrie frowned and tried to take Allister's hand "You aren't fine, I agree that we need more distance, but if you need a break, we can stop."

Allister shook his head and continued to ride on.

Chapter 16

Valkyrie and Allister rode two days, practically straight, as Allister refused to stop and rest, the horses had a few breaks for water and feed, but that was it. Valkyrie the whole time tried to get him to at least sit down and rest, but he refused.

Finally, as the night fell over their second day of riding Valkyrie got off her horse and grabbed Allister's arm, dragging him from Nightmare. "We are stopping and setting camp right now."

"No, we need to keep going." Allister tried to say as he reached back for the horse's reigns only to feel Valkyrie's fist knock him square in the jaw. He dropped to the ground stunned, he caught himself and then looked up at her, confused and shocked.

Valkyrie was fuming, Allister could almost the steam coming off of her fact as it was bubbling to a strong boil, she untied her hair and grabbed the horses, "We are camping for the night. I am done. Stop telling me you are fine, when you haven't stopped puking since we started this ride, I should clean and stitch up your head and we need food and rest, or I am going to hit you again. Do you understand?"

Allister just wide-eyed and nodded at her, "Yes Ma'am." He dared not say another word.

Valkyrie tied the horses and began to set up camp, Allister went to help but she bundled her fist together and he went and sat back down with his hands tightly together on his lap. Valkyrie wasn't the type of person that

Allister should be angering. Even after twenty minutes, his jaw was still sore, Valkyrie just sat down behind Allister, as the fire now blazed slightly and wrapped a thicker cloak around herself and handed Allister his own.

She soaked a cloth in water and pressed it against Allister's head, cleaning the blood that coated his neck and head, most of it was crusted and came off easily, but even with her being careful, she reopened the large gash that was about half the size of her palm. She sighed and kissed the back of his head, "That man really could have hurt you, Allister. You could have easily gotten out of that situation, why didn't you?"

"I couldn't have gotten out of it without hurting those people. They weren't bad people, just they were scared and they were doing in a way what they were told. I'm evil, inherently by my father."

Valkyrie wrapped her arms around Allister, her chest nestled warmly on Allister's back, as she laid her cheek down softly on top on his head, "You are much more than just a namesake." Allister placed his hand on her arm and just held tightly, welcoming her embrace around him.

Valkyrie finally managed to clean off the blood and carefully, yet crudely stitch the cut and the two fell asleep in each other's arm, using each other's body heat to keep them warm has the up incoming winter winds started to press harder and harder against them.

Another week passed before they finally reached the base of the mountain, snow had already started to fall and slowly the path that lead up the mountain started to be blurred by the white. As much as the pair wanted to enjoy the beauty of the freshly fallen snow they knew as the higher they got, the colder it was going to become and the more difficult it would become for the horses and themselves.

 With red faces and numb fingers it took them a month to reach the top, having to walk the horses up most of the way, as the ground iced over and they were worried about them slipping and hurting themselves. Valkyrie and Allister kept close to each other, keeping as warm as possible by their torches fire. But as the snow piled higher and winter stormed heavy it made the trek harder on them. They camped at the top for a week, hoping for the storm to calm and allow for a safer venture down the mountain.

 It seemed the winters weather was starteding to effect Valkyrie; first exhaustion and then nausea, once she started to get symptoms of a sickness, Allister knew they couldn't wait for the winter storms to pass. He placed Valkyrie on Nightmare and wrapped her in her cloak and blanket, leading her and the horses down carefully and slowly, about halfway down Valkyrie started to get a fever and cold sweats, she just held on to the horse. Valkyrie's mind was so fuzzy she didn't know what was going on half the time, Allister even wrapped his cloak around her trying to keep her as warm as possible, Valkyrie couldn't even argue with him. It wasn't long when Allister body started to go numb, Allister couldn't feel his fingers and he was slowly losing feeling in his arms and feet. Valkyrie had been asleep for three days straight; Allister couldn't even tell if his feet were still moving.

 They reached the bottom of the mountain and Allister knew it wouldn't be long till they reached the compound, but Allister legs buckled and he face planted into the snow, too exhausted to force himself up, he just laid there, barely conscious.

Allister blacked in and out of consciousness, he didn't know how long he had been laying there, the horses reigns had slipped from his hand and Nightmare along with Valkyrie asleep on his back continued forward, while Crimson hovered over Allister, nudging him with her nose. Crimson even laid down in the snow placing her head over Allister, attempting to keep him warm.

Allister woke to footsteps approaching, he couldn't do anything, he just laid there and lifted his head, trying to see who it was, but his vision was failing him and all he saw were green cloaks. Once again he passed out, he could feel the hands pull him out of the snow and then nothing.

Once Allister awoke, he shot up quickly, causing his head to spin and his stomach pained. Groaning he placed his hand over his stomach, his heart began to race. Tossing the blankets off of him he stared down at himself and then over the room, he was barely clothed, only his lower half covered by his thick pants, his hands and fingers were bandaged, as well as his chest. The room was bright and Allister covered his face with his hands, he was so light headed that even that slight movement made him dizzy and nauseous himself. Fully coming to realize that he was in a strange place he looked around. It was just a room filled with white beds and a few small tables with medical supplies, water dishes and clothes. Allister slowly stood up using one of the tables to support himself he stumbled over to the clothes and dressed. He barely tied his shirt before his legs collapsed on himself, both hands on his head, he tried to stop the room from spinning as someone approached. Allister forced himself to his feet and stepped back from whoever was approaching, he was almost shocked as he turned around and saw a woman, who was smiling at him; she was dressed in thick white robes, she was older, her faced warmed by wrinkles, as her long grey hair traced her pale face. "It's great to see that you are awake, but you should still be in that bed. Your friend and you are lucky that you have some smart horses, the dark one managed to make his way all the way to our compound with your friend on its back, but he refused to come in and he led us back, right to you."

Allister stumbled again and fell back landing on his butt, placing a hand back over his face he asked, "Is Valkyrie alright?"

"If Valkyrie is your friend yes, she is still in recovery." The woman walked over to Allister and offered him a hand feeling unthreatened by the woman he accepted and with her lead he stood back up, "Allister Ironfist, how you have grown child. You look so much like your mother." She smiled as Allister froze and stepped back from the woman. "You know better than to be fearful of me don't you? We clearly do not care who your father was." She laughed.

Only then did Allister realize they had reached their destination. He was at the sanctuary where his mother was born and grew up.

"I am Helena, I learned alongside your mother all those years ago. She was a visionary, she changed this place into what it is today. She was respected and loved, even after she left us to be a queen, we always kept her in memory. Even the younger girls here know of your mother's kindness. One of the women who followed the horse back to you apparently recognized you even in the snow, you do look a lot like your mother. Most people probably just see your father, but no, there is the softness of your mother all over your face."

Allister smiled as he finally managed to stand up on his own, "You knew my mother well?"

Helena smiled sweetly and sat down on one of the beds legs crossed over each other and her hands placed over her lap, "Yes, I probably knew your mother the best. We were both brought to the sanctuary the same summer. She was a loving and caring girl, but with this strange sense of adventure and something bigger, which she ended up being." Allister sat back down on the bed and smiled, how he wished he really got to know the woman that she spoke of, "How about I go get you some food and when you are a little more rested I will introduce to some people and show you around and I swear the second that Valkyrie is awake I will bring you to her. Deal, Allister?"

Allister just nodded and laid back down on the bed, his hands over his face once again, Helena laughed and left the tent.

After Allister ate, Helena let him rest for a few more hours before he and Helena started to walk around the village.

For the first time in Allister's life, no one seemed scared, everyone wanted to welcome him, the elder ladies approached, pinching his cheeks, telling him of stories of his mother, or when he was little, the one time he visited how much he had grown. It was something Allister had never experienced before and he couldn't help but smile and enjoy the moment, at the expense of his now sore cheeks.

A few days after Allister woke, Valkyrie woke in the similar panic; seeing herself in this strange place she threw herself from the bed and started to rummage through the tent looking for a weapon, it wasn't till the nausea hit her and she dry heaved as her stomach was empty that she heard two little voices behind her.

Turning around Valkyrie saw two little girls, one with light blonde hair and dark freckles and a red-headed girl with a pale complexion, both in long white dresses, holding hands and smiling back at Valkyrie. "Hi, miss."

Valkyrie stood up and placed her hands over her irritated stomach and attempted an eased smile at the girls, "Hello."

"I'm Lilianna and this is Reni." The blonde said with a small graceful bow.

"And I am Valkyrie, is my friend here with me too?" Allister being the first thing on her mind.

"Allister?" Reni asked with a smile and a clap, "Allister is with Sister Helena! I can take you to them after you see Lady Tyula. Everyone will be super happy that you are awake!" And with that Reni ran out of the tent before Valkyrie could respond. Lilianna stepped closer and walked over to a chest that Valkyrie had just rummaged through and handed Valkyrie a thick white fur cloak. "It's cold out there and your leather clothes are still being washed and mended."

"Thank you." Valkyrie looked down at the white loose dress she was wearing, it just passed her knees and it slightly framed her figure, but she just held the fur cloak in her hands and sat back down on the bed. "How long have I been here?"

Lilianna placed her finger to her lips and thought about it for a moment, "Maybe two weeks now?" She sat down next to Valkyrie, "You have been in an out of consciousness, Reni and I have been watching over you every day and even at night." She was so proud of herself and she just smiled.

"Is Allister okay?"

"He's been awake for a few days now, lots of the ladies around here have been swarming around him. This is the first time really that a boy has stayed in the compound for more than a few days." Lilianna smiled, "All he talks about is you and your grand adventure you have been on. Must be exciting!"

Valkyrie laughed, "Exciting is one word you can use for that."

The young girl just kept going on and on about how everything in the compound has been changed since Valkyrie and Allister came, everyone seemed so happy to see Allister. Cutting the girl off a woman entered the room, she was in red robes and she wasn't as old as Valkyrie would have thought, only being a few years older than Valkyrie by the looks of it. She walked over to Valkyrie and placed the back of her hand on Valkyrie's forehead, "I am Lady Tyula, I am the head nurse here. How are you feeling? Lightheaded? Dizzy at all?"

"Just nauseous."

Tyula inspected Valkyrie and asked a few more questions, "Did the nausea start along with your other symptoms?"

"It was the first to show up, I guess."

"Mind if I ask when you last bled?"

Valkyrie's eyes went wide as she looked at the woman who just stood up with her arms crossed over her chest. Feeling awkward about the questions she mumbled, "Why do you need to know that?" Seeing as the woman was waiting for a response she awkwardly noted, "A while, it's irregular, I don't keep track of it."

The lady nodded, "You seem alright, I will keep an eye on the nausea, but besides that, you seem to be in great health." She smiled softly, "Now please wear that cloak and Allister is in the dining hall, he will be thankful to see you."

Valkyrie wrapped the cloak over her shoulders and followed the woman in silence.

Chapter 17

Allister sat in the center of a large group of older women, all sharing stories about his mother, while he just smiled and listened carefully drinking hot tea. Allister's face was covered in a dark stubble and he was dressed a loose green shirt and dark pants, they were hand made by one of the ladies who were sitting with them now. He laughed saying Valkyrie was going to be jealous that he got to wear pants, where she would have to wear a dress.

Every day since he had awakened, he'd go and check on Valkyrie and then be whisked away by someone different, showing him their temple and telling him about every goddess and god that they worshiped here. It was beautiful. Every god or goddess there was a statue, the older ones were carved out of thick marble of many colours that towered even over their tents, where the newer ones were either made of thick woods or stone, but even those were grand and detailed that with the cheaper material, it was still a glorious site.

Allister had his head down, just listening to the grand stories these women were telling, when the oldest, Cassandra tapped Allister on the shoulder and with her boney dark finger she pointed towards the entrance. Looking up, Allister for a moment thought he saw a red-haired angel, Valkyrie walked through the tent door, her red curls tossed back against her pale face, her cheeks puffed red as the cold kissed them, she was dressed in all white as the fur cloak hugged her body. Allister stood up instantly, nearly tripping over himself as he rushed towards her.

Valkyrie only saw Allister when she heard someone hit their leg on a table and a few of the younger girls giggled. Valkyrie smiled and tried not to laugh as Allister half limped over to her, she quickly moved towards him and when they finally met, Allister pulled her close to him and nestled his head into her hair. For those moments' nothing else mattered; not the many eyes gazing upon them, not the fears of tomorrow, nothing. They just held each other in suspended animation. Finally, they pushed slightly apart only for Allister to pick up Valkyrie's chin and press her ruby lips against his, his stubble of a beard scratched against Valkyrie's face and she tried not to laugh as she placed her hands on both sides of his face.

"I'm glad you are okay," Allister said as he stepped away, grabbing Valkyrie's hand and entangling his fingers with hers.

Valkyrie looked down and saw the bandages wrapped tightly around Allister's hands, "What happened?"

Allister looked down and just shook his head, "Nothing to worry about, just some frostbite."

Valkyrie glared slightly, "I don't even remember how we got here." Allister hugged her again, he didn't want to admit that he didn't remember how they arrived here, not wanting to worry her.

"All that matters is that we are here," Allister said with a smirk as he led her back to the table where he was sitting before.

Together they sat and ate, relaxing and laughing with the fellow women at the table.

After a few long ours had passed and it grew dark, now only a few lit torches and the bright blue moon against the pure white snow glowed brightly. Valkyrie's face even glowed in the night as the pair walked hand in hand through the empty village. Allister wrapped one arm around Valkyrie, while she hugged tightly into his chest. Even the wind that was pushing against them was bitter and hard to withstand. Allister's fingers pained and started to bleed, but he didn't care, he just held on to Valkyrie and continued their walk, he explained all about what they were seeing, all that he had been told about. Finally, together they retreated to the medical tent, where they were to live until the women arranged more suitable quarters. Which the pair were fine with where they were, they moved two beds together and just held each other, stealing each other's warmth, Allister tucked her into his chest and whispered, as she swept off into sleep, "I wish you could understand how much you mean to me, I love you Valkyrie." She didn't hear a word, but Allister just smiled and fell asleep shortly behind her.

Valkyrie was swept off into her nightmares; a scene started to appear before her, dark fog washed over her, as hands of black grabbed her and pulled her into nothing, she tried to scream but the hands muffled her, she couldn't breathe this smell overwhelmed her, she tried to cough, but she was being smothered, the blackness just kept consuming her deeper and deeper into the hands. But there was a pale light at the bottom, she was being dragged towards it. Dropping with a loud thump, she was able to breathe again, gasping she held her throat, coughing and gagging she just sat on her knees trying to recover. Ropes wrapped around her arms and bound them together in front of her, Valkyrie tried to struggle, again hands grabbed her and forcing Valkyrie to her feet. She looked around, there were soldiers surrounding her, all faceless beings with nothing but white grins staring through her.

They stepped forward reaching for her again, she screamed and this time, her scream bounced off them and a broken voice broke through the darkness that was trying to consume her, "Valkyrie?" The broken voice spoke, Valkyrie turned around was confused and there was a man he was cloaked in the shadow of the men. Valkyrie was pushed towards the person, she fell on her face, just protecting her stomach as she hit hard, she could feel the fresh blood dripping down her face as she looked up, it stung, but what she was looking at hurt more than any wound ever could.

There sitting in the shadows, was a frail form of what looked like Zavier, his face was pale, his hair long and untamed, his face covered in dirt, blood and a poor excuse for a beard. His eyes were dark and broken, his lips were parted slightly in shock. Valkyrie stumbled back after she pushed herself to her knees, this can't have happened, this cannot happen.

Valkyrie turned around and the black shadows started to close in on her, she jumped forward and wrapped her arms around Zavier and just held tightly onto the broken idea of her brother. This wasn't her brother and she hoped and pleaded this was just a nightmare and not a vision to be unraveled. Hot tears and blood swept down her face as the shadows engulfed her and Zavier, darkness filled the air and smothered her, she gasped again, but she could feel no air in her lungs, growing more and number, she just allowed her body to go and drift into the darkness.

Valkyrie's eyes fluttered as a burning light in the distance reawaken the dream, a golden hand reached out for her. Without a seconds hesitation, she reached and grabbed hold; the blackness exploded into light and now she stood naked in the forest, standing in front of Allister, his hands both outstretched, Valkyrie took them. Allister squeezed them tightly. He was naked and bathed in light and she stared at the trees above them, "No matter where we go, we can always just be here. Together."

"I don't understand" Valkyrie answered, she tried to push forward into Allister's bare chest but he just held her at arm's length away and smiled.

"The time will come that one of us will be physically alone, but as long as we remember, we are never truly alone, right?"

Valkyrie frowned and released his hands, "I don't understand."

Allister smiled and looked back to the sky, tears falling from his golden face, Valkyrie went back to reach for his hands when his tears turned into blood and blood coated his whole body. Valkyrie screamed again, frantically reaching for Allister, but something was keeping her from him, every step she took, he was two steps farther.

The world around her went dark and the only thing that illuminated before he was Allister's body as it dropped to the dirt, the glow that had engulfed him disappeared and hovered above him.

"Allister!"

Valkyrie woke up panting, grabbing at her face she turned and sighed loudly, grabbing Allister and wrapping her arms around the suddenly waking Allister.

Allister didn't have to ask, he just grabbed Valkyrie and held her back, tightly, whispering softly to her that everything was going to be okay. Valkyrie panted and cried into Allister, this couldn't come true, she repeated over and over, Allister didn't understand a word she was saying through the tears and sobs, but he knew he just had to be there for her and maybe if she needed to she would tell him what she saw, but he knew that it didn't matter.

By the first morning light Valkyrie's eyes were dried and together they readied for the day, Valkyrie didn't share the pain of her nightmare with Allister, having to try and forget what she saw herself, but the horror of what Zavier might have become haunted her memory every time she closed her eyes. She tried to shake it with the fact that he was only a dream.

Valkyrie threw on another dress that the ladies had left her and glared as she could see Allister checking her out. She swung her arm and elbowed him in the gut, he keeled over slightly and laughed through the pain. "Stop laughing at me, or I'll make you wear the dress," Valkyrie demanded, but she couldn't help but smile slightly.

Allister stood up and grabbed Valkyrie by the waist and tossed her playfully over her shoulders, "But you are so pretty Valkyrie. Like an angel." Valkyrie kicked her feet and squealed for him to put her down but he just laughed louder and held onto her tighter. "You shall never be free! Wa ha ha!" Allister laughed spinning her around.

Helena stepped through the door, "Sorry to bother you, but Allister there is a man asking for you. He says you are old friends, we left him outside the gates."

Allister placed Valkyrie down and they just stared at each other and nervousness washed over the pair, as Allister tossed his cloak over himself, "Valkyrie just stay here."

As he walked out the tent having Helena lead the way, Valkyrie, of course, didn't listen, she barely took the time to grab her own cloak before trailing behind them.

Once at the wall, they climbed up the patrol ladder and looked down at the single person.

There was just one man, upon a horse, his cloak was dark red, the man didn't have to speak, he just looked up towards the group who stared down and him and Allister knew who he was, there was a two-headed snake and a mountain crest sewn onto his chest and a hawk sitting on his shoulder.

Allister looked down in shock, "Jessie?"

The man smiled wide and waved towards Allister, "Even after all these years? Haven't I changed at all from afar?"

With that Allister rushed back down the ladder and allowed Jessie into the compound, Valkyrie was confused, the man dismounted and Allister rushed over to the man, he looked a few years younger than Zavier. He placed his hand on Allister's head and laughed, "Guess you've grown and changed since I last saw you." He bowed and turned towards Valkyrie with another graceful bow.

Valkyrie paused and studied the man, the small scar on this lip caused bells to go off in Valkyrie's head.

"Now that I am allowed too introduce myself, I am Jessie Silvermouth." He smiled coyly towards Valkyrie, the hawk squawked loudly. "And this companion is Marcus."

"You are the man from the Tavern, the unmarked soldier who warned me of the Volcanic Spire's plan for Allister."

"Yes, Miss. At the time, I was still under orders not to enter into

Allister's affairs. As you may not know, I work for the order of the black serpent, but my allegiance lies with the Ironfist's." Jessie still speaking to Valkyrie as he finally turned back to Allister and spoke, "Your sister has sent me to protect you."

Allister's eyes went wide, "My sister? Kathrine?"

"She is the only sister that I know of, that is still with us of course. Her kingdom was one of the first to hear word of the Volcanic Spire's plans and sent me to at first warn and then now as the threat has grown, now to protect you."

"Why after all these years? How is my sister? I haven't thought about her in many years..."

"Well, her husband the king died to a plague quite a few years back, so she is the sole ruler of her kingdom, she is rather feared, stubborn, but respected woman. She has somethings that your father never had when it came to ruling a kingdom."

Allister and Jessie talked back and worth, while Valkyrie studied the man in silence, he had an overall approachable appeal to him, he was strong tall, bright warming eyes, smile wrinkles hugged his face, he was covered in deep dark scars, but it strangely didn't take away from the friendliness of the man, things she didn't see when she met the hidden man in the tavern months and months ago. Valkyrie knew just by watching the two talk that this man wasn't going to cause any harm to Allister, which caused her to smile and just watch the pair converse.

The ladies from the compound allowed Jessie to stay in the compound and he graciously thanked them.

That night everyone from the compound celebrated as a full moon hovered over their heads; with a large fire burning above their heads, they laughed, ate and told many, many stories.

Valkyrie didn't stop laughing practically the whole night, as Jessie had a million stories to tell about Allister.

Finally, when the fire was dying and everyone started to make their ways back to their tents, Jessie took Valkyrie's hand and kissed it softly, "Sleep well, Lady Valkyrie and good Night Prince Allister." He bowed and disappeared into the night, even though it was dark, Valkyrie could see the slight pinkish red on his cheeks from embarrassment, Valkyrie laughed.

"Looks like the cold is getting to you Allister."
Allister turned his head and nudged her gently to the side, trying to now hide is a clear embarrassment.

"It seems you have more allies than you originally thought, Prince Allister," Valkyrie laughed, with a sweet smiled as she took Allister's hand.

He turned and looked at her with a smile and kissed her on the cheek, "I suppose in the shadows I do."
"Maybe we were just born to live in the shadows," Valkyrie smiled leaning her head-on Allister's shoulders as they together walked toward their tent, her arms wrapped around his arm the wind softly brushing against their faces.

Chapter 18

As weeks went by, the bulk of winter passed but the worse of the storms started to pile down on the sanctuary, most of the people got bunkered together in tents to reserve warmth, even Jessie was welcomed into one of the bigger tents, it didn't take long for everyone to trusted the man.

Valkyrie and Allister started to get comfortable with this way of life, Valkyrie would help in the kitchen's and she started teaching some of the younger girls to fight, for defense the girls would tell their mothers, but Valkyrie and them would laugh that it was to show up the boy's later on in life. All the children had grown rather attached to the fiery-haired warrior, most of all Reni and Lilianna.

Allister and Jessie would help in the farms and the three of them would join a few of the gathering women on weekly hunts; every time they stepped out of the gates Valkyrie could feel her heart pounding, she wasn't use to being captivated in one small compound for that long, even when she was younger without Zavier's permission she'd climb over the cities walls and just run through the woods, she always just wanted to be free. Free to run. Allister, on the other hand didn't mind walls, he understood the purpose of strongly guarded walls, to protect one from the horrors and judgments of others.

Allister and Jessie crept side by side, bows at the ready, while Valkyrie and the two women were off on the other side of this large clearing, out of sight. Jessie pointed with two fingers at a noise about thirty feet ahead of them, Allister peeked around the tree and pointed his bow as a large buck appeared from behind a thick snow patch, he nodded and pointed his arrow, with a slow and calm breath and released the arrow as it sliced through the air and hit the target perfectly, the buck's head turned, his large antlers alert and proud even in his final breath. The arrow struck and the buck collapsed. Jessie and Allister waited for the clearing to turn silent, as the birds awoke into madness.

Jessie was the first to move from his position, they were dressed in long white cloaks to camouflage in the snow, but his dark rigid face made him stick out. Once Jessie was walking towards the buck Allister followed, Jessie was exactly as Allister remembered him, not shy, strong, protective and gave every person he met equal respect, royalty to commoners. "Prince-"

"Just Allister." Allister rolled his eyes with a smile, he hadn't had to remind anyone not to call him that since Savanna was still teaching him lessons.

"Allister doesn't sound right to me." Jessie laughed as he pulled the arrow from their kill's chest and wiping it off with a cloth. "What is your plan? Honestly, you could have been off this land and far out of the Volcanic Spire's reach, but you are still here."

Allister started to tie the buck's back feet, while Jessie tied its front, thinking about his reply. "Zavier is keeping me here. If the chance arises, I will give my life, for his."

Jessie frowned, but he understood, "He isn't likely even alive anymore Prince and if the Volcanic Spire takes your life, all war is going to break out. Is one man's life worth that of the many who may die in this war?"

"One life, shouldn't be worth more than another, but Zavier saved me all these many years ago, I feel the need to return the favor. As well as I believe this war is coming, with or without my head on a pike. It's just almost a poetic injustice, the last big war ended with my father's head and mine spared, which the new one might begin with mine on a pike as it should have been years-ago."

Jessie started to laugh bitterly and Allister just stared at the man in confusion, "Oh, if your father was here today to hear that. You are a different quality of man you are, I am proud of the man you have become." He firmly placed his hand on Allister's shoulder and shook him lightly, "Does Valkyrie understand the choice you would make?" The moment Jessie asked the question, he knew that Allister had thought hard about that, how Valkyrie would handle losing him, but gaining her brother back. Either way, Valkyrie was going to conflict with many emotions and possibly never forgive Allister, slightly how she's not forgiving Zavier for sacrificing himself in the beginning of all this.

Jessie stood up and smiled, "Prince, Allister, whatever fate you face before yourself. Remember you are not alone and you do not have to stand alone."

Allister just looked down at the buck and nodded, "Thank you."

"Now let's get this great catch back to those beautiful ladies, who again probably have shown us up! For being sanctuary folk, they sure know how to shoot an arrow!"

Allister snapped out of his own head and nodded, together they carried the beast of the buck over their shoulders back to their cart and waited for Valkyrie and the two others to return.

When they did, the three of them were carrying their weight in bounty; rabbit's, foxes, quail and still they managed to get a smaller sized doe. Jessie and Allister just smiled in amazement at the skill and talent of these women.

Valkyrie just stood tall and proud, sweat glossed her face, again she looked like an angel in the snow. Her red hair hardly tamed by the hood of the cloak, her porcelain skin in the dimming skylight and she breathed and with a smile as she stepped closer to the cart, removing the animals before turning towards Allister and Jessie, "Nice size buck you guys got."

Jessie smiled and took a small bow, "Don't need to shame us anymore my lady." Valkyrie just laughed and pushed Jessie slightly, before grabbing Allister's hand.

Allister was still lost in thought, he just smiled and squeezed Valkyrie's hand she could tell something was up, but Valkyrie also understood that sometimes it was best to let someone come to you when they were ready, rather than pushing to figure what was wrong.

Talia and Keyanna where their fellow hunters, they were both younger women and they were both brought into the sanctuary later than most of the other girls, they learned other skills before they learned the way of their religion. Talia and Keyanna were both tall, dark skinned women; sisters, they rarely found the need to speak. Keyanna was just smiling all the time, while Talia kept her calm composer at all times.

Keyanna placed the rabbits in the cart and stretched touching her toes, her leather boots stained dark from the melting snow, "I do enjoy having a larger pack to hunt with and we get a lot more meat with less time."

Talia shrugged, "Maybe it will mean fewer trips, later-on."

Valkyrie sat up on the cart and took a quick count of all that they had gathered so far, it was starting to get dark already as the sun began to set behind the trees and the winter winds still kept kicking harshly.

Talia looked towards the sunset and shook her head, "I do not believe we will have time before nightfall to head out for another quick search, we should head back."

The group just nodded, everyone piled onto the cart and make their way back towards the sanctuary.

Valkyrie even after all these weeks, her nausea hadn't gone away, if anything it had gotten worse, but Lady Tyula gave her this strange mixture that helped, for a small amount of time, she again was asking questions that made Valkyrie nervous, insinuating a terrifying thought. It couldn't be possible that she was pregnant, she didn't have the time for a child and what would happen to their child? Another born Ironfist? Would society welcome another? They barely welcome the one that they do have. Valkyrie thought as she glanced over at Allister, just slightly that he didn't notice, she grabbed the flask of the strange mixture and took a large swig while Allister was turned talking to Jessie and quickly slipped it back into her cloak. She held onto the reign's, her mind twisting with all these strange what if's, but the one that she paused and just kept on her mind the whole ride was what if I was pregnant, what would Allister say or do? She watched him from the corner of her eye, he was happy talking with Jessie, he was happy just holding her hand and spending his days here at the sanctuary, he was happy helping, he was happy not being afraid of what was around every corner, would a child change and take that away from Allister? Would the fear come back? Would the happiness that was written all over his face disappear again? Suddenly she scared herself and she clenched her stomach as the urge to vomit appeared again, she quickly took another drink, but it didn't go away. She passed the reigns off to Talia and climbed into the back of the cart, leaning over the edge, she emptied the contents of her stomach.

Allister from the second he heard her, stopped his conversation instantly and climbed to the back of the cart, placing his hand softly on her back, rubbing her gently.

Valkyrie finally leaned back into the cart and wiped her mouth, she was embarrassed that Allister and everyone had to watch that, but Allister just sat there with his arms, wrapped around her, holding her as the cart continued to bounce along the snowed over the path.

Once back at the compound Valkyrie dismissed herself, Allister tried to follow her, but Valkyrie kissed him on the cheek and asked him to stay and help.

Allister was left stunned and confused, but all he could do was watch as Valkyrie hurried out of sight. Jessie tossed his cloak at Allister with a smile, "You going to come and help, or stand there a look pretty?" He winked playfully and turned around grabbing a few of the carcasses and hoping off of the cart, Allister started to grab the supplies out of the cart, as the four of them brought everything back to the kitchen, where the animals were waiting to be skinned and stored.

Jessie saw that Allister was worried by Valkyrie's sickness, but he placed a firm hand on the boy's shoulder, "Come have a drink, if Valkyrie says she's alright, then let her be to deal with it. One thing about a woman you need to understand sometimes they need space. She's not a fragile little flower, that beautiful creature you got over there, if she needs you, she will ask for you."

Allister nodded, "I suppose, but that beautiful creature you are referring too, also doesn't always know when to ask for help, she's stubborn that way."

Jessie smiled, "The good ones always are." Grabbing Allister's shoulder, he lead him back towards his tent, where the two drank till they could no longer keep their eyes open.

Valkyrie was happy for the time alone, as the whole night, she had her head in a large bucket with Lady Tyula holding Valkyrie's hair back for her.

Finally, the last of winter was passing over the compound, the snow was melting and the bitter cold started to turn into just soft nip on the bare skin, nothing besides a howl, gusting through the evening.

Many weeks had passed by and Valkyrie found it even more difficult to deny the fact that there was a chance that she was pregnant; her sickness came back in flashes, she was overly emotional about small things and the slight weight gain. She hid the bump of her belly with her leather armor, tightening it just enough to not show, but the one thing Valkyrie couldn't hide from Allister was the abundant cleavage she had gained in the weeks they had been there, all considering Valkyrie didn't allow the fact that she may or may not be carrying a child affect her normal activities, she still trained the girls in the art of swordplay, helped around in the kitchen and still continued to go on regular hunts; the other women understood her symptoms and gave her the easier tasks, but besides that everything seemed normal.

Valkyrie was lucky that Allister had never been around pregnant women, he didn't see the symptoms like everyone else did, even Jessie understood what was going on with the girl, but Allister was just in sheer bliss, he was happy with how things had turned out, it seemed like all was going to be for the better.

Winter was finally over, the trees and flowers began to blossom and everyone began to feel the warmth of spring.

Reni and Lilianna followed Valkyrie around like lost puppies in the woods, everything Valkyrie was apart they wanted to also be a part of; they showed and taught Valkyrie all the god's they prayed too, many of the great stories of how things came to be and the three of them shared tales, for the girls stories of those who have wondered close to their lives, while Valkyrie told the girls some of her more tame stories. Valkyrie confided in the two girls and Tyula only, those three were the only ones to truly hear out of Valkyrie's mouth that she believed she was pregnant, Tyula gave Valkyrie herbs to help Valkyrie and advice, but as the days passed there was one thing on her mind, how long can she keep this from Allister?

Lady Tyula and the girls beaconed Valkyrie to tell him sooner rather than later, trying to tell her that Allister would be happy to hear the news of a child, but Valkyrie was scared, scared of the change that would happen the moment those words left her lips, but there was something else plaguing her, guilt.

Reni was speaking about a blind man who rode into the compound a few years back, the pair was sitting on the wall, legs leaning over the edge; he apparently was blinded by dragon's breath and then cursed by a dark witch; Valkyrie heard everything the girl was telling her, but she just rested her head on her arms and stared off into the distance, the trees covered everything. There could be a stranger approaching and no one would know until they were already upon them.

Valkyrie pulled her hair out from under her dark red cloak and placed her hand on her stomach, she was wearing a loose white blouse giving herself some breathe after constantly wearing her armor to hide the weight gain; but as she closed her eyes she could feel a soft kick against her ribcage, "Reni, Lilianna, have you even been around small children?" The two nodded and stared at Valkyrie wondering why she was asking, "I don't know how to raise a child. All my life I have watched many horrible things and I have done many horrible things. How am I supposed to care for something so small and fragile?"

Liliana spoke up, "Well, how the ladies always tell us, is when you have a child, you see things in a different light, because the being in your arms, loves you unconditionally, no matter what your past held.

Reni smiled and wrapped herself around Valkyrie's arm and pressed her ear against her stomach, "You will never have to be alone, you have everyone here to help you and most of all Allister to help you. I think he would be a great father because he loves you." Lilianna mimicked Reni's move, wrapping herself around Valkyrie's arm and resting her head softly on her stomach, Valkyrie just smiled and looked down at the girls.

Silence washed over them, but all silence is broken.

Jessie came up behind the girls, addressing his approach long before, wishing not to startle them, or ease drop on their conversation, "Lady

Valkyrie, I was wondering when you were planning on telling Prince Allister, of your condition?

"I don't know what you mean, Sir Jessie," Valkyrie spoke his name with such sarcasm that Jessie knew where he faulted. Valkyrie stood up and dusted herself off as the girls stood beside Valkyrie. They had a look of they were up to something written all over their faces.

"Valkyrie, I grew up in a brothel outside the palace of the mountain kingdom. I know what pregnant woman looks and acts like." Valkyrie crossed her arms over her chest and looked down at herself, Jessie smiled and bowed extravagantly towards the girls, "Lady Reni and Lady Lilianna, would you mind if I took Lady Valkyrie from your company for a short while? I have something I wish to discuss with her."

The two girls blushed and giggled with a nod, they took each other's hands and ran off, leaving Valkyrie and Jessie alone.

"Discuss?"

"Yes, would you care to go for a short ride with me?"

Valkyrie eyed Jessie carefully, honestly, she hadn't met a soldier before she could fully trust unless she counted her brother for the short time he was, but Allister did, so she had too. "Lead the way."

Jessie smiled and turned back the way he came, this thick cloak flowing around his feet with every step, he raised his hand as Marcus flew in and landed on him.

Valkyrie placed her hood up and they pair walked in near silence to the horses, Jessie giving her no clue on where they were going, or even what exactly they were going to discuss.

Valkyrie got on Crimson and followed Jessie's lead on his horse as they strolled calmly out of the compound and through the woods.

"I won't take you too far, I assume riding is uncomfortable."

"I'm fine, just go where ever. You are the one who wants to discuss something, not I."

Jessie smiled, "Fair enough." They continued to ride for another thirty minutes, they reached just passed the tree line, where the ground started to turn from grass to sand heading towards the forgotten deserts.

Once there you could only see miles and miles of sand and if you looked hard, you could just see where the great cavern starts as blackness starts to take over.

Valkyrie had never been this close to the Cavern, there were many stories and mythos that surrounded it and seeing it in the distance made Valkyrie's curiosity started to make her heart race, "Why here?" Valkyrie asked as Jessie dismounted looking towards the cavern.

"Mostly for the view," Jessie looped his fingers through his belt and looked into the distance, "What plagues your mind Lady Valkyrie?"

"That the more you call me Lady, the more I want to hit you." Jessie turned his head and raised his brow as Valkyrie dismounted and walked toward Jessie staring in the direction alongside Jessie as she thought for a moment, how to answer. "I'm worried that. That due to this possible condition, I won't be able to protect Allister, let alone this child. Already once, I woke up to find Allister off, trying to protect me in his own stupid way, what if I tell him and then the next morning he's gone and I am too late? I don't want to lose him, but he worries and he thinks very lowly of himself."

Jessie nodded and waited for Valkyrie finish her train of thought before speaking, "I haven't told Allister the truth of me being here. His sister was hoping he would be smart enough and seek her out himself, but seeing as he's forgotten of his ally from across the sea. I am supposed to bring Allister back to his sister, with or without his consent. His sister, Queen Kathrine of Stormwall wants to keep what family she has left alive, if I send word, I can have a secure ship here in weeks, to take Allister and you off this land and back to true safety." He pulled out a rolled-up parchment, holding it next to the bird.

"And why are you telling me this and not Allister?"

Jessie frowned crossing his arms again, with a sigh, "I have spoken to Allister, of his plans. He still has a hope of rescuing your brother, I feel that without news of your 'condition' he will not leave. You could convince him to leave." Valkyrie didn't know why but suddenly tears started to flow from her eyes, she kept trying to blink and rub them away, but they just waterfall down her cheeks. Jessie turned and looked at her, his face dropped, "I apologize if I upset you Lady Valkyrie, but -"

"All that you have said is true and I agree that we should leave. But I don't know if Allister will. I have mentioned leaving this land before, but Allister refused, this is his home, even if his people abandoned him, cast his family out, this is where he belongs and he doesn't want to leave and let this world, that was his home face another war, he feels he has a chance to prolong."

"War is going to break out with or without his head, but if he comes with me to his sisters land we can create an army to outnumber the Volcanic Spire, we can make allies, we can take back the Mountain Kingdom if we need too, Allister and you can live the life he was supposed to. You could be a Queen." Jessie placed a soft hand on Valkyrie's shoulder.

Valkyrie was now crying into her hands, "I just want Allister to live on." Jessie stood there in silence, seeing as her last statement was almost an agreement, Valkyrie bite down on her lip and rubbed her red, sore eyes. She took a deep breath and shook her head clear. "I will talk to Allister, but give me time. Send for your ship and I will try to assure he will board by then."

Jessie bowed and kissed Valkyrie's hand "Thank you, it's for the best." He tied the note to his hawk's foot and flicked the bird off his finger, "Fly home Marcus."

Valkyrie stood up straight and headed back to Crimson, as she mounted and waited for Jessie to also get on his horse and together they rode back towards the compound

When they finally returned the sun was about to set and Allister was still working away, a few of the younger ladies were watching him from afar as his pale skin glistened with sweat and dirt in the ever dimming light. Valkyrie had to smile because the moment she came into Allister's view, a smile crossed over his face and he gave a small wave. Valkyrie waved back and blew him a kiss, she was unable not to smile back, as the girls scattered away.

Chapter 19

Allister had been busy, the past week, Valkyrie had been all over him since her and Jessie went for a ride in the woods, it was strange. He wondered what they talked about, if they were planning something, or hiding something. Because it wasn't even just during the day, she would come up behind him and wrapped her arms around him, kiss him at all hours of the day, but at night, she couldn't take her hands off him. Allister and she had been rather physical with each other since the first, but not like lately, now it was every night, throughout the night.

It was funny, as soon as Valkyrie started to be in a great mood, Allister's seemed to dip; the past few nights he would wake up and sneak out of their tent and just wonder the compound, thinking, regretting.

This night was warmer then the last few, Allister found himself at the same statue as he finds himself most nights. It wasn't the most glamorous, or the biggest, it was off in the corner, mostly forgotten by passing eyes, but something about the woman made of oak drew Allister back to her every night.

Allister sat on the damp grass and wrapped his arms around his knees looking up at the woman's face; she seemed to look down at him, was she too judging him? The only thing Allister tonight could think of was this life wasn't even his to live. He was destined to die, that fateful day alongside his father and if he did it seems that everyone's lives would be for the better. Zavier and Valkyrie would be together and safe, all those people's lives who were ruined just to protect him in some way. He started getting these painful headaches, whenever he closed his eyes, he could see just a glimpse of Zavier's beaten and bruised face, staring into Allister's soul with those unemotional eyes, but he could see the pain, distanced in the dazed shine.

With a long pained sigh he looked up at the woman's face and he asked allowed, "Is there still a chance I can fix everything?"

"You cannot fix the world, Allister."

Startled Allister turned around and found himself looking at Lady Tyula, who stood there with her hands inside her robes, a soft warm smile placed across her face.

Allister wiped his eyes, unsure if he had been crying or not, "I'm sorry, I should be leaving."

"No it is fine, this goddess doesn't get to hear the many problems of her people anymore. It's a rather interesting choice that you picked to think here every night, she is the goddess of forgiveness. We call her Rem. It seems that you need to forgive yourself, Allister." She took Allister's hand and squeezed it gently, "You are a good person, just because bad things happen around you, doesn't make it your fault."

"Thank you, Lady Tyula," Allister smiled and sat back down as she walked away, leaving him alone again. He only stayed for another hour or so, before he decided to crawl back into bed with Valkyrie.

Tucking himself under the covers, he wrapped his arms around her and pulled her into his chest. Valkyrie still asleep smiled and curled up with him, he just listened to her breathe and waited until morning.

When Valkyrie woke, she rolled over and kissed Allister. "Good morning, my love."

Allister just smiled back, "Morning."

Valkyrie saw something hidden in his eyes, so she sat up and rolled her feet out from under the covers. "I have a few things to do this morning, but this afternoon, you and I need to talk about something."

Allister cocked his eyebrows at her and watched his tan lover dress herself for the day ahead; a long thin red dress and pale grey cloak, she didn't tie her hair back like she normally would, she just tied her belt around herself and wrapped the cloak around her, covering most of her stomach and chest in the fabric. She turned around and smiled coyly, "I believe you will like what I have to say."

Valkyrie once she exited the tent, loosened the cloak around her and looked down at her stomach, she was surprised that Allister couldn't tell, her stomach went from being flat and muscular, to being rounded and flabby, maybe he was lying and hiding the fact that he knew, maybe he wasn't as naive as she was leading him on to be. Allister did surprise Valkyrie now and then, even if she tried to deny it, honestly, this whole adventure with Allister had been one surprise after another. When she had visions hinting of this, she hated him, she wanted nothing to do with Allister and when she was younger she even thought some terrible things, wishing that he would die before these visions could come true, but now that it is, she just wants to protect him and be close to him, forever. Yet, only very recently did Valkyrie dream of a family, of a lifetime with Allister, maybe the strange hormones rushing through her veins were the cause of this, but either way, she wanted it to stay.

Maybe it was the fresh spring air, or the sun shining through Valkyrie's hair, but today she felt was going to be a good day. Valkyrie was preparing the horses, wanting to take Allister out of the compound to tell her the news, wanting to have a private moment to tell him, a moment to breathe and just know that it was the two of them, no other eyes upon them, a moment where they could talk about anything.

Valkyrie knew the time was nearing, Crimson and Nightmare we getting antsy after being in their harnesses for quite some time. By this time her heart was racing, her palms sweaty, she started second guessing herself, thinking maybe this wasn't the time, maybe it was too late, what if he isn't excited, what if he gets angry that she was even thinking about leaving this place and this and many more questions rushed through her head. Her heart pounded painfully in her chest, Valkyrie's breathing turned rapid and the room started to spin, she went to grab hold of the door to the stable and missed, falling on her butt, everything went black for just a few moments, but long enough to disorient her. Once the room stopped spinning, she sat there for a few minutes longer, Crimson dipped her head, brushing Valkyrie's hair ensuring that she was okay, Valkyrie smiled and placed her hand on the horse's nose and brushed her hair back into place.

Allister then walked into the stables, he was covered in dirt and sweat, his shirt was ripped from a long day, but Valkyrie just smiled.

"Why are you sitting on the ground?"

"No reason, just taking a break." She lied with a perfect smile that just caused Allister to laugh lightly, offering her his hand. She took it and as she stood up, she pulled herself into him and wrapped her arms around him, closing her eyes in a perfect moment; Allister wasn't stunned by her affection anymore, as he wrapped his arms around her and rested his chin on her head, holding her tightly.

"Where are we off too?"

"Just somewhere, anywhere honestly," Valkyrie smiled coyly as she pushed away and grabbed Crimson's reigns.

"Lead the way, miss" Allister smiled, mounting Nightmare after Valkyrie.

The two made their way through the compound, Jessie smiled and waved; Allister was confused on why everyone seemed overly cheerful for the fact the two of them were going for a ride together.

There was a redness in Valkyrie's face, Allister wondered if it was her overheating in her cloak, the ride was mostly silent, Valkyrie asked Allister how his day was and Allister asked her the same.

It gave time for the two to think to themselves, their minds set on two different things; Allister wondering about Zavier, if he was alive, if he wasn't, how he would have died, if he was in pain, where Valkyrie continued thinking about what she would do if he was unhappy with their situation, if it would change their relationship for the worse, or for the better, she wondered what a child would mean.

But they got to the meadow and their minds went blank, the sun broke through the leaves and the daisies, bloomed, taking over the grass filled meadow with white and yellow, Valkyrie dismounted and Allister followed, taking each other's hand they walked to the middle of the meadow and laid down, staring up at the sky. In that moment, their worries melted away, all they had was each other's hand tightly in their sweaty grip and it couldn't be more glorious. Valkyrie's hair went wild, bunching and tangling, Allister turned to her and smiled.

In that moment, she could feel his eyes on her face and the words just slipped from her mouth, "I'm pregnant."

Chapter 20

Allister's mouth went dry and it felt as if all time froze. Valkyrie bite down on her lip, he could see the nervous glance in her eyes. Allister looked down at her, as she removed her cloak from around her, now with the thought that she was pregnant he could see it, the roundness of her stomach. He let out a strange laugh, as his smile turned wide and in that instant, Valkyrie realized he was happy; he rolled over and placed his chest over hers, holding himself just above her, he shook his head, clearly unsure how to feel about the situation, "Are you sure?"

Valkyrie bit her lip again and looked down, pushing him off her as she sat up, taking his hand she placed it on her stomach. Allister's heart raced as it kicked against his touch, it kicked, it moved inside her. Allister was smiling like a love-struck child, he saw Valkyrie in this new and strange glow as her placed his hand behind her head, pushing her into his lips, as he just held her against him, the pair melted into each other; happiness and hopefulness where the only thing that crossed their love-struck minds.

"How long have you known?"

"The ladies suspected when we got here, but I've believed for a while know, I was just worried what you would do, or think about the situation." Allister shook his head, but he understood, he could feel the fear and anxiety in her shoulders, "I was afraid, I'm still afraid."

Allister laid back down in the grass and pulled Valkyrie to rest her head on his chest, "Together we can do anything," He lifted her chin as they looked deep into each other eyes, "We've made it this far, together, there is a finish line."

Valkyrie shunned away for a moment, "Our finish line could be closer."

"What do you mean?" Allister cocked his brow and sat up, crossing his legs in the grass, placing his hand on Valkyrie's back.

"Jessie was sent here to find you and bring you back to his sister." Valkyrie saw that Allister had realized this already, but with the hesitation in his face and the relaxation in his shoulders, she knew he needed convincing, "I know you don't want to leave because you are thinking about Zavier, but... The likely hood he is even still alive is slim at best. The volcanic Spire do not take prisoners."

Allister looked away from Valkyrie, he had to think of the facts and that was true. He couldn't just keep his head in the clouds hoping that there was a chance he could save Zavier.

Valkyrie frowned, "We can't just think about ourselves right now, it hurts me thinking that Zavier is gone and there is no chance I'll ever see him again, he's my brother, but I've painfully accepted it. He wouldn't want us to stay here, because as long as we are here, it's just a matter of time. Jessie has safe passage for us, he said even if you say no, he was ordered to force you."

Allister sighed, "I don't get a say anyways it seems. But you are right, Valkyrie. For you,-"

"For us," Valkyrie said placing his hand back on her stomach.

Allister smiled sadly, as he pulled her back into him, pulling her up on his lap as they sat in each other's arms waiting till day turned to night.

"Are you afraid? Of it." Valkyrie asked as the baby kicked again in her stomach, looking down at herself.

Allister thought about the question for a moment, "I'm scared, there is a lot that comes with being a parent. And this situation we are in doesn't make it at all easier... If I get the chance, to be there for the child, I hope to do justice, to our child." Allister leaned in a kissed her gently on the lips, today and forevermore Allister would see her differently, she wasn't this wild, fiery mess of a girl, she was a woman, she was the woman carrying their child. He wondered if he'd miss the way he uses to see her, but as he looked at her now, the sun setting around them, he smiled, change isn't always a bad thing.

Finally, the two hand in hand headed back towards the compound; everyone was waiting for them, all excited to be able to talk about it aloud. Allister was shocked how many people realized, where he had no clue, but seeing everyone so happy for them, was a warming blessing in itself.

Allister left Valkyrie as Reni and Lilianna swept her away for the evening, while Allister hunted for Jessie.

He was sitting on the wall the hood of his cloak over his head, he was almost like a shadow and Allister only knew where to look by the screech of Marcus Jessie had his back against the wall and one leg over the ledge, a pipe in his mouth and the bird on his hand. "How does it feel knowing you are going to be a father?"

Allister sat down beside him, with both legs over the edge, "I don't even know yet. This is overwhelming, but I didn't want to tell Valkyrie that." Allister's mind was spinning with everything that was happening, everything that could happen and this slight anger that was building up inside as he glanced over at Jessie, "Why didn't you tell me that the reason you are here was to take me back to my sister? Why did you use Valkyrie, to get me to agree."

Jessie untied his cloak and pulled out his pipe, lighting it while taking a long puff, looking out into the forest that seemed to protect and loom over the compound, "Don't act like I was trying to deceive you, Allister, I spoke of you leaving and I knew that with the guilt of knowing someone else risked their life for yours wouldn't let you leave without a push. I didn't want to force you to leave, like your sister requested. I respect you as a man, that you need to make a decision. It is for the better that you leave. There is nothing here for you. With what is left of your family is where you belong."

"Why now, why didn't my sister feel that I belonged with her before now? It's been over ten years since we've seen each other. After news our Father's death, why didn't she come for me then?"

Jessie laughed, "She did, it was a while after the fall of the Mountain Kingdom she sent me to retrieve you, I don't even know how long it had been and when I ride all time disappears in my mind. I actually fought with Zavier. It was pay back for that night, the night the kingdom fell and I won that time, but after the fight, Zavier showed me something. You'd been living there for some time and I saw something that I didn't while you were living in a castle. You seemed happy, you had bonded with

Zavier, you had a friend and you were smiling, enjoying yourself. When you are living in a castle with a court, you have expectations, there beside Zavier and Valkyrie, you had none. You could be just a boy. I used my better judgment and after a few weeks of observation, I decided it would be best for you to stay. Your sister wasn't pleased, but she respected my reasoning's."

Allister wrapped his arms around himself; he tried to find comfort in Jessie's words, but all he could think was if only, Jessie took him away from Zavier, their lives would be a million times different, possibly and likely a million times better. Allister tucked his head into his knees and his hands in his hair, he could feel the tears building up in the ducts of his eyes, "I'm a failure. All these people who have cared about me, have gone through hell."

Jessie placed his hand on Allister's back and smiled, pulling the pipe from his mouth, "You are not a failure. You are just one unlucky child, you've always been unlucky, but that doesn't make it your fault. Don't act like your friends going through all these troubles are a burden, most will gladly trek through hell and back, for an ally. I won't act like I knew Zavier well, but I know as long as you and Valkyrie was safe, he would be happy."

"His possible happiness doesn't lessen the heavy feeling of guilt in my chest."

"I know, that sometimes goes in time." Jessie took another puff from his pipe and with a long sigh, "Have you truly agreed? Will you get on the boat willingly?"

"I don't have much of a choice anymore, so yes."

"It is a smart move Allister and as much as you may feel that it's cowardly, it's not, survival is not cowardly."

Allister just nodded uneasily, as the pair sat there in silence.

Jessie bided Allister a goodnight, as he headed off to send a message to Allister's sister, to send a ship to retrieve them, as Allister headed back to the tent.

Valkyrie looked up as he entered, there was a soft, innocent happiness in Valkyrie's face that warmed Allister's worries away. "Are you okay Allister?"

He laid down on the bed beside her and placed his hand on her stomach, feeling as the being inside her moved around, he didn't answer her question, he just laid there.

Valkyrie bit her lip and brushed her fingers through his hair, she knew he had a lot on his mind, she had dumped everything on his plate that she had been thinking about for months, now he has one day under his belt, "Allister, I'm sorry I didn't tell you sooner-"

Allister placed his finger on her lips, laying back down, "Don't apologize. I'm fine Valkyrie, really." He closed his eyes and rolled away from her, Valkyrie heart sank as she blew out the candle and rolled over tucking herself into Allister's back, her face pushed in between his shoulder blades, as she draped her right hand over his hip. She whispered softly, "Allister, I love you."

"I love you too," Allister responded taking Valkyrie's hand as he pretended to sleep, feeling as she behind him drifted from consciousness. He was confused, his heart was trying to tell him he should be happy, he was going to be a father, that's supposed to be the happiest day of his life, but his brain was telling him no, it's a terrible idea to have the Ironfist legacy to live on, but mostly he the feeling of guilt was overwhelming Allister on the break of tears again, Valkyrie now can't do the things she wanted to do in life, she's going to be a mother, parenting was going to be their lives, what if that wasn't what she wanted, what if that wasn't what she wanted with him, everything he touched, he seemed to ruin in his own mind. Tears started to fall down his face and he just held onto Valkyrie's hand tighter and tried to stay quiet not to wake her.

One good thing came from breaking down in Valkyrie's arms, he found himself within no time, off into deep sleep, his cheeks still wet as they rubbed against the bedding. Still, he found himself plagued with nightmares, but he couldn't wake himself, he tossed and turned, his body drenched in sweat.

Valkyrie woke to his tossing and after she couldn't shake him awake, just held Allister tightly into her chest, holding him, whispering sweet nothings, until he finally calmed down, he stopped stirring, Valkyrie still held him, but laid down and closed her eyes, falling back into a lighter sleep, keeping herself just slightly awake encase Allister tossed some more.

The morning wasn't any better for Allister, finally after being able to wake he wiped his tired crusty eyes. Valkyrie turned her head; she was washing her naked body with a cloth, she turned and saw the blue under Allister's eyes and placed the cloth on the table sitting down next to Allister, she placed her head on his shoulders, "Nightmares?"

"It's nothing really."

"Allister-"

Allister pushed his lips against hers and smiled, "I know, I know." Valkyrie scorned him, but she could see Allister was putting his words together. "I've been dreaming of losing everyone lately, this time, there was a hanging tree. Savanna, Zavier, Jessie, you and a faceless child now. There were just bodies upon bodies hanging and swaying in the wind, the vines reached for me and I froze, all the voices of those I am going to fail echoed in my head, telling me everything was my fault and I'd never be able to be forgiven."

"Allister, it was only a dream. I'm here," She placed his hand on her bare stomach, "This child is here, Jessie is fine, everyone here in the compound is safe. You haven't failed Zavier. Zavier made his move to protect us, our safety was the only thing that mattered to him and it was the only way you could sometimes tell he cared. This was one final move Zavier wanted to make to show he loved you like a son."

"I should have just stayed, then Zavier and you escaped together."

Valkyrie stood up and stepped away from Allister, "Do you really feel that way?" There was a coarseness in her voice, which cause Allister to rethink his words, her back was straight and she clenched her shoulders tightly.

"Valkyrie-"

"Don't bother explaining, I understand." Valkyrie quickly dressed and left the tent without another word.

Allister was left stunned, he just sat on the bed looking down at his feet for a while longer, alone, in silence, he took a moment, before leaping from the bed and rushing out to follow Valkyrie. She had made it all the way to the main gate when he had finally caught her, Allister wrapped his arms around her, pulling her back against his chest, resting his hands on her stomach and he stuffed his face in her long curly hair. "I'm sorry, I don't regret falling in love with you, or the fact that you are pregnant with our child. I regret that Zavier had to suffer for our happiness, I regret I wasn't able to protect the only family you had left and the only man who cared about me. I love you and I want to be with you." Allister just held her tightly and fought the urge to cry, he was so exhausted, so confused, he just needed to break down.

Valkyrie placed her hands over his and just stood there, she understood his pain, as she felt it as well.

Chapter 21

Valkyrie and Allister informed everyone at the compound later that day that their time at the compound was ending, Jessie had word that a boat would be here in about two weeks; the boat had been delayed as heavy winds blew madly. Reni and Lilianna busted into tears and clung onto Valkyrie begging them not to go, everyone else understood that they had to leave, but everyone was going to miss them.

Allister and Jessie tried to help around the compound as much as they could in their last week's there if anyone asked anything of the pair they'd be on it at a moment's notice. The ladies pampered Valkyrie, on the other hand the women showered her with gifts for the baby and asked nothing of her; they understood the separation for Reni and Lilianna was going to be hard, so they let the girls take all of Valkyrie's attention. Time flew by and before they even realized the countdown began and continued to tick down.

Three more days before they headed towards the cavern and made their trek down to the shores. Off to a new land Valkyrie was scared, she had never been on a boat before, but the excitement of the adventure ahead kept her fears in a drug-like trance.

Her stomach was bloated, her body was sore and the thing inside her kicked and squirmed around, but she couldn't care, she just lived for the moments, Reni and Lilianna cried every day, wanting Valkyrie, Allister and Jessie to stay and live with them forever; but this life wasn't theirs to live, sadly.

Reni and Lilianna were dressed and ready for the day ahead, Valkyrie wasn't ready. Today was going to be the last outing with the two girls, final exam in a sense, after this, she had taught them all she could. The two girls ran up to Valkyrie both grabbing an arm, their practice swords strapped to their backs, Reni spoke quickly, "The horses are all prepped and ready to go! You ready?"

Valkyrie smiled and just nodded as the girls pulled her towards the stables.

They walked passed Allister who had been doing a lot of heavy lifting work over the past two weeks, due to the fact the ladies knew that once Jessie and him were gone, they'd have to return to doing it all, he was covered in sweat and dirt, Valkyrie just smiled and waved, as he blew a kiss towards her. The girls didn't even give her a moment to tell Allister where they were headed, she was just swept away and those two had been greedy with her time ever since they realized it was all coming to an end.

Once at the stables Valkyrie helped the two girls on Crimson and she mounted Nightmare, they slowly trotted out and through the compound, Lady Tyula was at the gate giving Valkyrie a scowl, "Valkyrie, you shouldn't be riding long distances, the bouncing isn't good for the baby."

"We are not going far and we will take it slow. We are just going to the hillside."

Lady Tyula frowned but waved her hand and pointed her long fingers at the girls, "Make sure Valkyrie doesn't overdo it."

"We promise Lady Tyula!" The girls replied together with a wave as the three of them exited the gates. The trek towards the mountain was easy, the horses now knew it by memory, Valkyrie nor the girls had to lead them, they just knew where to go.

Reni and Lilianna bounced beside Valkyrie and Midnight, Lilianna spoke softly, "Do you really have to leave?"

Valkyrie sighed, "We've been through this. It's safer if Allister and I leave. Maybe in the future we will return and visit, after I've had the baby and after the people who are after us give up on their crusade."

Reni scrunched her face and frowned, "Can't you just talk to them. Tell them Allister is a good person."

Valkyrie smiled and reached her hand on to the girl, Reni took it with a sad smile, "It's a lot more complicated than that, one day maybe you'll understand… Actually, maybe it is better that you don't, maybe one day these problems won't reoccur, someone should be judged on their actions, not the actions of others." Valkyrie released her hand as they continued on the path, slowly ascending towards the cliff clearing.

Jessie had been away from the compound since late that night, having to head to the cavern waiting for a message confirming that the boat would be there in a few days. After finally getting the confirmation he headed slowly back towards the compound.

Jessie was slightly uneasy as his horse walked tall, his ears perked and alert, even Marcus was uneasy clawing painfully into Jessie's shoulder. Jessie slowed the horse and kept an eye out in the direction the horse was hearing things, within ten minutes of riding Jessie dismounted and hushed the horse to stay as he stalked away from his position. A few hundred meters there was a small scouting party, in full military armor and armed to the teeth with weapons, Jessie knew instantly from the dragon on their sigil that they were from the Volcanic Spire and by the looks of it, he assumed there would be more not far. He quickly yet quietly, he returned back to his horse and quickly as he possibly could rush back to the compound, there was no time to waste if they were that far from the mountain's path, that means they could possibly be closer to the compound with another scouting party.

Once on his horse, Jessie pushed him as hard as he could back to the compound, the gates opened and he hoped off the horse, his first and only thought was where were Allister and Valkyrie, he saw Allister working hard in the fields and he rushed towards Lady Tyula, "Where is Valkyrie?"

Lady Tyula saw that there was a worry in the man's eyes and responded, quickly, yet quietly. "Reni, Lilianna and she went to the cliffs to train. Is something the matter?"

Jessie placed his hand on the ladies' shoulder, "It might be, do not let Allister leave the compound, keep the gates closed and scouts on the walls and do not alarm Allister."

"Yes, Sir Jessie." Lady Tyula nodded and hurried away, picking up her skirt as she whispered to the ladies she passed.

Jessie remounted his horse and rushed back out the gates, ordering Marcus to stay the hawk flew on top the wall and watched as his master disappeared into the deep woods.

Valkyrie was impressed with the girls, they had nearly perfected every move that she had taught them, yes they were still slower than they needed to be a real battle, but she was happy with where the two where for fundamentals. Their footwork was better than Allister's at their age.

"Girl's, come take a break," Valkyrie called sitting down, her legs crossed loosely as she rubbed her stomach, the baby was kicking her rib cage painfully causing cramps.

Reni and Lilianna rushed to Valkyrie's side, sitting down they crossed their legs and placed their blades neatly before them on the ground. "The baby bothering you?" Reni asked leaning in towards Valkyrie inspected her stomach.

"Slightly, they are kicking me in the ribcage at the moment."

Lilianna pressed her hand lightly where the baby's foot was and softly moved her hand around the imprint, "Movement is a good thing at least." Amazingly enough, as Lilianna massaged, they moved in Valkyrie stomach, relieving presser from her ribcage.

Valkyrie sighed happily, "What am I going to do without you two?" Valkyrie smiled as she placed her arms around the girls pulling them into her, they hugged her and pulled into her tightly.

"Maybe you could send us letters?" Reni asked lifting her head. Lilianna perked up as well, "We can send you some back too, tell us everything."

There was a gleam of happiness in the girls eyes that caused Valkyrie's heart to just melt, they were really going to miss her and she was going to miss them as well, "I will send you letters, I promise."

Valkyrie paused and hushed the girls as she stood up, quicker than she thought she could being the size she was and reached for the blade strapped to her back and turned towards the sounds of something through the woods.

Jessie appeared through the thick bush, dismounting the minute he stepped out of the brush, "Ladies, I am sorry to disturb you, but we have to leave. Now." He tried to sound as calm as possible not to scare Reni and Lilianna, but Valkyrie could see it written all over his face as he inspected the area above.

Valkyrie whistled loudly, Nightmare and Crimson trotted over quickly. Reni and Lilianna wind slightly, asking why, but Valkyrie and Jessie just said it's time to go home, as they placed the girls on the horses, Jessie gave them a smirk, "If you beat Valkyrie and I back to the compound I'll give you two a gift before we leave."

The girls smiled and nodded as they rushed away from the scene, once the girls were headed off into the woods Jessie was trying to push Valkyrie to mount the horse quickly, as his nerves started to get the best of him, "Jessie, what is going on?"

"There were some Volcanic Spire soldiers scouting near the compound, it was a very small group, so I know there has to be more, let's go and hopefully not find -" As Jessie went to finish his train of thought an arrow was shot from above, he heard it just in time wrapping his arms around Valkyrie and turning her away from the blow; the arrow just scrapped his back and cut his cloak and shirt clean.

Nightmare spooked and rushed off and Jessie's horse was now surrounded by soldiers, Jessie whispered to Valkyrie, "If you have an escape you take it, do you hear me? Even if that escape means my death you take it."

"I can fight-"

"Valkyrie, if they have you, Allister is going to come find you," Jessie spoke honestly as he turned and pulled his long sword from his back wielding it before him, still protecting Valkyrie with his body as the two backed slightly inching closer to the cliff's edge.

Valkyrie drew her weapons and stayed behind Jessie, they were out numbers two to fifty men, she knew Jessie wouldn't be able to defeat them all and she knew that she'd be a burden to him being his fear of her being hurt and failing his duty as a soldier.

One of the soldiers stepped ahead of his men, ten archers pointed directly at Jessie and Valkyrie, "Drop your weapons and surrender yourself, if you comply you may leave with your life. This is your last and only warning."

Jessie tightened his grip on his weapon and spoke softly towards Valkyrie, "Do you have a way out?"

"Sort of, the only way would be down."

Jessie breathed deeply, "Stick behind me, I will attempt to make you a path, then you run, hopefully, the horses haven't run far."

"Archer's aim." The commander yelled loudly, hoping to startle the two into surrendering themselves.

"I'm rushing to the left, you go first and I will cover you. Count to three."

Valkyrie nodded and counted just under her breath, then bolted to the left, as Valkyrie and Jessie rushed, the man yelled fire and the archers released, Jessie used his body to block whatever arrows came close, six of them piercing his body, but the adrenaline in him just kept him moving, as the soldiers pushed forward their weapons drawn Jessie stepped in front of Valkyrie, pairing with three soldiers, while she took on two, trying to just push past them, it was a risk they had to take, but it was a mistake.

A second wave of arrows fanned over the pair and Jessie pushed Valkyrie down to the ground, she protected her stomach, as he protected her, arrows cascaded around them and stuck painfully into Jessie, he screamed in pain and after the arrows stopped, they were swarmed by the remaining soldiers. Jessie was dragged off of Valkyrie and held by four different soldier's as well as another holding a blade to his throat as they pushed him down to his knees.

Two soldiers grabbed Valkyrie and pulled her off the ground, she didn't put up a fight knowing that if she did neither of them were likely to walk away from this encounter.

They tied Valkyrie's hands and attempted to do the same to Jessie, but he broke free with his right hand and connected with the closest soldier's face, only to be kicked to the ground, as his arm was twisted behind his back, there was a loud snap, that nearly echoed through the clearing. Jessie screamed in pain and Valkyrie screamed for them to stop.

The soldiers holding Jessie placed all their weight on him as their commander stepped towards him, placing his hand on one of the arrows sticking into his back and twisted, Jessie tried his hardest not to scream in pain, but as the man dug deeper into his flesh and leaned on his now broken arm, he had to give in. "I gave you a chance," the commander placed his heel on Jessie's shoulder, this time, there was a crunch of the bone under his foot, the man laughed, "Kill him, he means nothing."

They stepped forward raising their blade towards Jessie, Valkyrie screamed her face white with panic, "Stop! You need him!"

The commander laughed and waved his hand for his men to wait, as they stabbed their sword down, slicing Jessie's hip open, but not taking a killing blow.

"And why do we need him?"

"Who is going to relay the message back to Allister? Send him as a warning, a person to send a message is better than word of tongue."

The commander smiled and stepped towards Valkyrie, placing his hand on her chin, "You have a point."

One of the soldiers laughed, "Taking orders from a prisoner, sir?" He questioned.

"We are only after one person at this point, her and this other is not important to our mission, but if he's going to be a warning, he needs to be in worse condition than this." He smiled coyly as Valkyrie screamed for them to leave him alone, as the soldiers forced his hands tied and continuously beat Jessie to the point he was barely moving, blood was everywhere from the blade that sliced his side open and his face also was covered in blood and the arrows were still protruding from Jessie's body.

They gagged Valkyrie stopping her from screaming and begging them to stop, they tried to pull her away from the scene, but she was putting up a fight not waiting to leave Jessie until she knew he was still alive, that he would be okay. Tears were pouring down her face, she pulled and tossed herself around in the soldier's arms trying to break free, they even added four more men to contain her and finally, they stepped away from Jessie.

The commander stepped towards the man and picked his head up by the hair, "Still alive over there?" He laughed as he dropped Jessie back down on his face, "Logan, you are going to deliver their soldier here to that sanctuary, inform the Ironfist boy that in two days he is to surrender himself to us, here by nightfall, or his lady friend will be sent to him in a much worse state then his knight is."

Logan lifted Jessie off the ground and nodded, "Yes sir, commander, sir." The soldier picked Jessie off the ground with the help of one other soldier and stepped away from the group

Valkyrie screamed for Jessie behind her gag as they dragged her off towards their horses, they stopped for a moment and Valkyrie elbowed the man of her right and raised her foot into another crotch, the first man of her right cracked her once in the jaw, knocking Valkyrie off her feet, as he punched her once again in the face, before grabbing her by the throat and pulling her back up to her feet, "We aren't very kind to our prisoners, even more so when they are of your female gender, don't push it, girl." Valkyrie gasped under his grip but nodded as he released her, "Get her on the horse and let's get back to camp, Prince Jason should be pleased with us. Someone ride ahead and tell our prince the news."

Valkyrie locked eyes with the commander, as she was lifted on the horse and someone mounted behind her, she tried to squirm but that man wrapped his arms around her, resting his hand just touching her stomach and the only thought that came to mind was, she had to not just think of herself at the moment. Looking around slightly as the soldiers marched slowly, heading towards their camp.

Zavier sat with his head against the bars, the sun struck down on him causing his eyes to want rest, but he wouldn't allow himself, the camp around him was buzzing, rumors of them being near where Allister and Valkyrie should give him chills down his spine. There were only a small number of soldiers left at the camp, everyone else was out on scouting missions, every few hours a new scout would return with a message for Jason and every time that they did Jason would look over towards him and smile. Zavier understood that Jason felt that they were close and Zavier's stomach dropped every time.

Sitting up Zavier stretched, twisting the cuffs on his wrists; he had rubbed his skin raw with the iron binds that with just a little bit more push, he knew he could just slip out of the chains. He wondered to himself why he wasted the time and caused himself pain to accomplish this, he wasn't going to have a chance to escape, even if he managed to get away from the camp, the sheer number of soldiers Jason would send after him, he could never get far on his now weak legs. Thinking to himself, worst case scenario was maybe if he broke free they'd have to kill him. He was disappointed in himself for this thought, but maybe that's the reason he did it, subconsciously he wanted them to kill him, his worry and pain would be over, he wouldn't have to be strong, he could be in peace. For once. But Zavier's solitude ended abruptly today, a messenger scout rushed in on his horse, he didn't even dismount the beast before he spoke to Jason.

Zavier watched the scene unfold, he couldn't hear, nor read their lips to figure what they were saying, but he could see there was a twisted smile again, but this time it was different, Jason started throwing orders at his men and everyone went into a working frenzy, Zavier suspected the worse as he gripped the bars watching the men work around him.

After at least an hour four guards approached the door to the cell, while another guard came up behind Zavier, placing their arm through the bars and placing Zavier in a headlock as two soldiers entered the cell, unchaining Zavier from the cage and retying his hands with rope. The one guard released him, as the other two dragged him from his confinement. It had been days since he had been removed from the cell and his legs cramped and cracked with every step, but with only a slight wince every sixth step, he stood tall and acted as if he was fine. As he was dragged through the camp, he could now hear the approaching soldiers, he was pushed down to his knees and held there. Jason stood to the right of Zavier a few men away, arms crossed with a smug expression glued onto his face.

Zavier kept his eyes locked on the approaching soldiers, it physically was giving Zavier pain as he watched them approach in seemingly slow motion, trying to see through the many heads of people and he searched for Valkyrie or Allister.

Jason stepped forward as his men pulled their prisoner forward, the first and only thing Zavier needed to see to know who they had captured, was the bouncing red curls.

His stomach dropped and his heart beat began to rise as he struggled with the soldiers holding him back. Valkyrie was pushed forward in front of Jason, her face was flustered red, her jawline was bruised and her stomach was bountiful in comparison to her usual toned physic. Zavier froze, his baby sister was pregnant? His baby sister was in the hands of the man who hated him most.

Jason moved to place his hand on Valkyrie but she turned her face away from his touch and spat towards him, Jason went to strike her. Zavier broke free from the captors, only for a moment as he raised to his feet, "Don't touch her!" He yelled as the guards managed to get hold of Zavier once again.

Valkyrie's head shot towards Zavier the second his voice hit her ears, her jaw dropped and her eyes widened, tears formed in the corners of her eyes as she stared at her brother is sheer shock and disbelief.

Jason smiled and placed his hand on the back of her neck, as Valkyrie trembled barely remaining standing on her own, he whispered softly as they watched Zavier struggle to be released, "Allister and you left him for dead, is it like seeing a ghost of your failure?"

Valkyrie bit her lip and swung her head back into Jason's nose, tears still falling from her face, "Fuck you."

Jason pushed her to the ground and covered his nose, blood oozing between his fingers, he chuckled, "Zavier, your little sister is something. Nothing like you, she's controlled by her emotions," He grabbed Valkyrie by the throat and pulled her back to her feet as the guards held her up, "If I didn't need to use you for bait, I'd let every man here take you for a spin, while your brother watched till you begged for me to end it all and then I'd repeat it all again." Valkyrie gagged as he squeezed tightly, he whispered again to Valkyrie, "Watch what we've been doing to your poor older brother, while you've been running free like a robin." Jason snapped his fingers and the guards began to beat Zavier, Valkyrie screamed for them to stop, but they just laughed and continued to beat Zavier.

Time became irrelevant, Valkyrie just cried, screamed and pulled at her captors; finally, after Zavier stopped moving they released Valkyrie and she ran over to Zavier, kneeling beside him. "Zavier, Zavier!" His eyes fluttered and he gave her a winced smile.

Jason laughed, "Take them to the cage and leave them there for now." The guards grabbed Valkyrie, but she had lost her fight as she watched them drag Zavier through the dirt, she followed.

They tossed Zavier into the cage without care, Zavier's limp body just rolled to the back, with Valkyrie she stepped up into the cage and they cut her binds and locked the cell door behind her, not even a second after they cut her binds she crawled over to Zavier, untying his hands she rolled him to his side and placed his head on her lap. Again, the tears started to fall as Zavier rasped in her arms. Leaning against the bars she held onto her brother tightly, "I'm so sorry." She pleaded to Zavier softly, he reached up and grabbed her hand squeezing it as tight as he could.

Chapter 22

It had started to get dark and Lady Tyula wasn't sure how much longer she could keep Allister and everyone else in the shadows, Reni and Lilianna had returned, but she hurried them off into the medical tents without anyone noticing their distress, or questioning. After their return, she ordered some of the other ladies to keep Allister occupied at the other side of the compound and forced him to drink a sedative without his notice.

Lady Tyula paced back and forth, was it fair to not warn Allister of the possible threat? Lilianna and Reni had returned an hour before and with no sign of Jessie or Valkyrie, she understood what the likely outcome was.

Allister must have snuck away from the ladies somehow, as he climbed the ladder and tapped Lady Tyula on the shoulder.

Startled she jumped slightly and turned around to face the drowsy man before her, placing her hands on his shoulders she smiled, "Allister you look tired why don't you go rest?"

He rubbed his eyes and shook his head, "No, I'm fine, but I was wondering if you have seen Valkyrie and Jessie?"

Lady Tyula bit her lip as the most inconvenient time for her prayers to be answered happened, the scouts called out, "Who dares approach, halt!" Their bows pointed at their target. Lady Tyula tried to keep Allister from looking over the ledge, but he did.

The soldier dragged Jessie from the horse, he barely took three steps from the horse when he crumbled to his knees, the soldier placing the flag in his hand down in the dirt and a knife to Jessie's throat. "My Prince has given Allister Ironfist a gift and a warning. We offer the Ironfist boy a deal, himself for the life of the red-haired girl." Allister's jaw dropped and he threw himself towards the ladder rushing towards the gates, slowly they were opened and Allister could still hear the man speaking. "Here is your failed soldier he has the details of our bargain, if you fail to comply with our demands, we will return, with the girl's head on a pike and only after we've had our fun with her." He released Jessie and turned away to mount his horse, leaving the Volcanic Spire flag still in the ground beside Jessie.

Allister forced himself through the gate and ran over to Jessie catching him just before he crumbled again, "If you hurt her I'll-"

"You'll what?" The soldier laughed, "We are an army and you are just a boy."

Allister untied Jessie and threw his arm over his shoulder and pulled his friend off the ground and the messenger disappeared into the night.

"I'm sorry I failed to protect her, Allister." Jessie coughed on his own blood and pain.

Allister looked down at his feet, it took him a moment to respond and Lady Tyula rushed over to help Allister with Jessie, "It's not your fault"

Once inside they carried Jessie to the medical tent, where Reni and Lilianna were still crying in the corner when they stepped in, the pair stopped for only a moment as their stomachs sank only seeing Jessie be carried in and his bloodied beaten state.

Jessie smiled towards the girls as he was placed on one of the beds, "You two were very brave today." Oddly enough his bloody sincere smile helped the two girls.

They stood up and walked towards the bed tears falling down their face as Lady Tyula and two more nurses collected their supplies for Jessie, "Where is Valkyrie?" Reni asked her eyes red from crying.

Jessie turned his gaze away for a slight moment, "She'll be fine. She's a lot tougher than me." He smiled towards the girls before turning back to Allister who was sitting on the bed across from Jessie, he was heartbroken and Jessie could see the guilt written all over his friend's face, "This isn't your fault Allister-

"How isn't this all my fault?" Allister stood up and pulled at his hair pacing back and forth, "I should have surrendered when the Volcanic Spire first came for me, none of this would have happened."

"They still would have have came after Zavier and possibly Valkyrie still. The Volcanic Spire do not care if they get what they want, they always want more. The only reason they are making you a deal is because you beat them, they are at their last straw. They want you to make the trade in two days, maybe if the scouts and I attack the base tomorrow, we can free Valkyrie-"

"No. I am going to make the trade. You are in no condition to argue with me, or plan and execute an attack, you heard him, they have an army." Allister's voice was raised; he was stressed but determined. "Valkyrie is going to hate me, she will hate me for the rest of her life after I do this, but at least she will have a life. After I make this deal. Can you still take her to my sister? Where she will be protected..."

Jessie looked to the floor, he had failed his mission and he knew Allister was right, he was in no condition to argue or fight him. Jessie clenched a fist and looked at Allister, "With what honor is left, I promise you, my prince I will protect her till the end of my days."

Allister sat back down and Lady Tyula with the nurses helped bandaged and stitched Jessie up. Allister sat in the room with Jessie the hold time, even after the ladies had finished bandaging him up, the pair just sat.

The ladies took Reni and Lilianna back to their tents and recommended sleep for both Jessie and Allister, but none of the ladies were holding their breath.

Allister and Jessie knew these two days were going to feel like a week; but Jessie informed Allister of the details for the trade off, not even wasting any more breath in convincing him against it.

Allister looked down at his feet, hands together, "Will you be the one person I bring to the trade off, if you are physically able?"

"Is that even a question? I wasn't going to let you go with anyone else."

With a half-smile he stood up, "I'll be back... I need to do something and you need to attempt some rest."

"You should try the same," Jessie added in a wheezing sound as Allister walked out of the tent.

After exiting the medical tent everyone paused and stared at Allister as he made his way through the compound to his and Valkyrie's tent, he grabbed a quill and parchment and snuck out towards the statue Rem, where he sat by torch lite, scratching words on the parchment all night, he broke down at some point and his tears smuggled some of the words, he fell asleep clenching the words he had poured onto this parchment.

One of the ladies walked by and draped a blanket over Allister, no one dared to wake him.

Valkyrie sat with both hands on her stomach, the baby kicked and moved around, finally she composed herself and stopped the crying, she cursed the emotional aspect of being pregnant, but Valkyrie was saved of a lot of torment due to her condition. A woman approached the cage escorted by two guards, they unlocked the door, placed the girl inside and then locked the door and left as quickly as they came.

"I'm Silvia, if you would allow me to bandage Zavier, I can be out of your hair quickly Miss."

Valkyrie hesitated but nodded, resting Zavier's head back on the cage floor, but holding onto his hand.

Silvia tossed her hair over her shoulder and started to work on Zavier, cleaning off the dried blood with a cold cloth and bandaging the cuts after cleaning them with alcohol.

Valkyrie's face filled with worry as Zavier didn't even react to the burn of the alcohol, but Silvia reached out and placed her hand on Valkyrie's forearm, "He's never winched due to the alcohol, even when he's fully aware. He's been unable to rest for quite a few nights', his body is just catching up on the lack of sleep. I believe he will be alright, stress is bad for the baby Miss."

Valkyrie laughed, "Ha, stress is bad for this baby…" But she nodded sadly placing both hands on her stomach.

Silvia smiled, "May I feel?" Valkyrie hesitated, but agreed, Silvia placing both hands on Valkyrie's stomach lightly, the baby kicked her slightly and she smiled again warmly, "keep Zavier close to your stomach, maybe feeling the baby's movements will sooth him." Silvia placed her medical supplies at the door and turned back towards Valkyrie, "You are lucky to have Zavier as a brother, he is a very selfless person and he cares about the little people."

Valkyrie brushed Zavier's hair back and moved his head back on her lap, his ear pressed against her stomach, "I know. His selflessness drives me mad..."

"You weren't expecting to see him alive again where you?" Valkyrie just shook her head and half smiled, Silvia looked around and leaned into Valkyrie whispering in her ear, "If anyone asks to tell them that the soldier is the father."

Valkyrie nodded and the guards returned to allow Silvia out of the cell, all Valkyrie could do was wait, she spoke softly to Zavier about her and Allister's adventures together, hoping that the sound of her voice would wake him up.

An hour after the sun rose Zavier woke with a groan, "They are very active in there." Valkyrie laughed painfully as she wrapped her arms around her brother, he pushed himself up to a seated position and smiled weakly, "Did they hurt you?"

"No, I'm fine." Valkyrie said as she pulled herself into Zavier chest, "I'm sorry we left you." She fought the urge to cry again, as he wrapped his arms around her, his hand tangled in her hair.

Zavier's heart hurt as he held on to her, "You did what I asked of you, I understood the risks, Valkyrie."

"I never expected to see you again."

"I know." Zavier smiled and Valkyrie finally pushed herself off Zavier and wiped her eyes dry, "You should have left this forsaken land you could have been anywhere, why did you stay?"

Valkyrie laughed bitterly, "I wanted too, but Allister wouldn't. His theory was if there was even a possibility that you were alive and if the chance came, he'd trade himself for your life." Zavier sat up, with a silent groan and Valkyrie pulled her knees to her chest, "Looks like he might get his chance to sacrifice himself for someone…"

Zavier lifted his arm and Valkyrie tucked herself under it, he wrapped himself around his sister, keeping her close. "I'm sorry I wasn't there to protect you."

Valkyrie punched him in the gut, "Oh shut up." curling up into her brother's chest she closed her eyes and fell asleep in his arms, she felt safe knowing that Zavier was there watching over her.

Chapter 23

Even though Lady Tyula and the other nurses begged Jessie to rest more, he forced himself up, with the help of Allister.

Allister could tell just by the way Jessie stood, he was in pain, his back ached and was tightened, his face was still bruised and cut, his ribcage was swollen, purple and red, whenever he moved his bones would crack and ache. Jessie wouldn't show Allister the pain he was in; he was already guilty that he allowed Valkyrie and himself to be captured, he didn't want Allister to feel guilty of his condition, knowing that Allister himself was blaming himself, just as much as Jessie was.

Jessie received a message, the boat was ready to dock and waiting for them at the bottom of the cavern, they were early, why couldn't they be a few more days early is all Jessie could think as he read the message.

Allister was out of it, understandably, he knew very well what was going to happen after tonight, what his remaining days or weeks were going to be and mentally he was preparing himself for the worse. He was kidding himself, he couldn't prepare for what was going to happen and he was going to be paraded around like a trophy kill, dragged around his homeland like a haunting memory. Allister and Jessie sat in the kitchen tent, silently they avoided eye contact with each other.

Jessie placed his hand on his side and tried to think of something to say, he would start to say something, but then the words wouldn't escape his lips.

Allister finally managed to speak, "Is Valkyrie going to hate me?"
Jessie wasn't thrown off by the question, but he wasn't sure how to answer, "I don't think she can ever truly hate you, she will hate what you are doing for her, but she will grow to understand."

"She did hate me once," Allister placed his hands behind his head and placed his forehead on the table.

Jessie shook his head and sighed, "I can't predict how she is going to react, at first she is probably going to be angry, then she'll feel guilty, but I feel she will come to understand your decision." Allister looked up and nodded, he hoped that Jessie was right, "This doesn't have to be your nail in the coffin, maybe I cannot protect you from being captured and taken by the Volcanic Spire, but I will take Valkyrie to your sister and your sister will march to the Mountain Kingdom, we will come save you." Jessie placed his hand on Allister's shoulder, "Have hope, this doesn't have to be the end."

"Just keep Valkyrie safe and away. Far away from this, far from me."
Jessie nodded and the awkward silence washed over them again, time ticked slowly on, Jessie prepared the horses for the trek down the cavern and supplied himself with ropes, due to Allister's request, he had a feeling that Valkyrie wasn't going to leave without a fight. Some of the ladies left towards the cavern with supplies, gifts, for the boat and for the baby, Reni and Liliana dragged along, keeping them away from the sanctuary and occupied was the best option for the girls and if all goes well, they can say goodbye to Valkyrie.

Night finally was falling over the sanctuary and it was time for Jessie and Allister to leave. There were tears and short goodbyes but Allister kept a brave face, stiff upper lip, he tried to apply Zavier into himself, as he mounted his horse. Jessie and him left the compound, he knew this would be the last time he would see these gates; with just a small turn of his head, he silently said goodbye, he wondered if any of the gods whom statues rested there were looking down at him, glancing towards the skies he prayed for nothing more, then Valkyrie to be safe and for this to come to a quick end. For himself to come to a quick end.

Valkyrie awoke with a bang. Zavier had a leather strap wrapped around his throat through the bars, quickly she shook the tiredness from her eyes and she reached through the bars grabbing the guard, she clawed his face and screamed at him, as two more guards opened the cell door and grabbed her by the arms. She fought with them as they dragged her away from her brother, Zavier still struggling to catch a breath as they tightened up their grip on him. Valkyrie twisted around in the guards' arms and kicked one in the jaw, he released her and she went to give the other a right hook, but the guard got her first, dazed for those few seconds gave the other guard time to recover and grab hold of her, they pushed her down onto her stomach and quickly they tied her hands. Valkyrie kicked and squirmed, one of the guards pulled out his blade and placed it to Valkyrie's throat, he began to say, "Don't move, or I'll cut her," When Valkyrie jerked against the blade, slicing herself from the lower corner of her chin, halfway down her throat, she gasped and the guard dropped his blade as her blood started to ooze from the wound, Zavier lost it.

Everything flashed before him, his body moved without his control; grabbing the man's hands, who was holding the leather strap against his throat, he smashed his face against the bars and pulled away, grabbing the guard who cut Valkyrie, breaking his hand and flipping him over Valkyrie, into the cell, Zavier placed both hands around the man's neck, this ferocity as he squeezed tighter on the man's tiny neck. It took a moment and having the man pass out in his arms before Zavier turned around, the other guard had his hand on Valkyrie's throat with a cloth, slowing the bleeding. Valkyrie's breathing was panicked and loud, but she was breathing, she with a raspy voice stated, "I am not going anywhere without Zavier."

The rest of the guards looked at each other and complied with the girl's demand without consulting Jason.

Valkyrie's face was pale, but she nodded towards Zavier, "I'm okay." As the colour from his face had also disappeared, the guards tied Zavier's hands and lead him along beside Valkyrie, after tightly trying a cloth around her wound, luckily enough it just cut through the skin and not deeper. The guards took it slowly, as Valkyrie took every breath slowly, he heart pounded heavy as she looked down upon herself, before she turned to Zavier, they stared at each other as they were pushed through the camp.

They reached the horses, Jason was already mounted on his; he looked down at Valkyrie, Zavier and his soldiers and glared, but seeing the wound on Valkyrie's throat, he didn't even bother to ask, "Gag them both and let's get going." They tied a gag around their mouths and Jason grabbed Valkyrie by the arm, the guards pushed her up on the horse in front of him and then pushed Zavier forward, walking behind the horse, they trekked towards the meeting point. Zavier and Valkyrie in the dark but they both had a good guess of what was going to happen.

Allister and Jessie reached the hillside ahead of time, Jessie dismounted and walked over to his blood stains in the dirt, he was surprised by the amount of blood he had lost. Allister dismounted and scanned the area, turning around he looked over the tree tops and just barely in the distance he could see the small outline of the compound, "I wish I did more with my life Jessie." Allister placed his hands in his pockets, the wind blowing his cloak around himself, "The only thing I'll be remembered for is what my father did, nothing I've ever done has mattered."

Jessie shook his head and walked over to Allister, placing a firm hand on his shoulder, "The people who mattered to you will remember you for who you really are, not for what your father did."

Even though those were simple words, they comforted Allister enough to give a slight smile, only to be broken by the sound of horses approaching. Taking a deep breath the pair turned around to face their doom.

Jason at the front of the pack, he smiled as they approached, Valkyrie sat uncomfortable in his arms, she could see the distress in Allister's eyes that made her feel guilty and the bruised face of Jessie as he had to hold Allister still, in fear he'd might just rush in towards Valkyrie.

Valkyrie was pulled from the horse and she turned her face away from Allister as she was pushed forward; she was unsure how the bruise on her face was healing and the gas across her neck had begun to bleed again.

Allister's heart skipped a few beats when he saw Zavier be pushed out from behind the horse, he was happy for Jessie's hand as he needed it to steady himself from the shock, he was alive, Zavier had been alive this whole time. Jessie shook him slightly and Allister started to breathe again.

"I was told she'd be unharmed." Allister protested unable to keep his eyes off the two people he cared most about.

Jason laughed and pulled Valkyrie against him, his hand rested on her breast, "I promised you no such thing, I promised that if you didn't hand yourself over to me, I'd make her wish she was dead, or be dead." He pressed his tongue against Valkyrie's face, she squirmed and stomped on his foot. Grabbing Valkyrie by her hair he tossed her down in the dirt, Valkyrie twisting herself to not land on her stomach. Allister and Zavier both puffed up and jerked towards Valkyrie, both unable to actually move to her assistance.

"I will give myself up for Valkyrie and Zavier's lives."

"That's not the deal-"

"It's the deal now. You want me alive and I can end my life right here, right now without hesitation." Allister pulled his blade out of his sheath and stared Jason down, as he placed it against his throat.

"If you kill yourself, you all die. Is Zavier worth that to you?"

Jessie was thrown off, he released Allister's hand and backed away from him. Valkyrie screamed out behind her gag, pleading with Allister to not do it, but even as she cried, she knew he wouldn't be swayed as two guards grabbed hold of her, Jason snapped his fingers for Zavier to be brought forward. Allister took a deep breath and placed the blade tighter against his throat, even the slightest movement, the blade was going through his skin, "Zavier saved me, more times than I can count. He's worth my life and more to me."

Jason growled and grabbed Zavier by the throat, their eyes locked. "Sentiment makes you weak." He gave Zavier a right hook to the rib cage, where he collapsed, gasping through his gag. "Take them both, but hear this Allister Ironfist." Jason pointed his fingers towards Allister who stood tall, "You will publicly hand all claim to the Mountain Kingdom to me and if you try anything, I will make it my personal duty to hunt them both down and skin them alive, do I make myself clear?" Allister nodded and Jason snapped his fingers again, ropes were tossed over towards Jessie, "Hands tied tightly in front."

Jessie bent over slowly placing on hand on his ribcage as he picked up the binds and turned back to Allister, who had his hands out. With a whispered, "Are you sure?" Allister didn't even respond, he just stared ahead, he knew what would happen if he refused, he was lucky he was getting this deal.

Valkyrie screamed and kicked and fused about in the guard's arms, tears streaming down her face, while Zavier was pulled from the dirt and tossed forward. The two guards dragged Valkyrie forward as she fought them, another picked Zavier up and walked him towards the halfway point. Jessie walked forward with Allister one step ahead, at the midpoint they stopped, the guards reached out and grabbed Allister and Jessie grabbed Valkyrie pulling her into his chest, trying to keep her still and giving Zavier a free hand to use as support. Valkyrie jabbed Jessie accidently in the ribs, he coughed blood from the hit but didn't release her, Allister reached out, his fingers just grazing her face, "I'm sorry and I love you." that was all he could manage before he was pulled away from her, Zavier turned around and faced Jason and Allister.

Jessie removed Valkyrie's gag, giving her one chance to say goodbye, he whispered in her ear before she could say anything, "Don't make this harder on him, then it already is."

Valkyrie's lips trembled, "Allister! You fucking asshole!" It was all she could fester, she crumbled to her knees as Jason and his men marched away, Allister their new captive, they walked in victory.

Jessie cut Zavier's and Valkyrie's binds, Valkyrie ran into her brother's arms and sobbed uncontrollably. Jessie looked towards the ground, bent over and picked up Allister's dagger holding it loosely in his hand one hand over his ribs once again. Twice in his life, he had seen the person he was ordered to protect me taken away by the people he was supposed to protect him from.

After they reached their camp, the Volcanic Spire soldiers retied Allister's hands, tighter and placed a rope around biceps, hoping to restrict most upper body movement, all was futile, Allister wasn't going anywhere, he wasn't going to fight. He wasn't going to defend himself.

The guards sat him down by the fire pit and Jason walked over to inspect his prize. Grabbing Allister by the chin, he forced eye contact, "You put up a good fight these many months, you gave everything up for a girl and a worthless bastard elf?" Allister turned his head and looked away, Jason gave him a right hook to the eye and grabbed his chin again, "Don't turn your head from me, scum. You realize how easy it would be for me to send my soldiers to your friends." Allister took a deep breath and stared Jason in the eye, he didn't flinch or blink as the blood dripped down his face. Jason smiled, "See that's better." He punched him once more in the face, leaving him with a black eye and a swollen lip, but Allister just forced himself back into his seated position and looked down; all he could see were Valkyrie's tears. His lips began to tremble with fear, guilt, sorrow, every emotion you didn't want to feel rushed through his head, he pulled his face to his knees and tried to compose himself, Savanna's voice appeared in his head. Be proud of where you came from and never show your weakness, or that you are afraid. He felt sick to his stomach, but he sat up and composed himself, he wasn't going to break under the presser, he saved those who mattered and that is all that mattered. As much as he told himself that, didn't make any of this any easier... An hour longer had passed, the soldiers had packed up camp and one guard grabbed Allister by the arm and placed him in the cage and placed a shackle on his ankle, connecting to the cage. Again, the redundancy of everything, were they really scared he was going anywhere. Twisting the ropes he placed his cloak hood over his head and laid down as the cage bounced him around painfully, but the cold metal felt nice against his swollen face and being at the back of the convoy, no one's eyes prying upon him, Allister broke down, trying to keep as silent as he could, but he wondered to himself, an honest question, was watching Valkyrie cry and beg for him to not do this, the last time he was ever going to see her? He wasn't going to see her smile, hear her laugh, have her skin pressed against his, ever again... All he wished for was her hand she was always the stronger one. Alone, he was weak, alone he was nothing in his eyes.

This was the beginning, the beginning of the long trek home...

Chapter 24

Valkyrie sat with Zavier on the horse, he struggled to keep steady on the horse, as every step the horse took dug a rib bone into his lungs, but he watched over his sister, who blankly stared out like a comatose victim, he had to push his pain to the back of his head and support her, she's all who mattered at the moment to him.

The ride down the cavern was long, but the horses did well, even on the wet rocks closer to the bottom. When they finally got there, they were greeted by two scouts from the compound and six soldiers from the Northern Shores, they approached and bowed towards Jessie who jumped off the horse, quickly bowed painfully towards his men and turned towards Valkyrie and Zavier, helping them both off the horse, seeing Zavier's pain, due to the fact he was in similar agony.

"Kaston, prepare the ships to leave immediately and prepare me a messenger hawk."

"Yes, sir." One soldier rushed back towards the ship without a words question. Two took the horses two more helped Valkyrie and Zavier towards the ship and one stayed behind arms crossed behind his back, "What has become of Allister Ironfist, the last communication said you had him safe and ready for transport?"

"It went south fast, I need our Queen to prepare our troops if she still wishes to save her brother. We will be starting a war with the Volcanic Spire."

The man seemed surprised, "Our queen is going to start a war over this? Yes, he's her brother, but-"

"There is no but, he doesn't deserve to die and our Queen, his sister doesn't want an innocent man being prosecuted for someone else's mistake. She's lost one sibling to that already."

"Yes sir, I apologize. Shall I call our medic to attend to you?"

Jessie shook his head and stood straight, "Have them tend to our guest Zavier and ensure that Valkyrie isn't left alone. She might be. Unstable."

"Yes sir, anything else?"

Jessie shook his head no and headed towards the boat, the soldier hurried ahead of Jessie.

Zavier placed his arm around Valkyrie, while they walked toward the boat, thought there was one thing that broke Valkyrie's state of shock. Lilianna and Reni were sitting at the top of the ramp leading onto the boat, Valkyrie wiped her eyes and stood up tall, acting as nothing was wrong then the girls finally saw her. They waved and rushed down towards her. Valkyrie knelt and the girls wrapped their arms around her, tears filled their eyes instantly.

They sobbed their apologizes, while Valkyrie just hugged them while she spoke, "Shh, it's okay. You did nothing wrong, you have no reason to blame yourselves." She hugged them tighter, "Stay safe you two."

Reni and Lilianna were pushed back and Valkyrie stood up placing on hand on each other the girls head, Reni stared passed her and looked at Zavier who smiled at the pair, "Will you protect Valkyrie and the baby when we aren't around?" Reni asked innocently.

Zavier nodded, "I'll protect my baby sister and her child till the end of time, I promise you two that."

Reni smiled, Lilianna and her stepped over to Zavier and hugged him; thrown off he just stood there. Valkyrie smiled weakly and the two scouts came to retrieve the girls.

"It's time to leave." One said plainly.

The girl's hugged Valkyrie again, not wanting to let go, but they knew it was time. Valkyrie kissed both of their foreheads and the pair whisper into Valkyrie's stomach, "Grow big and strong little one." They kissed Valkyrie's bump and shook Zavier's hand waving goodbye as the two scouts took the girls towards the horses and headed towards the cavern wall.

Valkyrie held her arms and watched them leave, she wanted to say something, but no words came out, she was going to miss them, though she thought to say that would be redundant, there were going to be many things gone from her now she was going to miss. Finally, she turned to Zavier, "Do you think Allister..." She looked at her brother's bruised face and sighed, "Never mind."

Zavier wrapped his arms around Valkyrie, "He'll be fine because he knows you are safe."

"How long will that help..." Valkyrie asked before she broke away walking up the ramp, within minutes, the boat disembarked from the shores. Valkyrie leaned on the railing watching as the cavern got farther and farther away. She wasn't comforted by the fact that Zavier was only a few feet away watching over her, she knew he was in pain, but he was more worried about her, then he was towards himself that he refused medical help. Physically she was fine. She was fine, she kept telling herself and she was going to continue telling herself that till she believed it.

Digging her nails into the rail and held on as the waters continued to get rougher the rather away from the shores they sailed, Valkyrie blew a kiss into the wind and whispered goodbye into the salt sea air, before turning towards Zavier, "Maybe we should move indoors for the night."

Standing up, Zavier nodded and together they found their quarters, the pair tried to rest for the night, but neither of them got a moment's sleep. Valkyrie curled herself up in her blankets and silently cried; she was the reason that Allister got captured, if she was stronger, or didn't leave the compound, he'd be on this boat right now, beside her headed for a new life, a new start at something great. They were going to be happy. Now, what was he going to be to her? Just a memory, a shadow from her past reflected in the face of their child? Was this child now going to haunt her, was Allister's face going to haunt her forever as the man she failed? Her hands trembled as she placed her hands over her stomach, she whispered softly to herself, "I won't fail you, my child. I won't."

By morning Valkyrie stumbled out of their bunker; her eyes blood shot red, her stomach ached with hunger and the baby inside her kicked and turned around inside her. Jessie was leaning over the ledge of the boat, a bottle of whiskey that was near empty in his hand and Marcus perched on his shoulder, nestling his beak in Jessie's hair.

Valkyrie walked over to Jessie and brushed her finger along the hawk's back. She leaned over the ledge beside Jessie and just silently looked out alongside him.

Jessie sighed and took another drink from his bottle, "There is food laid out for you and Zavier in the mess hall, you should eat for the baby if not yourself."

"I will… But how are you holding up?"

Jessie laughed, "You are asking me how I am holding up? I should be asking you. You were captured by the Volcanic Spire, then traded off for the man who loves you."

"Thanks for rubbing it in."

"I'm sorry, but in comparison I am fine. I have plans to make this all right. Once the messenger hawk arrives at Stormwall, Queen Katherine will be preparing for war, I may have failed my mission to protect Allister, but that doesn't mean this battle is over, the war has just begun. My Queen is not fearful of spilling blood to protect an innocent, or family."

"Allister won't be happy, he wanted to protect those lands from war. Now one is going to be created to save him..."

"Either way there is a war coming. Does it matter who draws the first blow? The Volcanic Spire is searching for a war, which is the only way Jason is going to be able to claim the Iron thrown, through blood. He wants to ensure that his reign is secured among the history books. He wants to know, that no one will have any claim to the chair, beside him and his blood kin."

Valkyrie looked down at the dark unsettled waters, as it crashed against the boat, she struggled with what to say, she struggled with what to think.

"I apologize to you Valkyrie. I failed to protect Allister like I was supposed to, I failed to protect you, as I was supposed to. I'm failing everything over these years, it all started with Allister, wonder if it is going to end with him as well." Jesse mumbled his last few words.

Valkyrie turned her head, "Pardon Jessie?" He shook his head and smiled, "Don't apologize to me, I failed myself as much as you believe you failed me." Valkyrie placed her hand on Jessie's shoulder, "Come have breakfast with me. Get yourself slightly sober for the day ahead." Jessie laughed slightly, but he couldn't refuse the ladies request as they headed down towards the mess hall, it was nearly empty as the sailors had already begun their day.

Valkyrie and Jessie sat down and she bit down into a loaf of bread, with a long happy sigh she swallowed, turning back towards Jessie she asked, "What is Queen Kathrine like? What's Stormwall like?"

"Stormwall is a great land mainly fishermen and farmers, it's small but we have a lot of resources and a lot of allies nearby. As our name hints, we do get a lot of storms. But standing on the balcony during a heavy rainstorm, the wind and the water crashing against the shores, it's a rather calming experience." Jessie watched as Valkyries eyes brightened up, as he spoke to her about it, he calmed down and continued to speak, "Now, Queen Katherine is an interesting woman. She is fiery, she wants what she wants and she will fight tooth and nail to get it." Jesse placed his elbows on the table and crossed arms, "You probably don't know this, but when Allister and you were younger, I was supposed to take him from Zavier's care. I came back empty handed and oh man, did I get a strong word or two out of that woman. She is reasonable and she cares. She really cares about her people, about the people around her, when I explained why I left Allister in your brother's care, she started to cry, she longed to have a part of her family back beside her, her beloved brother back, but she knew the same thing as I did, he belonged with you. Allister wouldn't be the man became today, if he would have come with me back to Stormwall. Who knows what he would have turned into, all I know is it wouldn't be the man you love and for all, I know he might have fallen into what he fears the most, being like his father, the court changes you like that, it makes people cold. Allister was able to live a simple life, filled with people who cared about him. In Stormwall the court would have taken him in and changed him, trained him to become a leader, become a king. Looking at who Allister became, being a king isn't what he was meant for, then again, he wasn't meant for this fate that seems to be laid out for him. He's a good kid, he's always been a good kid and he loves you, more than anything."

Valkyrie smiled behind her tears, trying to dry her eyes as the waterworks kept flowing. Jessie placed his arm over her shoulder and pulled her into him, "I'm sorry. I truly am..." Valkyrie just placed her hands over her face and sobbed, maybe she needed this moment more then she realized. After a long ugly cry, the pair wondered off in their own directions, Jessie having duties he had to attend to, while Valkyrie wondered back towards her brother's side who was struggling to start his day.

Chapter 25

Days turned into weeks for Allister; he laid in the cell comatose to the world around him, he had nothing to live for, he had nothing to die for. He was going to be killed, for a pathetic reason that made no sense to him and he had no way to stop it. He had watched Valkyrie's heartbreak before his eyes, Zavier's sacrifice, all those months of torture were for nothing, they still ended up where the Volcanic Spire wanted them. Allister couldn't react anymore, he was just lying there, dead to the world, his body numb, was it from the beatings? Or was he broken on the inside? Even though he couldn't see his face, he knew it was black and blue, few days before he was refusing to eat, or drink and the soldiers were told to beat him into compliance. He never complied; they just had to stop before they killed him.

Allister knew exactly where they were, nearing the border to what was long ago the great Mountain Kingdoms, he wondered what had become of these free lands, he knew he wouldn't have to wonder long. If he sat up and looked passed the trees, he would have been able to see the Kingdom that he was born to rule, the Kingdom where his mother, father and sister all died. The home was the place he was going to die. He knew that in a few hours they were going to reach the first town; last he remembered it was a small farming village, mostly traded in wool, due to the abundance of sheep and mountain goats. Allister placed his face against the cold iron and questioned if Valkyrie, Zavier and Jessie had reached their destination, trying to keep his mind off the pending nightmare that was his new life.

The convoy stopped, Jason turned his horse around and trotted towards Allister's cell, "Get Allister changed and on a horse. I want to show him off to his, people." Jason coy smile twisted, smugly on his face as the soldiers complied. They had prepared red trousers and a thick white cotton shirt. Allister had no strength to fight as they stripped him bare and washed the dried blood off his body. Jason laughed at Allister, he was venerable and there was nothing he could do about it. Once dressed, they dragged him out the cell; Allister somehow managed to keep his legs straight as he weakly looked up at Jason, he tried to look brave but came off as pathetic. They dragged him towards his horse and threw him on, tying his legs to the straps, then his wrists to the reign's; the horse's halter had a rope being led by the soldier in front, where the saddle had a rope attached to the soldier behind, Allister wasn't going anywhere. Again, using all his strength, he tried to sit tall on the horse, but his posture slumped and he was defeated, he was once again a prisoner of war, this time at the beginning rather than the end. Jason rode beside Allister, he was proud of his achievements, he had captured and defeated the boy who was born to be the greatest tyrant this land had ever seen, or so he will tell everyone. Allister was fearful. It had been years since these people, his people had gazed upon an Ironfist, how much of an uproar would his face cause? He imagined the worse, he imagined worse than the day he was placed on trial, the day Zavier had saved him for the second time. Turning his head towards the skies he just let his body go with the horse, drowning out every sound, every look from the soldiers and every smile from Jason's mouth. Allister tried to find his happy place, a place he will never see, but a place he can pretend he could have. A place in Valkyrie's arms. A place where he was free of his past, free of the life he was supposed to have, free of what he was meant to be, free of the life he escaped. Free of the life he never truly escaped from, free from the expectations, free from stereotyping. All he ever wanted was to make a name for himself, not be Edward Ironfist's son, he didn't want to be known as Allister the son of a Tyrant, he wanted to be known for what little good, or what little bad he did, as long as it was his own and not the doing of another. Allister was just wishful thinking, but at the moment that was all he had.

Finally, they reached the outskirts of Halleen, a small village that laid just in what was one the Mountain Kingdom's boundaries; Allister managed to straighten his back, but he kept his gaze on the ground. The villagers had seen them approached for miles, as they were all waiting in the streets; families all stared at the army as it marched through. Allister bit his lip as he could feel it begin to tremble, he was afraid of these people. He was waiting for their reaction, waiting for the uproar, waiting for them to demand his death, to throw waste at him, to cuss as the even sight as if he himself was an offense to their very presence. It was what he deserved, he believed that because his father's blood ran through his veins because he couldn't stop his father, he was to blame for their pain. But something happened. They walked through the town and silence broke through the crowd, not even a word muttered between mother and child. Allister looked up, everyone was looking directly at him. Allister was confused, they all clearly recognized him, they all had to know who he was. Where was the angry mob he was so accustomed towards? Where were the death threats, the horror expressions on their faces? If Allister knew better, he would see the sorrow on the people's faces. They were not glad to see the heir to their kingdom being paraded around like a trophy.

Jason's smug expression disappeared, he looked at Allister then back to the people before calling out, "This man is Allister Ironfist! The blood kin of the tyrant who lead your brothers, sons and fathers into a war that caused your great depression!"

The crowd remained silent, eyes still locked of Allister as they rode deeper into the town, Jason snarled. The anger was building inside him and as the day continued and they reached the next town, it didn't get better, again the villagers seemed saddened by Allister, was it pity? Allister asked himself, to see an Ironfist, the name that meant proud powerful men, brought down to a pathetic boy painted black and blue with beatings? Allister was only seeing the worst possibility of this, he didn't see that they were troubled, he didn't see the truth that these people didn't want that they knew was coming. Allister was a son of these lands, his father was a tyrant, but they knew better, they knew he was just a boy, forced to grow up in a cruel world. He had done nothing wrong to these people, but what were they supposed to do? An army held him captive, they had to sit back and watch as their beaten prince ride on by. Even the children who knew him not by name, or by face, knew there was something odd about the situation as they looked upon their parent's expressions.

Allister managed to lift his head and stand slightly taller with every step.

With every hillside they passed every village they trumped through, Jason's anger built up and Allister's confusion built along with him.

Night came around and the convoy stopped at the top of the last hillside, the last hillside, in the very near distance, only a few hours ride. Allister could see the castle made of stone and iron. He didn't have time to enjoy the view as Jason, angered and flustered by the unsavory reaction of the peasants; he grabbed Allister from the horse and threw him down to the dirt. His left shoulder taking the hit on the ground he groaned as the bone popped out of its socket, biting down on his lips Allister looked up at Jason as the man's boot crushed down on his face, repeatedly. Allister took the pain and held in his cries the best he could, but he wasn't as strong as he wished he was. Tears of pain mixed with his blood, his nose broke, his jaw was dislocated and blood stung his eyes; finally when Jason grew tired of beating his prisoner senseless he retreated to his tent, while the soldiers dragged Allister to the cell. Allister blacked out even before they threw him in his metal cage. Lucky enough he couldn't feel the force of his body hitting the floor and rolling heavy into the bars, as his skull cracked loudly with such force, slicing another scar into his face.

Docking in Stormwall; Valkyrie and Zavier looked at the city before them, this land so foreign to them. Walls were built up all around the shoreline, protecting the city from the powerful winds and the massive storms. It looked like a fortress. And walking towards the boat was a woman; her hair raven black, pin-straight that flew behind her, a golden crown engraved with rubies and a white dress, with long sleeves covering her against the wind. Four guards in golden plated armor followed her every move. She was beautiful, with piercing blue eyes as she approached. Jessie disembarked the ship, Valkyrie and Zavier followed close behind.

Jessie bowed low and kissed the woman's hand "I am sorry I failed you, my Queen."

Lady Katherine's eyes were the only way you could tell her emotion, there was a slight hint of sorrow, but it was mostly hidden by the sudden glimmer of excitement as she turned her eyes to Valkyrie. "You child, are Valkyrie Dragonsbreath correct? The lover of my brother."

Valkyrie nodded and gave the woman a small bow, "Yes my lady, pleasure."

"And you must be, sir?"

Zavier gave a low, gracious bow to the beautiful queen, "I am just known as Zavier, Queen Katherine."

She smiled slightly with the corner of her mouth, "Pleasure. Jessie, you have duties in the war room, Valkyrie will you walk with me?"

Jessie turned to Zavier quickly and then back to his Queen, "May I allow Zavier to assist me in the war room, my Queen?"

"As you wish," Reaching her hand out towards Valkyrie, Katherine managed a full smile, as Valkyrie took her hand softly, confused, she was pulled away from her brother and Jessie.

The Queen brushed her hair back over her shoulder and pushed her way through her guardsmen, "Gentlemen, you may leave us."

The first guardsmen nearly spoke in rejection, but Katherine gave them a glare that caused the men to all stand tall and alert, without a word leaving their lips. She smiled towards Valkyrie, "I love being in charge." She whispered smugly.

They walked up a large stairway, leading to the top of the wall, turning back, they could see Zavier, Jessie and the guardsmen heading towards the palace, Valkyrie felt uneasy with the woman, she was Allister's sister, his family, but she never got along with women of status and she was afraid to offend the sister of the man she loved.

Katherine smiled, "Valkyrie, no need to be afraid. I never imagined I was going to ever be an aunt. That's exciting." She bit her lower lip and walked over to the edge of the wall, looking over at the long, never ending sea. "Will you tell me about my brother? Jessie, last I was truly informed about him he was just a scared boy, who was being well taken care of."

Valkyrie took a few steps closer to Katherine, her fingers crossed on her stomach, "He's a sweet boy and his selfishness drives me nuts, my brother taught him too well. He thinks that he is the most worthless thing in all humanity, that he is blinded by the fact he is a good person, he has a good heart." Valkyrie looked up as she could feel Katherine's eye's locked upon her. Katherine reached and brushed Valkyrie's red locks from her face.

"I can see the love you have for my brother. I have never heard anyone speak so kindly of my kin." Katherine turned away, "I always thought my brother was destined to grow up like our father, born to rule with an Iron fist." She laughed, "Our father tried for the few years he had my brother in his grasp, he tried everything to corrupt his mind. Those few years I tried to protect him from our father's corruption. Protect his soul from that monster of a man's harshness. I wonder now if Allister did take after our father if he'd be where he is now. Be honest with me, he traded himself for your safety, didn't he?"

Valkyrie paused a moment, then nodded sadly, "Yes. He did and I am I'm so sorry for that. When we were younger, I always found myself protecting Allister, he was a broken, sad boy… And then he felt the need to protect me."

"I'm not mad if that is what you are afraid of." The Queen chuckled lightheartedly, "I'm glad. Our father wouldn't have sacrificed himself for anyone, he'd rather watched his love ones be tortured and mutilated before him. Allister's humanity is what our mother cared about. She felt when he was born that he was meant to be a great man. It was her only wish of him before she died and him sacrificing himself for you, is something only a great man would do. Knowing that he did that for you, lets me know a little more about him." She smiled again. "I just wish we make it in time to save him. After all these years, I wish to at least lay eyes on my brother, to see the man he became." Katherine backed away from the wall and stood up tall again, "But dreaming doesn't bring action." Katherine clapped her hands and smiled trying to change the subject, "How due to your condition Jessie laid out in his message I have someone waiting for you."

Valkyrie was confused, but as Queen Katherine extended her hand she took it and together they made their way back to the castle.

Queen Katherine took Valkyrie to her new room and there standing in the room standing next to the baby cradle that the woman at the sanctuary had made her was a small, aged Dwarven woman. Savanna turned around and smiled at the shocked young woman.

"Valkyrie, it's been years."

Chapter 26

When Allister finally woke, it was to the sound of creaking iron gates opening. His head pounded, his vision was blurry and he was in pain, but he forced himself up to a seated position and looked before him. Some things never change, Allister thought to himself. Besides the overgrown shrubbery and the unkempt ivy climbing up the walls, the castle grounds looked the same. Allister was frozen in the moment, his eyes locked on the walls of the kingdom he once called home, within these walls, memories were locked away, memories Allister knew would soon be awakened again.

He didn't fight, or even react as the soldiers unlocked the cell and pulled him out, forcing him to his feet. He was standing and walking towards the large iron doors, but it felt more like a ghost taking his steps for him.

"Welcome, home Allister Ironfist." Jason laughed as his soldiers opened the doors and everyone slowly matched in. "Are all your happy memories of you being a boy, running through these halls flashing back to you yet?" He turned around and looked at the pale-faced prisoner, "Whatever happy memories you may have of this place. I will be sure to eradicate you of them before your time is up. Take him to his dwelling for the next few weeks and dress him for our special occasion, then bring him back down to the throne room."

"Yes, Sir." The soldiers holding Allister, plus four more broke away from the group, leading him up a spiral staircase. Allister hoped they weren't taking him where he thought they were, he remembered these passageways like the back of his hand and when they finally reached a large wooden door Allister forced them to halt.

Allister laughed bitterly as they released him, "Open the door." They ordered. Allister closed his eyes and reached for the cast iron handle, last he saw of this door there wasn't a handle as he turned the foreign nob, opening the door Allister found himself staring back into his past. It didn't look like before. The bed frame had been torn apart and replaced, the curtains leading towards the open balcony were gone and the balcony doors were nailed shut, all the dressers, the desks, the books, all gone. It was bare, with nothing but a bed and a cheap frame and a pile of clothes folded nicely.

"Our prince demands you dress in those clothes he has laid out for you. Either you dress yourself, or we dress you again and we are allowed to be, busy with you for a while." The soldiers smiled as they closed the door behind them, their hands crossed over their crotch, insinuating something that Allister didn't want to even think about.

He swallowed loudly and walked over to the pile of clothes. Allister's hands trembled as he looked at the clothes and reached for them, these silk and cotton clothes, were too familiar for his comfort and way too large in the shoulders. In his hands was the clothes of a king, the clothes of his father. "How did he even obtain this?"

"Our prince enjoys keeping treasures of his victims. We ransacked your father's wardrobe the night our Prince slayed him. Now enough questions, get dressed, or do we have to teach you a lesson or two."

Allister tore his shirt off and looked at the red shirt in his hand and threw it over his head, the silk felt strange against his skin, as he took off his trousers replacing them with the cotton ones his father once wore, that was all fine, but the last two items that laid on the bed made Allister sick to his stomach. His father's cloak, the red and black sigil of the Mountain Kingdoms embroidered onto it, the white fur lining and the gold colour ropes, the fur lining was stained in blood. The cloak he was wearing at the time of his execution and laying just under it, was Edmond Ironfist's crown. Allister held it in his hand only to drop it and fall to the ground, his heart pounded and he trembled.

One soldier marched over to Allister grabbing him by the throat, "Finish dressing." Allister just stared the man in the eye and forced himself off the ground, he tied the cloak around himself and grabbed the crown again, it took him a full minute to place it on his head, but he did.

The soldiers laughed, "He does look like his father."

Allister stood tall, his eyes red with near tears, grinding his teeth he turned to them, "I am nothing like my father." The soldier was closest to him cracked him on the back of the head and tied his hands in front of him, before dragging Allister's dazed state out of the room and back down the spiral staircase, tossing him down the last few steps as Allister landed on his face. The soldiers laughed as they picked him back off the ground.

They headed for the throne room, Allister wasn't sure what to expect, as he was pushed through the large doors, he stumbled and looked around the room. It was the same but in different colours, the coloured drapery of the Mountain Kingdom was replaced with the Volcanic Spire's coloured flags hanging from the high ceiling. Jason smiled as Allister studied them as he was pushed forward. "Do you like the decor? I've had men here for months preparing for this, special occasion. Now that you, my special guest is here, we can start sending out the invitations. Do you have a preference on how you wish to die? Hanging?" Jason stood up from the Iron throne and walked forward his hand resting on his chin, "Nah, for a king, hanging is not the way to go. Beheading would be fitting, don't you agree? Like father like son." Allister just looked at the man his chin held high as he breathed through his nose, "We could do an indoor ceremony, place you in the spot where I took your father's head off."

Allister dared not to speak, but his mouth twitched with anger. Taking another deep breath, he held his tongue and continued to look Jason in the eye.

Jason smiled, he could see he was hitting a nerve, so he kept poking. "If we did it inside fewer guests would be able to attend and being such a monumental day for the great the Mountain Kingdom, we should allow all to witness." He turned away towards the throne again and waved his hand for his soldiers to bring Allister forward, "I'll even send a formal invitation to your eldest sister and we can even dig up your sister Jasmine's bones,"

"Don't talk about my sisters." Allister pushed himself forward at Jason, managing to stretch himself to be inches from the man before the soldiers were able to control him again.

Jason smiled and placed his hand on Allister's chin, "I can do anything

I want to you like my men did everything they wanted to your late sister that fateful night. You were so young, did you even get to hear the details of what my men did to that girl? How they brutally deflowered her. Oh, it went on for hours." He slowly released Allister's face, wanting to see his full reaction, his full field of emotion.

"Stop!"

"Oh, she moaned and cried out, her body was so confused, conflicted with pleasure and pain, what a little whore, too bad she died so quickly."

"I said stop!" Allister cried out, his voice was mixed with anger and pain; he had heard some of the details of his sisters' death, but hearing them come out of Jason's mouth made his skin crawl. Allister spat towards Jason and the soldiers holding him dropped him to the floor, ones' elbow digging into the back of his neck.

Jason wiped his face and leaned down, placing his hand on Allister's head, he pushed it down into the stone floor. "Even after little Jasmine died, they still defiled her, in so many ways it makes any sane man's skin crawl. I wish I could have saved the image of her corpse just for this moment." Allister's eyes burned red, as tears of anger filled his face as he tried to fight the soldiers holding onto him. Jason stood up and walked behind the throne, "Stand him up and sit on the throne. The spot you were born to take Allister Ironfist." He laughed as the soldiers threw Allister into the seat.

Allister turned his face from Jason as he stepped around, "Doesn't it feel like you finally belong somewhere? This is your home!" Jason yelled out with enthusiasm, "You were an outcast most your life and now you are sitting where you truly belong, where you were born to be." His coy and condescending smile made Allister furious, but he didn't again dare act upon it. His mind still locked on the thought of what they did to his sister, what they could have done to Valkyrie. "Who am I kidding Allister? Even in the lands that are inherently yours, you are still an outcast. Your family is a black plague on the history of these lands and I am going to ensure that the Ironfist name is nothing, not even a memory." He grounded his teeth as he wrapped his hand around Allister's throat pinning him against the throne, "When this kingdom is mine, I will eradicate every person who dares speak the name Ironfist. Your family will not even be a myth, it will be nothing."

Allister swallowed and spoke truly, "You are only scared, scared that you have no right to these lands and you will never have a right to these lands. These people have survived without a king for years, do you really believe they will follow you now?"

Jason's smile disappeared from his face and he placed his second hand around Allister's throat, he lost his temper in that moment as Allister's oxygen was cut off. Allister gasped and clawed at Jason's hands, his face turning blue, Jason pushed Allister against the throne hard, leaning in as he whispered in Allister's ear, "Those who do not follow. Die. I have no problem with genocide."

"My prince." One of the soldiers snapped Jason out of his trance. Jason released Allister and turned away heading towards the door, furry was written all over the man's face. Allister just kneeled off of the throne, inhaling painfully and loudly. "I want him out of my sight, do with him as you please, we have a while till we need him presentable."

As Jason left the throne room, the soldiers smiled and cracked their fingers, removing the clothes from Allister's back they beat him senseless, then dragged his naked body through the walls, they tossed him around like a toy, taking turns abusing him, in very creative ways. They gagged him with old ripped cloth when they grew tired of his screams.

Finally after hours, they grew tired of him and dragged him back up to his old room, tying his hands to the bed posts they left him naked, bloodied and numb. Allister just closed his eyes, pulling his knees to his bruised chest and he tried to clear his mind of the pain, tried to remember good times, he tried to remember Valkyrie.

Another month passed, it was early in the afternoon and Valkyrie was terrified, her water broke and her body began contractions; the baby was coming. Valkyrie dug her nails into the bedspread and screamed. Zavier looked pale and terrified for the first time in his life, he didn't know how to react as he just paced back and forth.

Jessie opened the door, with three midwives, Savanna and Queen Katherine following his entrance.

Savanna turned to Jessie and Zavier grabbing them both by the arm leading them out, "Boy's are not permitted in the room while a lady is giving birth."

Valkyrie ground her teeth together and managed to say, "I want them here."

Savanna laughed, her bold dwarven eyebrows cocked as she placed her hand on Valkyrie's shoulders, "They will be near when the baby comes, but do you really want your brother to see your lady parts giving birth to a child?"

Valkyrie took a few deep breaths and shook her head no, Zavier walked over and placed a kiss on his sister's forehead, "I'll be just outside, you can do it." He didn't tell her how thankful he was to be relieved from the room. His heart was pounded, he was clueless on how to help her and that scared him.

Once Jessie and Zavier were out of the room, they closed the door behind themselves and sat with their backs against the wall, listening to the sounds of screaming and mild cursing.

Jessie pulled a bottle from under his cloak and handed it to Zavier, "It can possibly be a long night. Queen Katherine's first child took two days." Zavier's eyes went wide as he stared at the door and took a long needed swig from the bottle before handing it back to Jessie. He laughed and took a drink himself.

Every few hours the door would open and a midwife would leave, to retrieve something else and inform the boys of Valkyrie's condition and how the birthing was processing. Everything was going fine, as the woman told them.

Finally, the news that both Jessie and Zavier were waiting for came. It was well into the afternoon of the following day, they could hear a baby cry from inside the room, the pair stood up, even before Queen Katherine opened the door to the room, she smiled and with her long fingers beckoned the boys into the room.

Zavier stepped into the room first, Valkyrie was wrapped in many blankets, her face was pale and her red hair stuck to her face with sweat, but there was a stunned smile locked on her tired looking face as she looked into the eyes of the child she held.

Zavier walked towards the bedside and leaned in towards his sister, taking a good look at the baby, who silently laid in its mother's arms. It was beautiful, for a baby, with its face scrunched and its odd gray and red colouring.

Valkyrie looked up to her brother and smiled. "It's a girl. Want to hold her?" She offered her brother the baby, he froze for a moment looking at the bundled child.

Though he took her in his arms, being careful to support her head and tuck her into himself, he cuddled the child, a smile raised on his face, for once he cared not to hide his emotions, Zavier smiled down at the child in his arms, his niece, something he never imagined to see in his lifetime. "What are you planning on calling her?"

Valkyrie turned her gaze to Queen Katherine, "With your permission I'd like to name her after your late mother, Castriel."

Katherine smiled wide, "My and Allister's mother would have been honored, you have my blessing."

Zavier looked down at Castriel and smiled, "I won't let anything happen to you."

Savanna took baby Castriel from Zavier's arms and spoke aloud, "Valkyrie is going to need to rest if I may ask everyone to escort themselves out of the room."

Valkyrie rubbed her eyes and everyone left, besides Savanna holding the child proudly in her arms, placing the child in the wooden crib the ladies at the compound made her, Valkyrie closed her eyes. She was exhausted. It only took her minutes to fall into a deep sleep.

Chapter 27

It wasn't even days after Valkyrie had given birth to Castriel when a letter arrived, an invitation. Queen Katherine took the parchment and called her war counsel together.

She leaned on the table, the parchment clenched in her hand there was fury and determination in her eyes as she watched her men pile into the war room. She tossed the paper on the table, "We have a timeline now, is my army ready to move? If we are going to make it to the Mountain Kingdoms before the execution of my brother, we will have to leave in a weeks' time and no later."

Jessie picked up the parchment and read it quietly before handing it off to Zavier. Zavier paused and closed his eyes after reading the "invitation".

"Our ships can be ready tomorrow for sail, my Queen." Jessie said looking down at the map that was drawn on the large oak table, "They are clearly expecting us; should we dock in the cavern? We risk losing a few days, but we are more likely to surprise them, even though there are many farmers living in these parts, I do not believe anyone from the farm lands would comprise our location, no one has allegiance towards The Volcanic Spire on these shores yet."

Queen Katherine paused as the men discussed among themselves, "No, we will go to the Mountain Kingdom main port. We are formally invited you see. Jason wants a war, but most of all he wants the Mountain

Kingdom. He wouldn't dare harm the Queen of Stormwall. Myself and a large entourage will go to the main docks and my army will then take the cavern ways."

Jessie shook his head, "Queen Katherine, I cannot allow you to risk your life-"

"I am a queen, I do not need permission to do as I say. This is my brother we are speaking of. I have no rights to the Mountain Kingdom, my footing is here, I am no threat to his claim and he'd not risk my harm. He sent the invitation addressed to me." She was stern and Jessie backed away from the table, clearly seeing he wasn't winning an argument with her, but still not happy with the end.

"My queen, will you at least allow me to escort you?" Jessie asked, defeated by her stubbornness.

"I wouldn't have it any other way Sir Jessie. Zavier, I realize you are rather connected to my brother, as you raised him, would you as well like to join my ship?"

"Yes, Queen Katherine, if you welcome me that is."

"I'd be honored to have you aboard. I've heard many things of your skill with a blade," She flashed a smirk towards Jessie, who just gave her a look knowing that she was clearly speaking of his few encounters with the blade master. "Men, kiss your loved one's farewell, tomorrow we set sail." Slamming her fist down on the table the men cheered loudly and then exited the room. Zavier left to speak with Valkyrie, but Jessie stayed and waited till everyone was far gone and closed the door. "Queen Katherine, I apologize if I am speaking out of place, but how are you holding up?"

Katherine turned away from Jessie, her arms crossed, "As your Queen, I am unaffected by this news, as a sister, I am petrified. This is my baby brother we are speaking of. My baby brother who is going to be murdered because of our father's actions. It may have been years since we've set eyes on each other, he may not even remember my face, but his is still and always will be my baby brother, I loved him." She took a calming breath as she controlled her emotions, never letting her facial expression sway.

"Queen Katherine, we will do our best to save him."

She breathed heavy and turned around, her face strong but Jessie spotted a tear in the corner of her eye, "I just hope our best is enough. You may leave now Jessie."

Jessie bowed and paused, but did as his queen requested, leaving her to her thoughts, her dreads of the days, weeks ahead.

Zavier knocked on the door to Valkyrie and baby Castriel's room quietly, not hearing the baby cry, he assumed that she was asleep, Allison one of the midwives opened the door and glared at him, but allowed him to enter.

Savanna was sitting in the corner of the room folding blankets only looking up as Zavier walked in the room, she could read his face and she knew what he was going to say.

Valkyrie had blue bags underneath her eyes as she smiled, handing Castriel over to Savanna who rocked the baby softly, but Valkyrie's smile didn't last as she saw the serious expression on her brother's face, "What is it Zavier?"

He walked forward, not wanting to look his sister in the eye, he knew how this conversation was going to go before he even opened his mouth. "Tomorrow Jessie and I are leaving on one of the warships heading towards the Mountain Kingdom. An invitation for Allister's execution has been sent."

"I am joining you." Valkyrie didn't ask.

"No, you are not. You have just given birth, you have a baby to worry about."

"Castriel can stay on the boat with the Savanna and Allison, you are not leaving me behind." She was furious at the thought of them leaving her behind.

"No, I cannot risk taking you with us, if we are going to have any chance of success we need to ensure not to make any drastic moves if Allister sees you."

"Are you saying that I am too emotional to take? My emotions are in check Zavier." She stepped forward, only a few inches from her brother, stabbing her finger once against his chest, "You need me."

Zavier shook his head and grabbed Valkyrie's hand "This child needs you here, where it is safe and I am not fearful of your emotions. I can only imagine from my own experience," Zavier paused biting his tongue as a flashback came to mind, "I can only imagine what Allister is currently going through if he sees you and if our plan turns sour, he will do anything in his power to protect you again." Valkyrie's angry glare turned sad and Zavier pulled her into him, hugging her tightly, "I know you want to help Allister, but the way you can help him, is by keeping yourself and your child safe."

Valkyrie pushed away from Zavier and pointed towards the door, "Get out!" She screamed irrationally, Zavier just nodded and exited the room, he thought that was the end of it, he was playing naïve.

Late that night with the assistance Savanna and the midwife Allison, the four of them snuck on the warship. It didn't take anything to convince Savanna of Valkyrie's plan and Allison also agreed easily enough. Savanna and Allison led Valkyrie down to the maid's bunkers, they realized the Queen would be aboard this ship and new what bunkers would be occupied. Allison spoke placing a pile of blankets in a chest and then talking baby Castriel from Valkyrie's arms and placing the child in the bundle, "I am going to speak with Queen Katherine's chef tonight and warn him about the possibility of three extra passengers. He owes me a few favors; he will not speak a word to anyone."

Savanna smiled as she placed more baby supplies down next to the child.

"Thank you, Allison, I glad you understand."

"You have a chance to save the man you love, if you didn't do everything in your power you'd regret it for the rest of your life. I understand that very well, Lady Valkyrie." Valkyrie didn't even roll her eyes at the sound of her title, she just smiled and brushed Castriel's face with her finger. "We must leave for now. I'll make sure the other midwives keep everyone from your room, I'll say you are too distraught from being left behind to converse with anyone. I will be back before morning light, even if Castriel cries, no one coming on the ship will hear till in the lower decks. Don't worry about the noise."

Valkyrie nodded and sat on the bed, her arm over the edge, so she could reach over and place her finger in Castriel's hand the baby gripped lightly, while Savanna and Allison left the ship, silently and stealthily as they had boarded separating at the end of the docks.

Allison was heading towards the kitchen when she was stopped by a firm hand grasping her shoulder, she turned around and was face to face with Jessie. He had a folded up piece of parchment in his hand and he offered it to the woman. "What is this?" she asked, not looking away from the man.

Jessie brushed his hair back with his fingers, "It's for Valkyrie. From Allister; I've been waiting for the right time to give it to her, but haven't till now. Can you wait until after the boat leaves tomorrow?"

Allison glared at Jessie, then placed the piece of parchment in her pocket, "Are you expecting some emotional reaction after she reads this?"

"I am unsure, haven't read it myself. Allister wrote this the day before he was going to trade himself for Valkyrie's safety. With my best guess, I would assume she is going to be emotional after reading these pages."

"Thank you for the warning, I have duties to attend too, good night sir Knight."

She turned away and Jessie grabbed her one last time, "One last thing, how is Valkyrie holding up? Zavier said she was rather upset over the fact-"

"Over the fact that she might lose the last chance to see the father of her child alive? She is holding up as anyone would expect her too." There was a coarseness in the woman's tone that caused Jessie to back off from the woman.

He placed his hands to his side and bowed slightly, "I apologize for bothering you miss. Have a goodnight." Allison turned away with a loud click from her heels, Jessie just stood there, looking down at his own feet. He felt guilty for having to leave Valkyrie behind, she is the person who Allister cares about the most and her face in a crowd would be the one thing that gave Allister hope at the end.

Allison checked behind her still seeing Jessie standing blankly in the halls, she wondered if he suspected anything was off, or if his mind was lost on other things, causing his normally sharp mind, to be dull. Either way, she continued with her duties, first talking to the chief, then heading back to Valkyrie's room to inform the other midwives on what to do, before grabbing some more supplies and hurrying back onto the boat. When she made her way into Valkyrie's courtiers, she and the baby were fast asleep. Savanna was watching over the baby waiting for Allison's return.

"Did anyone suspect anything?" She asked Allison who looked at the piece of parchment in her hand.

Allison handed it over to Savanna, "Apparently, it is a letter for Valkyrie from Allister. Jessie asked for me to give it to her after the boat sets sail, but I don't think anyone suspects anything."

Morning came too soon for the restless, Zavier spent his whole time questioning his conversation with Valkyrie, but he dared not return to her room to apologize. He knew if he tried to speak to her now, she'd manage to convince him to allow her to accompany them, when, or if he returned he would apologize to her and he believed she would understand after giving the situation some time to clearly process in her mind. Zavier stared down at the leather armor Queen Katherine had given him, she offered him plate, but he refused, the suffocating restriction of plate never appealed to him, he was a fighter, who used his speed and flexibility to his advantage over his opponents. He sighed loudly, was he going to fight another war? Zavier knew in that moment he was a changed man, as the thought of fighting a war and the thought of having a chance to kill Jason didn't make him cringe. He clutched the hilt of his sheathed sword tightly, Jason had succeeded in his mission to break him. Zavier understood he would never be the same man he was over a year ago, but only now did he understand how much he had changed. Rubbing his face and eyes, his hands were sweaty, his heart races, more images of his imprisonment flashed before his eyes and he was ashamed of what he felt he was becoming, he hadn't acted upon the thought of killing, but he could and he was likely going too, he wanted too. Sickened with himself, he took a drink from a bottle of hard liquor that Jessie had left him, only to finished dressing and packing for the travel, leaving the room bare, he took another drink.

Jessie, Queen Katherine and three other guards; Sir Dave, Sir Calvin and Sir Matthews, met Zavier at the gates to the castle.

Katherine smiled extending her hand towards Zavier, her dark green cloak blowing lightly as she turned towards him, Zavier took her hand giving her a small kiss, as she spoke. "A good morning to set sail, do you not agree, sir Zavier?"

"Haven't seen one better." It was true, that morning the skies were clear and the wind blew eagerly, the waters seemed at ease.

"Let's hope this is a sign from the gods of a victorious encounter." Queen Katherine smiled as she began to walk forward.

Every villager was out in the streets to wish their queen and their soldier's victory. Katherine looked determined for this battle, her black dress, with a gold belt, made her look fierce, her hair tied back into a braid and her face had preparedness written all over it, by the scornful brows as she stepped through her city, head held high, as if with a chance this was the last time her people would see her.

Finally after reaching the docks they were welcomed by her two children, Jasmine and Edward. Jasmine smiled and bowed gracefully towards her mother, "Save sails, come back to us, mother." Her long blonde hair curled down her lavender dress.

While her son stood at the ready waiting for Katherine to address him. Kissing her daughter on the cheek then placing a soft, yet strong hand on her son's shoulder, "Protect your sister and your country while I am gone."

"I should be accompanying you, mother." Edward protested.

"You have other duties here to attend to my son. I need you to watch over your sister, ensure me she will not get to any trouble."

"Yes, ma'am," Edward smiled as Katherine kissed him on the forehead.

The siblings hugged their mother and watched her board the ship. Katherine waved to her people and heading to bow. The wind blew her hair wildly and she smiled at the anticipation.

Within the hour, they had set sail and it wasn't long before the boundaries of Stormwall were well out of view.

Jessie and Zavier were on the deck dealing with weapon maintenance and backup plans and the overall outline of how those days were going to lay out. Jessie informed Zavier of the tricks around the Mountain Kingdom, the servant's passages that were closed off for many years and the sewer system that laid under the prison cells.

"There is a sewer hole in one of the servant tunnels and through the servant tunnels we can get into and out of the prison cells in minutes," Jessie placed his finger on a wall entrance on the map and looked from Zavier towards another soldier Galvan, "Galvan here can pick the lock in under a minute, if we time it right, we can have Allister out and be back down in the sewers in under three minutes."

Zavier looked at the outline for the prison cells and where the doors and entrances were located. "There are going to be soldiers crawling at every inch of the prison, I'll go in first and clear the room. I'm the stealthiest."

Jessie stood back from the map and looked at Zavier, "I'm not denying that you are the stealthiest, but are you sure? Wouldn't it be better to just rush them, we are in and out in three minutes; we don't need too much silence. We can handle any guards who rush to the scene no problem."

Zavier shook his head and his eyes locked onto Jessie's, "No, we can't risk messing this up. I can do it."

There was an anger in Zavier's eyes that caused Jessie to agree, at this point, there was no reason to disagree with him. Jessie crossed his arms, "Okay, if we enter at night, even if you are tipped off by the guards, the reinforcement will be minimal. You, Galvan, Henry, Jorden and I will take a row boat ahead of the ship, there is an old fishing dock and on the shoreline, we can travel into the sewers from there. We should be unnoticed, then we can take Allister through the sewers and back on the ship without any complications."

"We hope," Zavier said looking down at the map.

Jessie was beginning to worry about Zavier on this mission, being captive in the Volcanic Spire clearly had changed him, was he going to be able to do this mission, he wondered silently.

Chapter 28

It was late into the second night of sailing, Valkyrie, Savanna and Allison still had been unnoticed by the crew; the chef brought food down to them and made sure no one entered the lower cabins. Telling people that it was all being used for extra storage, no one questioned him. Valkyrie was laying on the bed, her baby to her breast when Savanna sat down at the desk and pulled a folded piece of parchment from her breast pocket. Allison stood at the attention waiting for Valkyrie's reaction.

"What's that?" Valkyrie asked as Savanna handed it to her.

Allison took Castriel and rocked her softly in her arms before speaking for Savanna, "I was given to it from Jessie. He asked me to give it to you once they were out of sight."

Valkyrie sat up and unfolded the parchment; her hands trembled as she read the first few words. My dear Valkyrie, I'm sorry. She already began to cry, as she folded up the parchment again, "I don't want to read this. Reading this is admitting we will fail, reading this is admitting to myself that he is gone." Valkyrie stood and headed for the door, "Keep Castriel with you, I'll be back."

Allison hushed Castriel as she started to fuss in her arms, "Valkyrie, what are you going to do?"

Valkyrie turned around as she opened the door, "I don't know." And she walked out of the room and headed for the decks, Savanna following behind the irrational girl. She dried her eyes and pushed through the doors, it was dark and most the sailors were below decks, but at the bow of the boat, leaning on the railing alone, there was Jessie, she stormed over there, unsure of what she was going to say, or do. A few sailors noticed her, but said nothing, nor did anything. Valkyrie had already walked up the stairs, her red hair blowing everywhere as the wind pushed at her, her white shirt stuck against her body. Jessie has heard someone approaching and turned, surprised by the sight of the woman. He went to open his mouth, when Valkyrie punched him in the nose, as hard as she could.

Shocked, confused, bleeding and frozen he just stared at the woman. Valkyrie's eyes burned red, as she fought back the urge to cry and she pulled the letter into Jessie's view, "When did Allister give this to you? Why did you take so long to give this to me? Why were you such a coward that you couldn't give it to me yourself!"

Jessie looked at the girl and subdued the anger of that fact that she had managed on the boat to answer her, "He gave it to me the night before we went to rescue you, he asked me to give it to you, but I took it upon myself withhold it from you until the right time and the right time was when you were supposed to be safe back at Stormwall." Valkyrie clenched her fist, ready to hit him again, but Jessie grabbed her wrist and raised his hand "Let me explain, please?" Savanna stood behind the enraged girl, her arms crossed over her broad chest.

Valkyrie ripped her hand from Jessie's and crossed her arms, waiting for him to continue.

"You were collapsing under yourself, emotionally you were unstable and your stress levels were a risk to yourself and the baby. You didn't even want to care for yourself when we first boarded the ship. Would what Allister said in that letter have made it better? I doubt it, you would have begun blaming yourself more than you already had. You had your unborn child to worry about, but you were in such distraught, that you couldn't… I should have given it to you the day you gave birth to Castriel, but you were happy and I didn't want to ruin that happy moment for you. Then we got the letter from Jason, stating the day of the execution. I realized that if I gave you the letter than, knowing that we were leaving, there would have been no way to convince you to stay, seems that even without giving you the letter. Zavier was not able to convince you to stay."

Valkyrie turned away from Jessie, she hated that she understood his reasoning, she was absolutely distraught, she didn't want to do anything, but she was angry that she was agreeing with his reasoning. "I'm still mad at you."

"I am mad that you are on this boat, how did you even get on? Where is Castriel?"

"Chef's bunkers," Savanna added to the conversation.

Valkyrie looked away, "Allison and Savanna snuck us on shortly after Zavier came to inform me that you were leaving for a rescue mission."

Jessie laughed, "Are you telling me, that when I gave Allison the letter, you were already tucked safely on the boat?"

Valkyrie nodded and let out an awkward laugh as she started to cry again she trembled. Jessie placed his arms around her shoulders and pulled her into a hug, holding her there for a moment, before releasing her with a smile, "You are staying with Queen Katherine, at all times, can you at least agree to that?"

Valkyrie nodded and wiped her eyes, "If you need me, though."

"We need you to be away from the battle, if we do rescue Allister and say you are captured or harmed, Allister will not forgive himself again and we will end in a worst situation then we are now."

"Okay, I understand…" Valkyrie wished she didn't understand but she did.

"Let's go get Castriel and your brother. Some fresh sea air for the baby? If Castriel is here when Zavier sees you, I doubt he is going to get angry with you." Jessie smiled and headed down the stairs, he didn't want to admit how angry he was that she was here, now risking her and her child's life, but he had to try to understand her point of view, this was the man she loved, this was the father of her child. Jessie tried to think what he'd do in this situation and he couldn't. He wasn't a parent, he could never be the mother in this situation, he could never feel defenseless due to having a child in his body, no matter what he tried to think, he couldn't imagine how Valkyrie had been feeling, how she was feeling.

Allister knew he was luckier than Zavier, they needed him alive, they needed him presentable and able to speak before a crowd; but in the same sense Zavier was luckier then Allister, they needed him alive, meaning that this torture and torment wasn't going to end until his execution, he couldn't hope that one day they'd just grow tired of playing around with him and just kill him, end it there. Jason made sure not to bruise, or bloody Allister's face anymore, he wanted Allister to look perfect for his public appearance. When he beat him, trying to drill in the idea that Allister was no better than his father, that he was Edward Ironfist son and deserved the same fate as his father before him.

Allister was tied down to a chair, still stripped of his clothes, Jason's hand clenched around Allister's throat, while a knife marked his already bloodied skin. "Who are you?" Jason asked as he pressed the blade against Allister's abdomen. Allister looked passed Jason and bit down on his lip, trying not to tremble against the feeling on the blade rip through his skin. "Just tell me what I want to hear and I can stop this." Again, he said nothing, his body tensed as Jason dug the blade deeper, marking Allister's abdomen before moving up to his chest and scaring in the name Ironfist into his skin.

Allister tried to squirm away as it became unbearable; two soldiers grabbed hold of Allister as Jason continued to carve him. Grinding his teeth, one of the soldiers clasped his hand over Allister's mouth, as he screamed out, even muffled you could hear the pain down the hall. Eyes filled with tears, blood pouring down his body, Allister shook as Jason finally threw the blade to the ground and smiled, "You are your father's son, you may not admit it now, but we have time still, you will admit it. Want me to tell you the things we did to Zavier? The things you could have stopped us from doing, but that's in your nature. You and your father don't care about others. You just care about yourself. Zavier went through almost a year, of pain worse than this and you let him." Jason leaned in as the guard removed his hand from Allister's mouth. Allister's pained breathing excited him, as he leaned into a whisper, "We broke him, his mind, his soul, his body, but having you sacrifice yourself for him, after all, what he suffered through, it was what truly destroyed him. We left him with no reason to want to live when he managed to sleep, he tossed and turned with terrors of what we did to him and now he's going to have to live with that. Live with a year of torment, for nothing. You made his sacrifice meaningless."

Allister panted silently, looking down at himself, Jason was right, Zavier went through hell for him and look where it brought them? The same outcome he was trying to stop. Allister trembled and managed to speak, silently that Jason had to lean closer to hear, "No matter what you say. I am not, my father."

Jason laughed kicking Allister, his boot connecting with his chest, it knocked the chair over, Allister head hit the floor first. He could feel the blood pooling through his hair and the room went blurry. Jason pressed his boot into Allister's stomach, "What is the point in defying me? Say what I order you to say and that's the end of it!" Allister couldn't breathe as the weight pressed harder and harder against him, "You defying me makes no difference."

"If it makes no difference, why do you care?" Allister spoke, he closed his eyes the minute the words escaped his mouth and he regretted it.

The soldiers rolled the chair on its side, as Jason continuously kicked Allister in the stomach and ribs, coughing up blood and wheezing, as the room still spun Jason finally grew tired of this when Allister went limp his face pressed against the cold floor, blood covered him.

"Clean him up and get him out of my sight." Jason snarled sitting down on the throne and wiping Allister's blood off his shoe. Cutting the binds holding Allister to the chair, he just rolled limply, grabbing Allister's arms, they dragged the nearly unconscious Allister out of the throne room and back to his prison.

Throwing him inside, Allister slightly more aware tried to push himself from the ground, but his arms gave up and he just laid there, bleeding on his childhood bedroom floor.

Silvia entered the room, her black robes that barely covered herself, as she huddled over to Allister and placed her hand on his back. Allister flinched at first, but her voice calmed him and he allowed her to help him to his feet, "I'm here to help."

With her help, Allister managed to get to his feet, he reached for the bed frame, as he vomited, the room still spun. Silvia led him to the bed and sat him down before turning towards the door to grab her supplies. Placing a cloth into a bucket she strained it slightly, then placed it against the back of Allister's head.

"If you feel sick again, just tell me. I may be able to get something to help you with that."

"What's the point?" Allister asked leaning his head against the bed frame and Silvia had no answer for him. She was surprised on Allister's age, she had been told many things about him, many stories that her brother had been trying to drill into his men and the people around them about how much of a tyrant Allister would become if given power, but this man he spoke of was just a boy. "Just relax, I have you safe for now." Silvia sat down next to Allister, who limped over, but she caught him, keeping him from falling off the bed. Keeping Allister upright she cleaned his head wound and bandaged it tightly, she laid him down, keeping his head tilted to the side, as she began cleaning his chest and face, by the time she was halfway done, she had blood up and down her arms. She was horrified looking at this poor boy's body. There was no reason he deserved this.

Allister was barely conscious and he started to mumble as he started to black out, "I deserved this… I am my father's son."

Silvia slapped his face lightly to wake him up, his eyes fluttered for a moment, then he stared at her as she whispered softly, "You don't deserve this. Don't let him win, make him believe he won, but don't let him win. With your final breath, let your people know, that he will never win." Silvia softly wiped the blood from his chest and covered his lower half in a blanket, "Rest now, I'll be here to ensure the guards leave you be."

With that Allister closed his eyes and went limp, Silvia finished dressing his wounds, but remained at his side, as the soldiers' eyes bore down on her. She tried to ignore how uncomfortable she was as they watched her, but she knew what they had been doing to him and felt the need to protect him, as Zavier tried to protect her.

Silvia sat next to Allister on the bed, checking his breathing and pulse often, it was erratic, as if he was having a nightmare, but he seemed fine.

The guards tried to make a move towards Allister, but Silvia stood up and pointed her finger at the men, "Your prince as ordered no more harm to come to him till he's recovered. Back off." The guards laughed, but she stood strong, but they backed off from Allister. Instead, they grabbed Silvia by the wrist and pushed her up against the wall. She just closed her eyes as they pushed themselves upon her; she at this point wasn't affected by it, rather herself then Allister.

When the men were done, they tossed her back towards the bed and sat down on the two chairs smiling as if a job well done.

Silvia adjusted her dress and placed her hand on Allister's forehead, checking for a fever, before placing the blood-stained cloth on his forehead, sweat pooled down the boy's face. What was he dreaming about she wondered, trying to avert her eyes from the guards who stared at her and Allister smugly.

Chapter 29

Queen Katherine wasn't angry that Valkyrie had snuck on the boat, with Savanna, Allison and the baby, she was angry that Valkyrie didn't just come forward with her plan, as Katherine was all for her accompanying them. Katherine was glad to have her niece in her arms and she expected nothing less from Savanna.

The weeks had been long and finally, as midnight grew near, so did the Mountain Kingdoms, Queen Katherine, Jessie, Zavier and Valkyrie all stood at the bow and watched as the rocky-mountains grew near.

Jessie, Zavier, Galvan, Henry and Jorden all were dressed as their boat was prepared. The three soldiers were waiting by the boat, waiting for Jessie and Zavier.

Valkyrie frowned, "I should be with you. I am one of the best fighters you have ever trained Zavier."

"I know, but you have other things to worry about then crawling through a sewer. Take care of Castriel and we will be back. I promise." Zavier wrapped his arms around her and held her tightly. Valkyrie was worried about her brother, he was different, she could tell as he tightly held her in his arms and she was worried that he had been affected by what he had suffered through more than he was telling them. It was true, she loved having a brother who wasn't ashamed of showing his affection and a brother who wasn't afraid of shaming her by being related, but if that was different, was his morals gone as well? Valkyrie pushed her brother away and placed a hand on his shoulders, "Be safe. I don't want to lose both you and Allister." Zavier smiled and turned away, after he said goodbye to Castriel, her tiny hand gripping his finger as he turned to leave. Jessie started to walk behind Zavier, but Valkyrie threw herself at him, wrapping her arms around him, "Thank you and be safe as well."

Jessie was thrown off, but he thanked the affection as he placed a hand on her shoulder, "I will do everything in my power to make things right."

Valkyrie smiled and walked the boys' to their boat, as Katherine bounced Castriel in her arms, "Sail well men and may your mission be successful." Katherine called out as she bowed to her men, her soldiers and Zavier saluted her and entered the boat, as it lowered down into the black waters. Valkyrie leaned over the ledge and watched as her brother rowed off silently into the night. Queen Katherine handed Valkyrie back Castriel, as they all watched the five of them disappear into the darkness.

Once they could no longer see the ship in the darkness Jessie turned to Zavier as he took one of the paddles, "Zavier, are you alright? You were a prisoner for a very long time and you haven't spoken at all about it."

"There is nothing to speak about, I was a prisoner and many of the things you'd expect from that happened to me. No need to go into detail of the ordeal, while someone else is currently in need of our assistance."

Jessie sighed loudly, "You people are so stubborn when someone tries to help you, why don't you just take the help?"

Zavier laughed, "Thank you for thinking about my wellbeing, but I am fine. I can face my demons alone."

"But there is no reason to face them alone, the same thing I said to Allister." Zavier had to turn away from Jessie, but he spoke the truth, "You and I, have had our differences and our battles, but you spared me and my allies that day and you kept the person I was supposed to keep safe, alive. If you can't trust me, at least talk to Valkyrie about it, she really cares about you."

"I would think she'd need my support, more then I'd need hers."

"Sometimes caring about someone else, takes away from thinking about your own problems." Jessie left it at that and continued to row the boat towards the shore.

Zavier took a deep breath and questioned his words as he spoke aloud, "I broke." Jessie didn't direct eye contact towards the man as he spoke, "If it was someone else in my place, they might not say they broke, but I did. I showed them my hand."

Jessie finally looked up at Zavier's face, he wanted to say something but he didn't dare.

Henry turned towards Jessie, "Sir, the sewer opening is in view." Jessie nodded as they turned the boat slightly, adjusting their position, within minutes of spotting the tunnel, they were pulling the boat ashore and hiding it under seaweed and bush.

Jessie jumped into the sewer and lit a torch once far enough inside, "I'll lead the way, stick close, it's easy to get lost in here and if we do get separated, the person who ends up alone, try to make their way back to the boat, don't try to catch back up with the group. We won't leave without any of you."

Everyone nodded and followed Jessie silently. It took an hour to get through the castle sewer systems, you knew when you reached the end, as there was a large iron gate blocking the path to the servant tunnels. Galvan went to work, it took him thirty seconds to pick the lock, with a simple click, the door opened and they piled in.

Jorden was the second behind Jessie and he spoke softly, "Are we sure that guards won't be roaming the servant tunnels?"

Jessie shook his head, "I doubt they know about them, they were also used encase of an invasion, the servants would take the royal treasures and sometimes the queen and king down here for safe keeping."

Zavier raised his brow, "If they are for protection, why didn't you take Allister and the king down here when the Mountain Kingdom was taken over?"

"Edmond didn't think they would breach the castle, I asked him if I could take Allister, but he told me to barricade him in his room till it passed over. He was a stubborn, stupid man. The only good thing that came out of that war was his death."

Zavier wondered for a moment, what would have happened if Jessie had taken Allister through the tunnels, or even if Edmond didn't get killed that night. How different everything would be. Though he had to snap out of it, they were reaching the prison cells.

Jessie waved Zavier forward, "There is the opening, are you sure you want to go alone?"

"Yes, I'll be fine."

"Fine, just yell if you need us."

Zavier removed his blade from its sheath and pushed the door open a crack, slipping through. He was ready for at least six guards throughout the prison, but it was empty. The cells and everything was bare, knocking on the entrance, Jessie and them exited the servant tunnels. Zavier asked, "If he's not here, where would he be?"

Jessie inspected the cells, "It doesn't look like these have been used in years." He grunted angrily, "If Jason's aim is to break Allister, where would he keep him if not in the prison?"

Zavier rubbed his face, "He would keep him where it hurts the most. Where ever has the best memories, trying to ruin every happy thought he had."

"Fuck…" Jessie turned back and everyone piled in the tunnel, closing the door behind everyone, "There is a good chance they have him upstairs, the problem is you can't get to the upstairs tunnels through these tunnels. The only way to get into the servant tunnels for the upper levels is from the throne room."

"Is there a way to get to the throne room from here undetected?" Jordon asked as the group was unsure of what their next move was going to be.

Jessie shook his head angrily, "No, it's designed that you can't." He grunted with frustration, "The best bet would be to head back to the boat and think of another plan."

No one was happy with that option, but it was the only thing they could do.

As quickly as they had come, they exited the tunnels and pulled their boat from the seaweed and back into the water, sailing back to the mother ship, empty handed.

After explaining themselves to Queen Katherine, they waited until morning to inform the already sleeping Valkyrie.

One problem, their days were numbers, Allister's execution was closing in rapidly and now, they needed a new solution to their problem. They were beginning to lose faith in the mission, but they had to try, no matter what they had to try.

That next morning everyone was determined; Valkyrie tightened her dark leather armor around herself, placing a loose, green blouse along with black trousers and tying her black cloak over her shoulders, they were minutes from docking. A horn sounded loud, The Mountain Kingdoms knew they had arrived. Allison, Savanna and Castriel were tucked in the lowest half of the boat, hidden away for safe keeping. Even if you knew where to look, you'd not have found them. Valkyrie kissed her child farewell for now and headed up to the decks. Katherine stood tall and proud, her long golden gown flattered her tall, muscular figure perfectly. There was a determination in everyone's eyes as they docked.

Four Volcanic Spire soldiers dressed and armed to the teeth approached the boat. They dared not to unsheathe their weapons as they matched stares with Queen Katherine.

They reluctantly bowed low, "Our prince has ordered all persons for the execution of Allister Ironfist to be escorted to the kingdom personally by us." They stayed in their bow state till Queen Katherine responded.

"Rise, I am not your queen." She was cold and collected, "I wish to be escorted to your prince. In peace and respect."

The men stood tall and watched as they dropped the plank, Jessie refused to let Queen Katherine lead, as he stepped off the boat, placing himself and Galvan between the soldiers and their queen.

Katherine smiled as she could see the Volcanic Spire soldiers growing uneasy as Zavier and Valkyrie exited on the platform.

Zavier locked eyes with one soldier in particular who quickly turned away, acting as if he had nothing to do with the man.

Valkyrie could see Zavier grow tense, as she placed her hand on his wrist; Zavier took a calming breath. Zavier took Valkyrie's hand and squeezed it lightly, giving her a nod, in his way telling her he was going to be fine and she in returned smiled.

Katherine now pushed herself in between her two soldiers, "May I know your name, good knights?" Queen Katherine smiled gracefully.

The one who dared not to look at Zavier again was the first to speak, "I go by Julian and this is Yarven, Jax and Michael."

"What are your duties to your prince? Head captain?"

Julian shook his head, "No Lady Katherine, we are just foot soldiers."

"Well I should feel insulted, your Prince can't even spare the captain of his men to escort us?"

"Our apologies Queen Katherine, if we have news of your arrival ahead of time, we would have made it more of a spectacle. Not often a daughter of the Mountain Kingdom returns to her homeland."

Katherine's temper started to grow, but she just straightened her back and continued to walk as if the words coming out of the man's mouth didn't affect her.

Jessie watched the soldiers for even the slightest hint of them reaching for their blade, where Galvan and the other soldiers scouted above and around, even the slightest movement they were preparing to move.

"Are you inclined to tell me the condition of my brother currently?" Katherine asked as she looked behind at Valkyrie who had her dagger's hilt in her grip, still but barely sheathed.

Julian looked towards Michael who spoke turning his gaze towards Katherine as he spoke, "We personally have no details of the Prince Ironfist."

Katherine glared at the man and he turned around instantly. "One of you shall go ahead and inform your prince of my arrival, tell him I wish an audience. I shall bring three soldiers to this audience and he shall have no more than six. Or I will call his act, an act of war." The soldiers stopped in their tracks and all turned around the look at the woman, she crossed her arms, "Do I make myself clear?"

The soldiers looked at each other and together, "Yes Queen Katherine." Julian, could feel Zavier's glare on the back of his neck as he decided to rush ahead to inform Jason of the demands.

As Julian rushed away from the scene, the metal of his armor clanking away, Zavier closed his eyes and took his sister's hand once again. She looked up at him, his palms were sweaty and she could feel his heart pounding heavy in his chest. She stopped, forcing Zavier to stop as well and whispered, "Are you sure you are alright? You can head back to the boat and be with Castriel, Savanna and Allison."

Zavier kept his eyes closed for a second, holding his breath he calmed his heart and shook his head, placing his hand on his forehead, before releasing his sister's hand. "I'm fine, I just needed a moment."

Valkyrie wasn't sure if she believed him yet, but she squeezed his hand and continued walking, "I'm here if you need me."

It was three days before the execution. Jason was giddy with excitement; sprawled over the side of the Iron Throne, he had three girls naked standing before him; a blonde, a redhead and a darker skinned woman with black hair. The three girls looked down at their bare feet. Jason's eyes locked on the red-haired woman, he tried to compare her to Valkyrie, she was slightly tanned but frail and weak; Valkyrie had toned muscles, but he wondered if he dressed her up enough Allister would think of her while Jason took advantage of girl in front of him. He smiled wickedly as his dismissed the other two girls. The red head was pushed forward, as Jason grabbed her and pulled her onto his lap, he traced his hands down her body and in between her legs. The girl turned her head away from Jason. "Draven, fit and dress this girl for some leather armor, bruise her up a bit too." He threw the girl into Draven's arms, the soldier smiled as he grabbed both her wrist in one hand she screamed and squirmed but he pulled her into him and placed his hand over her mouth, dragging her out of the throne room. Leaning back against the Iron Throne Jason placed his hands behind his head resting, comfortably.

The Iron doors opened cautiously and Julian entered.

Jason didn't even turn his head towards the soldier, as the man approached and bowed low for his prince, "What is it?"

"The ship that docked had Queen Katherine of Stormwall and she is accompanied by Zavier and Valkyrie Dragonsbreath. Queen Katherine demands an audience with you, she proclaimed that she will bring three soldiers with her and you may have up to six, but no more, or she shall claim it as an act of war towards her."

Jason groaned and sat up on the throne, "She comes back after all these years and starts barking orders at me? Me of all people." Jason entangled his fingers together and sighed, "I will indulge the Queen; I shall meet her with five soldiers as a sign of good faith. Go order Allister dressed, he has a family reunion."

Chapter 30

Allister had recovered from the head wound and the abuse continued; one guard had him pinned against the wall, holding him up by his throat, reopening the scar of Ironfist on his chest. Any attempt to fight, Allister would get a knee to the groin. Flipping him over to have his chest against the wall the soldier went to reach for the ties of his pants. There was a knock at the door and the guard released Allister, who dropped directly to the floor, leaving a blood streak on the wall.

The soldier's conversation was inaudible to Allister who tried to keep himself steady on his knees, his head leaning against the wall.

Allister turned and looked at the soldiers as they approached, one man was carrying black trousers and a white skirt, Allister tried to laugh, but it hurt too much.

The soldiers tossed him the clothes and Allister dressed himself as quick as he could manage, which still took him a few minutes as his fingers were too tired and weak to grip the fabric. Within seconds of placing the white shirt on, it was coated in blood, slowly soaking with more and more as every second passed, but the soldiers didn't seem to care. They tied Allister's hands behind his back and dragged him out of the room and down, down the spiral staircase to the prison cells. After placing him inside, they forced him down into a chair before locking the door behind him they took a position at the door.

Jason entered the prison, he was dressed to impress someone, dark purple trousers and a blood red blouse, his crown sat upon his head, an off-shoulder cape flowed with every step. He laughed as he stepped forward to the cell, Allister didn't even bother to look up at him, "And who are you?"

Allister closed his eyes and spoke defeated, "I am the son of Edmond Ironfist and I deserve this."

"Perfect." Jason clapped his hands together, "I have a guest; Lady Katherine of Stormwall is here for an audience with me." Allister looked up, finally alert for that moment, Jason just smiled, "She brought along your friends. Maybe if you are good, I'll let your sister say goodbye." Jason bend down to be at Allister's eye level, "Who are you?"

Allister paused and looked away from Jason before reciting, "I am the son of Edmond Ironfist... I deserve this."

"Don't you forget that for a moment." Jason stood up and headed for the door, "Ensure that Allister remembers that for when his guests arrive. If he doesn't act to our standards, make sure to remind him of it at a later time."

The guards nodded and Jason left the prison, Allister dropped his head once again fighting back his emotions, he didn't want anyone to see him like this. Why would Valkyrie come for him, she had herself and their unborn child to worry about, he thought silently to himself, if she got hurt... If anyone else got hurt in his name he wasn't sure he'd be able to take it, his soul was already stained with others blood; he didn't want more pain, more death to taint him...

Valkyrie was in amazement as they walked through the city towards the Mountain Kingdom, she had never before seen the Mountain Kingdoms in person, the city was large and blooming with life, the first city to go so long without a ruler to guide them.

Katherine now took her place at the lead of their pack, even stepping ahead of the soldiers escorting them; villagers stopped and bowed low, some whispering in a gasp, "Queen Katherine." It brought a humble smile to her face, seeing the people her family had treated so poorly, showing her kindness and respect. Silently they reached the Iron gates, which was where Katherine's smile disappeared. The once luscious green grass was now dead and long, the roses that cascaded the walls was now replaced with overgrown ivy, every lawn statue had its head removed and had fallen to pieces.

Valkyrie started to feel the urge to run passed the group, run through the halls, breaking skulls and screaming bloody murder; but Zavier offered his arm to her, seeing her unsettled posture and she took it without hesitation. She didn't know where they were keeping Allister, this castle was a maze of doorways, halls and forgotten rooms; her only chance of seeing him again was to play the game.

They were halfway through the courtyard when Jason stepped out of the now opened doors, a large smirk on his face as he walked towards the group, "Queen Katherine of Stormwall, welcome and I welcome your allies, to the Mountain Kingdom." His sarcastic tone, caused all eyes on him, "I assume everyone here knows these halls well." He walked forward offering Katherine his hand she extended it and he kissed the top of her hand her retracting it back the second he released.

"Your tone does not amuse me," Katherine noted placing her fingers along her face and her other hand under her elbow studying her surroundings and Jason.

Jason snorted angrily, "Maybe a change in location will amuse you more, to the Throne room, Queen Katherine?"

Staring back at him, she waved her hand as if telling him to lead the way, he dismissed the escorts and turned back into the castle doors, heading towards the throne room.

A large oak table was set out, with five chairs, Jason sat at the head at the far end, while Katherine took the opposite head spot; Valkyrie sat on Katherine's left, Jessie of her right and Zavier stood up behind Valkyrie. Zavier stood straight and stared ahead of him, he couldn't look Jason in the eye. His heart again began to pound heavy in his chest.

Katherine placed her elbows on the table and leaned forward, "Now besides the change of colour, it looks just like it did all those years ago."

"Out of season, it was." Jason quickly replied.

Katherine placed her head on the top of her hands, crossing her fingers, "May I speak blunt with you, Prince Jason?" He waved his hand approving her to speak, "There is nothing I can offer you to have my brother back safely?"

He laughed loudly, then bluntly with a smirk, "No, nothing you have I want more than him. He is and has always been a prisoner of war, so I have the right to execute him and claim his right to the throne."

Katherine locked eyes with Jason, as he locked back, but he slowly grew unsettled with the interaction as she spoke again, "He wasn't a prisoner while under the watch of Zavier here? How do you justify that claim of yours?"

"He was forced into Zavier's custody, as his punishment for his war crimes. His people have not forgiven him for his crimes, so I am calling for a new judgment over him, a harsher punishment for his role in the murder of hundreds."

Katherine nodded, Jason finally broke eye contact and looked towards Zavier, who still wouldn't dare look at the man, in fear of how he might react. "Will you at least grant me and my escorts to see my brother?"

Jason turned back towards the Queen, "Oh course, but only you and one other may visit him, a precautionary move, you understand?" Katherine nodded, "Remember my lady, any act can be viewed as an act of war at this point."

Katherine smiled as she stood from her seat, "I wouldn't wish it another way, Prince Jason, of the Volcanic Spire." She condescending towards him, which caused Jason's smile to twitch.

"Men, lead Queen Katherine and her one escort down to Allister's cell."

Katherine waved Valkyrie up and she was to her side in a second.

"Sit Zavier, we have plenty of stories to catch up about," Jason smiled, his anger resided.

Valkyrie looked back towards Zavier, who reluctantly sat down where Valkyrie was sitting, across from Jessie. He still looked at the wall ahead of him, Jessie's face tried to hide the concern, but failed.

Queen Katherine whispered to Valkyrie, "Don't try anything while we are down there. I know it will be hard, but it is best if we remain calm and level headed."

Valkyrie nodded, she understood why Jason did what he did, he has all the cards in his hand any wrong move and Valkyrie was going to see someone she cared about hurt.

Katherine took Valkyrie's hand and held it as they walked down the halls together.

Three guards escorted the pair and when they finally reached the prison entrance they were greeted by two more outside and two more inside.

Valkyrie and Katherine walked down the stone stairs; center cell Allister sat, his hands tied behind his back, his head hung in defeat. Valkyrie fought the urge to run over to the cell, but calmly they walked hand in hand.

Katherine was the first to speak, "Allister? Baby brother." Instantly he lifted his head, his eyes wide he looked up at his sister and Valkyrie in shock.

"Valkyrie, Katherine?" His head filled with so many different emotions, he was speechless and frozen his eyes just going back and forth from the two.

Valkyrie placed her hands on the bars and held back her emotions; she conflicted whether she wanted to cry, scream, or rip at the bars, her eyes were locked on the blood-soaked shirt.

Allister shook his head clear, he managed to speak, "Why did you come here? It's not safe for you Valkyrie," He paused for a moment as he looked at her stomach, mouth open he looked back up at her.

"We had a girl. She's safe with Savanna. I named her Castriel." Valkyrie's lips trembled, but her eyes stayed dry.

"I bet she's beautiful." His voice cracked, it hurt him thinking he'd never get to hold his child, or even see her for that matter. Allister turned and looked at his sister, "It's been many years and you have to see me like this Katherine?"

"I'm sorry baby brother. I wish these circumstances were better, I really do."

"It's not your or anyone else's fault. This is my fault alone." Allister looked down at his feet as he spoke loud enough for all the guards to hear, "I am the son of Edward Ironfist and I deserve this fate." He started to cry as he spoke the words, his lips trembled slightly.

Katherine knelt down and placed her hand on the bars, "Allister, what have they done to you? You know this isn't your fault, you know that our father's actions does not define us."

Allister looked up at his sister and shook his head, "I don't know if I believe that anymore…"

Katherine snapped her fingers, "Allister, don't think this way. Where have they been keeping you?" She whispered just loud enough for Allister to hear. He replied and she continued to speak, "Do not lose faith in us Allister. I as a sister, may have failed you before-"

"You have never failed me, Katherine."

"Just understand that this isn't over. We have still have options."

Allister forced himself up from the chair, it strained him and caused him agony, but he stepped over to the bars, Valkyrie reached in and wrapped her arms around Allister, embracing him as tightly as she dared, worried that in his frail state she might hurt him more.

Allister looked at Valkyrie and they kissed between the bars, "Don't risk anyone else for me."

"Allister we aren't leaving you to be killed for something you didn't do," Katherine spoke standing up.

"This needs to happen Katherine." Valkyrie released Allister and he continued to speak sadly, "This will never end and I can't have you drag me back to Stormwall and think about what Jason is going to do to this place. This is where I belong, this is the fate I was born with."

"Either way, he is going to ruin these lands, my soldiers can stop this. Either way, we are going to war, it doesn't have to start over your death, Allister listen to reason."

Allister kneeled in pain, his voice was now raspy and labored, "I just don't want to see any of you get hurt anymore."

Valkyrie kneeled placing her hand on Allister's back, "And we don't want to have to watch you die for nothing." Allister turned and looked at Valkyrie and Katherine, "Allister, I love you and we all care about you." Allister had almost forgotten the look of love Valkyrie gave him, it caused himself pain looking at her, knowing that he had given up on a life with her, that's what he was telling her, he was telling Valkyrie to give up on their life together, because he didn't want to fight anymore. Finally, Allister realized that if he died, or lived, it was going to end the same way, the war was coming.

"Okay… I'll hold on a bit longer."

Katherine smiled and placed her hand on her brother's face, "Reserve your strength, you will need it soon." She whispered something to him, even Valkyrie missed it, while he just nodded. "Valkyrie, we should return to Jessie and your brother."

Back in the throne room, Jason was grinning from ear to ear, as he watched Zavier struggling to control his emotions. His nails were digging into his knees and he bit down painfully on the inside of his lip, Zavier could taste his own blood and that made everything even harder.

Jessie didn't know what to do, every time he tried to move Jason's topics from Zavier's ordeal, but the man would just turn it back around on him.

"Zavier, you haven't told anyone about what we did to you have you? Sir Jessie got to be the first to hear of your ordeals? Oh, how sweet, I bet you didn't even inform your lovely little half sister of all those cold nights, all the torture. Has she seen your brands? Have you Jessie? They are a lovely sight. We left him with nothing. He is just an empty shell, what was Zavier is left in a cold, wet dungeon back at the Volcanic Spire kingdom."

"For someone, you claim to be broke, he seems to be the most stable person in this room," Jessie responded quickly, he almost regretted it, he had to be careful with what he said to Jason. If he angered the man, Zavier and himself could be in a lot of trouble and seeing the colour leaving Zavier's face and the deep breathing he wasn't sure how much fight Zavier would have in him. He was genuinely concerned for him.

Jason tapped on the table with his fingers eyes still on Zavier, but Jessie could feel the anger turning towards himself. "Is it funny? That you went through all that pain, mentally, physically and look where we are? Exactly where I wanted." He placed a lot of emphasis on the 'I' and he leaned back in his chair.

Zavier turned his head towards the door, closing his eyes he took a deep breath, his heart was pounding hard in his chest, with every word Jason spoke, the room got smaller and smaller. He just needed to get out of there, or he started to question what he was going to do to Jason. His fury towards Jason caused him to be unable to see clearly, alongside with thinking.

"Sir Jessie, your ally seems rather unstable. Maybe being a bastard since he had no father to toughen him up."

"Leave Zavier alone. You are only bitter with him, because, in every way you have tested him, he has come out victorious." Jessie locked eyes with the shocked Jason and the pair just stared at each other for a moment.

Zavier took another deep breath and turned to the door as Katherine and Valkyrie walked in, there was a sigh of relief in him as he immediately stood from his seat.

Valkyrie and Katherine could see the distress in his eyes and Katherine spoke firmly, "We shall take our leave now. Thank you for being a gracious host."

Jason stood up from his chair and bowed his head to Queen Katherine, "It's my honor to host a Queen in her own home."

His condescending tone made Katherine want to walk over and smack the smile off the man's face, but she just bowed slightly and turned herself from the man, Zavier and Jessie both rushed to her side and just as they were about to leave Jason called out to them one last time, "I will look for you at Allister's execution tomorrow." No one reacted to Jason's call, they just walked away in silence.

Zavier took short strides, trying to calm himself down, telling himself he needed to be a strong brother for his sister, he had to forget his own problems and deal with what they were faced currently.

Jessie slowed down and walked beside him placing his hand on Zavier's shoulder, he walked beside him for support. Valkyrie couldn't even tremble, she couldn't cry, or break down, she just walked, head held high and strong, she had to be strong.

Zavier knew the struggle that Valkyrie must be feeling and he wanted to be there to support her; so with all his strength he tried to push his own emotions to the back of his head. Giving Jessie a quick nod, Zavier stepped up beside Valkyrie and placed his hand on hers. Valkyrie leaned her head on her brother and bit softly on her lip. It wasn't going to get any easier for the group, they had many more struggles to overcome.

Jessie kept his eye on Zavier, he was worried for the man; Zavier was a selfless person and being that way, in his condition, it was going to get himself killed.

Chapter 31

Allister was dragged back to his room once Valkyrie and everyone had returned to the ship; Jason was waiting on the bed staring at the now open balcony doors. The guards held onto Allister's arms tightly as they brought him forward to their king. "What did you tell your friends?"

Allister took a small shaky breath, "I said what you asked me too, I am the son of Edward Ironfist and I deserve this fate." He tried to be brave, but he was scared, he was already in pain and he knew more was coming.

Jason sighed and walked through the balcony doors, waving his hand for the guards to follow with Allister, "See, I want to believe you, Allister. I really do, but if you are like your allies. You grow, you find strength in each other and strength means defiance to me." Jason grabbed Allister by the hair and leaned him over the ledge of the balcony. Allister dared not to struggle, he barely dared to breathe. "Do you feel powerless? Your allies are so close to you, yet they can do nothing to save you if I wanted I could go have them all killed tonight." Jason pulled Allister back over the ledge into the guards' arms, Allister stumbled but they pulled him to his feet, "I won't have them killed tonight, but only because I want them to watch to die tomorrow." Allister's heart began to pound, Jason placed his hand on Allister's neck and smiled as he could feel his pulse race. "Where is that bravery I'd expect from an Ironfist, from one of Zavier's prized students?" Jason smiled and walked back into the bedroom, the guards followed with Allister, "Hold him down on the ground." Jason ordered pulling out his knife.

Pushing him to the ground, one guard pressed his weight on Allister's shoulders, while the over grabbed his feet. Allister squirmed and tried to pull himself away from Jason, but he stood over him, taunting him as he swung the blade back and forth. Kneeling now over Allister, he cut the fabric of his shirt and placed the metal of his blade on Allister's still unhealed wounds. The still bloody marks spelling out Ironfist were beginning to become infected and still oozed slightly with blood. Allister's lip quivered as the blade inched closer to his skin. Jason smiled as he stabbed the blade into Allister's chest recurving his outline over and over again. One guard placed his hand firmly over Allister's mouth and nose; blood and puss from the wound oozed down Allister body, his screams muffled and slowly he was being suffocated, Jason took his time on him.

Finally with his hands soaked in blood Jason stood up and snapped his fingers; the guys released Allister and he rolled onto his side gasping in pain as tears streamed down his face, with a quivering lips he muttered over and over again, "I am the son of Edward Ironfist, I deserve this..."

Jason laughed of course, proud of his work, "Rest up Allister, tomorrow we have an audience to please."

The guards closed the balcony doors and pulled Allister off the floor and tossed him onto the bed.

Jason walked towards the door, turning back at the guards, "Don't rough him up too much tonight. We do need him presentable tomorrow."

Allister just laid with his chest against the bed, his blood soaking into the blankets and closed his eyes; he wanted this to be over. Tonight, was likely to be his last, but as he closed his eyes he searched hard to find the little shimmer of hope that Valkyrie, Zavier, Jessie and Katherine would succeed and he held on to it tightly.

This night was just beginning for Allister and he knew it too well; luckily enough the guards needed him conscious in the morning, so their assault only lasted a few hours, as always being careful not to bruise his face. Finally, they stopped; themselves covered in Allister's blood, the smiled and strapped Allister wrists to the bed posts.

That morning when Zavier woke, he was drenched in sweat, panting he placed his hand in his hair and pulled trying to pull himself from his night terrors. When he woke in the dark cabin of the ship he thought he was there again, he thought he was still prisoned in the Volcanic Spire kingdom. It's not real. It's not your reality anymore, Zavier told himself as he tucked his legs to his chest and buried his face into his legs.

There was a loud knock at his door, Zavier sat up straight on the bed and looked as calm as possible. "You may enter." He said as calmly as he could. His words broke and his heart still pounded heavy in his ears.

Jessie hesitantly opened the door and walked in before closing the door behind him. Zavier couldn't hide the distress on his face and he really tried. Jessie stayed at the door and studied the mess of a man before him, he wasn't what he remembered from all those years-ago. He was a mess. "Zavier, do you need to talk about what happened? Is what Jason said true? Did they really do that all to you?" Jessie looked at the bare chested man and he could see the burned in brands and knew the truth in

Jason's words.

Zavier gripped his knees and looked down, "Don't tell Valkyrie what you heard."

"If that really all happened to your Zavier you need to talk to someone about it, deal with whatever you are going through with some help. I'm in the cabin next to you and I heard everything last night. You aren't okay. No one would be okay after what you went through"

Zavier stood up from the bed and sighed loudly, "I will deal with all this once this mission is over. Right now, I need to just push it to the back of my mind and be there for my sister. While trying to save Allister. That's all that currently matters." There was determination now in Zavier's eyes.

Jessie shook his head, "Are you sure you are mentally fit for this? I wouldn't blame you if you weren't, if I went through even half of what you did, I wouldn't have come back alive from it all."

"Jessie, I get that you are trying to be helpful, but like I said I am fine for now. I just need to do this. I can't sit back and do nothing."

Jessie crossed his arms and leaned against the door looking at the man, studying the man, looking for signs of instability. "Okay, I won't tell you to back down from this fight, but promise me one thing, for your sister and for Allister, if you start to feel distressed you will fall back?"

"I won't promise you anything. But I will say this, I have no plans to die today."

Jessie laughed, "Don't we all, Zavier. Now get dressed, we head for the city within the hour."

Zavier was the last to arrive; Valkyrie had Castriel on her boob while rocking the baby softly back and forth. Jessie was next to Queen Katherine directing his other soldiers on their duties. Zavier and Jessie were the only two soldiers to be hidden in the crowd, slowly without being noticed they were ordered to get on either side of the execution block, only to wait on Queen Katherine's order, or in case all goes sour at the last minute to save Allister's life. Jessie was uneasy about letting Zavier be the other person in the crowd, thinking that if Prince Jason didn't see him if he would be tipped off, but Jessie wasn't able to convince Zavier to stay back.

Castriel started to cry and all eyes went from worried thoughts of the mission ahead, to the baby, the baby in Valkyrie's hands was a symbol of hope in that moment, the innocence.

Savanna walked up and took the baby from Valkyrie, snuggling the baby warmly in her arms. Valkyrie tied her armor tightly and began to strap her weapons in their sheaths and on her belt's. Savanna looked at the group and then to the baby before speaking, "This isn't going to be the popular thought, but for the chance that you fail… And Allister's life isn't saved, may I bring Castriel? Give him the chance to see his child for the first and possibly only time?"

Zavier and Jessie both perked up and together spoke sternly. "No, out of the question." They both looked at each other then back to Valkyrie, who wasn't disagreeing to the notion.

Valkyrie paused looking towards the Mountain Kingdom, just beyond their view, "I want to say no, only because by saying yes I am admitting there is a change to fail." She took a long drawn out sigh and turned back to her child and Savanna, "I do not wish to be selfish here so just keep her safe, for me."

Jessie objecting instantly, "We are starting a battle today, do you really think it's a smart idea to bring an infant into a battle zone?"

Valkyrie cocked her brow and crossed her arms looking at Jessie, "Is this your child we are speaking about? No. She is mine and Allister's. I trust Savanna's abilities to keep my child safe and if it does happen that we are unsuccessful, I want Allister's to have a chance to see her."

"I think Valkyrie is right, bringing the child is a smart idea." Queen Katherine added, "Two of my guards will escort Lady Savanna in the crowd."

Jessie sighed placed his hand over his eyes, "Queen Katherine, do you understand what you are telling us to do?"

"Sir Jessie we have been over this, I am your Queen and I do not need to be patronized for my decision," Katherine smiled as she lifted her skirt and strapped a large dagger to her thigh.

Jessie just bowed, he was tired of arguing and their time was running up.

Morning came too quick for Allister; his body was stiff and every part of his ached.

Silvia entered the room; nicely folded clothes, a bucket and washcloths in her arms, she looked defeated as she walked through the bedroom and towards Allister. She looked over the bloodied barely conscious Allister and sighed sadly, untying his wrists from the bed post. She helped Allister to a seated position, he wasn't even able to keep his head up straight. "I'm sorry Allister, I wish there was something I could do to help you." Grabbing a cloth from the bucket she rinsed it out and carefully washed the dried and still wet blood off his chest, she has specific orders to ensure that the words carved into his chest were visible and well cleaned.

Allister didn't even speak to her, his eyes were glazed over; he was broken, emotionless and ready for this to end. Even though this end, was just the beginning for the Mountain Kingdoms. Allister wondered what fate had in store for the people he was once part of, for the people his family destroyed, for the people he failed. Allister sat with his arms limp at his side, finally he lifted his head and straightened his shoulders, "Do you believe in something after death?"

Silvia looked up as she strained the bloodied cloth into the bucket, "Yes, sometimes I feel envious of those who die; I imagine a place so much brighter than here. Even those who do terrible things, I wish them a better place in death."

"I hope you are right…"

"Don't you have any faith left in your allies?"

Allister managed the smallest smile on the corner of his lips, his eyes still glazed over, "I know they will try everything in their power to save me, but Jason is as determined as they are to have me killed."

Silvia finished washing the blood and handed Allister the clothes, thick black cotton trousers, a white shirt and a dark red cloak with a gold tie and white trim. With Silvia's help, Allister dressed and then she shaved his face and combed his hair back.

"Did you ever see my father?"

Silvia curiously looked at Allister, "I've seen a portrait of him."

"Do I look like him today?"

Silvia shook her head, "No, you look like an innocent boy named Allister, who happens to share a name."

Allister didn't even manage a smile there, as the guards pushed her aside, Allister placed his wrists out before him and they placed the iron shackles around him.

Noon was nearing; his time was running out.

Jason and six well-armoured guards entered the room, the soldiers were in the ceremonial plate, as the Volcanic Spire sigil was new and the armor was undented, unmarked and polished. Jason smiled as he pulled a crown out from behind his back, "Ready to face your people?"

Allister stood up on his own and walked towards Jason, "It's time to accept my fate."

Jason's smirk grew into a full smile as he placed the crown on Allister's head, two soldiers grabbed Allister's arms and with Jason leading the way, they made their way down the halls, towards the courtyard.

Allister took every second walking through the halls as a moment to reflect, to remember what good memories he had, to remember who and what he was going to lose today, but as much as he wanted to remember this castle in some light, all he could see was Valkyrie and what he imagined their daughter looked like, he imagined what their life would be if he was there, not walking to his death. Seeing her first words, first steps; Allister wondered if she had Valkyrie's eyes or her red hair. Allister bit his lip, he couldn't cry, not now, he placed a dead emotionless expression on his face and held it there.

Jason and the soldiers stopped at the doors leading out to the courtyard, Jason turned and placed his hands on Allister's shoulders tightly squeezing them, "I warn you Allister Ironfist, make a fool of me and I will never stop hunting your allies, I will ensure that your sister, Valkyrie and Zavier never have a moment of peace of me."

Allister looked down at his feet before looking Jason in the eye, defiance filled his eyes, "If I die here today, my allies will never give you a moment of peace."

Jason scowled at the comment, but Allister knew it was the truth if he was going to die today, Valkyrie, Zavier and maybe even Jessie weren't going to rest until Jason reign was ended.

Opening the door, the sun warmed them in the Mountain Kingdom's warm summer glow. Allister took a deep breath walking bravely to his final trial.

There was a large wooden platform, the deck was at head height above the crowd, then in the distance on top of the wall Allister saw Valkyrie, Katherine and some unknown guards, but Valkyrie could have been the only person there, as he was the only person he looked at. They locked glances and Katherine held tightly onto Valkyrie's hand unsure if she was going to make a run for him through the crowd.

Jason again was unpleased in the reaction of the crowd, as the villagers of the Mountain Kingdoms did not seem pleased, their eyes were filled with sadness as they looked at their defeated prince, silence washed over them.

Jason pulled Allister to the front and center of the platform and whispered in his ear, drawing his blade and placing it secretly against Allister's backbone, "Speak to your people."

Allister closed his eyes for a moment, as he looked away from Valkyrie towards the crowd of people, these were his people. The people he was born to protect. "I am Allister Ironfist. The one and only born son of Edward Ironfist," There was no emotion in his tone, he was just reciting what Jason wanted him too, " I am the one true and rightful heir to the Mountain Throne. My father and my father's father before me have wronged you in many ways." The crowd was dead silent, Allister lost his words as he tried to recompose himself, Jason's blade digging into the skin of his back, but he froze, in the crowd, he saw her. Savanna holding a little child tightly in her arms. Allister knew that was his baby and seeing her there, he wondered were Zavier and Jessie where.

The soldiers under Jason's cue cut Allister's shirt at the sleeves revealing the scars on his chest.

Allister looked towards Valkyrie whose hand was over her mouth, near tears, the crowd held their breath and Jason stepped forward, "This man is proud of his bloodline, these self-inflicted marks prove that to you, good people. If he was given the right to the throne, he would turn to be a worse ruler than his father before him. He has the blood of a Tyrant in his veins and today I am cleaning these lands of the potential for tragedy." Jason turned back towards Allister, the crowd not agreeing with Jason's speech, "Finish this Allister."

"I Allister Ironfist, the rightful ruler to the Mountain Kingdoms hand over all rights to the throne…" He paused again, frozen as Valkyrie leap from the edge, Queen Katherine having lost her grip on Valkyrie. Allister could almost hear the heel of her boots rushing through the crowd, as his sister signaled something with her free hand. Allister closed his eyes, unable to look towards the direction of the approaching Valkyrie as he spoke these words, "I give all right to the throne to the people of the Mountain Kingdoms," Quickly he tried to finish as he could feel Jason move the blade from his back, "Do not let the Volcanic Spire take the freedom-" His words were cut off as Jason's blade cut through his back and pierced through his chest and spine, choking on his blood Allister lost sight of Valkyrie, but saw Zavier, his face filled with anger and denial.

Jason held his blade deep inside Allister, holding him up in place as he spat angrily in his ear, "These people are still mine. You do not win Allister Ironfist." Pulling the blade out of Allister's back, Allister fell to his knees placing his trembling hands over the wound, as he fell forward, he was gone before he even hit the ground.

The crowd went into a frenzy as Zavier and Jessie reached the platform. Jason and his soldiers retreated quickly to the castle as the crowd and the soldiers of Stormwall went to war with the Volcanic Spire.

Valkyrie pushed her way through the mob and pulled herself onto the platform grabbing Allister's head she shook him, hot angry tears pouring down her face, ugly sobs and pleading, she begged and begged to every god that this was a dream, he had to be alive, she had to say goodbye, she had to have a last word with him, but this wasn't a fairy-tale. Allister was gone from this world.

The END

EPILOGUE

As the Queen Katherine's army stormed the castle gates, the land that was once her home, she knelt next to her brother's corpse. She rested what was once her baby brother on her knees and brushed his hair back until her guards beckoned relentlessly her back to the ship, along with her brother's body.

This day was a victory for the Volcanic Spire, as after hours of battle and many lives lost, Jessie pulled back his army and forcefully dragged Valkyrie and Zavier from the fight.

Stormwall was alone in the fight. No other kingdoms, colonies joined the battle against the Volcanic Spire, The Mountain Kingdoms new king. Despite the peace treaty that had been placed all those years-ago. The war was futile.

Fifteen years had passed since the death of Allister Ironfist. Fifteen years after Jason claimed his right to the Mountain throne everything changed.

Midnight had come. The worst winter in those years stormed heavy on the old Mountain kingdoms walls. The wind screamed and howled angrily, as a lonely shadow crept up the wall. Swinging its dark body over the railing, perching as it looked past the glass doors leading into the kings' bedroom. The balcony's doors wailed open and the glass shattered violently; as the king was stirred awake. The shadow disappeared as the now aged king emerged from his warm, cozy bed. Little did the king know as he walked towards the broken doors, he wasn't alone. The shadow watched him from the darkness. The king bent over and gripped a large shard of glass in his hand he proceeded to close the broken doors and re-latch the lock. He turned around the shadow revealed itself to him. The sad, lonely king went to call his guards, but it was already too late. Placing their boney hands over the old king's mouth, as he blacked out of consciousness.

King Jason then awoke to the shadow sitting atop of his chest. He was stripped off all clothing, his hands and legs were bound to his dark oak bed frame, sprawled out like so many of his own victims before him. An old smelly cloth stuffed in his mouth, unable to scream or call out. He looked up at the shadow, only it wasn't a shadow, wasn't black magic, nor was it a ghost coming to claim his soul; a woman, hidden by her black cloak, the old king could only see and stare at her twisted, proud grin. She looked down at the man. The shadowed woman lit a match, placing on hand over her prisoner's mouth, letting the wood of her match burn and slightly illuminate her face, giving the old king a hint. Jason could see her soft, young features, but this face, was never a face he's gazed on before. Once the fire started to singe at her fingers she dropped it on the king's chest, he tried to call out in pain, but was unsuccessful. Finally, she spoke seductively, placing her free hand where the match landed. "Do you recognize my face?" The woman, correction child removed her hood and freed her tangled blonde locks.

King Jason looked at this girl, she couldn't be even sixteen years old.

"Is it like looking at a ghost from your past?" She leaned in and whispered seductively in his ear. "Many people told me it was a curse and a blessing, my looks that is." She pulled a dagger from her blouse and twisted it around digging it into the soft flesh of her palm. He knew her, he knew her face. There was a long second where everything clicked in the old king's mind and the girl smiled placing the knife to his throat.

The woman laughed as she gripped the king's hair with her one free hand she slit and removed the king's head. She was soaked in the mans blood as she stood up from the now destroyed sheets and walked to the front door, carrying her trophy of the king's head and her blade she opened the door and walked through the halls as if she belonged here, she was meant to be here. The king's blood marked a trail of where she walked. Deliberately she clicked her heels loudly, the soldiers, the guards, they would do nothing to stop her. She was soaked in their king's blood and there was nothing they could do about it. Jason was dead. They had no king. No children, no wives, no one to claim his, throne.

The shadow assassin pushed through the throne room doors, she untied her cloak as it fell from her shoulders. The soldiers were in awe, they didn't know what to think of the girl who talked before them, aged far past her years. She stopped at the throne and traced her finger along the arm rest before turning around and taking a seat in the large, ill-fitting chair. The now fallen king's head in her lap, she laughed, she accomplished something no one else had. She looked at the large swarm of arms soldiers and guards, "Your king is dead. Under the laws of Tasryn as he has no rightful heir, I claim his right to the throne." She stood up and tossed the king's head towards the soldiers, "Bow to your new Queen. Today is a day to put in the history books, men." She sat back down getting comfortable in her new throne as she clicked her tongue, "Today once again, an Ironfist sits' upon the Mountain Throne."